*Brian Garfield's brilliant novel about
the spies who came in for the gold!*

"A rugged opus of prey, police, partisans and pursuit... Garfield uses his broadest canvas to date in this one, covering three continents and more than a half-century ... in a story about a quest. The object: valuable Romanov gold reserves that vanished in the Siberian wasteland in 1920." —*Newsday*

"Overlaid on the traditional structure of double agentry and subsequent disillusionment is the marvelously complicated narrative device—essentially Harry's notes sent on the lam to his "editors" who fill in the missing backgrounds with fascinating little-known info on such stuff as the Russian Civil War—a nice bit of authenticizing that gives this a huge lead on others of the genre." —*Kirkus Reviews*

"A sweet love story, a solid slice of contemporary and little-known history, and best of all from the point of view of this reader, a superb chase sequence along the Black Sea shores of southern Russia." —*Erie Times News*

KOLCHAK'S GOLD...

"This is a readable and well-written story of a love affair and a desperate search that spans continents and time—an epic of suspense that makes history a living part of the novel."   —*Fort Worth Press*

"Garfield has a fine feeling for history and his readers' knowledge of it; he neither gives too much information nor too little. The result is that the reader doesn't feel impatient or lost, and is swept along by the narrative. This is a beautiful blend of fact and fiction, accomplished with talent, craft, and imagination. The illusion of truth hasn't been this great since 'The Day of the Jackal.' "
—*Seattle Post-Intelligencer*

"Make room on the best-seller lists for 'Kolchak's Gold.' The author has woven an exciting, inventive story, vibrant with action, upon the tapestry of recent history."   —*San Rafael Journal*

"A cracking good suspense novel..."
—*Milwaukee Journal*

by BRIAN GARFIELD

"A superior thriller...Brian Garfield has built quite a tale...rich and complicated with historical overtones, but well done and fun."
—*San Francisco Chronicle*

"Not only is this an exciting, action-packed espionage novel, but it also gives the reader a good terse summary of the history of Russia since the 1917 revolution. It is an intelligent, interest-compelling book well above the category of the usual spy story."
—*Houston Post*

"This is a story with real suspense. Right up to the end the reader cannot know for sure who the good people are. The end is in fact a distinct surprise. Start a book like this and you will burn the midnight oil in spite of the energy crisis. The characters are real."
—*Best Sellers*

"A gripping novel..."
—*New York Post*

KOLCHAK'S GOLD

BRIAN GARFIELD

BALLANTINE BOOKS • NEW YORK

Library of Congress Catalog Card Number: 73-84062

SBN 345-24325-0-175

This edition published by arrangement with
David McKay Co., Inc.

First Printing: January, 1975
Second Printing: February, 1975

Printed in the United States of America

BALLANTINE BOOKS
A Division of Random House, Inc.
201 East 50th Street, New York, N.Y. 10022
Simultaneously published by
Ballantine Books, Ltd., Toronto, Canada

For Shan, with love

ACKNOWLEDGMENT

The editors gratefully acknowledge the important assistance, in preparing this manuscript, of Shan Willson, James O'Shea Wade, and Justin B. Scott.

John H. Ives
The Ives Literary Agency, Inc.
748 Third Avenue
New York, N. Y. 10017 U.S.A.

May 17, 1973

Dear Jack,
   Enclosed ms is not the contracted book
on the Sebastopol siege. I may never
finish writing that one. Hopefully you
will be able to persuade McKay to
publish the enclosed as a substitute
for it.
   The postmark will reveal I'm in Vienna
but I shall be in another part of the
world by the time you receive this
package.
   It's very hard to try to explain,
cold, how I came to this point. You'll
understand when you read the manuscript. I've backed into a game in
which I have no second chances--a game
in which I need to make the right move
only once. I've become the quarry of
a ludicrous number of security agencies:
they want what's in my head and
they'll kill to get it.
   It might be a torrid fiction loosely
based on one of my early books--the
Donovan/OSS chapters or the study of
MI-6 operations. But those were histories and I was only their chronicler.
Now I'm the protagonist, and I am
running scared. Armchair expertise

from researching those cloak-and-
dagger histories has kept me alive up
to now but it's the professionals
who are pursuing me and I can't warrant
how long my run of luck will last.
Two weeks ago in Athens I repeated
Heinrich's trick of 1944 virtually
move-for-move, as verbatim as I could
recall it; I must have written that one
in 1964, the Aeneas book. It threw
them off; it was three days before
they scented my trail again.

Maybe I shouldn't have dug in my
heels when I did. At times I want to
believe I didn't realize the consequences when I made that decision--
that series of decisions, really. If I
can persuade myself of that, it takes
the onus off me--it becomes _their_
fault entirely, and I their innocent
victim. It's rationalization, contrived
to absolve myself; actually I knew
what I was doing. I suppose I'm
stubborn after all: you were right in
your complaints. A man told me, a month
or two ago, "If you do this you'll be
an outsider forever, you know. You're
consigning yourself to exile--a blind
wandering to an unknown destination.
You're not the type, Harry." (I'm
translating that from memory but it's
close.)

Let me try to picture it for you;
you won't recognize me as the narrator
but that's the point of it. I'm a
different man--a better one in some
ways, but if I think about it too
much I feel cold terror.

'How I spent my morning'--class
theme by Harris Bristow--try this one
on your Harvard chums:

x

This morning for the fourth day I prowled the hotels searching for a man—not a specific man; any foreigner who resembled me at least superficially.

The tourist crush hasn't reached its summer maximum but the city is preparing for the annual June Festival of Wien and there's quite a bit of transient activity. Two film companies are shooting big-budget movies here and you find camera-clicking crowds gawking at stars. There's also a fair gang of up-country aristocrats from their mountain <u>Schlossen,</u> here to catch the tail end of the operatic and symphonic season. Fortunately for my purposes there are also several business conventions and a conference on East-West trade.

So there's a great deal of traffic inside the hotels and I didn't feel too exposed. I hit one of the bigger hotels this morning and had a piece of luck.

A number of guests were checking in; porters carried luggage through the fake-marble colonades and I waited in a corner chair like some ludicrous Marx Brothers prowler lurking behind potted palms. My man was in, but not of, a crowd that emerged from the lift-cage.

He separated himself from the group and crossed to the desk. A self-important business type, English or possibly American: fashionably fluffy hair, a hothouse tan, sideburns down to his jaw hinges. He was wearing one of those nipped-in suits that they tailor without regard for a man's need of pocket space. He had a lightweight raincoat over his arm, the transparent kind that air travelers prefer; there was nothing in its pockets. I sized him up as a movie assistant producer or a youngish hotshot in some burgeoning glamour conglomerate. He didn't have my tweedy trappings and he was stouter than I am; his shoes made him a couple of inches taller than he was and he still wasn't quite my height. But Europeans aren't accustomed to translating feet and inches into visual centimeters so it didn't matter that much. His face was as square as mine and the hair about the same shade of brown. He had a mustache but that doesn't matter.

He had an arrogant carriage and he looked careless: the type who wouldn't be very cautious about his possessions because he could always buy a replacement if he lost anything.

I watched him drop his room key at the desk. One of the clerks inserted the key in its pigeonhole. From my corner I couldn't read the number but I made a note of the location of the box—third row, sixth from left.

He went. I waited in the chair long enough to make sure he hadn't forgotten anything and decided to return for it. I felt exposed: every face seemed an enemy. I know they're close now with their noses to the ground—it's as if I can hear them breathing sometimes. (A paranoid melodrama: that's the flavor of it and I can't help that. Bear with me.)

I went out the side door, slipped into my topcoat and reentered the hotel by the main entrance. I walked straight

to the desk. As I approached it I
read the mailbox.

I chose one of the clerks: young,
chinless, harried. Not the same clerk
who had taken my man's key. I put
myself in front of him and in nondescript High German asked him for the
key to 724 and looked impatient. He
handed me the key with hardly a glance.

I was sweating. The lift-cage felt
like a prison cell. I found his room
and let myself in. It was the third
hotel in which I'd performed a burglary
in four days; I guess travelers are
wary nowadays, they carry everything
on them: but I counted on my man's
carelessness and that suit of his, the
one without many pockets.

Morality is the first casualty of
expedient needs, isn't it. Today I
needed something so I stole it.
('Cynicism is another word for experience.'--Machiavelli, I think.)

I found the prize in the pocket of his
Vuitton suitcase. His passport.
Canadian, as it turned out. Also a vac-
cination certificate, an International
Driver's License, a list of traveler's-
check numbers with half of them crossed
out; and an emergency fund, three
hundred dollars cash.

The passport photo was close enough
to get by a busy customs man in a
crowd; I could always say I'd shaven
off the mustache since the photo was
taken. I took most of his money as well:
he could afford it, I rationalized, and
the Canadian consul would replace his
passport quickly enough--he looked the
type who'd get things moving for him.
He'd have an adventure to relate to

his drinking buddies back in Montreal;
I had a ticket to survival.

I know how and where I mean to disappear and where I mean to hide. But
getting there's another thing: I'm
likely to get stuck in the flypaper
of my own mistakes; I'm still an
amateur at this kind of madness.

I left his key at the desk and walked
to the AmEx to cash the last of my
own traveler's checks. They were in
my own name and if I didn't pass them
now I couldn't ever do so. I have to
assume my pursuers will have traced me
as far as Vienna very soon. I cashed the
checks for Canadian dollars; maybe
that, and the theft of the Canadian
passport, will persuade them that I'm
going to try to get into Canada and
hide there. I doubt it but anything's
worth trying.

My flight leaves early this afternoon;
it's usually a pretty crowded plane as
I recall. I'll stay in the middle of
the crowd.

In forty minutes I've got to leave
this flat, drop this and the ms in the
postal exchange and taxi to the airport.
By that time the Canadian may have
discovered the theft of his passport
but there'll be time wasted while they
question hotel maids before a bulletin
goes out, and while the passport details
filter through channels to the airport
desks. By then I'll be in another
country destroying the passport. I
have a scheme for obtaining something
more like a permanent valid passport in
a new name but it'll take more time
than I've got now.

Anyhow they may nail me before I

get that far. But I'm giving them a run for it.

If they get me, or if they don't, I mean to have something to show. Partly it's sheer rage—the need for vengeance: I want some prominent noses to bleed, I want to blow the whole stinking mess ten miles in the air. And I keep rehearsing Burke's dictum that the only thing necessary for the triumph of evil is for good men to do nothing.

The manuscript is my act of defiance. I've spent every available snatch of time on it. When I've had access to a typewriter I've used it; the rest of the time it's been pen and even pencil. As you can see, parts of the thing are scrawled on both sides of scraps of hotel stationery—a mapping of my peregrinations through the flea-bags of Asia Minor and Europe.

It's a very rough draft. I've spent no time polishing or cutting. I'm going to ask you and the McKay editors to be my collaborators on this book: not merely polishing the enclosed wretched scrivenings, but doing many things I haven't been able to do. I can't carry around with me the contents of my files on the Kolchak and Sebastopol books, for example; they're still down in Lambertville.

I want you to go down there and burglarize my office. Rick knows you, he'll let you in; if he balks show him this letter. (Rick—let Jack Ives in.)

By now I'm sure those files have been rifled, possibly more than once, by the buffoon henchmen of my erstwhile buddy from Langley, and maybe by some of the others too. But I doubt they've

stolen anything, that's not their style.
They're all trained to take microphotos
and leave things as they found them.
And even if they've absconded with a
few items they thought vital, they've
had no reason to steal the things I
want you to get.

You're going to have to put it together and make a coherent book out of
it. In the enclosed ms I've had time
only to relate current events, together
with the pages of transcription of my
interviews with two or three people in
Israel and elsewhere. For the lay
reader to understand all this he's got
to have background. Particularly he
needs to know something of the events
of the Kolchak years and the events
of the Ukrainian disasters during
Hitler's war. I don't know how you'll
decide to fit it in: in separate chunks
or filtered piece by piece as inter-
polations into the narrative. Either
way it must be included in order for
this book to make sense; and it must
make sense—it must be heard.

In the second drawer of the steel
cabinet in Lambertville, in the manila
folder marked 'Kolchak,' you'll find the
rough draft of my manuscript on the
history of the White Russian debacle.
It's quite short; of course it's far
from complete—I'd intended doing
further research. But it does cover the
ground and it contains quite a bit of
history that's never been published
anywhere. You'll want to take the appropriate portions of the Tippelskirch
interviews (transcriptions enclosed
with the file) and fit them into the
Kolchak document where they belong in

the chronology; perhaps those passages
should be set off somehow to distinguish
Tippelskirch's narrative from mine.

Unfortunately all my Crimean-based
notes on the Ukrainian campaigns were
lost before I could get them out of the
Soviet Union. I've related as much of
that information as I can recall; some
of it is probably faulty in detail but
the drift of it is accurate enough.
They key documents I destroyed myself;
the only record of those specifications
is in my head. That's mainly why they're
after me.

Both Tippelskirch brothers are beyond
anybody's reach now. I'm the only living
link to what they're after, and I hope
to disappear and take my knowledge
with me. Doubtless a good many governments are indulging in ecstasies of
speculation over its whereabouts, but
they're not going to find it without me.

It sounds shaggy-dog, I suppose.
You'll have to set that right; this is
to be my last book and if nothing else
it must stir people's hearts. If there's
indignation left anywhere in the world,
we've got to seek it out and induce
its outcry.

I'm leaving it to you and the McKay
editors to select a title; to arrange
the organization of chapters and
whatnot; to rewrite and add explanatory
notes wherever they seem needed; and
to find a sensible concluding wrap-up
if circumstances don't permit me to
send you further material.

There's more, but I feel them breathing too close to me. The enclosed is
enough for an understanding and I

must at least be sure that you receive
this much of it.

I wish there were more time. I
must run.

As ever,

Harris Bristow

EDITOR'S NOTE

The various narratives which go to make up the body of this volume are all the product of one hand: that of the distinguished and popular historian Harris Bristow, author of nine successful books since 1962, including *The Aeneas Scheme* (1965), *The Nazi Spies* (1967), *The War in the Aleutians* (1969), and the bestselling *The Master Spies* (1971). It should also be noted that his first book, recently brought back into print in a new hardcover edition, was *The Civil War in Russia: 1918–1921* (1962), and that for many years Harry Bristow has been regarded as one of our outstanding authorities on modern Russian military history. (His long article on Marshal Zhukov in the *American Historical Review*, March 1964, is regarded as a classic.)

The unique circumstances underlying the publication of the present volume—which we sincerely hope will *not* be Harry Bristow's "last book"—have left no doubt in the publishers' minds that the book must be published essentially as Harry Bristow wrote it: that there be a minimum of editorial tampering. We believe this to be one of the most alarming publications the United States has seen since the revelation of the Pentagon Papers by *The New York Times,* and it has been our feeling that any efforts to "smooth it out" or "polish it up" would merely run the risk of destroying potentially important material. Further, it has always been our policy to make no substantial changes in an author's work without the express consent of the author.

The obligatory copy-editing has been done, of course, under close supervision of the editors; and we have added explanatory footnotes where it was felt they were needed. We have attempted to follow as closely as possible the instructions in Harry Bristow's letter to his agent. Beyond that we have taken no liberties with the book. If its organization appears haphazard or arbitrary, that is more the editors' fault than Harry Bristow's.

KOLCHAK'S GOLD

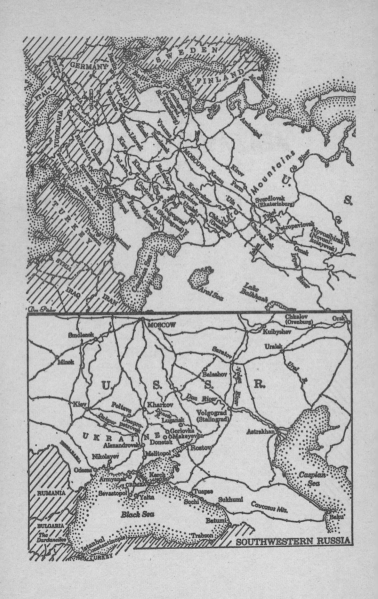

SOUTHWESTERN RUSSIA

Arctic Ocean

Bering

ALASKA
(U.S.A.)

Bering Sea

S I B E R I A

U.S.S.R.

Yenisei River

Lena River

Amur River

Kamchatka Peninsula

Sea of Okhotsk

Petropavlovsk
on Kamchatka

TRANS-SIBERIAN
RAILROAD

Krasnoyarsk

IRON
MINES

Lake
Baikal

Mt.
Piramida

Sayan Mts.

Irkutsk

Manchuria

Harbin

Sakhalin

Vladivostok

MONGOLIA

Sea of
Japan

Peking

NORTH
KOREA

SOUTH
KOREA

JAPAN

Tokyo

Pacific Ocean

Shanghai

RUSSIA
today

0   200   400   600   800

Scale of Miles

THE VIENNA MANUSCRIPT

I

1

A VAST GLOOMY BUILDING stands along the Potomac waterfront in Alexandria. Originally a torpedo factory, it now houses many of the military records belonging to the National Archives. I've been familiar with it for a dozen years; masses of research for all my books have come out of those miles of microfilm and documents.

The National Archives is supposed to be a civilian department—our government's historical librarian—but access to its military records is controlled and limited by the Pentagon. I had my first clash there in the 1960s when I began to compile material for a history of the Aleutian campaigns in World War II. Those campaigns ended in 1943 and the records I sought were twenty-five years old; yet they were locked inside "Classified" cabinets and it took nearly a year before I was able to wheedle the Pentagon into declassifying them so that I could use them for publication. The opposition was not based on argument, merely on bureaucratic inertia; but that made the obstacles all the more maddening, because they were unreasoning.

There was nothing sensitive in those files. It was only that no one had asked to see them before I came along. They'd remained under lock and key. When you took them out you had to blow the dust off them.

In the course of researching that book and others in the long warehouse, I developed a fair working knowledge of the scope and coverage of the NARS collections. I came to know the pale people who worked there, and the ways in which I could trace the erratic paths of reference in their muddled index of dusty possessions. In the end I followed those paths too far, I suppose: being a writer made me a scholar of sorts;

3

being a scholar forced me to be a detective; being a detective made me a fugitive.

My mother was Ukrainian, perhaps I should explain that. She lived in Sebastopol until 1935, when freak circumstances permitted her to leave the Soviet Union. She immigrated to England. My father in those days had a minor post with the American Embassy in London.

They met one evening at the Haymarket Theatre; they were married in 1936. I was born in 1938 on board an ocean liner at a spot south of Iceland on a voyage from Southampton to New York; since my parents were of separate citizenships and I had been born on the high seas, I was allowed my choice of nationality when I reached my majority in 1959. I have carried an American passport ever since then but a good part of my childhood was spent outside the United States: Ottawa during the war, then London again—my father then Second Secretary to the Ambassador to the Court of St. James—then Bonn for two years, and a further two years in Switzerland. I went to a variety of schools and acquired four languages including my mother's native Ukrainian dialect, as well as German, English and St. Petersburg Russian.

During the war my mother's relatives managed occasionally to get letters out to her. She saved these carefully in a leather case and in later years she would let me read them. As far as any of us knew, all her relatives in the Crimea and the Ukraine had perished in the war. I'm sure it was those letters, and my mother's childhood memories, which inspired me to write my first book on the Russian Civil War and to lay elaborate plans to write the definitive history of the Nazi siege of Sebastopol—the project which took me into the Soviet Union in February 1973 and culminated in those alarming events with which this account is concerned.

When I was researching my book on the Nazi spies I first encountered German documents that referred to the Sebastopol siege. I had thought that such docu-

4

ments would be in Russian hands today, but that isn't altogether the case.

The Germans were compulsive paperwork addicts; our own Pentagon can hardly match the Nazi mania for record-keeping, which helped doom many of the war-crimes defendants: their bestiality was attested by document after damning document, many of them sealed with their own signatures.

When the Wehrmacht advanced it sent back its records to the Fatherland. When it retreated it took its records along. Nothing was left behind. Amazingly few records were destroyed, until right at the end of the war a belated effort was made to erase the evidence they had so carefully amassed against themselves. But at that point everything was collapsing around them and the ranking officers fled to preserve their skins while their subordinates found more pressing engagements than record-burning, so that a vast body of Nazi history fell intact into Allied hands at the end of the war in Germany.

Among these records were voluminous files from the Crimea. Even in rout; even under siege; even in the panic of desperate flight from the Red armies, the Germans threw their own wounded off trains and ships in order to make space for the transshipment to Germany of their paper records.

These trainloads fell into American hands, mainly in Austria, in 1945. Most of them were taken to Berlin (the American sector) for examination. Harried men, assigned to the Strategic Bombing Survey and the Allied Military Government in postwar Germany, had the jobs of sorting these endless millions of documents; collating them, indexing them, finding places to store them. (For a while many of them were kept in the bombed and burnt-out remains of the old Reichstag.)

Many were not indexed with any care. The principal target of the hunt was documents to incriminate those accused of war crimes; anything that didn't seem to have a direct bearing on that objective was discarded and consigned to the oblivion of "miscellany." Later, when the military occupation ended, the American forces brought the captured material back with them. Most of it was stored intact and unopened; in the intervening years it has been examined piecemeal but there has never been any systematic attempt to get it sorted out. There is still enough unopened material to keep historians busy for a century.

When I came across the first clues I was tempted to shelve the book on Nazi spies and plunge straight into the Sebastopol material. I did abandon the spy book for several weeks until it became obvious that I was not going to get enough material from those files to justify doing that particular book. The key material was Russian; and of course it remains in the Soviet Union.

Clearly I had to have access to the Russian archives. I began to make approaches to the Soviet government, by mail and through their embassy in Washington, while at the same time I returned my immediate attention to the Abwehr and Gestapo records and proceeded to complete that project.

Predictably the Soviet authorities were obstructionist; I knew it would take years to break down the barriers, if it could be done at all. At that time no Western historian had been allowed into any Soviet archive.

I hoped my dual nationality would help. Also there was the fact that I had treated the Russians fairly in all my books, particularly my history of the Russian Civil War—my first book. I hoped that would count for something. (Since then some things have changed. Even then I was dabbling with material for a book on Aleksandr Kolchak and the White armies. But the Soviets weren't to know that.)

I completed the manuscript of the Nazi spy book in the autumn of 1965. After that there were the usual revisions, the work of obtaining photographs to illustrate the book, the preparation of the bibliography and index, all the other irritating post-partum chores that go into the publication of a book which from the author's point of view is already completed. It was well into 1966 before I had breathing space in which to begin the next project.

The Soviets still hadn't budged. I was making pleas through intermediaries by then—old friends of my father's, people in the diplomatic corps—but none of it had worked; the Russian archives were still closed to me. It was going to take years, if it was to happen at all. To the Soviets history is not a source, not a tool, but a god. Like all gods its interpretation is subject to revision—periodic expedient changes to fit the requirements of the present. No crime, regardless how heinous, can be condemned if it is performed in the service of Red history—a system of rationalization which is reminiscent of the Inquisition and the Crusades. But as long as history is the Red religion it is small wonder that the Soviets resist incursions by outside students, and I had few illusions about my chances.

So I turned to the Aleutian campaigns and spent two years on them (1966–1968), after which I assembled the vignettes that went into *The Master Spies.*

Those were years when my daughter died in a stupid accident and my marriage broke up. I mention those things only to explain why I did not devote more wholehearted efforts to opening Russian doors a crack. I had too many problems. For a while my work took a back seat; in fact for more than a year I was drinking too much to do decent work. But I don't mean this to be a confession or an *apologia;* my personal life has only a limited bearing on the facts that must be divulged here.

For one reason and another it was near the end of 1970 before I returned to Washington to begin work on what I intended to be the definitive popular history of the Siberian Civil War in 1918–20—Kolchak's War. It was shortly thereafter that all this began. I remember the date quite clearly: January 26, 1971.

George Fitzpatrick, who has a Boston Irish sense of humor and a practical joker's temperament, was throwing one of his bacchanals. He detested the hoary Washington practice of throwing every party "in honor of" someone. This one, I recall vividly, was thrown in commemoration of the date of Oscar Wilde's death.

I had been weeks sorting the boring files of Graves' Expeditionary Force in Siberia and I welcomed Fitzpatrick's invitation in the hope the party would pull me out of my dulled mood.

Fitzpatrick is a Boston lawyer, a registered lobbyist; he keeps a suite of rooms year-round at the Hay-Adams. In the lobby that evening, conventioneers with name-tags on their pockets swarmed like prisoners of

7

war and it was with great difficulty that I made my way to the bank of elevators.

A man arrived there just ahead of me; he put his finger on the depressed plastic square and it lit up. He turned and we looked at each other with the tentative smiles of people who think they recognize each other but aren't quite sure.

Then he said, "Harry Bristow." He pumped my arm in a politician's handshake, left hand on my elbow. "Been a hell of a long time."

I still didn't remember him well enough to put a name with the face.

"I didn't realize I'd put on *that* much weight. I'm Evan MacIver. Remember?"

I had to do the self-deprecating laugh and disbelieving headshake; he was right, I should have remembered him—we'd roomed together one semester at Columbia.

MacIver brightened; we asked each other how we were, after which he said something complimentary about my books.

I remembered him as a self-possessed jaunty youth; a magpie with a raffish way. Now he had the somewhat defeated air of a worn-out roué: a big rumpled man with the jowls of a bulldog, the rheumy eyes of a bloodhound and a hard round belly on him. In profile his nose was an exact right triangle with a bit of a point on it. He was only two years older than I but he looked badly used at thirty-five. He wore a beet-hued tie and a gray flannel business suit as if he had been born in them; there'd been a day when he wouldn't have been caught dead in conventional attire. And his manner somehow suggested that the good education he'd once absorbed had gone stale through shiftless indifference.

At Fitzpatrick's floor the elevator doors slid open with a soft scrape. The hallway was wide and carpeted, intersected at intervals by painted doors. MacIver said, "You going to the Fitzpatrick bash? You know the way?"

"I've been here before," I admitted and led him along the corridor. I made conversation: "What have you been up to?"

"Oh hell, you know how it is. A little of this, a little of that. I did time at grad school after you left. Few

8

years overseas—Kyoto and Darmstadt, mainly. Married a German girl while I was stationed over there, got my inactive papers, came back here."

"Any kids?"

"I got my wife and she's got me." It was wry because, evidently, there was truth in it. "Other than that no, no children. How about you?"

"No ties at the moment." I saw no point in going into detail. I rang the bell and a laughing girl let us in.

Among those who know, an invitation to a Fitzpatrick party is a privilege. There is always a White House crisis or a Capitol Hill scandal to fuel conversations and the guest list insures that a good number of animated and heated disputes will break out in the course of the bibulous evening.

You never see quite the same crowd there twice; you're kept on your toes by the presence of strangers who throw lethal darts into your best set-piece opinion speeches. A bore never gets a second invitation. There's a slight artificiality to it—Fitzpatrick's principal aim is to recreate the Algonquin round table—but nobody minds. The best sarcasms are honed here. Tomorrow's political-humor newspaper columns often have their geneses around George's bar. I believe it was at one of his early parties that the phrase was coined, "Would you buy a used car from this man?" Or at least legend would have it so.

Evan MacIver and I were separated almost instantly on entry; I found myself marched into the center of the main room with George Fitzpatrick's thick arm thrown across my shoulders. Around me vied the fumes of his Black Label Cologne and Cutty Sark whiskey. George stopped to introduce me to a trio of allegedly beautiful people and left me there to find my own way to the bar; I don't recall speaking to him again at all that night.

I was in the wrong mood for it; I knew that right away. I'd been immersed in dry research too long; wit, like love, is something you have to keep working at—otherwise it withers. I constructed some sort of drink and found a neutral corner in which to swizzle it reflectively. Across the room I saw a glamorous woman, the wife of a young Senator who wasn't here with her, take offense at something someone said to her; she took a reef in her floor-length dress and swept straight out the door. When it closed behind her the entire room burst into raucous laughter: there was no such thing as an embarrassed silence at one of these bashes. Manners were suspended; anything went; she had broken the house rules and nobody had sympathy for her: the room echoed with ridicule when she returned for her forgotten coat.

A columnist buttonholed me and tried out a funny idea he was thinking of using. Evidently he was speaking to me but he seemed to be aiming somewhere over the top of my head. I laughed in the right places.

Another drink, too fast. I saw MacIver drifting through the crowd, looking curiously like an eaves-dropper: he was out of place here, the company was too fast for him. I wondered where Fitzpatrick could have come across him. What did MacIver do nowadays? He hadn't said. I had thought he was taller than he seemed now; perhaps events had shrunk him. He was burning his cigarettes away in long drags.

I found a chair in the lee of conversations; someone had just vacated it to charge into the midst of a spirited argument nearby. Laughter hung in the room in waves that bounced from one end to the other; the various knots of joke-tellers seemed to have found synchronization. I settled into the chair and went through the time-consuming ritual of getting my pipe going.

For a little while I let things drift by me. Then my attention drifted toward a young woman who sat in the corner opposite me, beside the window. Her head was bowed so that her dark hair shielded her face; people went by and there was an undrunk glass of something in her hand but she paid nothing any notice.

"She's Israeli. Separated from her husband, not divorced. Twenty-eight, I think."

It was Evan MacIver, suddenly at my side, sitting down hipshot on the arm of my chair. "She's got a son in some Swiss boarding school. She's staying in a consulate apartment out in Georgetown."

"Why tell me all that?"

"Because you wanted to know." His smile was cynical: he had a salesman's knowledge of human weaknesses. "She speaks five or six languages but as far as I know she doesn't know how to say 'yes' in any of them."

"I gather you don't like her much."

"I can't stand argumentative women," MacIver said. "Her name's Nikki something, I forget exactly. Weinstein, Eisenstein, something like that."

"Nikki?"

"She's only half Jewish. French mother, I think. Probably short for Nicole. She's over here with some kind of fund-raising group, trying to get shekels out of the New York Jews to help spring Jewish emigrants out of Russia."

I drained my drink down to the ice cubes and set the glass down.

MacIver said, "You really ought to talk to her about that Russian stuff you're always writing about."

I could tell by the way the girl squinted at her newspaper that she was nearsighted. I looked at MacIver. "Why?"

"She's hipped on it. Talk your ear off. You don't know what depressed is until you've listened to her number on pogroms and atrocities. You've never met such a relentless memory for dismal facts and figures."

"How'd you meet her?"

"On business. I should have left it there."

The girl had opened her handbag. She took out a pair of large dark-rimmed glasses to read the news more closely. She was quite oblivious to her surroundings. She looked bright and quick; MacIver's droll attempt to characterize her didn't quite jibe with her appearance. Her eyes, magnified behind the glasses, seemed slanted with a somewhat rancorous irony—wary, suspicious, but the sort of face that would hide sooner behind clever mockery than behind heavy literal fact-mongering.

MacIver's lip-hung cigarette bobbed up and down when he spoke. "What are you working on right now? Another spy book?"

"No. I'm doing a book on the Russian Civil War."

"You already did one. Didn't you?"

"This one's on Kolchak. I passed him over lightly in the first one."

"The admiral, I remember." He beamed as if proud of his memory. "You do pick the grim ones, don't you?"

I let it lie. "What kind of line are you in these days?"

"Cloaks." He dragged avariciously on his cigarette and poured thick slow rivers of smoke from his nostrils, and gave me the familiar grin for the first time. "Cloak-and-dagger business. I'm in the cloak end of it. Civil service, you know. Years ago I decided I was the sort of bureaucratic hack the civilian world would eat alive, so I stayed with the government when I got out of the army. Now I'm just another fool exercising my petty authority around Langley."

His candor surprised me. It was not *de rigueur* for people in that line to advertise their calling. This was long before the celebrity of E. Howard Hunt.

He seemed to feel he'd gone far enough. He changed the direction of the conversation: "Some of us at The Firm were reading your last book. We got a few yocks here and there, but you didn't find half the jokes in that Haitian business. Not half."

I grunted to encourage him and after he found a place to stub his cigarette he went on: "It was Lansky, you missed that part."

"Meyer Lansky?"

"Let's say people associated with him. Miami types." He lit up and blew smoke at his match. "Come on, Harry, you should've figured out that Papa Doc knew what our mental retards were up to. Lansky had a little meet with the Duvalier people to talk about those Mickey Mouse exiles we had flying B–Twenty-fours over Port au Prince."

"You're kidding."

"Why should I? Look, the mob was looking for beach resorts for their casinos, and Papa Doc offered to trade beach-front property for antiaircraft guns. Where'd you think he got his artillery on the roof of the palace?"

"The *Mafia?*"

"Shot down two Liberators, too. Those clowns trying to fly airplanes—eighteen tons of bombs and they never hit the palace once." His chuckle grew into a bray of laughter.

"Why tell me all this?"

"Ancient history. It's what you write about, isn't it?"

But it was something else, I knew. I had a feeling he was doing it to establish his bonafides but I couldn't fathom what reason he had for doing that.

The girl in the corner was quite indifferent to the party swirling around her; it wasn't an act.

MacIver said, "Remember old Gilfillan, the time he mimeographed that fake sociology exam and hooked half the class on it?" And then he was off on a rambling discourse of nostalgic reminiscence which I endeavored to curtail by making a gesture with my empty glass and carrying it away toward the bar.

He came along unshakably. "You had dinner yet?"

"Yes," I lied.

It made him pause. "Too bad. There's a place down the block, the steaks aren't too bad. Christ, I don't know about you but I can only take so much of this ruckus. I think I'll take off. Listen, we ought to have dinner soon—have a few yocks over the old times."

"I'd like to," I said politely.

He gave me a card after scrawling a ballpoint number on the back of it. "That's the home phone. I've got a little house just the other side of Arlington. Come out and visit sometime. The little lady makes a hell of a sauerkraut."

I looked at the card as if I really intended to call him sometime.

MacIver drifted away through the smoke; I was still waiting my turn at the bar. He stopped by the young woman's chair in the corner and I saw her stiffen and nod with recognition but not pleasure. MacIver spoke briefly and the Israeli woman's eyes turned toward me. I had no choice but to smile and wave my glass in their direction.

When I'd got a fresh drink I looked again and MacIver was still there with her. He waved at me and I dodged through to the corner.

MacIver made some sort of blurred introduction and hurried away while the young woman stared at me out of cool agate eyes.

I glanced back through the room. MacIver reached the door, turned and smiled with conspiratorial vicious-

13

ness, and left; as if to say, *I really stuck you with one this time, old buddy.*

"Well then," I said.

The girl's femininity, MacIver to the contrary, was not sufficiently atrophied to enable her to resist what I thought of as my fetching smile; she gave me a deep and luminous smile, albeit brief, in reply.

"MacIver tells me you're steeped in Russian Civil War lore," I said. I smiled again to show I was ribbing her and she smiled to show she understood that.

Then her face changed. "Oh of course. You're *that* Bristow."

"You've heard of me. That's too bad—I was hoping we could be friends."

"It's a hell of an obstacle," she said, "but maybe we can overcome it." She moved subtly into the corner of the chair—she was quite tiny—making room on the overstuffed arm so that I could sit down there.

She had a soft and slightly breathless voice; I had expected something with more bite to it. The accent was minimal: without MacIver's briefing I'd have known that English wasn't her native tongue but I'd have been at a complete loss to identify the accent.

She looked amused but not impatient. She was under no compulsion to hurry into conversation; silence was not awkward to her, she was too self-assured.

I said, "MacIver warned me against you."

"I'm an iceberg and a bore, yes?"

We both laughed; she took off her glasses and squinted her big nearsighted eyes at me. "I'm afraid I disliked him instantly. I took him for FBI—I assumed they'd sent him to keep tabs on me."

"When was this?"

"Oh, six weeks ago I suppose. Two months. It was soon after I came over. I'm afraid I must have taken a blowtorch to the poor man. He was trying so desperately to be a man of the world. At one point he started to talk about some Czechoslovakian Communist friend of his. It might as well have been a Jew, or a black man—you know? Some of my best friends. . . . I'm afraid I slapped him in the face with a cold fish—I reminded him of the half-million Soviet troops that invaded Czechoslovakia in the summer of sixty-eight and

14

I reeled off a few statistics on the women and children they murdered in Wenceslas Square. The gang that contrived the so-called suicide of Jan Masaryk. Then I spent ten minutes telling him how the Russians exposed Dubček to a massive dose of radiation to give him leukemia. I'm afraid he wasn't amused. But he seemed so—banal, so gullible. He infuriated me, his small unconvincing arrogance. It was only the conceit of a petty man, trying to believe he deserves better than life has granted him. But I was new here, I'm sure I was on the defensive. I treated him badly. Why am I telling you this?"

"Maybe I look harmless enough."

"Anyway you're a good listener. Do you live in Washington?"

"No. I have an old farmhouse on the Delaware River in New Jersey—more or less across the river from New Hope, if you know the area."

"Bucks County. Someone took me to the playhouse there once. It's lovely."

I waited for a burst of party laughter to subside. "Have you lived in Czechoslovakia?" It sounded lame.

"No. I have an annoying memory for facts, that's all. Particularly facts that show the Soviets in a bad light."

"That's candid enough."

"I do hate them. But I don't limit my being to that alone. I'm afraid I let MacIver think I did, and I'd prefer to have him go on believing that."

"My lips are sealed."

"Do you know him well?"

"We roomed together in university for a few months. But I didn't remember him when he introduced himself to me tonight."

She changed the subject abruptly. "Are you writing another book on the Civil War in Russia?"

"On Kolchak. He was the Czarist admiral who——"

"I know who he was." She didn't snap; it was a kindly rebuff: *Don't waste time explaining things that don't need explaining.* "Do you think you can add much to what's already been written about him?"

"We have quite a bit now that wasn't available before. I've gone through Deniken's papers, for example —the family only turned them loose a few years ago."

15

"Ah, but he was only another general. You really should talk to the survivors who really knew."

"They're a bit hard to find. It was more than fifty years ago."

"I know a man in Israel," she said.

2

HER NAME, it turned out, was Nicole Eisen, *née* Desrosiers; it was her father, not her mother, who had been French. (Her mother had been a Ukrainian Jew.) She did in fact have a seven-year-old daughter, a severely retarded child, in a Swiss institution; but there was no husband. Ben Eisen had been dead for nearly two years. When I observed that MacIver was a rotten spy she agreed with amusement; MacIver had accepted everything she'd told him. It left me wondering how much of it I should accept: did she tailor her fictions to fit each audience?

She was doing some sort of work for a refugee group, an Israeli-sponsored mission in Washington which lobbied for the relaxation of Soviet restrictions on Jewish emigration. She was a bit vague when it came to what precisely she did there, or how long she expected to stay.

At five the next day I picked her up at her organization's rented office down C Street from the State Department; I drove her home so that she could change for dinner and give me the name and address of the old man in Tel Aviv who she said had survived the White Russians' Siberian disaster in 1920.

She had a small flat a few blocks from the water in Georgetown. In the next weeks I came to know it well.

We had dinner that night and the next; we were at ease with each other from the very beginning. I liked talking with Nikki; she was a stimulant: when I talked with her my voice became quicker, my perceptions brighter, my mind bright and analytical.

Her face was animated, full of vitalities and subtleties that inhabited the swift constant changes of responsive expressions: wisdom, sophistication, alert shrewdness, avaricious impatience. To a painter's eye I suppose

17

she would not have been beautiful but I found her extravagantly bewitching. Her *rayonnement* was irresistible. Her enormous amused agate eyes; her soft and always slightly breathless voice; her good-humored pride in her quick little body—she was willing to give frankly when it pleased her, when the touch of my hand pleased her. She was the kind of girl who enjoyed being with a man but did not define herself only in terms of men; you had to meet her as an equal. That was one reason she had turned MacIver off. He was too much of a scorekeeping womanizer.

She knew she was generous; she expected to get hurt sometimes. If you wanted to avoid being hurt, she said, you never took emotional risks but then you might as well be comatose.

Like her accent, her taste in things was hard to pin down in terms of place. She enjoyed *haute cuisine* and took a bawdy delight in wolfing hamburgers; she wore floor-length dresses and Levi's with equal aplomb. She was not an expatriate in America; she simply lived there for the moment. She was at home anywhere.

I brought her to Lambertville on the weekends. She loved the woods; she went barefoot into Alexauken Creek. But she said she felt guilty about being there because she had not brought a few of her own pots and pans; somehow that would make it all right. The old-world proper side of her character, which came out strongly when we were in company with other friends, was amusing to me: I knew how utterly wanton she was in bed.

When we had made love she liked to lie warmly against me and talk of idle things until she felt stirred to make love again. At first we sought each other's bodies with the insatiable appetites of adolescents; we drowned in each other but it was always rescued by laughter.

It is important to the rest, how this dark-haired *chayelet* Sabra and I felt about each other; otherwise it gives me no pleasure to expose these personal things— this is not a memoir. If I hurry past these intimacies it's because of two things: first that I'm a private person not given to public soul-baring, second that I'm a prosaic historian without practice in detailing the lyrical

18

facets of sexual relationships. Whatever I write will take on the appearance of a banal Technicolor love affair no different from millions; yet it is important that to us there was nothing commonplace about it. We were in each other's thoughts at all times. We couldn't wait for the working day to end. I had not been so single-mindedly infatuated since college days; everything—utterly everything—was colored by my love for Nikki.

Her image intruded upon the screen of my vision at all times, yet this didn't make my work more difficult; only more pleasant. Work, to me, has never been an ethical virtue; it has been the great pleasure of my life, my *raison d'être*. But with Nikki there was additional reward: the promise of happiness at the end of each day. The quiet talk, the candle-lit dinners and always the laughter. We regarded anything, no matter what, as a challenge to our sense of humor.

But from the beginning we both knew that was a defensive barrier. Laughter is an expression of existential feelings: it is of the present. Rely on it too much and you preclude a view of the future. It was because both of us, for our own reasons, wanted to ignore consequences: we didn't want to think of tomorrow.

Tomorrow held no specific threat for me; whether it did for Nikki I had no way of knowing then. For me it was only the fear of repetition. I had helped ruin my marriage to Eileen and I was afraid of it happening again. There were vast differences between Eileen and Nikki but it was myself I feared.

My marriage had been poor almost from the beginning; I had several tormented years with Eileen's jealous hysterics but it was hard to forget her because I couldn't help remembering the good times as well as the horrors. But it had always had a tentative quality. Eileen offered an American woman's brand of love, which was about half the whole thing; she was presentable, she was sexually agreeable, she made a dutiful mother and hausfrau; and she was singularly unexciting. Wherever we lived she always put me in mind of a neat gadgety little house, a neat lawn blooming with roses, gravel driveways, Early American mailboxes. That was her background and she never escaped it. I

19

kept an image of her laying the baby down wet in the bassinet, her mouth cooing, her hair done up in ugly curlers, the tails of one of my old shirts flapping around her hips.

Our daughter was killed in a school bus that went over the edge into the Delaware River. She was eight years old. I suppose it was afterward that everything flew apart but the seeds had been germinating for years and there was nothing left to hold us together: the more bored we became with each other, the more jealousy ruled Eileen's imagination. She became fixated on a wholly false idea that I had turned into a satyr; she asked constant idiotic questions in a demanding voice and finally it drove me in defiance into the very kind of meaningless affairs she dreaded. I made no great secret of them. There were three or four histrionic scenes and finally, having justified her near-paranoia, she filed for divorce. I did not contest it.

It's distasteful to write these things but it seems necessary. When I met Nikki I had convinced myself of my own unreliability; I did not regard myself as being capable of sustaining anything more demanding than a brief affair.

Nikki had lost her husband two years ago and I assumed she too was not yet ready for anything like a serious relationship. We never mentioned marriage. It was as if the word had been erased from our lexicon. We made no plans more than a few days ahead. We delighted in each other in a broken instant of suspended time and gave no thought to what might come after. Yet it seems important to try and convey an understanding that we had no sense that it was temporary. That would have implied an anticipated ending, and we had none; we reserved nothing, withheld nothing—nothing intimate. There were things we did not discuss very much (our own backgrounds for example) but that was because those topics didn't fit into the style we had adopted with each other, or so it seemed at the time; I had no feeling she was keeping deliberate secrets and I know I kept none.

The idyll extended into the cherry-blossom spring; we took our exercise on horseback in Rock Creek Park, we drifted down the canals, we picnicked on the

Blue Ridge with my outrageous friends: uproarious games of Botticelli, insane evenings of puns and character assassination, quiet nights in bed when we only lay warm together and listened to each other's breathing.

Early in May she told me she had to return to Tel Aviv for two weeks; something to do with the organization she worked for.

I immediately said, "I'll go with you."

I had written to the old man in Israel—his name was Haim Tippelskirch—and he had replied by air-letter that he would be happy to grant an interview if I should happen to visit his country. The invitation hadn't excited me; he said he had been a subaltern in Siberia and I'd had enough experience with old men's recollections to put very small stock in their veracity. It hardly seemed worth a long expensive trip merely to interview one man whose function in those historic events had been one of low-ranking unimportance. That his revelations would draw me into a terrible trap was something I had no way of suspecting until much later.

Nikki's trip changed my mind about Haim Tippelskirch's unimportance. I rationalized that there might be useful records in the Palestinian archives; I had never seen Israel, it might be worthwhile to talk to the old man after all; it was still a cool spring in Washington, cloudy all the time it seemed, and I looked forward to a blaze of desert sunshine; I had not been away in months; and so on. The truth was I wouldn't have gone without Nikki.

3

THE OLD MAN lived in a modern block of flats in Tel Aviv. I hadn't expected such Scandinavian architecture or such crowds along the commercial thoroughfares; somehow I'd created a picture of Israeli austerity and was amazed by the hell-bent rush for consumer goods I saw on all sides. Certainly on the streets of the city there was no sense of fear; you didn't feel an Arab air force lurking beyond the horizon, you didn't suspect every alley of harboring an Al Fatah fanatic. It was almost as if all that must have been a fiction of the Western press. At the time of course I was unaware of what went on behind closed doors, except insofar as the government-censored newspapers covered it. The Jewish Defense League, which had terrorized New York so recently, was regarded as a pathetic joke; the press was filled with political cartoons ridiculing not only pompous Arab windbags but also the American Zionists and to some extent Israel's own politicians.

It was quite hot and the proximity of the Mediterranean only made it seem even drier than it was—like the parched feeling you get when you come in sight of a man-made lake in the middle of the Arizona desert.

Haim Tippelskirch had a tiny apartment on the fourth floor overlooking the playground of a modern school. He and Nikki were very glad to see each other; they embraced and their laughter mingled.

She had told me he had a great deal of vigor for a man in his seventies but to me he appeared alarmingly frail at that first meeting. He was very tall but thin as a sapling, with oversized grey slacks cinched up around his middle chest; he leaned on a polished cane. His wispy hair was in pewter-grey tufts and his cadaverous face appeared to have few teeth.

Yet there was dignified authority in the poise of his

22

head, the angle of his physical attitude when he greeted me. With Nikki he had spoken Hebrew; we now had a brief go-round of tongues—he had no English—and we settled on German, with which we were both comfortable. He spoke with a good High German accent and did not need to hesitate in search of the right word.

Later after that first meeting Nikki told me how hard it had been for her to conceal her alarm: he had wasted badly since she had last seen him six months earlier. We had no way of knowing it but he was already quite ill with the cancer that would soon take his life. I don't know if he had the diagnosis yet; he knew he was ill.

She was remarkably good. She gave no sign. She teased him girlishly and the old man gave as good as he took. He was her surrogate uncle, they told me; he had known her mother well. They were not related but they might as well have been.

He didn't seem a religious man; there were no artifacts in the apartment. The furnishings were inexpensive and Scandinavian in style but hardly spartan; he had arranged the small flat pleasantly and the sun streamed in with clean strong light. One entire long wall of the sitting room was given over to bookcases and the volumes on the shelves were in several languages; I saw none in English but apparently he read French, German, Italian and two or three others besides Hebrew and Russian. There were the classics of Russian and Continental literature and philosophy; there was also a substantial library of history and military studies (including three of mine in translation); he had Clausewitz and an extensive shelf of Nietzsche and Goethe.

The two of them made tea and Nikki brought it into the sitting room on a silver tray. It looked quite valuable. I remember the old man catching my eye and smiling. "This is one reason I am no longer in Russia. I fear I lack proletarian sympathies. I enjoy as much comfort and luxury as I can afford—and I've never had anything against privilege."

Nikki had to leave. We both saw her to the door. "Take good care of him," she said to the old man; we kissed and she went.

He waved me to a chair and went to the bookcase where he took down a book. It was my first, the one on the Civil War in Russia. He laid it on top of the case; stopped to glance out the window at the sky and then pivoted on his cane to face me. "Of course I have read this."

"A very youthful effort," I said.

"It's quite well done. But it's seen from a great distance. You must have done it all from libraries."

"Libraries and official archives," I said. "I didn't know of any other sources then. It takes time to learn one's way around, in my craft."

"In any craft." He hobbled to a chair with wooden arms, settled into it and bent forward to pour the tea. "Do you take sugar? Cream?"

"No thank you."

I didn't rush him with questions; I've learned they tend to close up on you if you do that. He knew what I was there for. I let him do it his way.

He indicated my portable cassette recorder. "Do you always use that?"

"When I can. It reduces the possibility of misquoting."

He stared briefly at the machine. Recorders frighten some people. I said, "I won't switch it on if you prefer."

"It doesn't matter. Please yourself." He had a curiously engaging smile; it was a bit absent and never quite complete but there was a tremendous warmth in it.

He handed me the tea. The cup rattled on the saucer. He sat back and sipped his own, regarding me over the rim of his cup. "I confess you took me by surprise. From your book and your recent letters I took you to be an older man. What does a young American have to do with these events in Asia of so long ago? Are you Jewish?"

"No."

"Of Russian parentage then?"

"My mother came from the Ukraine."

"As did I," he murmured.

"I've always had the feeling that we in the West need to know more about these things," I volunteered.

"Americans know nothing of the Russian Civil War. Nothing at all. Most of them never heard of it."

"Perhaps that's just as well, isn't it?"

"Those who do not learn from history——"

"Yes yes. I know all that. But the fact that you teach them this history is no warrant they'll learn from it."

"I only want to give them the opportunity. They can't make a choice if they don't know any facts."

"Which facts? What do you expect this to prove?"

It was hard to answer; really I had no grand purpose. "I enjoy the act of discovery," I said lamely. "Possibly my books don't do much more than entertain, but the readers do learn something. What they do with this knowledge isn't up to me."

He wasn't particularly pleased with that. "This land where we are right now," he said. "During the First World War this was Turkish territory. History shows us that the British promised Palestine to both the Jews and the Arabs, at different times, in return for Jewish and Arab help in capturing it from the Turks. So the British captured it from the Turks and now the Jews live on it and the Arabs want to take it. The fault is England's. The English know their history, they know this. Has it helped us?"

"It provides you with a scapegoat," I said; and we both laughed at that.

"I have lived most of my life in Palestine," he said abruptly. "I came here in nineteen twenty-four."

"That long ago?"

"I'm something of a pioneer." He was proud of it. But it was an endearing pride, not at all arrogant. He stabbed a finger in the general direction of my book on top of the case; the pointing finger was frail and avian. "That war of yours drove me here. But I suppose I can be thankful for that much. Although I can think of very little else to feel kindly toward, in that war."

"It must have been horrible."

"The cost," he murmured. I noticed that his hand was shaking. He noticed that I noticed; he hid his hand in his lap.

I thought it was the right time to press gently. "I

understand you were with Admiral Kolchak's gold train at the end."

He looked up with dignified astonishment. At first he did not reply; he covered his confusion by drinking tea. When he set the cup down he cleared his throat. "I'm surprised Nicole would have told you that."

"I'm sure she didn't mean to betray a confidence."

"It isn't that. It only means she trusts you—more completely than I have known her to trust anyone in a long time. Nicole is . . . brilliant in many ways of course, a remarkable woman. But she can be very vulnerable and she knows this. That she chooses to trust you—I hope you will take that as the great compliment it is."

"I do."

He studied me before he nodded his head; then he said, "The gold train. Yes, I was with it. Up to the very end." He went on appraising me, sizing me up; impulse wrestled with caution on his face, and finally won. "It should be told, I suppose. *Gott in Himmel,* if it had been told forty years ago my brother might still be alive." An abrupt nod of decision. "I shall tell you, then. There are no longer any secrets worth keeping."

He reached for his cane: balanced it on the floor between his knees and rested both hands over the curved handle. He leaned forward and nodded toward my recorder and I obeyed, switching it on, testing the levels.

"The treasure was only gold in part. The largest part to be sure. I have never forgotten the count we made. There were five thousand two hundred and thirteen wooden boxes containing gold bars. I believe the value of that bullion was stated at the time as being six hundred and fifty million rubles. In addition there were some sixteen hundred bags that contained securities and other valuables—one hundred million paper Romanovs, nearly four hundred millions in platinum, and what one could call a miscellany of state treasure. This was the entire treasury of Imperial Russia—the Czar's liquid reserves. The total value at that time was very close to one billion one hundred and fifty million rubles. In your dollars of that time this represented approximately nine hundred and fifty million, but some of the securities would be valueless today of course.

26

The platinum and gold alone, however, would today be worth nearly two billion dollars on the world market."

He tapped his chest. "I have made an amateur study of the gold market in my retirement. But you do not need to have a sophisticated knowledge of international monetary exchange to understand what this much raw wealth could do to the economy of nations if it were suddenly to appear."

I said, "Not much likelihood of that, is there?"

His smile this time was edged with irony. "Herr Bristow, do you know what happened to the Czar's Imperial Treasury?"

"Not for an absolute fact, no. The published histories conflict. One suggests the Czech Legion got it, another insists Kolchak handed it over to the Bolsheviks. One of them even says the partisans mined a bridge over the Angara and the whole train went to the bottom of the river. But it seems obvious it ended up in Lenin's hands. They've got those underground vaults in the Urals. . . ."

"They do, yes, and those vaults contain great quantities of gold. But not the Imperial Treasury."

I felt the first tingling of excitement. "Then what happened to it?"

"A great many things happened to it, Herr Bristow, but so far as I know, the entire treasure remains intact to this day—hidden.

"I will tell you about it—as much of it as I know." He settled back now and let the cane lean against the chair; he spoke with self-assured candor and quiet composure.

"On the seventh day of February, nineteen-twenty," he began, "I did not die."

KOLCHAK'S WAR*

1.
BACKGROUND TO A CIVIL WAR

"Westerners prefer to believe [Haim Tippelskirch told Bristow] that the Russian Revolution was decided in a few weeks of October and November nineteen seventeen. They think the Revolution was a simultaneous uprising of workers and peasants who revolted against czarism and the needless slaughter of the World War.

"It isn't true.

"Czarism was already collapsing when Kerensky came to power in nineteen seventeen. The Bolshevik Revolution was not a triumph of workers and peasants; quite the reverse. It was a high-level coup in which the workers and peasants were betrayed, Marxist ideals were forgotten, and a Bolshevik dictatorship assumed power.

"The Russian proletariat never had a chance. And the nineteen seventeen Revolution was the beginning

---

* An incomplete manuscript from the New Jersey files of Harris Bristow. For continuity's sake the editors have added, within brackets, summaries of those events which Bistow undoubtedly would have covered had he been able to finish the work. This survey, which runs hardly fifty manuscript pages in length, is not even a "rough draft" in the usual sense; rather, it is a skeleton—an outline for a book, upon which Harris Bristow intended to build tenfold.

As Bristow instructed, much of Haim Tippelskirch's narrative has been included. The Tippelskirch remarks are set off with quotation marks. Other factual material from the Tippelskirch interviews, where it could be confirmed by secondary sources, has been included in the editor's bracketed summaries and in the occasional footnotes.—Ed.

28

of a three years' bloodbath which makes your American Civil War a minor skirmish by comparison. From nineteen seventeen to nineteen twenty-one we were engaged in the bloodiest civil war of human history. Twenty-five million human beings died. *Twenty-five million.*"

The empire of the last Czar of all the Russias was the largest of all nations. It contained one-sixth of the world's land area and was inhabited by 175 million people who spoke nearly two hundred dialects and languages. Until the mid-nineteenth century* the people of this land were absolute slaves, and the formal abolition of serfdom in 1861 did little to change their lives: they went right on being regarded as vermin and the only important change was that they now had to pay taxes.

Toward the end of the nineteenth century, socialist thought swept through the cities. (It had little effect on the vast rural countryside; among the peasants and among their masters an indifference to violence and repression was ingrained.) There were strikes, there were demonstrations and appeals, there was the revolt of sailors and workmen in 1905; but there was no mass movement from *hoi polloi* and it was the liberal aristocrats, not the commoners, who agitated most stridently for reforms.

The first three years of the Great War were unspeakable on the Western Front but on the Russian Front they were worse.†

The Czar's empire was an archaic fiefdom. Its military leadership was a proud and backward officer corps, a thoroughly lazy and corrupt general staff and

---

* One assumes Harris Bristow had plans to expand his summary of pre-twentieth-century Russian history; it has been the editors' decision, however, to add no material not clearly needed for an understanding of the text.—Ed.

† Russian dead numbered 4,000,000 in 1914-1917. Compare casualties of the Western Allies for the entire war through the end of 1918: Great Britain, 950,000 killed; France, 1,400,000 killed; United States, 115,600 killed (more than half of them by Spanish Influenza).—Ed.

a multilayered, absurdly parasitic bureaucracy. Its primary fighting strength was Russia's Cossack horse cavalry; the Czar's armies simply were not equipped to meet the modern German war machine.

Germans swept into the Russian breadbasket; by the end of 1916 hunger and suffering had infected the towns and cities, where Marxists fueled the common people's bitter rage with propaganda that insisted the war was a plot by capitalist munitions cartels to slaughter millions for profit.

Revolutionary fury ramified through the cities of Imperial Russia. Rasputin was assassinated on the night of December 30, 1916—a warning of the coming uprising. Finally the awful food shortage in Petrograd brought out the riots of March 1917: and the Czar abdicated on March 18.

"It wasn't a Bolshevik rising that forced Nicholas to abdicate, you know. The Bolshevik party had fewer than fifty thousand members. [When it came to power a few months later it still had only seventy-six thousand members.] In March it was the liberal republicans, many of them aristocrats who'd been exposed to Western progressive ideas; they took over, and it was orderly. The Duma [the provisional government of Prince Lvov] was very anti-Bolshevik. Its ambition was to elect representatives to a Constituent Assembly and create a constitutional government along Western lines.

"The Bolsheviks did not want any part of that. But they weren't strong enough to dispute the Duma, until everyone began to see that Prince Lvov wasn't going to sign an immediate peace with the German invaders. Then things changed."

Alexander Kerensky, the strongest member of Prince Lvov's coalition, ordered a full-scale offensive against the Germans in July and this was what broke the back of the republican movement. The offensive collapsed, a blood-drenched disaster, and the defeat allowed the Bolsheviks to turn popular passion against the liberal coalition.

"Lenin's promise was simple and very appealing: he promised peace.

"Lenin said, 'The revolutionary idea becomes a force when it grips the masses.' But that was not it, you know. What gripped the masses—you saw it everywhere in Russia—was the promise of peace. The Bolshevik opportunists dashed right in. They seized the factories and consolidated their revolutionary soviets. Even in our village they were throwing up placards and slogans.

"In Saint Petersburg there was a palace coup. It wasn't a revolution, it was a ruthless coup—Lenin's junta unseated the Duma, that was all there was to it. That was November of nineteen seventeen. Kerensky had to flee the country disguised as a sailor.

"Lenin was the dictator of the Bolshevik Party. He wanted to be dictator of the empire, but that took three years.

"In the beginning he did two things—he confiscated all private property and he made a tender of peace to the German Kaiser."

The Duma's elections [to form a Constituent Assembly] were scheduled for November 25 and communications in Russia were too slow to enable Lenin to cancel them. They took place, and the non-Communist liberals won by a landslide: they took nearly 60 percent of the more than forty million votes cast in what was, and still is, the only free election ever held in Russia. (The Bolsheviks garnered only some 29 percent of the vote, even on their peace platform, and the bourgeois and conservative parties accounted for the rest.)

"Lenin had lost at the polls but it didn't stop him. The elected representatives arrived in Saint Petersburg —Lenin was calling it Petrograd by then—and a few hundred of Lenin's shock troops sealed off the palace. The representatives never got inside and the Assembly never was called to order. Of course we never heard about this until much later."

Denied their elected place in government, those who opposed the Bolsheviks took up arms. Thus, in January 1918, began the Russian Civil War.

2.
BREST-LITOVSK AND CIVIL WAR

On December 3, 1917, the Red regime signed a temporary cease-fire agreement with the Germans.

For the Western Allies it was a bad time for Russia to defect from the war effort: it meant Germany's eastern divisions now could be thrown into combat in the trenches against the Allies on the west.

Infuriated, the Allies sought to undermine Lenin's government by infiltration and sabotage and by lending aid to anti-Bolshevik military movements that sprang up in Poland, in Finland, and within Russia itself, where Lenin's enemies were forming coalitions under the banner of "White Russia" (a term coined mainly to offer a simple contrast with "Red"; it had little to do with the geographic origins of the movement).

"I have studied this for many years. I think Lenin really wanted to stabilize relations with the West. But he had great danger at home. Only by carrying out the promise of peace could he remain in power. 'Peace' was the one promise he could not afford to break.

"One can't help but observe that this Communist Party, which came to power on its pledge of peace, has been responsible for the brutal massacre of more human beings than any other political organization in history, the Nazi Party included."

The truce continued but a permanent peace had yet to be signed. Lenin delayed as long as he could: to placate the Western Allies and to salvage what he could from the impending negotiations with the Kaiser's representatives.

But anti-Bolshevik pressure finally forced Lenin to sign.

Germany's demands were voracious. The Treaty of Brest-Litovsk, signed on March 3, 1918, was a horrible blow to Russia. Germany took away nearly half her industries, a third of her population and a quarter of her territory.

The cost of the peace was so harsh that indignation flared up once again and White Russian units everywhere were mobbed with volunteers.

"Whole regiments were defecting en masse to the Whites. They felt Lenin had betrayed the Motherland at Brest-Litovsk.

"The peasants rallied to the White banner because of Lenin's confiscation of private property. The peasants had never wanted communism, you know. What they wanted was ownership of the land. That was precisely what the Reds denied them. Serfdom was the same whether your master was an aristocrat or the State."

Military resistance against the Reds flickered into existence all over Russia. It had no central leadership and no governmental structure; at first it was partisan warfare and recruiting contests, with both sides hastily daubing the giant Cyrillic characters of their slogans on walls and barracks.

Then for a while it became more orderly: traditional warfare, great armies drawn up against one another on vast battlefields. The Whites were encouraged significantly by the victory of Mannerheim, who defeated the Reds in Finland, and by the victories of Marshal Pilsudski's hard-riding Polish cavalry against Trotsky's ill-supplied and ill-organized Red infantry.

But in 1918 as the Whites spread their enthusiastic forces across a great part of Russia's acreage, no fewer than nineteen separate White Russian governments came into being in different areas, each claiming legitimate franchise from the deposed Czar. From the very beginning it was this lack of central organization which threatened to destroy the anti-Bolshevik movement in the Civil War.

3.
THE CZAR'S TREASURE

On the night of July 16, 1918, in a large manor house in the Ural Mountain village of Ekaterinburg, occurred the murder* of the Imperial family: the Czar, the Czarina, the Czarevitch, four grand Duchesses and four servants. Lenin did not want the Whites to have a figurehead to rally round.

At the same time there was a battle fought at the city of Kazan on the Volga. The White forces won—and captured the city, which unbeknownst to the Reds was the repository of the monetary reserves of the Imperial government.

The gold and treasure had been transferred to Kazan to avoid its falling into German hands in Petrograd. According to most sources its value was estimated at 1,150,500,000 rubles; it was composed of platinum, stock securities, miscellaneous valuables and approximately five hundred tons of gold bullion, each ingot stamped with the Imperial seal.

It may well have been the greatest tonnage of raw gold men have ever moved in one shipment. When the city of Kazan fell into White Russian hands the treasure was loaded onto a train after several episodes reminiscent more of comic than of grand opera (a Red counterattack, misdirected reinforcements, the arrival of a pack of bickering White bureaucrats, the dispatching of confused plain-language telegraph inquiries that were intercepted but not understood by the Reds). Finally the gold train was taken away by members of the [anti-Bolshevik] West Siberian Commissariat. This group seems to have obtained the gold merely because it sent a more numerous delegation than any of the others.

The gold was shipped to the city of Omsk and was parked on a siding in the marshaling yards; it was placed under guard by a flimsy detachment of White Army troops. Before long, everyone—White and Red alike—knew it was there. But neither side seemed to attach very great importance to it and it stayed in the

* Several students of the subject insist there is room to believe the bodies, jewels and blood that were found at Ekaterinburg were planted fakes and that the royal family was spirited away alive by sympathetic conspirators. But no real proof has been offered. (*From Bristow's notes.*)

marshaling yards aboard its weather-beaten goods wagons for the next four months without incident. In the meantime both sides suffered for lack of funds.

4.
KOLCHAK: SUPREME RULER
OF ALL THE RUSSIAS

Aleksandr Vasilyevich Kolchak was born in 1874, the son of a Russian army officer. Why he decided on a naval career was a mystery to his family but—oddly, in the light of forthcoming events—Aleksandr Kolchak became a first-rate naval officer.

During the war against the Central Powers he commanded the Black Sea Fleet. His crews regarded him as a compassionate man; they were among the few who did not mutiny during the March 1917 naval revolts. Kolchak was also courageous (he had led several bold forays of exploration into the Arctic) and even efficient (he had been a key reorganizer of the Russian navy after its catastrophic defeat by the Japanese at Tsushima, a decade earlier).

In June 1917 the revolutionaries finally took control of his Black Sea Fleet. They demanded that Kolchak disarm his officers and surrender his sword to them. He expressed his contempt for these demands by tossing his sword over the side into the waters of Odessa harbor and stalking ashore. None of the revolutionaries had nerve enough to stop him.

Kolchak was diminutive and birdlike: impatient, pale, nervous in his quick movements. He always dressed impeccably and shaved with care. His small round head was dominated by a great curved prow of a nose which separated a pair of grey eyes of ferocious and penetrating brilliance. Precise, cold, mercurial, aloof.

In 1918 he was a vice admiral without a command. Toward the end of that year he made his way to Tokyo in order to offer his services to the British Royal Navy in whatever capacity they might see fit to employ him usefully, whether against the Germans or against the Bolsheviks. But the British hadn't much use for him and Kolchak languished as a near-charity case in a second-class Tokyo hotel: alert and energetic, but without purpose, he simmered in stunted hope for a reprieve from boredom. He did not drink very much but he came to know the pleasures of narcotic drugs and was known to use the stimulant cocaine; General Pierre Janin later insisted Kolchak was an addict.

Kolchak's constant visits to the British Embassy brought him to the attention of the British Military Representative in Siberia, Major General Sir Alfred Knox.

There was none of the robust bearded-warrior quality of Russian ruthlessness about Kolchak and possibly this endeared him to Sir Alfred. The British general listened with interest to the diminutive admiral's views on the conflict in Russia. Kolchak impressed the British general to the extent that Sir Alfred went away insisting that Kolchak was the great White hope.

[The Whites themselves at this time had incredibly few anxieties about their chaotic lack of organization, but the Allies—particularly the British—were desperate in their insistence that the Whites produce a single leader upon whom the Allies could rely for coordination, command and liaison.]

The Allies finally got what they wanted. An English major general, supported by Czech and Japanese and French and American officials, succeeded in imposing upon Russia a one-man government in the person of Admiral Aleksandr V. Kolchak, Supreme Ruler of All the Russias.

"I do not believe that [General Sir Alfred] Knox reckoned on Kolchak's temperamental character. The Admiral was undoubtedly on his best behavior in those early days, but he had an erratic and violent temper. Much later, when we were aboard his train, I remember that the Admiral's desk had to be resupplied every morning with pens and inkwells and that sort of thing, because during the course of a day's business he would

36

fly into at least one rage in which he would smash everything breakable he could lay his hands on.

"He had what you would have to call an intransigent sense of principle, but he was filled with unstable energies. I'm convinced he was honest, but he was weak; he was determined but rather adolescent—he would react to bad news with an almost catatonic frown, like a child's—solemn and innocent. He really was uncontrollably neurotic. And I had the feeling he was always inclined to be persuaded by the last person who talked to him."

Kolchak traveled with a retinue that included several personal servants and his mistress, whose husband was one of Kolchak's officers. [Kolchak's wife and children were safely ensconced in Paris for the duration.]

Kolchak was undoubtedly a man of naïveté and excesses. But he saw through to the realities of the Civil War to the extent that he quickly realized the uselessness of the Whites' strategy of evasive harassment. His armies were soloists who could not harmonize; they had Lenin outgunned, outmanned and outsupplied, yet they had made virtually no progress toward Moscow.*

Unfortunately Kolchak's early efforts to set this right were undermined by his own command structure. His government, of which he was "supreme ruler," had little actual military control. The Allies had imposed upon White Russia a commander in chief of armed forces in the person of General Pierre Janin, the ranking member of the French Military Commission. Janin took his orders from Paris.

The American Expeditionary Force in Siberia was commanded by Major General William S. Graves, who stayed in Vladivostok almost the whole time and, under orders from President Woodrow Wilson, refused to intervene in Russian internal affairs except by using his troops to guard the Trans-Siberian Railway. General Sir Alfred Knox, having installed Kolchak, seemed to feel his responsibility had been met and he made no apparent effort to help clarify the command structure

* The Bolshevik government had moved the national capital from Petrograd to Moscow in 1918.—Ed.

between Janin and Kolchak. Janin himself was a gruff soldier who spoke poor Russian and was as inept at strategy as he was expert in tactics.

"Admiral Kolchak was a liberal. It was not through his own design that he found himself put in a position of dictatorship. I felt he regarded it as an enigmatic position—he never seemed to decide how to handle it. He lacked a tyrant's personality, the despotic inclinations; he never seemed to realize the extent of the powers that had been given to him.

"He didn't have the ruthlessness or force of will to make subordinates submit to his demands, and he had no effective means of contact with the ordinary people —he was a remote sort of man, he had no public personality, he spoke at gatherings only with great awkward discomfort.

"Many of our generals in the field were characterized by a suicidal and hysterical incompetence. When they made decisions that were obviously wrong, the Admiral would let them have their way until it got too late, when inevitably he would relieve them of command with utmost regret and then replace them with equally incompetent generals who were additionally handicapped by their total ignorance of the field situation.

"He never knew whom to trust. He believed everyone and no one. He had altogether the wrong political philosophy for the circumstances. As an example, one of his first acts in office was to call for a National Assembly to be freely elected as soon as the war ended. Naturally this incensed most of his officers, who regarded such ideas as useless democratic political euphemisms, mysterious to soldiers of more cynical persuasions. Many of the officers wanted to restore the monarchy and he bowed to their wishes and dropped his proposal instead of ordering them to quit disputing him."

He was burdened impossibly from the very beginning with a staff of more than nine hundred* beauti-

---

* The Russian tendency to infect every organized activity with a terminal case of bureaucracy is not a creation of the Communists; it is a traditional Russian disease and was partly

fully tailored and extraordinarily dishonest subordinates, most of them completely unfit for military duties. White officers and politicians engaged in incredible profiteering schemes and speculations. There was a black market in *trains:* whole trains were stolen, their contents sold in back alleys. Kolchak's Northern Force at gunpoint stole shipments of supplies earmarked for his Western Force. Officers couldn't be bothered to feed or clothe their men; staples and military medical supplies were sold at incredible prices.

Kolchak was aware of the corruption in which he was engulfed: He appointed several investigatory commissions, but none of them produced any results. No officers, regardless how guilty or incompetent, ever got fired. The moody Admiral seemed to feel there was no point in dismissing the corrupt because the vacancies would only be refilled by men equally corrupt: there was no other kind.

What is remarkable is that for the first months of his tenure Kolchak enjoyed as much support as he did. Nearly all the bickering factions seemed willing to pay him lip service if not real loyalty. Perhaps he was so well accepted because people found it easier to confirm credentials than to assess character; at any rate he gave the White Russian movement the appearance of a central authority and for a while, in spite of everything, that was enough to elevate morale and produce a string of White military victories.

Kolchak has established his government in Omsk, a dreary city of vast gloomy state buildings on the barren plains of western Siberia. It had the flavor of a frontier camp, laid out along exact 200-meter square blocks with wide streets and single-story frame houses painted vivid hues. The city lay about two miles behind the railway marshaling yards, on the right bank of the wide Irtysh River, and was surrounded by a huge farm area of dairies and grain. In normal times it was a four-day train journey from Omsk northwest to Moscow.

The houses here were widely separated. Each had its

---

responsible for the lethargic ineffectualness of the White armies. (*From Bristow's notes.*)

pigsty or chicken coop, its stable or cow corral, its courtyard and cart shed. The big public buildings were Byzantine brick. There were a few cobblestone streets at the center but most thoroughfares were unpaved impacted dirt, powder-dusty in dry weather and muddy in wet. The wooden sidewalks were bordered by deep gutters and in the springtime each house pumped its cesspool out into these gutters so that the smell throughout Omsk was indescribable.

It was anything but a sophisticated capital. Yet for a brief time there was a spirit of elegance. Czarist officers in their grey greatcoats marched the walkways in polished boots; Kolchak's own officers made splendid visions in their white uniforms with purple epaulets, their leather heels clicking on the marble floors of the state buildings. The city flapped with the banners of the new government: Kolchak's colors were white and green and the banners were ubiquitous.

"My brother and I were subalterns together. We were assigned to foot companies guarding the railway yards at first—this was before the Czech Legion came. I remembered the first time we saw the Admiral. He came with the French General, Janin, to review us. Our Captain at that time was a brute called Grigorenkov, a Muscovite. He saluted the reviewing officers with colonial violence. (Once, later on, I remember Grigorenkov actually groveling on his knees to kiss the boots of a superior officer when he was reprimanded. But of course when he returned to the battalion he cursed and kicked the subordinates there, myself included. I suppose that got it out of his system. Cringing and brutalizing are equal parts of the Russian character, I should say. We were always burdened with the kind of vermin who leap from your feet to your throat. Have you read Alexander Werth? He has the audacity to insist the Russians are a fundamentally unaggressive people!)

"I recall that walking along with General Janin, the Admiral could not get in step. It seemed to unnerve them both. I confess I always thought of General Janin as a thoroughly poisonous man, although I did not know him really at all and have no basis for that belief.

We were being inspected in barracks and he hurried right along—his flapping greatcoat made the oil lamps flicker. He scowled a great deal and kept rubbing the back of his neck with his swagger stick. As for the Admiral, I was struck by what a small man he was. He had a watchful, alien sort of impassivity—it discouraged one from speculating, from inquiry. Certainly he had none of that, what you call *charisma*.

"Not too far away from me he stopped and asked one of my men a question. I did not hear it, but I heard the reply from the soldier. The Admiral must have asked something about our rations and the soldier had the temerity to complain there was not enough to eat.

"I heard the Admiral's reply. He said, 'Hungry dogs bite well.' It was rather sad really, because I don't believe he meant that; it was expected of him to say something like that, you see. Our company was in no fit shape at that or any other time for real fighting. The favorite joke around the barracks was that we should invite the enemy in and let them laugh themselves to death."

"It is late enough in my life that I can admit this now. My brother and I were officers only because we were somewhat educated men, we did not 'look Jewish,' and we had falsified our backgrounds and our names. Our village in the Ukraine had been overrun by waves of Germans and Russians and Czechs. We had a great fervor to survive, Maxim and I. It shamed us both, unspeakably, but we took Russian names and pretended to be *kulaks* who had joined the White Army because the Reds had confiscated our farm.

"The Whites were as anti-Semitic as the Reds, of course. They were all Russians, weren't they? The Whites tended to blame Jews for bolshevism. A few Red leaders were Jews, that's true, but after a while the Whites were convincing themselves that Lenin himself was Jewish—a canard to which I imagine Lenin would have been the first to take offense, since anti-Semitism was no small part of his nature. At any rate the Whites persuaded themselves that all Jews were Bolsheviks, and the terror of pogroms—particularly

41

the massacres by Cossacks—went on and on, on both sides.

"Some of the Admiral's own people were particularly vile in that respect. You know of course about the rumors that spread after the assassination of the royal family—that the Czar had been murdered by Jews. Even General Knox believed those rumors, he reported them as fact to London. And at Ekaterinburg some White Cossacks butchered thousands of Jews in reprisal after the Romanovs were killed there. But the Admiral himself was rather indifferent, I think. Certainly he wasn't visibly anti-Semitic.

"In any case they did not know we were Jews, my brother and I. In those days no one had much documentation and you were taken to be what you claimed to be.

"There were five of us, brothers, in my family. Three had been killed—two by the Germans, the youngest (he was sixteen) by the Bolsheviks. My brother and I, you see, had made a pact to survive. Nothing else mattered."

5.
THE CZECH LEGION

After the Treaty of Brest-Litovsk the Germans moved swiftly into the ceded territories. German troops occupied much of the Ukraine and this penetration was the cause of the remarkable odyssey of the Czech Legion.

"I think there were about fifty thousand Czech partisans. They had wanted to free Czechoslovakia from the rule of the Austrian Empire, but they were fighting in the eastern Ukraine when the treaty was signed, and the German occupation cut them off from their homeland.

"They retreated slowly and in good order into the Ural Mountains. For a brief period the Czechs found themselves at war against both Austria and the Bolsheviks; and since they had these enemies in common

42

with the White Russians it was not surprising they joined forces.

"But then there was the Armistice of November eleven, nineteen eighteen, and the Legion was no longer at war with Austria. The Legionnaires were no longer pariahs. They were citizens of a new free state, they had a homeland to which they could go, and they wanted to go to it.

"The Czechs asked for passage home along the Trans-Siberian Railway but the White Russians insisted that such aid would have to be paid for. The required payment was in the form of indentured service: the Whites offered rail transport, and the Allies offered to grant diplomatic recognition to the new Czechoslovak free state, *if* the Czech Legion agreed to remain in Russia for the time being and fight the Reds. I believe that General Knox suggested that the Czechs could get home merely by eliminating the Red armies that stood between them and Czechoslovakia.

"As a military unit the Czech Legion was probably the best fighting force to do combat on either side in the Russian Civil War. They were as ruthless as Cossacks, as well organized as Germans, as up-to-date as any army in the world. And their motivation for fighting was stronger and more clear-cut than most others': victory was their ticket home."

[For a few months the Legion fought spectacularly in front-line battles throughout the western Urals. But then Admiral Kolchak consolidated his command at Omsk.]

"The Admiral distrusted the Czech Legionnaires and their General, Syrovy; they were not Russians, and he felt it would be unwise to rely on an army which at the first opportunity would simply stop fighting and go home. So he withdrew them from the front lines and assigned them to guard the Trans-Siberian Railway, pending their evacuation to Czechoslovakia."

By the spring of 1919 the Legion had moved east as far as Omsk and had begun to disperse its units along the railway eastward. Some of the Czechs thought of seeking their own way home by way of Vladivostok, but inadvertently the Japanese prevented it by encouraging their Tatar warlords to interfere with railway operations along the easternmost 2,000 miles of track. The Japanese felt Kolchak should be kept weak because otherwise he would challenge their territorial ambitions in the Far East.

It was the depredations of the Atamans that convinced the Czechs that the railways really did need their services. [If the Atamans succeeded in interrupting traffic it meant the remainder of the Legion would never get out of Siberia.] So the 40,000 Legionnaires stayed, most of them unhappy about it, and—with token American assistance—provided the only real defense of thousands of miles of fragile rails.

6.
THE EARLY TRIUMPHS:
VICTORY IN SIGHT*

[By early 1919 the Bolsheviks were in an almost impossible trap. They were surrounded.

[To the south of Moscow, Denikin, with his Cossacks—supported by Allied units of White troops led by British, French and Italian officers and noncommissioned officers—had moved into positions previously occupied by the Germans. On the west stood Yudenitch with his mixed assemblage of White Russians, Poles, Germans and Letts. On the east, in Siberia, the Reds faced swift advances by Kolchak's big White Army: his Cossacks, his Czech Legionnaires and the

* The material in this section is needed for an understanding of the whole. This chapter was to be written after Harris Bristow gathered more details concerning the battles fought at this time. (No military engagements have been fleshed out in the existing manuscript, which was intended as a skeletal working structure by the author. The book, as planned, was to include detailed coverage of all significant individuals and engagements.) The editors have assembled the material in this chapter from Harris Bristow's work notes and, to some extent, have adapted parts of the material rather freely from his earlier book, *The Civil War in Russia: 1918–1921*, New York, 1962.—Ed.

small forces of Allied powers. To the far north—Murmansk and Archangel—access to the vital seaports was denied to the Bolsheviks by British, French and American Expeditionary Forces.

[And in the northwest stood Mannerheim at the Finnish border: Smirnova danced at the Petrograd Conservatoire while White Russian guns muttered within earshot. The battle lines were drawn less than twenty miles from the city.

[The area controlled by the Reds had shrunk to a circle around Moscow about seven hundred miles in diameter. It was a fraction of the nation. Estonians, Letts, Lithuanians, Ukrainians, and particularly the Poles, led by their pianist Prime Minister Paderewski, were in open revolt against Lenin's regime. The Whites now held the lion's share of the world's largest nation, an immense territory with a periphery of ten thousand miles. They had conquered the Don, the Kuban, the outer provinces at all compass points; Kolchak controlled all of Siberia except for the Japanese areas and Kolchak's forces were as far along the road to Moscow as Perm. The slogan of the day was *"Na Moskva!"*—"To Moscow!"

[The Bolshevik Revolution was at the edge of collapse. It hung by its claws, bottled up in the center of Russia, and Lenin knew the Revolution would be destroyed irrevocably unless the Reds could reconquer a good portion of the nation by autumn.]

Somehow the Revolution tottered into February, then March, then April without falling. That it survived its own blunders and atrocities is far more remarkable than its having survived the attacks of its enemies. Russian industry suffered particularly under the heel of the new soviets. The workers had assumed power but lacked the managerial ability to go with it. They voted themselves shorter hours and 200 percent raises in pay. In the new "communist workers' paradises" the workers' soviets made all managerial decisions and this meant that a worker, regardless of his offense, could not be dismissed or degraded, nor a new man hired or promoted, without the approval of the workers' council. Inevitably the soviets upheld the workers against the administrations. And every time a vote was required, the entire

45

work force of the factory was called out to an assembly, which meant shutting down the plant. Inevitably, the productivity of Russian industry under workers' control dropped to a pathetic fraction of its former output. Yet somehow the new Red nation stumbled on.

Rumor and appearance were as important as reality to the minds of the people. Slogans were daubed on every available wall in Red-controlled areas. In White areas there were enthusiastic war maps in the shop windows, and photographs of the Czar. Incited by rumor more than dedication, whole platoons—even companies—went over to the opposing side and within hours would find themselves facing their former comrades on the battlefield. Rapidly the Civil War tore families apart. No one trusted anyone; chaos replaced order in vast areas of the countryside. Everyone was forced to pick a side—or be shot for treason.

[Along the endless track of the Trans-Siberian these factors were more disheartening than anywhere else.*]

"The Admiral's government assigned each village a quota of conscripts or volunteers to serve in his army. If the quota was met voluntarily, eventually the Reds would arrive in the village and when they learned that the village's men were in the White armies the Reds would raze the village to the ground and massacre the inhabitants. If the quota was not met, on the other hand, White generals would send our Cossacks out on area sweeps to punish those villages which had failed to meet the army's levy, and the Cossacks would slaughter the entire village.

"These conscription squads and punitive expeditions were far more responsible than the Reds for the rise of partisan bands. Siberia came to be filled with bands of Socialist revolutionaries, monarchists, partisans and ordinary bandits. The Reds were willing to try recruiting them; the White Russians took them all to be Bolshe-

* In Siberia the war was fought solely along the railway. Go a hundred miles to either side of the line of track and you would find relative peace; go two hundred and you would find remarkable disinterest in the war; go three hundred and you could find people who didn't even know there was a war on. (*From Bristow's notes.*)

viks. It was one small difference, but it hardly meant anything.

"You saw these vicious recruiting practices done by both sides equally. The issues of the war were of little importance to most of us, particularly those outside the cities. The Bolshevik insurrection had been almost exclusively urban and the Civil War was always a war between two minorities. Neither side enjoyed any support except what it could command by extortion, threat of force, or benefit of hate and reaction (that is, if the Reds wiped out your village you would probably join the Whites, and *vice versa*)."

When Kolchak began to look as if he might win after all, many of the Siberian Atamans made belated overtures to him. The warlords wanted to be on the winning side because in that place and at that time it was probable that being on the losing side would lead to a firing squad. (British pressure on Japan to modulate the Atamans' brigandage also had an effect.) Nevertheless no one—Red or White—trusted the warlords; and the Czech Legionnaires kept their posts along the Trans-Siberian. Kolchak's principle source of supply was the British, who during the campaign delivered to him the contents of seventy-nine shiploads of war matériel from Vladivostok and the northern ports; keeping the railway open was vital.

By April 1919 the Whites had everything in their favor and the Allies happily felt that it was only a matter of weeks, a few months at most, before the Red menace was annihilated permanently. The membrane of Bolshevik control was so fragile that it was hard to comprehend why it wasn't already ruptured.

Victory was in sight for Aleksandr Kolchak. No one could credit a reversal at this point; the Whites were just too strong.

No one could credit it. But it happened.

7.
THE WHITE RUSSIAN DEBACLE

In April 1919 Kolchak's lines, spread too thin and supported poorly by supply lines that were too long, staggered to a halt in the Urals.

Now the war went into a state of deadlock which was to the Reds' advantage. The Whites were scattered across two vast continents without adequate communication and their only means of achieving a juncture of forces was to destroy the Bolshevik center. Until that happened the Whites could not coordinate their efforts and it left the Reds free to deal with each White force in turn—a tactic which Trotsky made splendid use of, rushing from front to front in the armored train that was his headquarters.

"For more than a month I can remember fighting there in that awful frozen muck. We were toe-to-toe in the mountains, neither side giving ground, each attack foundering on the insensate resistance of the enemy's defenses. Our troops would march wearily to the front, herded by Cossack warders who ran swords through those who moved too reluctantly toward the battle. There were many who froze, or went out of the lines with frostbite and trenchfoot.

"There was no real net change up there until the fourteenth of May. Trotsky's counterattack. It was sudden and ferocious. We were thrown into complete panic.

"By the middle of June we had lost every foot of ground we'd taken during the past six months."

[At the same time Wrangel fell back in the south, Denikin couldn't reinforce him sufficiently to prevent the retreat, and the Kuban fell to the Reds.]

"When the Reds captured our officers they would nail their epaulets to their shoulders with six-centimeter spikes. It was an awful retreat. The Admiral's slogan, 'To Moscow', disappeared from the posters and marquees, and I suppose that part of the world which had watched all this began to realize that those posters would never be displayed again."

[July 1919:] The Reds infiltrated the small high passes of the Urals and swung around behind the Whites to take them from the rear. A sudden thaw had turned the frozen canyons into quagmires but the Red drive continued, and the haphazard White defense was as fatuous in execution as it was in design.

At this point the British ceased their deliveries of aid to Kolchak. They gave him up as a lost cause—which he was, of course, as soon as they gave up supporting him.

Three rivers crossed the paths of the retreating Whites between the mountain battlefields and Kolchak's capital at Omsk: the Tobol, the Ishim and the Irtysh. Within the next several weeks the White armies would make a stand at each of them.

In military terms the falling back of Kolchak's regiments could be called a retreat only with some serious abuse of that word. Desertions, disease and death by combat had squandered his front-line forces; Kolchak's generals presided over a flimsy holding action with an army whose strength had been reduced to fifty thousand men and the only accurate term to describe their brief defense of the Tobol and their panic-stricken rush to get across it is "rout."

Everything had splintered. Kolchak, Supreme Ruler of All the Russias, was the leader of a "government" that was a mere cohesion of weakness and exhaustion and terror; no longer did it have the slightest hope of survival.

"The officers tried to encourage recruiting by publicizing Red atrocities on shop posters, but it only scared people off. You saw money lose value by the hour—goods were scarce and there was a rush to buy *things*—portable valuables. People moved through the dark alleys looking for black-market contacts. You saw the deserters crowd past with their sullen faces and muffled starving people huddling in the doorways.

"Finally the Admiral gave orders to retrench the

rear guard—many of them unwilling or unfit to fight—in defensive positions along the Ishim River, some one hundred miles west of Omsk. My brother and I went out with them. Somehow we held, we fought back the Third and Fifth Red armies.

"In the meantime we understood that the Admiral had pumped a little confidence into his people and they had 'recruited' enough replacements to start planning a counterattack, intended to drive the Bolsheviks right back into the mountains.

"But before that, we had a respite. There was no overt agreement that I ever heard of, but both sides suspended the fighting for the harvest season. Russia would starve without her crops. The soldiers went home to reap the harvest, and we held the lines with token forces.

"We lay in the trenches for nearly a month above the Ishim, waiting for them, and waiting for the Cossacks to herd our own armies back to us."

8.
THE TRANS-SIBERIAN RAILWAY
AND THE ATAMANS

By mid-1919 the Siberian railway towns had become training camps for Kolchak's armies. Recruits and conscripts were assembled in them; the market squares were used for drilling and training, the storehouses for billeting them and equipping them with uniforms and arms. As soon as they had received a minimum of training and equipment these troops were thrown right into the lines in the Urals. In the meantime the Czech Legionnaires and a handful of American soldiers provided sentry cadres for the protection of the towns and the railroad itself, the prime umbilical: the only source of supply, and the only escape to the East.

Past the Urals the track extends four thousand miles east across the steppes to Vladivostok. In many places the rails dwindle away in both directions in a perfectly straight line as far as a man can see. For many long stretches there is but a single line of tracks; opposing traffic must pull off on sidings and await the passage of a priority train. Part of the line—mostly in the west, from Irkutsk through Omsk—had been double-tracked in substantial sections but was still insufficient for the traffic engendered by modern warfare and the support it required.

The Trans-Siberian had a poor roadbed; the ballast tended to spread and sag, and the tracks with it. Workmen had to be constantly at work with spiking hammers to tighten loose rails against the floating ties. The spring thaw almost always meant the line had to be closed down for more than a month for repairs.

Stopping the transport of an entire continent was merely a matter of blowing up a few yards of track or putting a torch to one of the thousands of small wooden bridges that dotted the line. Guarding the track against such depredations by partisans and bandits was the job of the Czech Legion; repairing the tracks was the job of labor battalions of conscripts—old men, women, adolescents too small or too young to bear rifles. These unfortunates were herded at gunpoint along the length of the Trans-Siberian to work until they dropped, keeping the roadbed in fragile repair.

The long Siberian winters were hell for railroad men. Sometimes the big 2-8-2 snowplow locomotives were not sufficient to clear the track of blizzard falls of drifted snow. Locked switches had to be thawed with pitch fires and torches. To get started from a standing stop each engine was equipped with a sandbox that could be opened to scatter sand under the driving wheels. At all times the engine fireboxes had to be kept alight and the boilers had to be kept in water; if the fire went out the pipes would burst from freezing and if the water ran out the mechanism would melt.

That the railway kept operating as long as it did was nearly miraculous. In the end, inevitably, it was destined to collapse.

"It was a war that divorced men from the restraints of decency. Massacres, tortures, rapes and atrocities were the rule and it soon became tiresome to object to these things on moral grounds because that would be

51

like objecting to the force of gravity. They were simply the conditions of life, and life was the cheapest thing in Russia.

"Nevertheless the depravity of the Siberian Atamans stood out. These Atamans were Tatar Khans with little private armies of rural Cossacks. They were independent bandits, like the Mexican road agents of fifty years ago, but the war in Siberia made great opportunities for them and they became very powerful in their little fiefdoms. In a way they were the inbred dregs of the descendants of the Mongol hordes, the last of the petty heirs to the empire of Genghis Khan. They had been allowed to run wild in Siberia for centuries, beyond the reach of civilization.

"I remember one of them. Ataman [Grigory M.] Semenev [warlord of the Trans-Baikal Cossacks]. He operated west of Lake Baikal, mainly as a bandit but at least he professed to be an anti-Bolshevik bandit and therefore he received support from both the British and the Japanese, who apparently felt he could be useful in helping them get control of Manchuria and eastern Siberia. The Japanese were terribly ambitious out there.

"These Atamans and their Cossacks would loot towns and trains. That was their occupation, looting. They found ready markets for their spoils in places like Harbin and Chita.

"Early on, when the Admiral signed an order that was supposed to force the Atamans off the line, the Japanese informed him very coolly that the warlords were under Imperial Japanese protection. The Allies tried to change the Japanese minds, but that had no effect—it was only the Czech Legionnaires who kept the Atamans from seizing complete control over the entire eastern two thousand miles of the railway."

It was the *broneviki* that gave the warlords their awful strength. The *broneviki*—armored trains—were not a Siberian invention but the Atamans had carried their development as machines of destruction to a new extreme. Even the massive locomotives of these menacing juggernauts were encased in 3-centimeter armor plate. The barrack and stable cars for the Cossacks, machine-gun cars with slitted traverse ports, turreted swivel-gun platform cars and armored flatcars for the chain-drive lorries and command cars and motorcycles were armored with incredible thicknesses of steel.

The *broneviki* could be stopped by derailment and they couldn't travel faster than about fifteen miles per hour because the roadbeds were uncertain and they were excessively heavy trains. Nevertheless they were the scourge of Asia. When the rumor of an armored train rumbled into a railway town the citizenry would gather up its portables and leave instantly. Those who remained were exposed to the sight of the grinding black behemoth scraping to a ponderous halt with a hissing sigh of brake shoes; gunports slamming open; rifles thrusting out through armored slits; artillery swiveling in its turrets; machine guns running their muzzles out their slits and traversing the town with wicked deliberation; stable-car ramps slamming down and Cossack cavalry thundering forward, sabers high.

Service aboard the *broneviki* was not unlike penal servitude and not many volunteered for it. Except for the Cossacks most of the troops were impressed forcibly by the warlords and for the least offense were whipped to death. Only the Cossacks served by choice.

"Ideology meant nothing to the Siberian Cossacks. Fighting was their way of life and its object was the opportunity for looting.

"You saw them in their karakul hats, festooned with sabers and ancient Krenk rifles, and they were terrifying to look at. But unlike their western Cossack counterparts in Russia and the Ukraine, they were nearly useless in modern combat since one or two properly positioned machine guns could cut them to ribbons —they had no tactics to counter that, they were very primitive. The water-cooled machine guns of the Czech Legion held them at bay. Nothing else did—certainly no moral scruple. If any human tribe of our century can be said to be utterly without redemptive qualities— other than horsemanship and physical courage—it is the Siberian Cossacks. Those *stanitsa* villages where they were raised on the steppes were breeding grounds for every conceivable depravity.

"If they had been too long without women—a couple
53

of days or more—they would lasso adolescent boys and bring them along to camp at the neck end of ropes tied to their wooden saddles. They would subject them to homosexual gang-rapes and then slaughter them with sabers and hack off the victims' genitals and leave them pendant in their mouths. If the Cossacks had been too long without action (a day or more) they would get bored and would practice their long-range marksmanship on whatever moved within eyesight, whether it be wolf, woman or infant."

On August 19, 1919, Ataman Semenev's Cossacks captured a train in the Trans-Baikal. When they learned it was a White Russian prisoner-of-war train the Cossacks were incensed: no booty. The fifty carloads of Red prisoners were slaughtered to the last man by Cossack sabers. Three thousand dead.

Ataman Rozanov in the Far East—a Kolchak supporter—rounded up whole village populations as hostages and whenever one of his own men was killed he would kill ten of the hostages. Later in history this extortionate technique would be put to use by the Nazis but it is useful to note that Hitler did not invent it.

The Allied Expeditionary Forces which had landed in Vladivostok to support White Russia's efforts were exposed to these Cossack bestialities at closer range than were most Russians, let alone other outlanders. It was in large part the revulsion experienced by men like General Knox and the American General Graves which, as much as any battlefield reverses, encouraged the Allies to pull out of Russia. They no longer wanted any part of the Russians—White *or* Red. To their Western minds it was no longer possible to extend assistance to any nation regardless of leadership so long as it fostered (or even permitted) the existence of beings as verminous as Grigory Semenev and his Cossacks.

So the assistance was withdrawn, and White Russia collapsed; and in Siberia, in the end, the only surviving beneficiaires were of course the Cossacks.

9.
THE COLLAPSE

"Our soldiers went from house to house in Omsk, that September, begging for food. I think all the livestock disappeared almost overnight. On the streets you saw orphans who'd starved to death and old people frozen dead on the boardwalks. The soldiers' wives were prostituting themselves for the price of half a loaf of bread. Everywhere you saw wagons abandoned in the mud of the streets, it was up to the axles. So nothing moved in the streets, they were all stoppered that way. Half the stores in the city were looted empty.

"Epidemics infested every overcrowded building in the city. The sick overflowed the public buildings and hospital trains; in the hospitals, reserved for the war-injured, men lay three to a bed and the floors were carpeted with half-dead bodies.

"You saw Jews in gabardines and threadbare frock coats trading their last possessions for food. A silver samovar for two eggs, some ornate lamp for a few slices of bread. Some of those Jews had come from far away —I think some even came from Saint Petersburg and Moscow, they'd got through the lines somehow. The Reds were purging again you know, there were new pogroms up there and everybody was trying to get out.

"You have to remember everyone in Asia lived briefly and wretchedly in those days. It wasn't just the war, although that made it much worse. There is such a thing as being worked to death—literally worked to death—and also there is such a thing as being too impecunious to survive. My brother Maxim and I had no money but we had learned to degrade ourselves by toadying to our superior officers and somehow we didn't starve. We were desperately hungry but we didn't starve. We stole, yes.

"Our job at this time was to guard the horses. You see we all knew there would be a retreat and we needed draft animals, there weren't enough trains. But the starving people wanted to kill the army horses and eat them. We had to fight them off. In the morality of

55

the time, Maxim and I felt we had honored ourselves because we never killed anyone who tried to steal a horse. We only sent them away. But I'm sure some of them starved to death because of us. You can't live with that knowledge and remain sane. We became insane, of course. No more so than anyone else around us, but insane just the same. You were insane or you were dead."

Those few with possessions and money stayed in the taverns, stayed drunk, stayed oblivious. The debauched gaiety in the cafés made an unspeakable contrast to the horror all around it.

Rumors from the front were increasingly despairing. But if the appearance was bad, the reality was even worse. In October the Reds rolled over Kolchak's holding forces and marched into Petropavlovsk with nothing much left to restrain them from moving right on into Kolchak's capital.

Kolchak's armies, dressed in rags, fell back as far as the Irtysh, just two miles west of the city. Here they stopped. The Irtysh had refused to freeze, there were no boats of any size, and the railway bridge had floated away.* The White armies could not march across the river and so they had to remain where they were and prepare to fight with their backs to the river.

"We had been in the front lines a good part of that summer before they had rotated us back to Omsk to guard the horses. Then I think it was early November that they sent our two companies of infantry back across the Irtysh in rowboats, a squad at a time. It took all day to get three hundred men across. We took up positions facing the west and waited for the Bolsheviks.

* Most Siberian river bridges, like those at Omsk and Irkutsk, were floating bridges which were removed from service before the winter freeze-up to prevent their being destroyed by grinding ice movements on the rivers. Temporary sand roadbeds were constructed on the thick ice for winter rail installation. After the spring thaw the bridges were replaced; to do so earlier would have been senseless. The Siberian rivers are very wide: The Irtysh at Omsk is more than a mile wide and during the spring floods can become as wide as ten miles, flooding entire valleys. (*From Bristow's notes.*)

"It snowed every day, at least a little, but during the afternoons it would warm up a little. The river never froze hard. Everyone said such a mild autumn meant a terrible winter ahead. It turned out they were right, you know. But in November the river wouldn't freeze and there was some panic in the lines about what we would do if the Reds fell upon us. We knew they had several full-size armies around Petropavlovsk and by this time I think we were down to something like thirty thousand men in the lines."

[On November 8, two Red armies marched down the plains toward the river—a hundred thousand men or more. The Fifth Red Army made a direct advance on the Irtysh while the Third moved obliquely past its rear to prevent retreat to the south.]

"You could hear their guns, bombarding our tiny rearguard out on the plains. At night you could see the greenish German-made flares they used."

[Normally by the end of October the river would have frozen. But it was still loose ice, floating floes, on November 9. That morning, displaying some of the courage for which he was noted, Kolchak made his way across the Irtysh in a steam river-tug, accompanied by a handful of aides including General Janin.* Twice the tug was rammed by heavy ice rolling downstream on the swift current; once it almost broached.]

"The Admiral wore a belted fur-lined coat of grey leather; its fur hem hung around his boots, almost scraping the ground, and he looked as if the boat trip across the river had soaked him to the skin.

"We were in a dugout we were using for battalion headquarters. The Admiral came down from what passed for army HQ—it was just upriver a few hundred meters from us. He came with four or five officers. The whole time he was with us he did all the talking, none of his aides spoke a word. General Janin only stood watching. He kept flicking his trouser thigh with his quirt.

---

* After the first few months Janin had received instructions from Paris to obey Kolchak's orders, with certain restrictions; he was free, for instance, to pull out at any time. Oddly, however, he remained loyal to the cause longer than most Russians did.—Ed.

"All the battalion combat officers were assembled and it was quite crowded in the dugout—fifteen of us, perhaps eighteen. The enemy was not far away. I remember just as the Admiral opened his mouth to speak, we heard a mortar fire. You know what an old tennis ball sounds like when it bounces? It was like that, the noise. One of our own mortars, I think.

"There was a growing rattle of rifles off to the northeast—some advances by the Bolsheviks, but most of it was indiscriminate shooting of a very poor standard. Our soldiers tended to fire several rounds at intervals just so they could warm their hands on the hot barrels of their rifles.

"I suppose it wasn't later than half-past two or three o'clock but there was an early-gathering winter gloom and one had the impression the Admiral was in a hurry to get back across the river before dark. We all stood around in our long winter coats and listened to him talk. He made very little effort to be civil. He lambasted his generals, none of whom was present—he blamed the losses on them, he said now it was up to us in the lines to hold out as long as we could. He had already ordered the civilian populace to flee the city but it was much too late for most of that, there wasn't any transport for them because the Admiral had requisitioned every horse and of course every train.

"He asked our battalion commander how many ablebodied we had in the lines. We had I think a shade more than four hundred. Then the Admiral smiled and asked, 'And how many of them are on our side?' Some of us laughed; the battalion commander only said, 'I hope most of them, sir.' He was rather gallant, our commander—an old-line Czarist professional soldier. He was killed the next day.

"The Admiral said it was likely to freeze hard within twenty-four hours but it was going to take several days to evacuate Omsk. He confessed he had been urged by some of the bureaucrats to negotiate for a cease-fire with the Bolsheviks, to spare the city from destruction. Then he said—I remember the words—he said, 'A decision must be made.' He said it to the face of our lowly battalion commander as if he were putting the decision up to him.

"Our commander answered in a very calm way. 'It does no service to put that in the passive voice, Excellency.'

"And the Admiral drew himself up. I think he had needed that from someone, from anyone. 'You are right,' he said. 'I must make the decision.'

"Somewhere inside his rigid exterior I think an emotion had been provoked. Pride—perhaps he had forgotten it up to that moment. He was so accustomed to having officers toady up to him. When he left, he seemed far more resolved."

With the Reds a thousand yards from his last defensive trenches, Kolchak tried to negotiate for a cease-fire; when that failed he offered to surrender.

But the Reds had victory in their nostrils and refused to accept his surrender. The word came down: "The Reds don't take prisoners." The Bolshevik armies meant to destroy the Whites, utterly.

There was no choice but to run.

10.
RETREAT FROM OMSK

"In the city the local Bolshevik sympathizers grew more daring by the hour. I saw it soon afterward. Dead Czarists lay in street doorways while refugees rushed past carrying their few belongings toward the rumor of an eastbound train.

"On the night of November ninth the temperature dropped well below freezing. By sunrise it had stopped snowing and the thermometer was still dropping. The river was frozen solid by midnight of the ninth; by noon on the tenth General Dietrichs decided the ice was thick enough to support the weight of our foot soldiers.

"I believe we were the first company of foot to be withdrawn from the lines and sent across the river to the city. It was no special favor to us.

"Our company had been decimated, really—of the two hundred we had started with, there were forty of us left. My brother came with me because his own company was nonexistent, it had been absorbed into another unit. I had eleven left in my own platoon.

"It was snowing lightly when we pulled out of our entrenchments. Enemy soldiers made a confused flitter through the falling snow west of us—they must have been as close to us as two hundred yards. The men who replaced us in the trenches had been withdrawn from other line companies; we were spreading the line thinner and thinner, you see, trying to cover the withdrawals. Most of the firing was rifles and machine guns, there wasn't much artillery—the visibility wasn't good enough for the spotters. As we pulled out they were beginning to put mortar into our trenches, though.

"I think we were guinea pigs. Particularly my brother and I. In spite of the food shortages we were still big strapping men—I must have weighed a good fifteen stone even then. We were sent out, as much as anything else, to test the ice—to make sure it would bear our weight.

"Because of our fear it seemed to take forever but I suppose it didn't really take more than half an hour to reach the eastern bank of the river. No one fell through the ice, it was quite solid. We made our way into the city.

"At some point it stopped snowing, because I recall it was not snowing when we marched into Omsk. The streets stank of battle debris—the Reds had been lobbing seventy-five millimeter across the river for two or three days. Buildings had collapsed. Shells had made ruins of some walls. Here and there you'd see a three-sided room standing open to the street like a stage set, curiously undisturbed with the furniture intact. Trees had been stripped of their branches and the street surfaces were cratered by the artillery. That morning it was accentuated by its silence. There was a kind of slow grey smoke that kept rolling through the streets and it made no sound at all. It stank of cordite and death, you know. There was one interruption I can recall— we came across a soldier who was wasting a lot of ammunition trying to shoot down a portrait of the Czar that hung above a bar in one of the cafés that had been half destroyed.

"We went along to Government House but we found

nothing but smoke hanging in the halls there, so we made our way through the refugee crowds down toward the marshaling yards below the city.

"I have never seen such a crush of people. We lost half our party in the crowd—most of them chose never to rejoin us. My brother and I were the highest ranking officers left in the group by the time we reached the yards.

"I forget how we found out what the real situation was. I know there were as many versions as there were mouths. But somehow we learned that the Czechs and General Janin's home-guard troops had gone ahead down the railway to clear it, and the Admiral with his retinue had commandeered seven trains on which they intended to flee the city.

"By this time you could hear the Red guns again, they had resumed shelling our trenches and the city.

"There was a train pulling out when we got there. I think some of the Allied missions were on board it. They must have been jammed in at least twenty-five to the compartment. The engine wheels kept screeching on the cold rails—it took a long time to get moving and I think it ran down quite a few refugees who couldn't get off the tracks."

The evacuations were hampered by railroad men who sold seat space at huge prices to the wealthy, some of whom bought entire compartments merely for space enough to carry away their valuable possessions. In South Russia, under similar circumstances, General Wrangel discouraged this profiteering by sending his Cossack Guards into the trains to throw the rich off and smash their harps and commodes and crystal and even pianos, and by hanging the profiteers publicly on the spot. But in Siberia Kolchak took no effective action and the transportation black market continued to flourish right up to the end.

Crowds bayed in panic in the railroad yards. Kolchak watched the trains depart and his tongue must have been bitter with acid. He stayed, nearly to the last; he was a naval officer and seemed to have some sense of duty to the ship of state that was sinking under him.

By now the roads leading east out of Omsk were

jammed night and day with wagons, carriages, sleighs, sledges, donkeys, camels, oxen, men and women and children. Whole regiments of deserters were among the refugees and there was no hope of reorganizing them to defend the rear. The dead lay a hundred to the mile along the tracks, rotting and contaminating the road. The refugees were like army ants, plundering every farm and peasant house, stripping every vermin-ridden corpse. Kolchak witnessed this macabre ritual of lemming-like flight and was seen to weep openly.

"On the morning of November fourteenth—one does not forget such a date—we were under almost continuous artillery bombardment from the far bank of the river. Somewhere General Kappel had recruited a number of Cossack squadrons and you saw them galloping across the snow toward the river on their wiry Siberian horses. I imagine they must have been wiped out within twelve hours.

"General Kappel had withdrawn all the Czech soldiers from the yards and the Admiral was looking for a trustworthy small unit to perform a special service. I suppose ours was one of the few groups of soldiers that remained together that morning—it was mainly because my brother and I had developed somewhat ruthless means of insuring that our men did not starve. There was a slight *esprit de corps* left among our remaining men and we did stay together much longer than other units. One can take no pride in that, in view of the cost to our integrity. At any rate one of the Admiral's aides chanced upon us in the throng and my brother and I were ordered to report to the Admiral at once.

"He was on the observation vestibule of his train in company with his mistress, Madame Timireva. She was a striking woman, full-bosomed and dark-haired. She had kind eyes.

"The Admiral must have been out among his followers all night. A great deal of heavy snow was matted in the creases of his coat. He hadn't shaved.

"I don't think he recognized us as men he had ever met before. We saluted and I told him an officer had told us to report to him—we had twenty-five soldiers still at our command.

62

"The Admiral pointed out a train adjacent to his own, on the next siding. It was one of those armored trains, not a *bronevik* but a train with armor-plated goods wagons. He told us the contents were of great importance and our unit was to guard it with our lives. We would be provided with machine guns and food; all we had to do was get aboard that train and never leave it.

"Of course it was the national treasury. The gold train, the Czar's reserves. Maxim and I were placed in command of it. At all times we were to place our train immediately behind the Admiral's.

"The Red artillery was shooting in greater volume all the time, but it was still only pot-luck fire—they hadn't got spotters across to our side of the river yet, General Kappel had prevented them crossing. But everyone could see it was a matter of hours at most. It was just past noon, I think, when our trains moved out. We were among the last trains there, and of course the last to leave Omsk."

The Fifth Red Army entered the ruins of Omsk on November 14, 1919—the same day Kolchak left.

11.
INFERNO

The *trakt* was the old overland trail that travelers had used for centuries. In most places it ran alongside the rails of the Trans-Siberian.

Down this road the refugees poured in terror with their valises and parcels, in what is perhaps history's most bizarre and massive single-line retreat: at least 1,250,000 men, women and children fled east from Omsk that November:* east into thousands of Siberian miles, their destination unclear even to themselves.

Tatars in their sashes and pantaloons, bearded Jews in worn-out black coats, foreign soldiers in puttees, Orthodox priests in their robes, deserters in assorted

* According to most sources there were 750,000 civilians and approximately 500,000 men in uniform, of whom most were deserters from both sides.—Ed.

uniforms, Russian aristocrats in shredded finery, Chinese with their hands muffed inside the sleeves of their quilted jackets, women in mud-caked heavy skirts, *kulaks* in farmer corduroys, Cossacks in long heavy coats, children in rags. . . .

There was a thaw on November 18–19 and along the *trakt* the huge ungainly peasant carts mired down to their hubs and blocked the road every few hundred meters. The tide broke, swirled around them, came together again like water in a flash flood. People lay jammed on the roofs of railroad cars; people competed savagely for scraps of food and fodder.

Kolchak's seven trains had been almost the last to leave Omsk but once out of the city Kolchak felt no compulsion to continue acting as rearguard for the avalanche of refugees he had triggered. He began to make remarks to his staff officers that the one million pounds of gold bullion aboard the twenty-eight armored goods wagons of the treasury train were a "sacred trust" and must be safeguarded at all costs because without these funds there would be no hope for a rebirth of the White movement. With this rationale as his justification he ordered the tracks cleared ahead of him so that his trains could pass through to the front of the line of march.

It was not easy. That it was done at all is flabbergasting. Kolchak's officers had to threaten to shoot stationmasters dead on the spot before they could get the seven trains shunted through. The sidings in every hamlet became jammed chaotically with refugee and hospital trains that had been pushed off the main line to allow passage for Kolchak and his gold. Nevertheless, traffic jams held them up for days in some places. The confusion was augmented by the Allied Expeditionary Forces which were scrambling for transport ahead of him, so that Kolchak kept being held up by them—mainly by the Czechs, who were passing their own trains down the line ahead of Kolchak's. Meanwhile on the sidings, in the stalled trains, hundreds lay dead—starved or frozen or diseased.

Kolchak had taken a decision to retreat as far as Irkutsk and set up a new capital there. Irkutsk was the midway point along the Siberian Railway—approximately equidistant between Omsk and Vladivostok. It lay at the head of the great inland sea of Lake Baikal on the Mongolian border. Here he would reorganize his forces, he said; he would prepare for a long war. The Reds could not take Irkutsk because if they marched that far they would be at the precarious end of a supply line so easily interdicted that they wouldn't dare try an attack. At the same time the move would put Kolchak that much nearer his own principal base of supply at Vladivostok; and the gold treasury would be dipped into in order to keep the flow of incoming supply alive. Once the Allies saw him stabilize the White government at Irkutsk they would climb back onto the bandwagon; he was confident of that, the Allies hated the Bolsheviks.

But two thousand miles of Siberian winter lay between Omsk and Irkutsk. And Kolchak's trains were making a bare fifteen miles a day.

In the chaos of Kolchak's wake any man who could command a few followers, a machine gun and a handful of rifles was a government to himself. In every town and village there were lawlessness and riots, looting, marauding, fires, massacres.

Through the month of November the temperatures kept dropping until it became so cold that vodka froze solid in its bottles.

It was the coldest Siberian winter in fifty years. By December the thermometer had dropped to minus sixty degrees Fahrenheit and Cossacks were found frozen to death in the saddle. Thousands lost limbs and even genitals to frostbite. Corpses froze solid in less than thirty minutes (and for sanitary reasons it was desirable that there be no thaw in the weather). To fall asleep was to freeze to death.

In their initial flight from Omsk or points west these refugees had put on as many clothes as possible, one on top of another, and this saved some of them; the rest stuffed their shirts with moss and hay to ward off frost. Many had rags tied around their feet. The sick died untended where they fell; cholera and smallpox epidemics raged; thousands of people broke out with the livid red pellets of the spotted fever, typhus.

Along the *trakt* the dead were stripped of their boots and coats. The corpses were heaped in patternless mounds—human bodies treated less carefully than cordwood; but then they were of less value. Everywhere the dying writhed, chrysalis-like, ignored by the hundreds of thousands who went past them in empty-eyed hopelessness. Driven beyond human endurance this mass of doomed souls trudged endlessly through Siberia with their frozen wounds and starving bellies, slipping on the ram-packed dry snow that squeaked under their boots, maggots in their wounds, lice in their clothes and hair. The infinite featureless horizon daunted whatever spirits they had left; their legs shuffled and flopped in a loose unintended mockery of drunken dances.

In this hard-lying snow the fugitive line moved slowly and without end and the frozen air created a clear separation of sounds, the crunch of frosted boots and the crisp rattle of horse gear, the grind of cartwheels and squeak of frozen leather. Pots clattered and hoofs thudded the packed snow as if wrapped in muffling cloths, but there were no voices—none—and along the hundreds of miles of march a million exhalations of breath hung clouded in the air, freezing quickly and visibly into brittle puffs of mist that shattered and shifted and clouded their clothing like tiny hailstones.

Even among the still-organized units there was no military supply service left. The soldiers requisitioned food at gunpoint. On the trains the passengers burned anything flammable: candles were worth the price of a life—for their heat, not their light.

Every few days the *booran*—the high wind that came with the Siberian blizzard—whipped across the steppes and blew dry fine powder-snow which could choke a man and blind him. The deep winter slaughtered them by thousands: by hundreds of thousands. They marched obliviously through the snow, sliding on the slippery flesh of corpses underfoot. The *trakt* was a macabre putrefaction of rubble and derelict human remains.

By mid-December Kolchak's seven trains had passed down most of the length of the column and he had left some three hundred evacuation trains behind him. Nearly all of them froze, broke down, or were derailed by partisans. Each had to be pried off the tracks so that following trains could proceed.

The dead capsized trains became shelters for refugees who lived in them and burnt all their wood and then moved on again, clinging to passing sledges and carts or walking.

At rare intervals a passing train would toss food to the refugees. But hundreds were trampled to death in the rush to claim it.

The news reached Kolchak that Red cavalry had interdicted the track only a few hundred miles behind him. Trains back there were cut off and the Communists were methodically butchering the passengers, burning the hospital trains with the sick and injured still inside them. Thousands of passengers were clubbed to death because the Reds wanted to save ammunition.

Toward the end of December the Red Army behind them was capturing a dozen trains a day and those who could escape the trains took to the mountains south of the railway to avoid capture. By now less than one tenth of the railway's rolling stock was usable. Kolchak forced his staff officers out into the gales to gather snow for his engine boilers because the pumps of railway water towers had congealed in the cold. Morphine and all other medical supplies ran out. Axes would not cut frozen trees; farmhouses and barns were chopped down to fuel the Admiral's locomotives. Each depot was stripped and razed for food and fuel but there was not enough; each of the old convict stations became a graveyard and the unburied dead lay along the tracks in mountains. On December 14 the Reds entered Novonikolayevsk and found in the buildings and streets of the city the corpses of thirty-five thousand men, women and children.* At Taiga they counted more then fifty

Because of the war—still being fought in the Ukraine and elsewhere throughout Russia—the harvest had been minimal (despite the informal harvest-season truce) and in this horrible winter of 1919–1920 millions—literally millions—died of disease, famine and cold. They

_____
* By the following April another thirty thousand had died of typhus in this small city alone. (*From Bristow's notes.*) thousand dead.

were not battlefield casualties but nevertheless it was the war that killed them.

In the meantime the retreat stumbled on. Beyond the frozen Ob and Yenisey rivers the terrain began to crumple and heave. It was the boundary of the central Siberian uplands; the Sayan Mountains formed a high barrier along the Mongolian borders and long ridges shouldered out far into the steppes. The Kuznets, Siberia's rich iron and coal region, was timbered and jagged: Mount Piramida, eleven thousand feet high, loomed just south of the Trans-Siberian tracks.

Somewhere in this district, Aleksandr Kolchak played out his penultimate gamble.

"Twice around Christmas our locomotive had run out of fuel and the boilers had frozen and burst. The third time it happened we were in the Kuznets, I think it must have been two or three days after Christmas. We uncoupled the locomotive and concocted some sort of cable truss with which we heaved and jacked and tipped the locomotive off the rails, and then the Admiral's train reversed into us and we were coupled onto the caboose of his train. But we were too heavy and his locomotives—he had two of them in tandem on his train—only slipped their wheels on the tracks. You see, we were on the upgrade there, it was miles and miles of two or three percent grade. Even putting sand on the rails didn't help. Our train was simply too heavy. The gold itself weighed five hundred tons—one million pounds that is—and there was all that armor plate, we had twenty-eight armored goods wagons filled with treasure. It simply wouldn't budge.

"Our detachment—my brother's and mine—was still manning the gold train, of course. We were not alone there, the Admiral had assigned several of his officers and their staffs to us. The gold was the most important thing in his existence then and of course he wasn't going to trust it to two dozen worn-out soldiers like ourselves. We were knee-deep in colonels and brigadiers and it was a curious arrangement because officially my brother and I—subalterns in rank, you know—were in charge there but we had more high-ranking officers than enlisted men on our train. Natural-

68

ly none of them took orders from us. But we were all in the same hopeless situation and there was very little friction—the officers were as terrified as our enlisted troops, no one had the strength to be abrasive.

"All the officers on the Admiral's staff kept vying for assignment to our train. There were a number of reasons. We were always the first to receive food and firewood, for instance. The Admiral meant to insure that we stayed in good fighting health in case we had to defend the train against an attack. Then too there was the fact that our train wasn't overcrowded. The gold weighed so much that it hadn't been possible to jam people into every available space. There was elbow room—each of the goods wagons had only part of its space filled with treasure, there was a good deal of empty space because of the weight. And also everyone knew that if any train got through it would be ours, so that everyone wanted to be part of it. There were squadrons of Cossacks aboard the trains in front of us and behind us and their sole assignment was to prevent our own people from climbing on board this train. I have no idea how many were murdered by those Cossacks; it must have been hundreds at least.

"When we were stalled that final time in the Kuznets the Admiral called a conference—the ranking people on his staff. My brother and I were not privy to it of course, but afterward it was easy to see what they had decided. I don't know whose idea it was—I doubt it was the Admiral's, he was too jealous of the treasure, he wouldn't have volunteered to part with it. But someone—or some group—must have convinced him that it simply wasn't possible to go on carrying it with us. We were still a thousand kilometers short of Irkutsk.

"At this time we had progressed ahead of the vanguard of the refugee column on the *trakt*. I suppose it must have been two or three days behind us. We did not know then, of course, how many of them had perished.* But in spite of our special treatment we had lost several lives even among our own small privileged

* At this time—late December 1919—probably three-fifths of the refugees had died; half a million humans struggled on, with the Reds at their heels.—Ed.

company and we couldn't believe that those poor wretched beings had much chance of survival in the open.

"I don't excuse our actions; it was a time when you chose between your charitable impulses and your need for personal survival. You can debate the philosophical consequences of such a decision endlessly in hindsight, and God has witnessed the guilt with which all of us who survived must have struggled without cease. But you didn't think about such things then. You didn't think at all. You existed from moment to moment, you armored yourself with indifference to everyone's suffering but your own. If there was privilege or advantage to be had, you siezed it or you perished.

"In a way the ones who died had an advantage—at least they were spared the unavoidable torture of guilt that goes with the knowledge that through no virtue of your own you've lived through hell simply because you happen not to have died in it, and that your survival has been achieved at a cost of hundreds or thousands of the lives of your fellow men.

"I think the only thing that has prevented me from committing suicide many times since then has been the rationalization that they would have died whether or not I had survived. The Civil War and the awful winter were disasters as arbitrary as hurricanes; I had not caused them to happen. Yet so often this sounds to me like the echo of the voice of some SS beast from the Second War who answers all accusations with the cry that 'I am not responsible!' In some way, you see, I *am* responsible—I'm responsible to every human being who died as a result of my existence. I must be called to answer for them. But how in the sight of God does a man do this?

"To return to what we were talking about—the gold train, yes. When we stalled in the Kuznets.

"The burnt-out locomotive lay on its side at right angles to the tracks where we had pushed it over. There were trains stalled behind us, I suppose for hundreds of kilometers—I don't know how many trains were left. There must have been at least forty or fifty. We were holding them all up. The track ahead of us was clear, however. There were perhaps two dozen

70

trains ahead of us—the Czechs and some others. They were well on their way to Irkutsk by then.

"I cannot describe the ferocity of that winter. Of course I was not a native of Siberia but I was accustomed to the climate of the Ukraine which can be incredibly severe; but nothing like that. The tears would freeze to your eyelashes. Even inside their railway wagons the horses had great balls of ice on their hoofs. If you went outside the train for only a few minutes your coat would turn stiff as a board. If lubricating oil dripped from a locomotive it would form a strip you could pick up like a piece of stiff steel wire. And the blizzards, the gales . . . One simply cannot comprehend how any of the refugees afoot were able to survive at all. Yet thousands of them did, for a time at least.

"The train behind ours was filled mainly with high-ranking officers and privileged civilians—wealthy people and civil government administrators and some of the gentry. Now and then you saw ladies tottering about on their high heels when the air inside their stalled coaches became so oppressively close that they simply had to get out for a two-minute respite. And there were two squadrons of Cossacks riding the horse wagons of that train. They were Don Cossacks as I recall.

"The Admiral gave some orders and this train of which I speak was brought forward to the rear of our own train. Then with the Admiral's tandem locomotives pulling at the front, and the uncoupled engine of this following train pushing us from the rear, we were able to make very slow headway up the grade. After about two hours we had covered some three kilometers in that fashion, and we came to a fork in the tracks where a branch line fed off into one of the ravines that made a groin into the higher mountains to the south of us. It was one of the rail sidings that led off to an iron-mining district.

"The frontmost locomotive of the Admiral's train was detached here and ballasted with tons of sandbags which my troops were employed to pack on board it. Then the engine was switched onto the branch siding and began to clear the rails. In many places the drifts were as high as the locomotive smokestack and our men had to dig by hand. You could see, as the track was cleared

71

away, that the line had not been used for quite some time—the tops of the rails were rusty.

"We had a bit of luck. There were no storms just then. The sun had come out in the morning and the ice cracked like rifle fire. The air was frozen so still that it was too easy not to notice how cold it was. You had to remember to keep batting your hands together and thrusting them under your armpits—even our fur-lined gloves were insufficient protection.

"In thirty-six hours we must have cleared nine or ten kilometers with the aid of the Admiral's plow engine. We had six or seven casualties during the effort—one man broke his leg in a crevasse and I had two soldiers make a stretcher for him by putting their rifles through the sleeves of two coats, but I think the man froze to death on his way back to the train. Two or three men fell asleep in the snow and we would find their still-breathing remains, but they were too far gone with frostbite to do anything for them. You developed a bovine indifference to all their sufferings.

"As for my brother, fatigue and pain had become so much a part of his face by now that they almost seemed to add to the glory of it. He was a bigger man than even I. Rather clumsy muscles but a splendid body and he would move among the men, wearing his white *papakha* fur hat and an ankle-length greatcoat trimmed with fur that he had taken off a stalled train somewhere back along the line; at least it had been ankle-length at first, but I seem to recall that he had cut off part of its skirt to keep the snow and mud from weighing it down. But he was a magnificent sight, looming among us. We were all so exhausted and yet he seemed to go on and on—I never discovered where his strength came from.

"Maxim and I had developed differences—we found we reacted to all this in different ways, and it began to draw us apart. We were very close in age—I was one year his elder—and we had always been as inseparable as twins. Of the two of us he had always been the more sober-minded, he had been a very deliberate and serious child where I tended more toward the pragmatic and expedient. I suppose it's true he had a more profoundly developed moral sense than I, but the difference

72

had never been very marked—as I've said, we had together made our pact to survive however we could. And regardless of all the horrors we experienced, I think we always felt our most unforgivable sin was our denial of our Semitism. From this grew all our other guilts, you see; it was the cause of everything.

"And as our days grew steadily more appalling we began to react differently, as I said. My own defense was to withdraw—I simply went into the kind of catatonic state you sometimes experience when you've gone too long without sleep and you see everything as if it were at a distance and without reality. I lost my initiative after a while; I just drifted with things. Fortunately by that time we were under the Admiral's protection. Otherwise I surely should have died quickly. I had lost most of my will.

"Maxim on the other hand had toughened. This is hard to describe because I don't mean to suggest he became ruthless or hard. It was a very moral kind of thing with him. It was as if he realized all this was punishment for his great sin, and he had decided to face up to it and accept the challenge because it was his obligation and responsibility. And so he not only endured the hardships, he became a leader among us.

"This change in him flowered visibly at this time when we were clearing the branch railway. For the first time you would see him organizing the entire effort, giving orders to the locomotive driver and all the colonels and majors among us. He was far beneath them in rank but he had this resolve, you know, and all the rest of us had lost our own wills as if a drain plug had been pulled. Maxim did that job alone, really. He carried it all on his shoulders. The rest obeyed him without question.

"One of the staff brigadiers had discovered on a map that there was an abandoned iron-mine shaft along the siding. That was what we were aiming for. When we reached it we went back to the train and spent the next twelve hours bringing the gold wagons along the siding to the point below the mouth of the shaft where they had dumped the ore carts in the old days. From here we had to manhandle the treasure up into the shaft. We

73

did that with winches and block-and-tackle hoist which we powered from the steam locomotives.

"Once the plats had been lifted to the mouth of the tunnel we had to carry the gold deep into the mountain, and Maxim organized a train of horse-drawn ore carts which carried a good deal of it inside. But the horses were in terrible condition and the last of them was spent before we had completed the task. And everyone was dismayed, particularly the Admiral, until Maxim started in to do the animals' job, putting his shoulder to one of the carts and heaving it up into the tunnel.

"We were all defeatist about this mad scheme. Those mine shafts are all constructed with a slight upgrade going in, you know. They are designed to bring heavy-laden carts *out,* not *in.* The slope was against us, you see? But Maxim shamed all of us into following his lead. And it wasn't on account of the gold; he had very little interest in the Czar's bloody gold. It was this penance he was doing, this purgatory he saw himself in—and his pride, the need he had to accept this punishment like a man.

"We weren't equipped with proper miners' lamps, of course. Candles kept blowing out and half the time we worked in a frozen darkness or near darkness. The tunnel was perhaps four hundred yards deep and we were packing the treasure into the tributary shafts that sprouted off to either side. Some of them were in a state of collapse and the rest threatened to cave in on us at any time. We didn't spare the time to shore anything up. There were no materials for that anyhow. The forests were frozen so solid they would turn the blade of an axe, or shatter it. Inside the mine, of course, it was not quite so cold—the earth insulated it quite well. Some of us were reluctant to leave it in spite of the fetid stale air and the claustrophobic fears we all had.

"The Admiral planned to return in the summer for the gold. He kept saying it was vital if the White forces were ever to recapture Russia. I don't think any of us cared who ruled Russia, by then. It was only Maxim who kept us going.

"Men dropped in their tracks from the labor of moving the treasure up those rails. We had already suffered so much—our constitutions were too far gone, these exertions wiped men out by the scores. I have no idea how many bodies we left up that ravine and around the mouth of the mine. I doubt more than forty of us returned to the main line of the railway after we had secured the gold inside the mine and closed the mine to seal it in. We—one of the brigadiers, that is, an officer who had had some engineering experience—placed a great number of demolition charges inside the tunnel and collapsed a good part of the mountain over it when we left. We were quite some distance down the track when it exploded but I have never heard such an ear-splitting noise in my life. My ears rang for days afterward.

"We had been holding up traffic on the line for at least four and a half days. The refugees on foot were beginning to straggle past. We got aboard the Admiral's train and set off down the railway on, I believe, the last day of the year. We made quite good time for the next two or three days because there was nothing on the track ahead of us. Then we began to come upon trains that had broken down and been abandoned on the track, and we had to jack them up one at a time and push them aside before we could proceed. There was a terrible blizzard on the first of January, I recall, but the generals seemed happy about it because it would obliterate all the signs that we had left along the cleared branch line where we had hidden the Admiral's treasury.

"On January the second we were ambushed by a band of partisans who had thrown roadblocks across the track. Maxim and I had remaining under our command some eighteen soldiers and since we were the lowest-ranking people on the Admiral's train we were sent out to do battle with these partisans.

"Mercifully I cannot remember those few hours in much detail. I recall our mission was to drive the partisans back far enough for our people to clear the tracks so that the train could proceed; as soon as the train began to move, that was to be our signal to return to it and get aboard. The Admiral's remaining Cossacks—there was a small squadron of them, perhaps twenty-five or thirty and their horses—the Cossacks went out

75

with us but they were so exposed on horseback that the partisan machine guns cut them to ribbons.

"Our foot soldiers clung to the ground and we moved from rock to rock trying to push the partisans back. We did manage to gain enough time for the track to be cleared, but I have no real recollection of how we did it. In the end I do know that when Maxim and I ran for the moving train we had only three followers.

"I almost didn't make it; Maxim had to reach out from the train and pull me on board. I had taken an insignificant wound in the thigh but it had made running difficult.

"As the train picked up speed I was at one of the gunports and I cannot ever forget the sight of a wounded Cossack who was trying to get to his feet in the midst of the carnage where his squadron had been slaughtered by the machine guns. The man was up to his knees in blood. The partisan machine guns were still firing as we pulled away. The Cossack was hit again and screamed soundlessly before he fell."

12.
KOLCHAK'S END

[In December 1919 Kiev fell to the Reds. Within a month the Allies lifted their blockade of Bolshevik Russia. They wanted to trade; the war was over as far as they were concerned and they were willing to deal with the victors.

[The war was not in fact over. General Denikin was still putting up strong resistance in Rostov: his Don Cossacks, with Wrangel's infantry, defeated Budenny's Red assault along the Don and briefly there was room for hope that the White cause was not dead.]

Early in January the Admiral was still struggling through the terrible Siberian winter en route to Irkutsk where he planned to set up his new capital. But ahead of his arrival, on January 4, revolt broke out in Irkutsk and after several days of vicious streetfighting the Kolchak sympathizers fled the city and abandoned it to the mobs.

Apprised of this fact by Czech dispatch riders, Kolchak stopped three hundred miles west of Irkutsk on January 7 and made his final command decision: he submitted his resignation.

Officially he passed the mantle of Supreme Ruler of All the Russias to General Denikin; Kolchak signed a formal instrument which was then forwarded to Denikin via Vladivostok and took months to reach the Crimea, where Denikin accepted the hollow throne.

There was nowhere to go but Irkutsk and Kolchak proceeded there with the remnants of his staff; the seven trains with which he had started were diminished to two. Behind him with a ragtag miscellany of troops General Kappel held out for a few more weeks in a hopeless rearguard action which only served to delay the advancing Reds for a few days. When at the end of the month Kappel died of frostbite the last organized White Russian army in Siberia dispersed.

Kolchak was interrogated in Irkutsk by partisan and socialist street leaders. For nearly a month he was beaten, starved and degraded by his captors. General Janin, who had reached safety a little farther down the railway past the Trans-Baikal tunnels, attempted to make a deal with the Red sympathizers in Irkutsk to exchange the Czarist gold reserves for the lives and freedom of the Admiral, the Czechs and the rest of the Allied personnel still in Siberia. Janin, however, did not know where the gold had been hidden—he had been on one of the trains ahead of Kolchak's—and neither Janin's emissaries nor the Reds were successful in forcing the Admiral to reveal the location of the treasure.

In their eagerness to capture Kolchak the Reds had ignored many of his top aides and these men rapidly flitted through the city and fled south, joining a growing throng of pedestrian refugees who were making their way around Irkutsk in an attempt to escape across the border into Mongolia.

The Red Army entered Irkutsk early in February aboard trains it had captured from stragglers among the White Russians. The army quickly took over the administration of all affairs in the city. Kolchak was brought before the commissars and sentenced to execution for treason.

Early on the morning of February 7, 1920, bundled in a heavy coat with a muffler wrapped around part of his face, Kolchak stood against a wall, pinned there by the headlights of two armored chain-drive lorries. It was a scene which has become a cliché throughout the world: he was offered a blindfold but refused it; he stared calmly into the gun muzzles, probably unable to see them very well because of the glare in his eyes. Witnesses said he looked relieved, almost grateful. He stood up quite straight and removed the muffler from his face, draping it carefully across his chest: a bedraggled little man trying to cover the nakedness of his failure with his remaining rags of dignified courage.

He was executed by a detail of five men armed with automatic pistols.

Later that day those eighty or ninety of his officers who had been captured with him were brought from their cells. By twos and threes they took the last short walk to the same bullet-chipped wall.

In February 1920 the Whites in Archangel broke up into packs of looting drunken mutineers. Most of the White forces in Murmansk fled into Finland and the rest capitulated to the Reds. By March, Denikin was once more in retreat in the south and the Soviets drove him back out of the Kuban. But millions continued to die in the names of causes that were already foregone conclusions. On November 15, 1920, when the last of Wrangel's army was evacuated from the Crimea by the French navy, the Civil War officially ended; even then, scattered outbreaks of warfare continued well into the next two years. The famine of 1921, caused by the war, added to the casualty lists. It was not until 1922 that the Red Army finally took control of Siberia, marched into Vladivostok and evicted the Japanese.

In the meantime anarchy prevailed throughout Russia: casual brutalities, pogroms, massacres, speculation and corruption, mass drunkenness, murder for sport, suicides precipitated by disease and lice and despair.

When the White Russians lost, it was total. With savage malevolence the victors impressed upon them the consequences of defeat: the barbarous and vicious bestiality of reprisal, executions, revenge on a horrible scale. In the end the only single crime which distinguished the White Russians from the Red Russians was that they lost.

After Kolchak's capture the spent remnants of his refugee column dispersed beyond Lake Baikal. Some managed to survive the trek to the Orient; most died, or joined up with bandit armies, or finally gave it up and joined the Reds.

Of the 1,250,000 who had begun the trek from Omsk, approximately 200,000 people survived as far as Irkutsk. Most of these fled Irkutsk ahead of the oncoming Red Army. They fled into a final nightmare: they tried to walk across the ice of Lake Baikal into the sanctuary of Mongolia.

Lake Baikal is a vast inland sea surrounded by craggy mountains 5,000 feet high. The lake is 400 miles long, some 50 miles wide at its center, and it is the deepest lake in the world—6,365 feet at the deepest point.

The refugees did not survive the crossing. A terrible blizzard caught them in the open on the lake. More than 150,000 people lay dead on the ice until summer melted it and they sank to the bottom. They are still there.

Somewhere in the Sayan Heights the gold of the Czars remained hidden. Of those who had helped bury it, and thus knew its location, nearly all had perished: the eighty executed with Kolchak; and the rest frozen to death on the flat windswept ice of Lake Baikal.

"Maxim and I survived it by happenstance. When the partisans took the Admiral off the command coach we remained with the train until nightfall. January the fifteenth, that was. It snowed early in the night. We walked down the roadbed in the direction of the lake.

"Someone—partisans or perhaps the Atamans—had blown one or two of the Trans-Baikal tunnels and the railway was blocked, there were no trains going out in either direction. We found a narrow foot-track at first light and made our way up into the hills in search of

79

food. We still carried our sidearms. There was the risk of being set upon by bandit groups; we moved carefully but we kept moving because of the cold.

"Two days I think we walked. We came to a little mountain farm which had been abandoned, but not very long abandoned. It's strange, I recall we shot some wild animal for food but I can't remember what sort of animal it was, or which of us bagged it. We took shelter in the farmhouse and demolished half the barn for firewood; we stayed there at least a week, I think, burning clapboards from the barn and shooting game when we could. Some of our strength began to return.

"After the first few days it was as if our minds had begun to thaw out, along with our bodies. We began to think. For the first time in our recent memory we began to conjure with the possibility that we might survive beyond the next few hours. We began to suggest plans.

"All my instincts cried out for one thing: that I put this unspeakable horror behind me, get away from Russia, from Asia, from what I considered to be quite literally Satan's Hell on earth.

"Different voices spoke to my brother. His guilt was the overriding influence inside him. He felt we were obliged to stay, to suffer—and to acknowledge our Judaism.

"That week in the mountain farm was a different kind of crucible from the one we had just escaped but in its way it was even more affecting. The more we talked, the more each of us became obsessed with his own chosen route to exoneration. For that was what we really sought, you know: an escape from guilt, a means of erasing our sins. I believe now that my brother was far more mature than I. I did not realize it was impossible to escape from yourself; somehow he had made the discovery, but he was unable to persuade me.

"We did not quarrel violently; there was no violence left in either of us. But the gap was not to be bridged, it only grew wider with every hour.

"In the light of what happened years later, I have wondered frequently—which of us was Cain, which Abel.

"We separated there in the mountains above Lake

Baikal. It was after the great blizzard. My brother and I embraced and I watched him set off to the north, toward Irkutsk. I know we both wept. I picked up my homemade knapsack and went away to the south. I never saw Maxim again.

"I heard from him, in the years between the wars. We exchanged a few letters—not many. Of course he may have sent more than I received; the Soviet authorities tend to confiscate the letters that Jews write to people outside the Soviet Union. Later on, during the Second War, I came to know what befell him in the Ukraine because I went there from Palestine on a mission for the organization which employed me in Jerusalem. But I never saw my brother; I only learned about him from others who knew him. He had become a leader in the village—a Jewish leader, you know; a respected elder by that time, the nineteen forties. He made every possible sacrifice for the Jews in his town. That was his penance.

"Mine took a different form but I suppose it served the same purpose of the heart. I made my way into Mongolia and went from farm to farm. In the spring I joined up with a Tatar caravan. Curiously now I recall only the beauties of those months—the glorious sunsets, the beauty of the steppes in the springtime when the grass was green and long, and we would travel through miles of crocuses, violets, buttercups. The simoons carried dust across the summer, I recall.

"It was August when I reached Harbin. I took a job there for a while, interpreting for a merchant at meetings with Russians. Then I made my way to the coast of China.

"I was quite a long time at sea. I took jobs on passenger liners—first on coastal runs with a Japanese line, then with one of the small British lines that ran ships out of Hong Kong into the Indian Ocean. I made a few ocean crossings to San Francisco. I began to hear about the Zionists and Palestine—the promises the British had made there.

"I visited Palestine first in nineteen twenty-two, I believe it was—we were going up through the Suez to Constantinople on a cruise ship. I was assistant purser.

81

I settled in Jerusalem in nineteen twenty-four; it has been my home ever since.

"As for the gold, it remained buried in that iron mine for more than twenty years before the Nazis came and took it away."

THE VIENNA MANUSCRIPT

II

4

MY CONVERSATIONS with Haim Tippelskirch were nearly six weeks in duration. He had the rambling tenden-
cies of age, and sometimes the querulousness. But
perhaps he was aware of the hungry cells that were
consuming his life; he kept repeating to me his desire
to get it all said. If he had been a Catholic it would
have been his final confession before asking for last
rites, I think.

There were several evenings when he hardly touched
on the subject of the Civil War—evenings when he
talked of pre-war life in the Ukraine, of his village and
his family; or of events between the wars, or his fifty
years in Palestine, or the Second World War. His mind
was remarkably retentive and he had a gifted analytical
memory.

Clearly he had resolved to be candid with me from
the outset—largely because he trusted Nikki and he saw
that she trusted me—but for the first ten days his habits
were stronger than his resolve. He had decided he
would tell me only what it was good for me to know,
and so he censored himself and spoke with an air of
rueful formality.

He began at the end, with his memoir of the gold—
how, why and where Kolchak had hidden it. The first
time he told me the story it was related in impersonal
terms, as if he and his brother had been observers
there. Yet the subject of the gold was a constant source
of excitement to him.

At that time I felt occasional impatience with him;
I had less interest in the gold than he had. I'm a his-
torian, not a treasure-hunter. The disposition of the
Czar's treasury was a matter of academic interest; I
was more concerned with the human truth of the events.
Nearly a hundred million people have died in the

conflicts of the Russian twentieth century* and I had become obsessed with seeking the causes of that serial armageddon. Perhaps it was hazy reasoning to study cruelty in terms of numbers—the Russians had been involved in more bloodshed than any other people on earth but they hadn't systematized it the way the Nazis did, nor did they put to use the technology for destruction which the United States employed on Dresden and Hiroshima and the Indochina villages. But more than any other modern nation, Russia had indulged in an unparalleled and nearly unbroken succession of mass human obliteration—sometimes aggressive but often as purely self-destructive as a rabid animal which, finding nothing else to attack, turns upon itself in a foaming fury and tears itself to bloody pieces.

I wanted to find the roots of that. I had reached a point where I was compelled to go beyond the idea of history-as-source material; history—the human record —was beginning to look like a substance with shape and motive and direction. I never took a Leninist view of History as an Entity to be worshiped and lied for; but as I probed the Russian century I began to take a Freudian view of it: I began to think it might be possible, by analyzing the causes of Russian behavior and gaining an insight into the contemporary Russian psyche, to predict the direction of future events.

This wasn't an intellectual game. It was an earnest pursuit. I arrived at it slowly and in retrospect I'm sure Nikki had a lot to do with it. We talked incessantly: most of it was light and frivolous but there were times when we sat together in the room or the cafés of Tel Aviv and discussed ideas. Ideas had more reality in that setting; you had a sense of living in the center of

* Bristow's figures are not exaggerated. Nearly thirty millions died in Russia in 1914–1921 (Russians, their enemies, and their allies). A like number, or something very close to it, perished in the Second World War on the Axis fronts with the Central Powers and with Japan. And the Stalinist purges between the wars destroyed tens of millions of lives. Taking into account a number of "little wars" (like the Russo-Finnish War of 1940 and the Russo-Japanese war of 1905), the total war-associated deaths of the Russian twentieth century number very close to one hundred millions.—Ed.

things, there was none of that blasé insulation against hard truths which you get in the States. Israel lives always under the poised threat of a suspended axe and it heightens the reality of pleasures, the savor of simple things, the intensity of everything. In that atmosphere it is still possible to discuss the ultimate questions of good and evil without feeling ludicrous.

And so we talked. Sometimes the two of us, sometimes the three; sometimes whole groups—friends and associates of my two companions. We thought it might be possible by puzzling out the Russian destiny to know whether the Russian urge toward self-destruction could determine the odds for, or against, the Kremlin's willingness to risk war. We asserted that it was no good studying the political and rational counterpressures in the Middle East without taking into account the character of Russian leadership and its relationship to the Arab neurosis. Reason was seldom a guiding principle in international affairs and never was it less so than when you were dealing with peoples as volatile as the Jews, the Arabs, the Russians, the Americans. How much was behavior predictable on the basis of biological urges toward domination and aggression? How much was peculiar to the nations individually? Was it possible the Russians were no more aggressive or self-destructive than anybody else—that they'd simply had more provocations and opportunities than, say, the Brazilians or Canadians? Was it possible, by the same reasoning, that the French or the British, given their Versailles and their Hitler, would have been as murderous as the Germans had been? How much different would the Soviet Union have been without Stalin?

They were questions for cocktails and cigarettes and charades; but for the first time in my life I was sincerely looking for the answers.

Partly it was Nikki's influence; partly it was the fact that I was well into my thirties and it was no longer possible for me to subsist on the kind of critical notices that inevitably began by saying, "For a writer so young, Harris Bristow has produced a remarkably impressive output. The latest of his many books is . . ." After more than ten years writing professionally I could no longer use my youth and prolificity as accomplishments of importance; I needed to do something solid—and churning out more and more summaries of historical events had become too easy because I knew how to do it, I knew which levers to press and which narrative gimmicks to employ.

I wanted more from the old man than dry facts about the burial of Kolchak's gold. He and his brother had spent those times in the company of officers of the old Russia and I wanted to know about those men—their sensibilities, their behavior, their attitudes. Russia and its leadership were still in the hands of men like those: their sons and brothers. The Soviet generals who fought the Wehrmacht in 1941 were former Czarist officers, most of them; the Kremlin leaders of 1970 were men who had grown up in a Russia that was still feudal or near to it. Especially among the leaders, old traditions of thought and attitude slip away only slowly. The psychologies of the men in the Kremlin today could be measured according to the prejudices of their fathers, I believed; I wanted to know about those men with whom the old Jew had lived and fought and survived.

But he didn't give me much satisfaction during the first few weeks of our interviews. He withheld judgments even when I asked for them. He kept coming back to the gold:

"You must understand this. The gold is of the utmost importance today—more than at any time ever before. As I have told you, I have made a study of this thing. As recently as July of nineteen seventy the price of gold on the free market was not far out of line with the official monetary price of thirty-five dollars U.S. But today suddenly there is inflation throughout the world, there are devaluations everywhere you look, the currency exchanges are madhouses of profiteers. No one trusts the currencies anymore, you see. And loss of confidence in national currencies is the entire basis for the gold market. Currencies today are in a state of collapse, and the farther they fall the farther gold rises. The price of gold has already gone up to something like forty-two dollars, which is an increase of some twenty percent in one year. You understand what I am saying?"

I suppose I understood well enough; I understand it

more vigorously today than I did in June of 1971, when these interviews took place; in the interim the free-market price of gold has shot up to seventy dollars a troy ounce, and on the clandestine exchanges of Beirut and Macao it is selling at nearly a hundred dollars an ounce.* This means the Kolchak treasure today is worth at least twice what it would have been worth in 1971, in dollar-exchange terms; the five hundred tons of bullion would command somewhere near five billion dollars today, depending on who sold it to whom.† There is more than one nation whose entire national treasury is only a fraction of that.

"You must understand what this means." His hand made a loose fist. We were at a small table in a dairy restaurant, the three of us, eating blintzes. "What it must mean to any government which still has the pretense of a gold basis for its currency—even unofficially."

"Like the United States, you mean."

"The United States, or the Soviet Union. Yes." *Ja.* Explosive, emphatic. We were still speaking German. Nikki's attention flickered from my face to his; her smile was fond.

"A large sum in gold has a way of pyramiding its power," he went on. "You can't merely think of it as two billions or two and a half billions. It is not paper currency, subject to inflation. In Beirut where the world black market has headquarters and the trading is for opium and heavy weapons, gold is the only accepted medium of exchange—they have been stamping out new gold sovereigns for years, and the transactions are in millions and hundreds of millions of dollars. This is true in all the smuggling capitals of the Near East and the Orient—only gold is used. No currencies at all. Can you imagine the effect of *billions* in gold on those markets? It would be far, far beyond anything you can measure in dollar equivalents."

I said I could hardly picture a private gang of

* At press time the free market price of gold on the European exchanges was fluctuating around one hundred and thirty dollars.—Ed.

† At press time it would appear to be as high as eight billion dollars.—Ed.

smugglers and thieves trying to heist five hundred tons of gold bullion for criminal purposes. The logistics alone were prohibitive; it would require the manpower and transportation facilities of a national government.

"Or a big corporate enterprise," he countered.

"On Russian soil?"

"I have not said the gold is still on Russian soil, Harry."

"Oh? Then where is it?"

He drew back. "I have not said it is *not* on Russian soil, either."

Nikki said, "You shouldn't play games with us, Haim."

"The truth is I do not know where the gold is. I have an approximate idea. Very approximate—you must measure it in thousands of kilometers. But that is not the point. I only mentioned the smugglers' black market as an illustration of the power that can be exercised with this much gold. An even more telling illustration is the use to which a government might put it."

I was dubious. "There are departments of the American government that spend that much money in a matter of days."

"In *gold?*"

"Gold or not, it's still purchasing power."

"You mistake it, Harry. The leverage of bullion wealth is many times its value. For how many years did your government support a three-hundred-billion-dollar economy on the official basis of thirty or forty billions in gold reserves? The political and economic power of large sums of gold is a factor of eight or ten times the actual value of the gold. A small country with two or three billions in gold reserves is in a position to wield the same economic pressures as a substantial but gold-poor country with an economy of twenty or thirty billions a year. Do you understand the reasons for this?"

"I'm not sure."

"It's a question of credit, more than anything else. A nation with piles of gold in its vaults gives the appearance of being a solid credit risk. When the world money market is uncertain, when currencies can't be

90

depended on to hold their values for any length of time at all, a reserve of gold becomes magnified out of all proportion to its real value—simply because it is there. It isn't going to wear out, it can never be inflated to the valuelessness of a Weimar Deutschmark. It is always gold, always measurable by the troy ounce, always valuable."

Nikki caught my eye and made her private signals of love. The waiter's arm flashed in past our shoulders; he took away the plates and replaced them with *espresso* cups. Haim Tippelskirch was drawing tracks in the tablecoth with his fork.

He said, "A country with that much uncommitted gold in its vaults could go a long way toward destroying the economies of neighboring states. It might behave very boldly because it would know that no internationally sanctioned blockade could succeed against it when every greedy trader in the world was eager for gold credits. Or it could buy munitions—enough to build the most powerful and modern small army on the face of the earth. Do you begin to see what I'm driving at?"

I said, "You're talking about Israel now, aren't you."

He made no reply; he only watched me until Nikki broke the silence: "If the shoe fits."

His intensity made me uneasy. He was driving at something, as he admitted; I was not yet certain what it was, and I didn't altogether want to know. I steered the talk away from the subject of the gold and, for a while, he was content not to return to it.

During the next week or two he began to open up with me, far more than before. Later I realized he was doing this partly in an effort to gain my confidence; at the time I felt he was warming to me, loosening up with familiarity.

He told me about his wife, Hannah Stein. I recognized the name at once but though it might have been a coincidental duplication—it was not an uncommon name for a German Jew—but very quickly I realized he had been married to *the* Hannah Stein, the forthright woman who had worked so closely with Ben-

91

Gurion and Golda Meir in the thirties and forties to bring about the nation-state of Israel.

When I realized this, the old man changed in my eyes; he was more than the quaint relic I had taken him for. In fact it turned out that for several years—the years that counted—he himself had been an agent for the Mossad. I felt terribly foolish; I took to casting back through our discussions in an attempt to recall whether I had appeared patronizing at any point. Now he was no longer a garrulous old man still living in a forgotten war of fifty years ago; he was a veteran Israeli security agent who had helped forge a nation in what must have been one of the great adventures of the mid-twentieth century. For the first time I realized that the importance of his life had not drifted away after the fall of Kolchak: that in terms of his own accomplishments the Russian Civil War had been a minor youthful training ground for the hard important events in which he had figured in his maturity.

He showed me a photograph of himself and Hannah Stein that had been taken in 1949; I knew her face from all the old newspaper photographs but I found Haim Tippelskirch barely recognizable. For the first time now I understood why Nikki had been so alarmed when we had paid him our first visit together. In the photograph he was a strapping giant in his prime: a man of fifty or thereabouts, towering over his sturdy wife, the big chest and shoulders filling the poplin of his new Israeli uniform. Today he was nothing more than a bookmark left in place of that man. His color was faded, a kind of powdered yellow; the skin hung in brittle folds from his skull and the spidery hands were always atremble, mottled with small brownish-blue spots of illness and age. He was still tall but the shoulders seemed to have curled inward, the chest collapsed; he was gaunt and tired and only the pale eyes reminded you of life, like bright coals in the ashes of a dead fire.

Hannah Stein had been a physician in Hamburg until the Nazi rumblings had alerted her. She had been a Zionist even before that; in 1934 she had immigrated to Palestine and Haim Tippelskirch had met her in Jerusalem. They had been married in 1936 and the marriage lasted thirty years until her death. They had three children, all of whom were alive: one was a minor functionary with the Israeli mission to the United Nations, and the other two, both girls, were married and living in Israel. I met his younger daughter when she came to visit him on a Sunday afternoon. She was a handsome woman, large-boned, in her sixth or seventh month of pregnancy, radiant with the flush of impending motherhood but deeply troubled by her father's visible deterioration. I gathered that both daughters had asked him to come and live with them but the old man was having none of that.

Hannah Stein had kept her maiden name and he told me it had amused her to refuse to answer to the appellation "Frau Tippelskirch." Until the war of 1948 she had kept up a medical practice and had served on hospital staff in addition to her work as a nationalist; after the 1948 war she had been forced to give up her practice by the pressures of membership in the Cabinet and leadership of the new nation's fund-raising apparatus abroad. It was Hannah who had recruited Nikki into that movement, shortly before her death in 1967.

I was unfamiliar with Jewish ritual and tradition and was uncertain of my forks, particularly when it came to Sabbath practices and dietary laws; fortunately the old man was more nationalist than religious and he did not keep a kosher house. He regarded the Orthodox beliefs with a worldly, kindly cynicism; to him they were useful but quaint, he didn't quarrel with them but he had no personal use for them. His god was the Jewish people; he told me that, insofar as his sins allowed it, he regarded himself as a humanist first, a Jew second and a Zionist third.

You had to credit him with the compassion and goodness he aspired to. Yet there was always a shadow over him and it was more than the long-ago memory of the crimes he blamed himself for during the Siberian terror. I began to feel he must have done things as a Mossad agent that he was not proud of; but for a long time he steered away from that subject, always reminding me that I was a historian trying to do a work on the Russian Civil War and that was our proper field

93

of discussion. The same argument seldom kept him from returning to the subject of the gold, however; he was always coming back to that—the importance the Czar's hoard could have in the modern economy. I began to have the strange feeling that he was trying to persuade me to do something about that. What it was, I had no idea at the time.

By the end of the third week of our interviews he had fallen into the pattern of beginning the discussion with a lecture on gold, and then good-humoredly allowing me to steer him back to Siberia; he would talk—ever more freely—about his brother Maxim and the months with Kolchak. Then after an hour or two he would tire of that. Sometimes we would have tea together; sometimes Nikki would come at the end of her day in the office and the three of us would take tea in his flat or go out to a café. He wasn't talked-out yet; he would dominate the conversations, even when others joined us, and the rich variety of his interests was constantly surprising. Once he launched into a half-hour monologue on the effect the Beatles had had on modern popular music; another time he participated energetically and knowledgeably in an argument with a visiting American museum curator on the relative merits of half a dozen post-Impressionist painters, half of whom I had never heard of. And there were several evenings with friends when there would be long heated post-mortems of the Napoleonic wars or the North African campaigns of the Second World War or the repercussions of the Marshall Plan.

Finally after we had been at it for weeks he started to broaden the topics in our private interviews: he carried the story forward past the Civil War into the Stalin years and began to talk of his brother Maxim, whom he had never seen again; but he had received a few letters and had heard of his brother's doings indirectly through friends and fellow agents, during the war.*

---

* There follows a series of interviews on the subject of Maxim Tippelskirch and World War II in the Ukraine and the Crimea. To eliminate unnecessary duplication of material, we have transplanted this material to a point farther along in the book where it fits more logically into place.—Ed.

Toward the end of June 1971 the old man's health began to fail more rapidly and obviously than before. Nikki insisted on calling in a doctor even when Haim Tippelskirch objected. He was still investing great enthusiasm into our interviews but finally on July seventh he was taken away to hospital.

We continued our talks there for more than a week but he was fading quickly and I could not bring myself to press him; after a while I went to see him every day only in company with Nikki or others of his friends, so that he was forestalled from launching into long talks which only left him limp and in pain. They had him on drugs—tranquilizers and painkillers for the most part; the cancer was everywhere in his system and there was no point attempting surgery, although he was being subjected to cobalt treatments.

I had far outstayed my plans. But there were no pressing engagements at home, Nikki had still been unable to finish the work for which she had been summoned back to Tel Aviv, and I felt a responsibility to the old man now; I could not leave until the end. None of us pretended there was any hope for his recovery; not even the old man himself. The doctor was a close friend, an old colleague of Hannah's, and he knew the old man far too well to lie to him.

Haim Tippelskirch did not take it easily or cheerfully; it depressed him and made him angry but I saw no evidence of self-pity and he did not become maudlin. He did not take the attitude that he had been betrayed; he behaved as if cancer were a straightforward enemy, worthy of his rage and hatred but not his fear. Sometimes he would roar at the nurse to take the medications away: he didn't mind losing the fight but he wanted to go down with a clear head, using his brain to the end. And he did so as long as he could.

His body wasted away horribly. He was covered with spots of a cyanotic blue; the flesh melted from his skeleton. His hands no longer trembled but he had no strength to lift them from the sheets. He lay propped up on pillows fighting for breath, very angry that he was too debilitated even to read. Conversation was the only stimulus left; he detested the television they had offered him and had refused to have the set placed in the room. There was a small radio by the bed and he listened to the news with active interest; the rest of the time he left it turned to a rock-music station from Luxembourg which came in by way of a relay broadcast antenna somewhere in Greece, I believe.

I can't pretend he didn't become cranky and childish; he didn't die a hero's death. But I was in awe of his courage and this only made the inevitable end more heartbreaking. By then I was as fond of him as if he were my own uncle and I felt that he loved me a bit as well; he was always pleased when I appeared at his bedside.

The Mediterranean summer was viciously hot; we went through the streets, Nikki and I, in wilted flimsy clothing, trying to avoid the crush of swarming tourists. There was an air conditioner in her flat but it did not work very well; we hardly spent a moment in the place except to sleep. The old man had put me in touch with three others survivors—a Polish Jew and two old women from South Russia who had watched the Red and White armies chase one another across the farm fields—and although none of them had been in Siberia I interviewed all three for as much background detail as they could provide.

Nikki and I were tourists now and then; we visited Jerusalem and Haifa and we drove out into the frontiers as far as one was allowed to go before being turned back by the military roadblocks. We swam off the beaches as often as we could; we enjoyed it all, and enjoyed each other, as much as we could under the shadow of the old man's dying. We took in concerts and movies and I appeared three or four times on radio and television panel programs at the behest of my Israeli publisher. Nikki spent the weekdays in her office, obviously working very hard but not burdening me with the tiresome details of whatever she was doing there. She had an ability which I envied, to compartmentalize her life; but then I didn't need to compartmentalize mine. My work couldn't be separated from my life by time-clock hours. Nikki understood this because she too was immersed spiritually in her work, mainly organizing refugee efforts; it was more than a job for her and she knew how it was to carry one's profession around as a built-in component of life rather than a separate entity, a mere source of economic sustenance.

On an afternoon in early August we went to visit Haim and found both his daughters at his side. They informed us that their brother, Haim's eldest, was flying home from New York. It could only mean the doctor had passed final sentence.

He was in strong spirits, although hardly cheerful ones. He complained of the brevity of one daughter's skirt (the unpregnant one) and made pointed remarks about his younger son-in-law, the father-to-be. Evidently Haim didn't think much of that one. I think he was employed in a curio factory in some shirtsleeve capacity. The other son-in-law managed a *kibbutz* and the old man was happy enough with him, one gathered. There was awkward affection in the room but neither the old man nor his daughters were expansive types by comparison with the stereotypes of *Fiddler on the Roof;* they were not clutching one another's hands or weeping loudly. It was a quiet sadness in the room, mature and deep, broken only by Haim's growling complaints and the fierce rock music of his radio.

After a short while he said he had to speak privately with Nikki. He waved the rest of us from the room.

We waited in the outer hall. It was not a time for getting acquainted and none of us had any small talk then. The two women were in their thirties and not very attractive. There were a few strained remarks; one of them said her father was very fond of me—she said it almost sharply as if she meant to impose on me an obligation to prove deserving of his fondness. I said something vague by way of thanks. Nearly a quarter hour went by before Nikki appeared in the door and we returned into his presence.

Afterward Nikki wouldn't tell me what he had said to her. She said it was something of no importance to anyone but the two of them. If I make issue of it now it is only because of hindsight; at the time it passed from my mind very quickly but I recall noticing that it was the first time she had withheld anything from me deliberately, as far as I knew.

Two days later he died.

5

NIKKI WAS VERY QUIET that day and the next. There is an old Jewish saying: The deeper the sorrow, the less voice it has.

They had not been related but they had been more than friends. She helped his three grown children make the funeral arrangements; he was cremated on a Thursday afternoon.

We gathered afterward in his flat and the "children" —everyone called them that but they were at least as old as I was—were very busy making everyone comfortable and going around the place talking about what the old man would have wanted done with this possession and that. The rest of us milled about in a strained way and people drifted out of the place after the decent interval had been observed. Finally the elder daughter came to me and announced to my surprise that a week ago Haim had directed that I receive the military-history portion of his library and certain other books—he had made a list. She gave it to me and asked me to select a convenient time to come and pack the books for shipping to America. I ended up making an appointment to come around on the weekend. Nikki said she knew where to find small packing cartons.

That evening I had a look at the list. In addition to the two or three hundred volumes on warfare he had bequeathed me a sizable collection of books on Jews, on Russian Jews, on Israel, and on gold. I can't honestly say I realized there was a message in that; I realize it now but a great deal has happened in the meantime. But at the time—this was almost two years ago—it was merely the generous act of a man whom I had befriended.

He left me one other thing. Nikki transmitted it to me one evening that weekend. She was at the little desk in her flat, going through bills and letters. I was reading over some notes I had made and she was bent over the pile of paper on her desk, tapping a pencil against her teeth. She was wearing a faded housedress and her hair tumbled loosely over one shoulder; I set my notes aside and watched her. The light from the desk lamp made highlights in her hair and she was lovely in that glow, like a Flemish portrait.

She plucked a slip of paper from the pile and turned her face toward me; she caught my stare and smiled immediately.

"You're very beautiful."

"No. That's silly."

"*Je t'adore.*"

She shook her head impatiently in that pert way of hers; she pushed her lower lip forward to blow hair off her forehead. I said very theatrically, "Ah, my beauty, let me be your batman, your orderly, your serf. Let me kiss the hem of your skirt and polish your shoes."

It brought her laugh but her slim fingers were at war; in the end she picked up the slip of paper again and flapped it up and down at me. "He meant you to have this."

"What is it?"

"Just a name." She read it off: "Otto von Geyr."

I crossed the room to take it from her; I brushed her neck with my lips and straightened to read the note. It was in his crabbed hand:

Otto von Geyr—SS Gruppenführer, RSHA,
General—see Ukraine 1941–42,
Crimea 1943–44—Sebastopol. Lives in Bavaria,
gov't post of some kind. Re Czarist treasury.

I said, "That's kind of cryptic."

"He didn't mean it to be. He was having difficulty holding the pad. He only made enough of a note so that I would remember what it meant. This General von Geyr had something to do with the Nazi effort to find the White Russians' gold during the Second World War."

"And?"

"He thought you might want to find this man and talk to him."

"What for?"

"To find out what happened to all that gold, of course."

"He had an obsession with that, didn't he?"

She began to say something, but curbed her tongue. "I suppose he always felt he had a vested interest in it." It wasn't what she had meant to say.

She tapped the note. "This general was also at Sebastopol during the German evacuation. You'd want to talk to him about that, wouldn't you?"

"If I could find him. Bavaria's pretty populous. I'm not a detective."

"Of course you are. What else would you call what you do?"

I put the note in my pocket. "If I get to Germany I'll try to look him up. Was that all there was to it?"

"The Germans found the gold, you know."

"Yes, he told me about that." I didn't add that it was not the kind of thing you could put in print on the unsupported testimony of one old man who hadn't even been there at the time.

"Aren't you curious what happened to it after that?"

"I suppose I am. I'm not burning up with it. It's only a sideshow at most. I mean, millions—"

"I know," she said, amused. "Millions of people were dying. Just the same, they're dead and there isn't a thing you can do to bring them back to life. But the gold is still there, somewhere. You *could* do something about that."

"Like what?"

"You could try to find it."

I laughed at her and in lovemaking we both forgot about von Geyr and Sebastopol and the gold and everything else that was not of the flesh and of the moment.

We had come to our lusty passion fiercely and quickly and without reluctance; if there was a level beyond which we did not delve, I was not aware of it then. We played the games of children in love, sometimes courtly and sometimes bawdy. Nothing prudent or fearful about it: love turned the two of us into one, in the way that two sheets of glass lie one on the other—hard to distinguish where one ends and the other begins, and harder still to pull apart.

Yet a night or two later—it was the night we packed up the books in Haim's silent flat—we came home from dinner and she threw herself across the couch in an abandoned sprawl. "Do you think you could be an angel and get me some aspirin from the loo?"

She'd had a headache for hours; I'd seen the pain across her eyes. I brought the aspirin and a glass of water. "Ready to serve milady at all times."

She sat up to swallow and when she lay down on her back with her breasts diminished she looked girlish. Her eyes were closed. "Harry you can't stay in Israel forever."

"My work's finished here. I'm only waiting for you, you know that."

She took a breath. "You'll have to go without me."

It was her job, she said; they weren't going to let her go back to the States for a while—she had too much to do here and she wasn't needed in Washington just now. She didn't know how long it might be before she could come to America.

She sat up and talked rapidly at me: "It would be ridiculous your staying here much longer. Your work isn't here."

"I don't want to leave without you, Nikki."

"We've got to be sensible. You'd come apart if you stayed."

I folded her hand between my palms and she drew the back of my hand against her side; I could feel the soft rhythm of her breathing. She didn't open her eyes.

Finally she said, "I won't give up my work, Harry. No more than you could."

There was more talk; it kept going in circles and after a while we sat in conflicting silences until she said, "Oh, dear, now you're really angry with me." She was watching me and I saw the shadow across her eyes; it was not the headache. I remembered something Haim had said to me once—probably one of his old sayings: *Take care not to make a woman weep, for God counts her tears.*

I asked her how long she thought it might be; she

101

said she had no idea. I said I could wait awhile until we found out; she said it might be months.

"Look. Suppose I go back and finish up in the archives. I could bring my notes back here to write the thing."

"Could you really? Don't you always need to go back to the archives to look up things you missed and double check other things?"

That was true; it was the way I always worked and I'd told her that. Now I felt she was using my own words against me. "You want me to go," I accused her.

"No. My God, no."

"Do you love me, Nikki?"

"With all my heart." She turned her face against my chest; her words were muffled: "With all my heart, Harry."

Finally I said, "I'll have to think about it. There must be some way."

But there wasn't and she was right: after another week I was restless and growing irritable.

It was a Sunday morning in her flat. The hot sun through the venetian blinds laid horizontal bars of light across the bedclothes. I remember her face, childlike with the drowsy innocence of first awakening. I said something cranky, something about the sun waking us up—why couldn't she put drapes across those windows? And she got up without a word and padded to the chest of drawers and pawed through her open handbag until she found an envelope.

It was an El Al folder with a ticket inside. The flight was scheduled to depart at two o'clock that day, that Sunday.

"I bought it early in the week. I knew you'd be ready by today."

"You know me too well, Nikki."

"I know it's possible to manage to live without the people you can't live without." She pressed the ticket into my hand. "I know how it is, Harry. I understand."

"Do you? Well, maybe you do—I guess I'm not the only idiotic fool you've ever met."

"Oh Harry . . ." And I stopped her with a kiss and

we made a frantic kind of love and sometime afterward she said, "You'll miss your plane—you'd better hurry."

"I suppose I'd better."

She went with me as far as she was allowed to the customs departure gate. "I'll come soon, darling."

"Promise me that."

"Yes—it's a promise I'm making to myself too."

"Wangle it, Nikki. You're good at that—twisting men around your finger."

We both laughed but it was brief laughter. We understood, both of us, that it might be a long while.

Abruptly I kissed her very hard. "That's to make sure you don't forget me."

"I have a very poor memory," she said. "You'd better do that again."

I obeyed but when I kissed her I felt the warm tears on her cheek and then she was wheeling away from me: *"Ciao,* Harry . . ." and she was running away through the airport. They were calling the flight; I couldn't follow her. I had the impulse to throw the ticket on the floor and go back with her but in the end I went through the customs and emigration line and boarded the flight with stinging eyes and an empty weight in my throat that wouldn't go up and wouldn't go down.

I knew it was foolish, immature. But that didn't ease it. I think I was sad because it made me realize we were not complete romantics at heart, either of us. If this love had been paramount we each should have been willing to make nearly any sacrifice for it but we hadn't been willing to do that. We both understood we'd have no happiness together if it meant sacrificing our individual *raison d'être.*

She'd seen it faster than I had; she'd known the day when I would no longer reject the airplane ticket. Another month and we might have been bickering, at each other's throats. Nikki had been wise enough to make the decision for us and I should have been grateful.

Love is meaningless without dignity and it is self-destroying wherever one's success means the other's failure. Nikki and I were too well aware of that. I think we both regretted it. It seemed unfair and at times I grew angry with both of us, I felt we had made a selfish and petty decision; I felt we must be small people

103

crippled by unheroic realism—it wasn't that this was the wrong age for the grand passion; it was that we were the wrong people. We were too ordinary, too hidebound in our commitments to ephemeral occupations, too egocentric in our smaller-than-life way.

In that manner I alternated between extremes, sometimes maudlin and sometimes confident that we had made the best decision. But underneath it always I felt we would find our way together again. I trusted that; I believed it with all my heart.

6

I SPENT a good part of that sweating August at home in New Jersey avoiding getting splendidly drunk. I had a secretary in to transcribe the tape recordings from my talks with Haim Tippelskirch and the others to whom he'd introduced me in Israel; I went over that material as it came from her typewriter and I spent two or three weeks going back over the material on Sebastopol and the Kolchak retreat. I had been away from it all long enough to discover some new things in it; I made some notes to take with me to archives and late in the month went down to Washington.

My first act there was to visit the Soviet Embassy. There was some encouragement: they had not shut the door on the possibility of my visiting the Crimea for the purpose of looking at their archives and interviewing survivors. Neither had they opened it wide, however. There was a bureaucratic wall of rules behind which the embassy and OVIR (the office of visa registration) took refuge. There were more applications for me to fill out, more questions to answer. The Soviets had thwarted my efforts for years but I was determined to outlast them.

At the same time I had more procedural battles to fight in the Pentagon in my attempts to get access to several cartons of Wehrmacht and SS records, particularly the stenographic minutes of daily staff meetings —records that were essential to my Sebastopol book. These initially had gone into the West German central archives but some clerical mistake had moved them into the Political Archives of the Foreign Ministry in Bonn and a supervisory clerk had discovered them, decided they didn't belong there and shipped them out to the Americans shortly before the end of the Occupation. So far as I knew they had never been examined in any detail. Nor would they ever be unless I could find some lever with which to pry them open.

The machinery was in motion but there was no rushing it. I needed the records of British Intelligence and Expeditionary Force operations in the Russian Civil War for the Kolchak book; I flew to London in the fall and spent weeks in the Imperial War Museum and the archives of the Ministry of Defence in the Old Admiralty Building. I had it half in mind to swing down to Israel before going home; I put through an international trunk call and finally, in spite of everything the telephone service could do, I reached Nikki.

It was a poor connection but it was wonderful to hear her voice. "They must have routed this call through Johannesburg."

"Oh, Harry, I can hardly hear you."

"I'm thinking of coming to Tel Aviv next week," I shouted.

"Oh dear—I won't be here. They're sending me to the Far East for several weeks. Oh crap."

"It's a conspiracy against us. Christ."

"I'm so sorry. I'll see if I can get it changed—can I call you back tomorrow?"

We arranged that she would; and she did so but she hadn't been able to change the schedule of her mission to Tokyo and Peking. There's no purpose in recounting the details of our conversation; we said our disheartened farewells and I returned to my work with somnambulistic determination.

She had never given me a clear picture of her position or function in the refugee organization. I knew she had to do with fund-raising but obviously there was more to the job than that. I took it for granted she was engaged in clandestine dealings to some extent—the efforts to get Jews out of Russia had always been tinged with the coloration of espionage and intrigue but the business of espionage was far more humdrum than the moviemakers would have us believe. Whatever her job, it didn't put her in any evident physical danger. But what began to concern me now was the realization that her position in the organization must be a good deal higher than I'd taken it to be. Perhaps because of her youth and vivacity I'd taken it for granted she had an ordinary minor post of some sort; but you didn't send your minor clerks off globetrotting to Washington and Tokyo and Peking. Nikki was nobody's secretary.

So it now appeared that I was in love with a person of some importance in the political scheme of things.

I found this discouraging, not because it created any sense of competition but because it made me realize how seriously committed she must be. This was no mere youthful enthusiasm for a cause. She had to be fairly high up in her organization; it stood to reason she must have had decision-making authority. At any rate if I had used my head earlier I should have known she was no fuzzy-headed do-gooder. She was not merely serious; she was dedicated to whatever she was doing and it was no passing fancy. It was becoming very unlikely she would ever decide to throw it over and come rushing into my arms to stay.

There was the alternative of continuing an intermittent affairs but that held very few attractions for me. I'd had some success but my income wasn't unlimited and I couldn't afford to keep up a zany schedule of globetrotting, particularly since I had to conserve money for my possible trip to Sebastopol; and it looked as if Nikki had no idea when—or if—she would be able to come to the States.

For nearly a year we kept in touch—long letters and the occasional extravagant phone call. We were neither of us at ease with gushy sexual prose; often it was a strain to write because I was too verbally inhibited to put my feelings on paper adequately, and writing long paragraphs to her about the progress of my work was no decent substitute. Nevertheless we looked forward to each other's letters and I sometimes got angry when more than a week went by without a few pages from her. She kept me appraised of the unexciting doings of the handful of people I'd met in Israel; she wrote nice chatty letters about some of the eccentric characters who shared her suite of offices; at intervals she went off to Stockholm or Vienna or Belgrade and I would get incisively witty travelogues from her with those postmarks on them. She never talked about her work in any detail; only the occasional reference to a conference of Jewish organizations in Brussels or the rather

107

proud statement that three hundred Jews had been able to emigrate from the USSR in a month's time.

After several months I began to fill with hopelessness. Gradually I started to suspect that there was no good end to this, that our long-distance affair was only a form of self-flagellation. The odds against us were high and I began to defend myself against ultimate heartbreak by thrusting Nikki away from the center of my emotions.

I began making the rounds of the Washington parties again; in time it became a series of casual beddings that lasted a night or a fortnight. It didn't work. I found no distraction strong enough to threaten Nikki's place in my soul.

I became talkative and argumentative and found myself slinging opinionated remarks into the smallest cocktail-party opening. I must have become a pill. I discovered that I had opinions on everything and anyone who didn't share them was a fool.

I offered pat simplistic solutions to the problems of crime and drugs and race relations. I insulted bureaucrats and diplomats with equal obliviousness. Curiously, I became something of a lion that season—very much in demand—and I suppose it was partly because I had a successful spy book on the market and partly because my outspoken brashness was taken to be forthright and refreshing at those gatherings of pious discreet woolgatherers. The only parties at which I ceased to be welcome were George Fitzpatrick's; wit was too highly prized at those bacchanals and it appeared I had traded in my rapier on a broadsword—suddenly, literary celebrity or not, I was too gauche for Fitzpatrick and the invitations stopped. It was at this same time—the late spring and early summer of 1972—that my publishers booked me onto several network television talk-shows and my forceful assertions about the Russians brought a ton of mail into the Dick Cavett offices while several officials—one of Cabinet rank—hinted to me that it would be wise if I tempered my pronouncements in view of the current Nixon *rapprochement* with Moscow.

I hadn't been making political remarks at all, but they were taken that way and with some justification: you can't divorce nations from politics. But I wasn't a political person. I'd grown up in the post-McCarthy era; it was no longer commonplace to be vocally anti-Communist and although I thought communism to be a system that was (if anything, and if possible) even worse than capitalism, I was not riding an ideological hobbyhorse. My outpourings were more like racist prejudices than political ones; at this time I was writing portions of the rough draft of my book on Kolchak and my feelings toward Russia were hardening. I was unable to find any consistent history of immorality in the West that matched the habitual behavior of the Siberian Cossacks, the Red Army and the Stalinists. I don't cling to those views now. But my feelings at that time had an important bearing on the decisions I soon had to make. I think it's important that in those days when I hadn't yet begun to penetrate this nightmare I had got myself into the habit of making righteous distinctions between Us and Them. I was able to believe, somehow, that the longevity and numerical hugeness of Russian atrocities made them wholly different in kind from the American atrocities in Vietnam or the absolute and thorough corruption of the entire police department of New York.

In retrospect I find it pathetic that I even made any pretense at objectivity in the things I wrote at that time. My bias was as clear-cut as the bias you find in the output of Soviet historians. It wasn't long before I was deliberately seeking out evidences of Russian perfidy. That sort of selectivity can't lead to a balanced report but when you're in the grip of bigotry you don't make those distinctions.

The cause of it must have been my frustration with the way things were going between Nikki and me. I couldn't bring myself to take out my anger on her; therefore I took it out on everything and everyone else. Yet perversely I chose as the main target of my hatred the very people whom Nikki herself regarded as The Enemy. Perhaps I was unconsciously trying to reassure her that I was on her side.

A writer's professional decisions often are the result of happenstance. Probably my mother's nationality prefigured my interest in Russian history; but I didn't hate my mother—the bias came from somewhere else. The shape of both projects—the Kolchak book and the Sabastopol book—had been changed considerably by several coincidences, mainly my chancing to meet Nikki and then, through her, my meeting Haim Tippelskirch.

Because of these accidents my mind was attuned to things I wouldn't have noticed otherwise: specifically the gold, in which I should have had a very limited interest had it not been for Haim's obsession with it.

Whenever I came across the remotest reference to Kolchak's gold in my researches, my attention would rivet itself onto the reference. I ended up with a surprisingly thick file of notes on the subject.

During the Second World War the German war machine made its deepest penetrations into southern Russia in the summer and fall of 1942. In the far south the Nazis had swallowed up the Black Sea and the Panzers were within striking distance of the shores of the Caspian. These penetrations took the Germans to a point nearly four hundred miles east of the longitudinal parallel of Moscow: the Wehrmacht pushed a great bulge into the lower belly of Russia.

That year of 1942—as all the historians point out —marked the high point of Axis expansionism. We have wiped much of it from our memories with the hindsighted rationalization that manpower and productivity made the Allied victory inevitable, but that was not necessarily the case in early 1942; the issue was still seriously in doubt before the strategic turning points at El Alamein, Stalingrad, Midway and the rest. Hitler and Mussolini and Tojo did have world conquest within their grasp for a brief while; it slipped quickly beyond reach but it was not inevitable that this happen.

Nevertheless, even in those months there were noticeable weaknesses in the German system of conquest. In spite of their masses of imported slave laborers from the conquered nations, the Germans had a limited manpower of "pure Aryans" who were thereby qualified, according to the sick standards of Nazi bureaucracy, for service to the Fatherland. Limited manpower meant limited productivity, even in a nation as highly industrialized as the German Reich. Technological advances and the use of slave labor helped to offset these weaknesses but technology was hideously expensive and the German economy became daily more unstable because its real productivity never matched its monetary needs for financing the war.

The result was that Hitler was chronically broke. Theft—even the wholesale rape of national treasuries in the conquered lands—was not enough to feed the ravenous war machine. There were vital foreign products and raw materials which had to be imported from neutral trading countries. The neutrals always demanded hard currency and the Deutschmark was not considered a hard currency anywhere outside the Axis sphere. Hitler needed gold.

He thought he had it in 1938: five hundred and ten tons of gold that had belonged to the Spanish Republic. Most of it was earmarked by Franco for payment to Germany in return for Nazi aid in the Spanish Civil War. But the Republicans in Spain had followed the example set by the Russian monarchists: they had taken their gold into exile with them. It went from Barcelona to Odessa aboard several ships and was taken to Moscow "for safekeeping."*

In 1940 the French treasury had been spirited to England via a roundabout route, a few jumps ahead of the *blitzkrieg*. The other occupied territories in Europe and Africa had no vast hoards of gold or hard currency with which to support Hitler's needs. In the meantime steady inflation was doing morale no good on the home front and Berlin was increasingly hard pressed to meet its foreign-payment commitments.

Under those conditions it isn't surprising that any rumor of billions of reichsmarks' worth of gold bullion, no matter how far-fetched, would trigger an eager response among the leaders of the Third Reich.

In the Alexandria archives I found several directives from General Franz Halder, Hitler's army chief of staff, to von Paulus and Guderian and other field commanders in the spring and summer of 1942, indicating Hitler's avid interest in the Soviets' treasure vaults in the Ural Mountains. I found one top-secret memoran-

---

* It is still in the Ural vaults; only recently have Spanish and Soviet ambassadors in Paris begun to discuss the possibility of Moscow's returning the gold to Madrid. In mass and value it is almost identical to the Kolchak treasure. (*From Bristow's notes.*)

dum from Halder to OKH Headquarters Rostov, requesting a feasibility analysis for implementing a coordinated parachute and armored raid into the Urals. The memo suggested a meeting between von Paulus, Guderian and one of Goering's visiting Luftwaffe generals; the suggested plan was to drop a parachute *commando* that would break open the Russian mountain vaults while one of Guderian's crack Panzer units made a run across the Volga to rendezvous with the parachute team. Then the Soviet and Spanish treasure would be brought out of the USSR aboard armored troop carriers and tanks.

I found no record of any such meeting taking place, nor did I find any reply to this memo. One can guess what such a reply would have contained. The distances were far greater than Hitler seemed to imagine (and the pipe dream has an unquestionable flavor of Hitler about it; clearly it wasn't Halder's idea—he was too level-headed an old soldier). There was no possibility of getting an armored column that far behind Russian lines, nor was it likely that a paratroop invasion would have cracked the well-guarded Russian vaults. In fact I found no evidence that the Germans had any decent intelligence of the location, let alone the defenses, of the Soviet gold vaults.

In any case nothing came of it, but I did find a fair number of OKH directives urging the Wehrmacht to drive across the Don and the Volga in a spearhead aimed at the Urals. The gold vaults were mentioned several times among the various strategic reasons for pursuing this dubious plan. (The German army did in fact reach the banks of both rivers, but never crossed them.)

Then on September 12, 1942, Halder directed von Paulus to "proceed with an investigation" of the "reported Tsarist gold"—its validity, location and accessibility. In the light of later discoveries I decided that this directive was only supplementary to investigations that were already under way by Gestapo and SS officials, but this Halder cipher was the first reference to Kolchak's gold I had come across and I felt a disturbing excitement.

Halder and the Führer had a falling-out at about

112

that time; Halder was relieved of his position as chief of staff on September 24 and was replaced by General Kurt Zeitzler, an arrogant youth from the Western Front who removed the last vestiges of Officer Corps dignity from the high office and became nothing more than a rubber stamp for Hitler. From that point forward in the history of the Third Reich, up to Guderian's replacement of Zeitzler, the records of the C-of-S become much less enlightening and it isn't surprising I didn't find any further references to the gold in Zeitzler's files. Very little of any importance went through his hands; for all practical purposes Hitler became his own chief of staff.

My next encounter with the gold was in a dispatch from Waffen SS *Standartenführer* Heinz Krausser which had been forwarded to Himmler in Berlin over the countersignature of *Gruppenführer* Otto von Geyr, with endorsements by various SS *Sturmführeren* and an *Obergruppenführer*. The dateline—September 13, 1942, Poltava—placed the writer in a town that had recently fallen into German hands on that date; and von Geyr, to whom it was addressed, was at that time in Kiev headquarters on the staff of a Waffen SS combat division. Krausser, the writer, evidently was a full colonel in command of a battalion of killers, *Einsatzgruppe* "E," and therefore it was clear that von Geyr was not Krausser's direct superior officer; both were members of the Waffen SS but there was a vast distinction between combat soldiers and *Einsatzgruppen.*

The *Einsatzgruppen* were battalion-strength (700 to 1,000 men) units of Gestapo, SD and Waffen SS commandos. They were originally under the direct control of Reinhard Heydrich and had been trained in the techniques of annihilation at a police academy on the Elbe at Pretsch. They had been indoctrinated chiefly in master-race ideology and the methods of genocide; the stated purpose of these murder battalions was the extermination of Jews in the conquered territories, under the authority of the Führer's order of March 3, 1941, that the Jewish Question was to find its Final Solution in mass executions.

Krausser's dispatch was attached to a dim carbon copy of a summary battalion report over his own signature which coldly spelled out the massacres of several thousand Russian Jews and summarized the incredible fact that over the past year this single *Einsatzgruppe* had murdered more than three hundred thousand Jews.* Krausser's letter expressed pride in these accomplishments, mentioned that he hoped von Geyr was in good health—evidently they shared in-laws in common or were otherwise distantly related—and went on to explain in some detail the information he had unearthed concerning the Czar's gold treasury.†

Krausser's dispatch was several pages long. It covered without much detail, the removal of the Czar's gold from Omsk by Admiral Kolchak and the subsequent decision to hide the gold in an abandoned iron mine along the Siberian *trakt*. Krausser was not specific in naming the sources of this information; he used some such phrase as "Our interrogations have produced the possibility." He then went on to say he had no way to evaluate the truth of this information but in view of the tonnage of gold involved, he thought it might be wise to bring it to von Geyr's attention. The implication was that von Geyr had access to certain ears in Berlin; evidently Krausser was as paranoid as most of his kind and distrusted his own immediate superiors, who were people high-up on the SS staff.

The number of endorsements on the Krausser dispatch indicated clearly that it had been read with interest by a number of officers, going up the chain of command from von Geyr. The last endorsement was

---

* The text, from Bristow's files, reads as follows:

EINSATZGRUPPE "E" REPORT NO. 1761

9 SEPTEMBER 1941

"Area now reported cleared of Jews. During period covered by this Report, 11,692 Jews (adult), 6,843 Jews (adolescent), 273 Partisans, 18 felonious criminals, 310 Communist functionaries shot. Up to 8 Sept. 1941, therefore, Einsatzgruppe 'E' has dealt with 329,241 Jews in all."—Ed.

† The Krausser dispatch is not among Bristow's files; neither, evidently, did he have it at hand when he was writing the above passages. Therefore either it was stolen from his files in New Jersey or, more likely, he had it with him in Sebastopol and lost it there along with most of the materials he gathered in Russia in early 1973.—Ed.

114

that of a member of Himmler's staff; I no longer recall which officer it was.

Obviously the intriguing thing about the Krausser dispatch was that it spelled out in remarkable detail the exact location of the iron mine where Kolchak had hidden the gold.

The description in Krausser's letter was uncannily similar to the description Haim Tippelskirch had given me; Haim and I had spoken mainly in German and even the phrasing of Krausser's directions was very much like Haim's. Even if Haim hadn't told me his own version of the German episode, I should have guessed that the Krausser information could only have come from a survivor of the Kolchak expedition.

7

THE FALL AND WINTER of 1972 were disagreeably grey and rainy in the Northeast. It was a dreary time of record rainfalls, and after the Presidential election and its post-mortems there were no urgent topics of conversation around the capital. Of course this was before the Watergate revival. I was seeing a good deal of a gangly cheerful divorcée whose name it would be pointless to mention here. Nikki was on my mind almost constantly although it had been a year since we had last seen each other.

In Lambertville around the end of November I had a phone call from Washington. It was Evan MacIver. I was surprised to hear from him; I'd seen him four or five times at parties in the course of the past year but we hadn't much to say to each other. He called to suggest we have lunch the following week; he named a time and a restaurant. I don't recall the conversation; in substance he said he had something of interest to discuss with me and he made it intriguing enough for me to accept the invitation.

It was the middle of the week. Heavy rain had brought traffic to a crawl and I was late getting to the restaurant. MacIver was watching for me; he got my eye and waved me to his table and I found him spooning the skin that had formed on his cup of hot chocolate. When I sat down my nostrils informed me there was whiskey in the chocolate.

It was one of those mock-Polynesian restaurants with jungle décor where middle-class women in absurd hats took a lunch break from their holiday shopping; this was the week after Thanksgiving and the Christmas boom had started. Waiters were serving sweet potent concoctions in imitation coconut shells with drinking

116

straws. I ordered a Bloody Mary to keep MacIver company.

He looked rumpled and jowly but there were traces of the old raffish humor in the lines that exploded from his eye-corners. "Well Harry, just between us suspicious characters, how are things going?"

For a while we reminisced about campus days—the bad food in the university cafeteria, the Japanese restaurant he'd taken me to once where I'd gagged on raw fish, the J. D. Salinger stories and Castro and the banning of *Lady Chatterley's Lover* and the Powers U-2 incident, and the swap of Powers for the Soviet spy Rudolf Abel. Memoirs which dated us both, and which led—as if by aimless free association—to the subjects of intelligence and espionage. MacIver was pretty good, he was at ease and casual; but the invitation had been his and I had let him guide the conversation and I was aware that it probably was no accident he led us to that point. Each for our own reasons we were interested in espionage but clearly his motives were more specific than that.

I found something vaguely edible from the menu; it was not until we were drinking coffee after the meal that MacIver began to come to the point.

"Well then how's the little Sabra?"

"Nikki?" I gave him a closer look. I hadn't spoken to him about Nikki at all since the night I'd first met her. Yet he knew.

There was a crafty gleam of guile in his eyes; I was meant to see it. "You do keep in touch, don't you?"

Suddenly I was determined to know what he was getting at. I contrived to look curious.

But he refused to be drawn. "Well she wasn't my cup of tea, I can tell you that." He put his cigarette on the edge of the ashtray and I watched it smoulder there. He said, "You know I got interested in something you were talking about a couple of months ago. Where was it, Huddleston's party? You were talking about that far-fetched Russian gold story you're writing. Sounded like a hell of a yarn. I'd like to know more about it."

"And that's why you arranged this lunch?"

"Partly. There was something else, but it can wait.

You're not in a hurry, are you? Am I keeping you from anything?"

"I've got some work to do this afternoon up at State. It shouldn't take too long—no, I'm not in a big hurry."

"State," he said, and made the connection. "Sure. You're still pushing for that Russian research visa, aren't you? Maybe I could help."

"You?"

"Us suspicious characters have a few contacts here and there. That's our main excuse for existence, you know. I might be able to help pull a string or two."

I knew he wasn't referring to the State Department; he was talking about the "other side"—OVIR and the Russian Embassy—but you had to be circumspect in MacIver's line of work. It hadn't occurred to me that he might be in a position to exercise any influence over there; I still had no idea to which desk he was assigned at the Agency in Langley. All I really knew about his position was what little he had told me a year ago.

He said, "Where is it you're trying to get to? Moscow?"

"Moscow and Sebastopol."

"You figure to hunt for the Czar's gold over there?"

He said it with a smile but he was waiting for an answer and I gave him a truthful one: I was doing a historical research, not chasing wild gilded geese.

"Well sure, Harry, but the way I've heard you talk about that gold, you seemed pretty excited about it."

"It's an interesting yarn. But that's all it seems to be —a yarn."

"What makes you so sure of that? The gold was real enough."

"Yes . . ."

"And it's never turned up, has it?"

"It has, though. The Germans found it during the war."

"I thought you were telling Huddleston they found it and then lost it again."

"It's all speculation," I said. "I'm getting pretty tired of that gold. It's threatening to become a tail wagging the dog. This job's hard enough without distractions."

"Come off it, Harry. A good strong dose of gold bullion's just what you need to beef up the book's appeal.

Otherwise who's going to buy a thousand-page history of the siege of Sebastopol? Who the hell cares about *Sebastopol,* for Christ's sake?"

There was truth in what he said. The story of the gold was dramatic and it was completely new; no other historian had come across it at all.

He scowled at me. "You won't sell eight copies of a book on Sebastopol unless you've got a hell of a hook on it. Why kid yourself? I was listening to you at Huddleston's—you weren't talking about sieges and politics and Panzer battles, you were talking about *gold.* You're trying to make yourself feel like an important scholar with all this serious research, but your stuff wouldn't sell the way it sells if you were just writing textbooks for history department libraries. You're a yarnspinner, Harry—you're an entertainer. And now you want to tell me you've got your hooks into the biggest money-caper story in history and you don't want to be *sidetracked* by it? Harry, I wouldn't buy that if it came with an American Motors guarantee."

He stubbed out his cigarette and beamed at me in triumph. "You know what I think, Harry? I think you get your nocturnal emissions from dreaming you'll find that gold of Admiral Kolchak's."

"You're pushing it pretty hard, aren't you?"

"Am I? Why should I?"

"Suppose you tell me."

"Tell me something first. Would you think of asking me that question if you didn't know who my employer was?"

I saw his point.

"Okay," he murmured. "Look, I just think you're in danger of taking yourself too seriously. You could end up on the wrong track. I think I've read every one of your books—I read the first one or two because it was a cheap thrill to say I knew the author, but after that I got to be a fan of yours. I still am. I also think I'm kind of a friend of yours and I hate to see you talk yourself into a mistake."

One of the crosses a writer must bear is well-meaning advice from people who know utterly nothing about the craft. But MacIver was leading up to something in his

119

transparently devious way and I let him set his own pace.

"That lost treasure—that's the dog, Harry, it's not just the tail."

He blew smoke at his chest. "End of kindly advice. Okay? Still friends?"

I didn't think that was the end of it at all. I said, "You said you wanted to talk business."

He toyed with the burning cigarette. "I'm sorry, I kind of did this wrong. I can be a bull in a china shop. You're not in much of a mood to listen."

"As long as it's not another piece of literary criticism."

"Why don't we have a drink?"

"You talk like a man with bad news." My mind leaped to his earlier remarks about my visa.

"Not bad news. A little off-the-record information and some advice, that's all."

"About what?"

"You want a drink? I'm going to have one."

"I think I'll pass."

MacIver summoned a waiter who took some time reaching us; he didn't say anything until after he'd ordered another bourbon. Then he plucked the cigarette pack from his shirt pocket, found it was empty, crushed it in his fist and excused himself to hunt for the cigarette vending machine. I saw him intercept a waiter who gave him directions.

He returned simultaneously with his drink order; he asked the waiter for the luncheon check and sat down stripping the cellophane from the cigarette pack. I said, "I gather your department doesn't have close rapport with the Surgeon General."

"I try to quit now and then. Every time I do, we get some kind of crisis. I figure if I keep smoking maybe it'll deter the start of World War Three. It's a small enough price to pay. That girl Nikki, she smokes, doesn't she?"

I was taken aback. "Now and then."

"You keep in touch with her, don't you?"

"Why?"

"How deep and heavy did it get between you two?

120

I've got a reason for asking. Somebody told me she was pretty deep in your guts, but that was a while ago."

I was knotting up slowly, inside. "Evan, if you've got a point to make . . ."

"How much do you know about her, Harry? What she does for a living, I mean."

I stared at him. "That's a cheap shot."

"I'm not trying to pry, Harry. I promise you I already know a lot more about it than you do. I'm not pumping you for private information, I only want to know how much she told you."

"I don't see where it's any of your business."

"Well it's exactly my business, but you're right—you don't have to answer the question. Suppose I give you some information, instead. This is off the record—I want that understood. We're not supposed to go around giving out information to people who aren't in the Firm. But you look like you're on the way to Russia on this book of yours, and I'd better set you straight. This wasn't the Agency's idea, my boss doesn't know anything about it. I'm talking to you on my own. That's why it's off the record. You understand?"

"I don't understand at all. You haven't said anything yet."

"Well I assume at least you know she works for the Israeli government. Specifically, she works for an agency that gets Jews out of Russia."

"I know all that."

"Uh-huh, it wasn't likely you didn't, but when people are working her side of the street you never know how much they're willing to spill to their lovers. For all I knew she told you she was a fund-raiser."

"She does that sometimes."

"It's only a cover, Harry. On the surface it's a legitimate agency—they do raise funds, they agitate for publicity and demonstrations wherever they think they can arouse public opinion against Soviet policy. That's on the surface. They also grease the wheels inside Russia —they get out pamphlets that tell Russian Jews how to get through all the red tape they have to go through to get an exit visa."

"You haven't shocked me yet," I said. "I don't see what you're leading up to."

"It's an underground railroad. They work with Jews who can't get official permission to leave the country. They print up false documentation and they falsify records in some of the local OVIR offices. They've got a fair-sized fifth-column staff inside the Soviet Union. It's very Jewish and very efficient—an organized operation. It's an agency of the Mossad, out of Tel Aviv."

I had half guessed that much months before. I still wasn't stirred much by his revelations; only by his intense air of conspiracy, which seemed an unjustifiedly melodramatic pose.

The waiter brought the check face-down on a saucer. MacIver took out a credit card. I said, "Expense account?"

"Sure."

"Then I won't fight over it."

"Anyway, I invited you." He signed the check and put his credit card on top of it. The waiter took it away. MacIver said, "You're not Jewish."

"Riddle me no games, Evan." I was angry with his pointlessly roundabout attack—like a dog that turned several full circles before lying down: a ritualistic habit, indulged in whether there was a need for it or not.

"They break their asses to recruit non-Jewish help. You'd be a perfect courier if you got your visa. They need couriers badly."

"And?"

"I just want to warn you. It's off the record, as I said. Screw her eyes out if you want to, Harry, but don't let the little bitch con you into joining her pack of running dogs. The chances are you wouldn't come back from Siberia before the year two thousand."

8

BEFORE CONTINUING this account I must interpolate a few explanations.

First, in reconstructing conversations that took place a year and more ago I have used the device of placing dialogue within quotation marks. The need for accuracy compels me to explain that I do not have an absolute memory for exact words that may have been spoken months or years ago. I do, however, have a fair ear for speech patterns, and when important things are said I remember the substance and flavor, if not the exact words. The device of direct quotes is admittedly a contrivance but I find it both more readable and more writable; it saves time and avoids the need for awkward circumlocutions. And I believe it provides a fuller measure of the nuances of real exchanges.

Second, I am resuming the writing of this manuscript after an interruption of nearly two weeks during which I have been almost constantly on the run. Prior to that I was writing under circumstances far less pressing than those which obtain now. During the early part of April of this year* I went into hiding, in a manner of speaking, and I had no idea how long I might have to remain in that place. There was nothing to do but write. Under those conditions I felt an obligation not only to make a full account of these events but also to interpret them wherever I could, to provide background information and to explain all the circumstances as completely as possible.

That luxury is no longer available. I am hunted; I may have a very limited time in which to complete these pages. My present hiding place is not very secure. It is likely I will have to run again soon. The most im-

* 1973.—Ed.

123

portant thing now is to complete this recitation of events.* If the remainder of this narrative appears disjointed and hasty it is for that reason; I shall have time to relate only the most important events.

---

* At the end of this section of manuscript, Bristow wrote a twelve-page summary of the events covered in more detail by the remainder of this book. He then went back and fleshed out that account; it is the second version which we publish here. But his deciding to write the twelve-page outline first is an indication of his urgency and sense of peril.—Ed.

6

IN FEBRUARY 1973 Evan MacIver telephoned to congratulate me on having won my fight with the Soviet bureaucracy. My visa and clearances had been granted by the Russian government.

It was the first I knew of it. I am morally certain that MacIver's calling me with the news was his way of taking credit for the victory. He didn't say so, but I had to assume he had been responsible, at least partly, for the breakthrough; otherwise how would he have known about it before I did?

I immediately called the Soviet Embassy to find out if it was true. They had nothing new to tell me on that day; but two days later they called me back and I went in to pick up the papers they had waiting for me. There was an absurdly thick sheaf of documents and I had to buy an oversized wallet to contain them.

I left Kennedy Airport in New York on February 9 aboard the Aeroflot flight to Moscow.

In the meantime I'd been at work. It had gone well except for one setback. Since November I had been making active efforts to locate Otto von Geyr, recipient of the Krausser letter and the former Waffen SS officer whom Haim Tippelskirch had indicated I should meet.

I had sent inquiries to three former German officers whom I had interviewed for earlier books. I was still ambivalent about the story of the gold, but less so than before; I was prepared to make a special trip to Germany to talk with von Geyr.

But von Geyr was dead. He had died within the past month. Arteriosclerosis, at age sixty-four. He was buried at Munich; he had been survived by a daughter and three grandchildren.

I learned this in January. It closed a door I had only

just begun to try to open. I was depressed and angry: if I had gone directly to Germany after Haim's death I'd have had the chance to talk with von Geyr.

But MacIver's news pulled me out of my depression and very quickly I was inside the Soviet Union.

I had a limited volume of work to do in Moscow but it took more than a week. I spent much of the time in waiting rooms of the *Arkhiv Dircksena* and the A.M.O.S.S.R.—the Defense Ministry Archives. They didn't admit me to the stacks or allow me to browse in any of the collections but they did give me access to a number of records which had never before been seen by an outsider—and for that matter probably had never been used by anyone other than the Soviet-controlled body of historians which compiled the *Istoriya V.O.V.S.S.**

Some of my requests for specific records were denied; a surprising number were not. Mainly I wanted to see records of the southern campaigns of 1942–1944 and the siege at Sebastopol. At this point I still wasn't primarily interested in the German attempt to unearth the hidden Czarist gold, and at any rate if there were to be more documents to shed light on that subject I wasn't likely to find them in Moscow—partly because the Moscow archives didn't include any captured German records, and partly because even if there had been such records in Moscow I wouldn't have known which ones to ask for.

I wasn't sure how much censorship was applied to mail sent out of the USSR by foreigners; nor was I confident that the Russians would let me out of the country without inspecting—and possibly confiscating—some of my notes. For that reason I tried to protect myself with

* The *Istoriya Velikoi Otechestvennoi Volny Sov. Soyuza* is the Communist Party's massive and monumental official history of the war. It was published during the Khrushchev regime and is characterized by a distressing number of bald-faced, self-serving lies and distortions. Still, it is the best basic source on World War II in Russia. Elsewhere in his notes, Bristow indicates he had studied the *Istoriya* at length, and that part of his purpose in Russia was to confirm from the primary field sources some of the statements he thought suspect in the *Istoriya.*—Ed.

a triple note-taking system. I had brought with me two reams of carbonset note-forms—the kind of blank pads with self-carbon backing which many companies use for invoices. In that manner I made three identical copies of each note. One copy I kept with me. The second I mailed home to Lambertville. The third set I took to the American cultural attaché's office in Moscow on the day before I left. The plan was to have my notes delivered "through the bag"—in the sealed diplomatic pouch which was not subject to Soviet scrutiny—to a contact of mine in the State Department in Washington. This meant my notes would be subject to examination by my own government but I didn't have anything to hide and I put up with the invasion of privacy because anything worthwhile in the notes was going to be published anyway; there was no point making a fetish of secrecy about them. It was obvious the Russians weren't going to let me see anything they didn't want Washington to know about.

I established the habit of making all my notes on the triple-sets so that I could feel sure of having everything intact when I returned home to write the book; it wouldn't be feasible to return to Russia again merely to double-check some obscure note I might have lost somewhere along the way.

It was my plan, even then, to include no significant notes on the gold in these shipments. I wasn't quite sure how I was going to handle the situation if it did come up. (In Moscow it did not; I came across nothing pertaining to the gold there.) I felt highly secretive about that topic, for reasons which perhaps are obvious enough not to need explaining. I planned to keep any gold-related notes on my person until I was ready to leave Russia; then, on the eve of my departure, do a cram course, memorize the notes and destroy them; then, after leaving Russia, reconstruct them on paper as quickly as I could so that I wouldn't forget anything. It was a melodramatic plan but these are melodramatic times.

I hadn't meant to get into such detailed explanations of my working methods; I have mentioned this only because it has an important bearing on what was to happen within a matter of weeks.

The Soviets had assigned an Intourist guide to me in Moscow; this guide was relieved of my charge upon my departure for Kiev on February 19. Whether I was watched by agents aboard the internal flight I have no idea. I was picked up by a new Intourist guide in Kiev, a pleasant young man who spoke a fair grade of English. He insisted on practicing it although my Russian was considerably better than his English.

It was not a particularly severe winter in European Russia although I suppose out in Siberia it must have been as miserable as it always is there. A great deal of snow covered the city of Kiev—more than I'd seen in Moscow, oddly—but it wasn't terribly cold and I had four or five sunny days in Kiev.

The War History Archives of the Federal Republic are housed in what used to be a large Byzantine church near the center of the city; I spent my days there and it must have bored my Intourist companion to tears. He never complained; he was well disciplined. As in Moscow, I arrived with several specific requests for documents and a study of these documents led me in turn to others. The people of Kiev are characteristically less formal and hidebound than those of the north and I found I had less difficulty and delay than I'd experienced in the Moscow archives. I was waited on with reasonable efficiency. A Communist Party functionary named Gorokov had to check each individual request of mine against a vast list of document numbers in a bound typed volume he had brought with him from Leningrad; evidently the State had gone to considerable expense in my case and I wasn't sure whether I should be flattered by it or irritated by their caution. In several cases he refused to let me look at documents which could have been of no conceivable harm to Soviet prestige, reputation or security. But apparently the numbered documents listed in Gorokov's book were coded according to their security classifications and Gorokov went religiously by his list.

I found quite a lot of good material in Kiev but very little of it is worth describing here; I have to repeat that my mission was Sebastopol, not gold.

Official policy was to guard Soviet records far more zealously than German ones. The Russians had captured trainloads of Nazi documents just as the Western Allies had; but the Soviets classified very few of their captured German documents—only those that had some bearing on the Hitler-Stalin pact, on political matters, and on events and people whose existence has been erased from the official version of history by the revisionists. Both in Kiev and in Sebastopol I actually *saw* far more German records than Russian ones. (Partly this was because their defensively brutal pride compelled the Germans to itemize their atrocities for posterity. The Nazi war records are a staggering exercise in self-incrimination. The Russians are not reluctant to expose this.)

I was given all but *carte blanche* with the Nazi documents. I suspect the same access would be available to any historian, whether Russian or Western, but I was the first Western one to get into those archives at all. My circumstances were unique; that is important.*

I won't stop to specify the clues I found in Kiev. They were indirect in any case; they mainly told me what I should look for in Sebastopol. There were strong indications of what I might find there and it was exciting to anticipate but I did not hurry my other researches on that account. I stayed in Kiev until I had what I wanted—or as much of it as my *apparatchik* overseer, Gorokov, would permit me to see. It was February 26 before I departed by air for Sebastopol.

I am writing now of events that took place only six or seven weeks ago and they are fresh in my mind. The twenty-sixth was a Monday; I had spent the previous day in my Kiev hotel making separate envelopes for my triple-copy notes, mailing one set and preparing the second set for delivery to the American consulate (where I dropped them off Monday morning on my way to the airport). My young Intourist guide remained in Kiev. I didn't see Gorokov at the airport or on the plane. I arrived in Sebastopol in midafternoon

_____

* It is obvious that the Soviets regarded Bristow as a test case. This explains why he was kept under such close supervision and surveillance. Spy fiction to the contrary, most visitors to the USSR are not shadowed and tailed twenty-four hours a day. Not even the KGB has that much manpower. —Ed.

and was met at the OVIR turnstile by a stout man who greeted me with a grin that revealed a chrome-hued tooth, trilby hat lifted high above his head.

He was my new Intourist "assistant"; his name was Timoshenko and I was to get to know him rather well in the next few weeks. His mournful smile showed that he wanted to be liked; he had unkempt grey eyebrows and the distressed air of a shy nervous man who tended to see every little disturbance as a major calamity. He spoke Russian with a strong Georgian accent and his voice had the effect on my ears of a nasty child's fingernails scraping a blackboard. From hairline to toes he was a peasant but he was conceited about his vocabularly; self-educated, I learned—a compulsive reader. He had ploughed his way stubbornly through whole libraries, often understanding only a fraction of what he read. He had the habit of ending every other sentence with *"Da?"* which, in a Russian, is the same as an American's annoying tendency to sprinkle every clause with a "You know?"

When I first met Timoshenko I found him forbidding. He was a large man and he wore an ankle-length black-leather coat with vast lapels into which his round chin was sunk. (It was a dyed German officer's greatcoat, lovingly preserved ever since the war.) In his coat and his round hat he looked like one of those Grade-B thugs in spy movies who devote their scenes to bouncing the Good Guys off walls. I soon learned better; he was anything but intimidating. There was an ingratiating likability to him, his eagerness to be friendly, his enthusiasms for scenery and history (his parochial version of it) and books. Of course he knew I was a writer; it made him both diffident and fawning at first. After only a few hours he had become confident of me and was not deterred from digging an elbow into my ribs to make a sly point about a passing girl.

On my own home ground I wouldn't have given him a second glance; I'd have thought him a boor. But here, in spite of my international and somewhat cosmopolitan background, I felt isolated and faintly fearful: I was in a place that was not only foreign but vaguely threatening. Timoshenko's cheerful open offer of friendship —especially after the cool courtesy of my previous

Intourist guides—was a welcome human contact. I clutched at it gratefully. In a very short time I became fond of Timoshenko. I hope my recent actions will not have discredited him with the organization in which he is an indentured servant; nothing that has happened was Timoshenko's fault.

Sebastopol is a modern city, a phoenix upon the ashes of its total destruction in the war. It has a nearly Scandinavian flavor; it is no longer the city my mother lived in. I arrived in a grey drizzle but a warm breeze tousled the air, coming in off the Black Sea, and there were no traces of snow; the climate there is quite temperate. Timoshenko had a car assigned to him for use in chauffeuring me around—a squat ugly Volga sedan —and he drove me around the jaws of the harbor, pointing out sights. I made it clear I was more interested in what had stood there twenty-five years ago than in the modern egg-crate structures which stood there now; but Timoshenko wasn't much help in that respect since he had not lived in Sebastopol before or during the war. His knowledge of local history was limited to gossip, salacious ribaldry and his memorized guidebook spiel. At one point he gave me a ten-minute lecture on the climactic battle at the Russian strongpoint of the Grand Redan.*

My visa allowed me five weeks in Sebastopol. I had hoped for more time but I was fortunate to get that much. Timoshenko settled me in a small modern hostelry not far from the embankment. My room was on the ground floor and my door was within full view of the registry desk where a formidable woman—or several identically formidable women in shifts—kept a vigilant and rather forbidding watch on my comings and goings. Undoubtedly this particular room had been assigned to me for that reason. There was no way to

* A battle that took place in 1855 during the Crimean War. Mention "Sebastopol" today to a university history class and it is still that nineteenth-century siege that comes to mind, even though it was insignificant by comparison with that of World War II. It was partly to rectify this imbalance of geo-historical perspective that Bristow was writing his book on the 1942–1943 Crimean campaign and the siege which literally destroyed the city of Sebastopol.—Ed.

leave it undetected; the window gave access to an air shaft. There was a view only of a cinderblock wall six feet away. It was a depressing habitation, too reminiscent of a prison; but I had very little time to brood about that and none to complain. The room itself was comfortable enough—square, stark, unrelieved by any decorations other than the colorful eiderdown on the bed; but they had provided me with a writing desk and lamp, a sufficient wardrobe and even an attached bathroom. By Crimean standards it was a luxury accommodation.

On the assumption that my possessions (and especially my notes) were subject to constant search, I was keeping all gold-related jottings on my person; after I began to find more significant clues to the gold story I actually took to slipping them inside the pillowcase at night.

The gold episode was a completely new discovery, never even hinted at in anything that had ever been published. When a writer comes across such a discovery he lives in professional dread from the moment of discovery to the moment of publication, lest by plagiarism or by pure coincidence someone else should happen to publish it first. I didn't want the Soviets to know about my investigations into the story of the gold because I didn't want *Pravda* or the Soviet Historical Association to publish it ahead of me. Admittedly this was a farfetched anxiety. I can't really excuse it except by reasoning that I must have had a subconscious awareness that there was a remote chance I might actually stumble across clues that would reveal the whereabouts of the gold; that such knowledge could be very dangerous to me if the Russians learned I had it; that therefore it was best to drop no hints at all. Whether I actually felt that way I don't really know; it makes sense retrospectively but that doesn't prove much. I don't pretend to understand why I did all the things I did; in the end all I can do is report them as they happened.

Timoshenko took me to a tourist restaurant for dinner; we were entertained by a troupe of folk dancers. I joined him for a chilled glass of vodka but I demurred when he made it clear enough that he had a drinking contest in mind. I let him get mildly potted by himself.

We were surrounded by visitors—mostly vacationing Muscovites, drawn south by the mild winter climate of the Black Sea. I found myself seeking a familiar face in the crowd—Gorokov's—but I didn't spot it; I had to assume if I was still under surveillance they must have brought in a new man. (In fact I never saw Gorokov again.)

I retired to the hotel as early as I could and prepared my notes for the next day's assault on the Military Archives. My plan was to work solidly for three weeks or so in the museum-library and then devote the rest of my visit to interviews with veterans of the siege. I had posted notices to the city's two newspapers, through State channels; I hoped the responses would begin to come in before my three weeks' paperwork was completed. On a job like this you need only make contact with a few veterans—a dozen or so—and they in turn will give you more names and references; it can easily pyramid like a chain letter and once the door has been opened the job is much easier than one might expect. People are delighted to talk about their experiences.

Timoshenko lived in a flat not far away. He collected me at seven forty-five in the morning and we were on the museum doorstep precisely on the dot of eight. It was a cool sunny morning and I spent it near a window in the reading room with two young women delivering cartons of dusty documents to my table. By half-past eight I had the company of four or five other patrons—sometimes there were students; quite a few old men used the place and after the first couple of days it was obvious the number of readers in the library was a direct function of the weather outside. When it rained the place got crowded.

Timoshenko did not watch over my shoulder. He would drop me at eight and arrange to pick me up at four when the museum closed; I was on my own for lunch. Although there were cafés in the neighborhood I soon took to bringing a cold lunch and a flask of coffee with me so that I didn't have to interrupt the precious hours of work.

From a researcher's point of view the Military Archives were a treasure of dreams. The Russians had carefully preserved every scrap of paper relating to the

133

siege. Candid snapshots, railway timetables, propaganda leaflets, even restaurant menus with penciled dates on them to show the progression of the siege—with more and more items being scratched off as time went by until there were no more menus. The Germans at the last had taken out an incredible volume of material in the evacuations—that was the material I had already seen in Washington and London—but a great mass of it had been left behind nevertheless. Some of it had been abandoned by fleeing Germans, and other bodies of documents had been captured by the Russians along with the Germans who had them in their possession at the time when the Red onslaught overran and swallowed whole rear-guard regiments.

I had taken the better part of eighteen months to go through a similar volume of material in the West; I had three weeks to do it here. There were the usual bureaucratic delays—it was a middle-aged woman at the desk, an employee of the museum, who now had a spiral-bound list of document numbers from Moscow in which she had to look up the classification of each request of mine before she could release it to my table or deny me access to it.

It goes without saying I became very shortly a victim of backaches, headaches and blurred vision. The concentration of work unnerved me and I came to dread that hard wooden chair each morning. With dinner I took three or four straight chilled vodkas. The first few nights Timoshenko took me out on the town after dinner but soon I was too exhausted for that; at any rate I was trying to keep ahead of my notes and sometimes the work in my hotel room kept me up well into the small hours. Once, at three in the morning, I emerged from my room and limped toward the front door to go outside for a breath of air but the stern woman at the desk shook her head mutely at me and I returned chastened to the room; from then on I had to satisfy myself with five minutes' pacing back and forth around the bed at irregular intervals to keep my bones and muscles from cramping into irrevocable knots.

Toward the end of the first week I learned I was under surveillance. It took that long because they worked it in relays and I didn't see the same faces all the time.

There were at least three of them, possibly others as well. I can't say exactly what put me onto them. Perhaps it was the fact that they made a point of not looking at me. Most Russians tended to stare at me out of curiosity. By my clothes and hair, perhaps by my face and carriage, I was obviously a foreigner; they didn't get many Westerners in Sebastopol and I was studied with great interest by most people. These fellows only shot covert glances at me when they thought I wasn't looking at them. By the beginning of the second week I knew who they were and I knew at least one of them would always be in the reading room while I was working there.

After that it took two or three more days before I realized they were not there so much to keep an eye on me—although I'm sure they did keep watch, to make sure I didn't purloin any records; their main purpose was to find out what I was looking at, or looking for. It was a slipup on the part of one of the girls on the desk which gave that part of it away. I turned in a batch of documents, picked up the new batch and returned to my table; and as I sat down I happened to glance back toward the desk and the girl was handing a man the sheaf of papers I'd just turned in to her. He took them back to his table and went through them quickly, occasionally jotting something in a pocket note pad by his elbow.

Usually they were more circumspect than that. At no other time did I see the documents turned over to a new reader but on occasion I would glance around the room and see a folder I'd read the same day on the table in front of one of the men whose faces I'd come to recognize.

It was a bit of a charade; once one of them even smiled at me in a shrugging helpless way as if to say he knew it was silly but what could he do, he had his orders. I don't imagine there was anything sinister in it; in a way it was a kind of courtesy they were doing me. I was a distinguished guest and it simply wouldn't do to have some snarling KGB thug wrench the documents out of my hand and go riffling obviously through them to see what I had found. The effect was the same but they were trying to be polite about it. The result was a sort of comic pantomime in which we all knew what was going on but none of us said a word about it. Such are the devices of diplomacy.

I should have been more good-humored about it but I was engaged in what I thought of as a major duplicity —I was still doing everything I could to mask my interest in Kolchak's gold—and the surveillance meant I had to use even more caution in selecting the documents I wanted to see.

I did my best to deceive them while still managing to look at all the documents I thought might be relevant to the gold affair. I would sandwich a request for a potentially gold-related document into a multiple request for a whole group of documents, all very similar but the others being of no significance to me or to the gold. Thus if I wanted to look at one of von Geyr's latest letters on the subject of the gold, I would request an entire folder of von Geyr's reports. Twice I made a point of smudging thumbprints on documents that had nothing to do with gold.

Steadily I formed a picture of the events east of Kiev that had been precipitated by the Krausser dispatch in 1942. I put the new facts together with those from the American and British archives; together they confirmed and expanded what Haim Tippelskirch had told me in Tel Aviv. His aged ramblings had been vehemently querulous and I'd been tempted to discount much of what he'd said (partly because even Haim admitted a lot of it was hearsay); but everything I'd learned since then only added proof to his story.

Details were missing. Some of the evidences were mildly contradictory but that was only to be expected. There was still work to do; but by the end of my second week in Sebastopol I knew how and when the Germans had removed the gold from Kolchak's iron mine and brought it west across southern Siberia into Russia; I had enough clues to make a shrewd guess at what had happened to it after that; and for the first time I saw that it might be possible to find out exactly how it had disappeared—and where.

10

TIMOSHENKO HAD very kindly offered to make regular visits to the offices of the two Sebastopol newspapers to see if my notices in them had brought in any responses. After my first ten days in the city I had accumulated a little stack of letters—seven or eight, of which about half had come from addresses in the city and the others from outlying villages.

On Friday evening* Timoshenko drove me to my first meeting and we talked for several hours with a sixty-eight-year-old retired Red Army major who had participated in the final weeks of the decisive Russian counteroffensive that had driven the Germans out of the Crimea. His anecdotes were useful, he had a good wry sense of humor, and he gave me the names and addresses of three fellow veterans in the Sebastopol area. I counted it a well spent evening.

Saturday we went quickly from one interview to a second to a third; and a telephone call at lunchtime established a fourth meeting for me, after dinner, with one of the retired captains whose name I had obtained only the previous day.

It was a full day and I gained a good deal of information, particularly from one factory foreman who had driven a tank in the war. He was one of those people who had a fascinating memory for the kind of detail a writer is avid to have.

I had arranged by telegraph two Sunday meetings with correspondents from nearby towns. Timoshenko collected me very early in the chill morning and we drove out of the city at an hour when it was still necessary to use headlights.

Timoshenko participated in all those interviews—

_____
* March 9, 1973.—Ed.

mostly as a silent observer; now and then he would offer a question and sometimes it was a question that made sense. I'm sure he had orders not to let me out of his sight. But he was a genial companion. So far as I know, he wasn't armed; and I'm quite certain his masters had not told him to eavesdrop on my interviews for purposes of censoring them. He didn't have the sensitivity for that—although I suppose it is possible he had some sort of miniature transmitting device or recorder hidden away somewhere in his bulky clothing.

In any case I wasn't inhibited by his presence. In those interviews I had no secrets; I'd resolved to play the game by the host country's rules.

Anyhow I expected no information on the subject of gold to come out of these interviews. These people were all Russians; presumably the Russians had known nothing at all about the gold episode or the German attempt to spirit the treasure out of the country.

My first Sunday interview was something of a washout. He was an old man who ran a dairy farm about fifteen miles from the edge of the city. He had served seven years in the army—most of them as a cook in a regimental field mess. He was proud to be a veteran and, although he didn't seem overly indoctrinated with Communist notions, he was nevertheless a flag-waver at heart and his rambling reminiscences were all designed to laud the heroism of Russian soldiers and the glory of the motherland. He lacked the anecdotal spirit and a sense of detail; he told me far more than I wanted to know about the operation of a field kitchen; his recounting of his only real battle experiences— emergencies when every warm body available had been pressed into rifle service against German attacks—was so subjective it was useless, and had the unmistakable flavor of habitual repetition and embellishment.

Ordinarily I wouldn't have been disappointed. You expect bad interviews and bad interview subjects. You listen to them, you thank them kindly and you go home. Maybe you use one or two lines of the material they gave you. It's all part of the job and I'd been prepared for a much poorer average than I'd obtained thus far; one dud out of six is much better than usual. But I couldn't help chafing because my time was so limited and I couldn't afford to waste it on fruitless trips and courtesies.

We left as soon as possible but not before the old farmer had insisted on feeding us a hearty lunch heavily lubricated with dark ale. Timoshenko must have consumed at least half a gallon of it and his driving was noticeably less precise when we started down the road toward our second rendezvous. Once he almost ran into a farm cart that was wobbling down the road on enormous solid wooden wheels.

We only had twenty miles to go but Timoshenko interrupted the journey twice to get out and relieve himself by the side of the road.

He was in boisterous high spirits but I clung to the handholds inside the car and winced in terror at his misjudgment of curves and his lead-footed recklessness.

By the mercy of his Slavic gods he delivered us intact into the village of Bykovskiy, not too many miles above Yalta. My appointment was with a man called Vassily Bukov whose letter to me in care of *Gazeta Sebastopol* identified him as a postal official who had served in wartime as batman and orderly to General Tyulenev, who had commanded the Trans-Caucasus front against the Germans in 1942–1943. I had high hopes for the interview; a general's batman is as good as a prime minister's butler for providing the kind of human glimpses of key leaders that can make the difference between a dull story and an exciting one.

I had made the appointment by telegram and it had been confirmed the same way; I had suggested the time and Bukov's reply had named the place—his flat in a communal boardinghouse on the square opposite the railway station in Bykovskiy.

We had no trouble finding the place although when he attempted to park the car Timoshenko bumped right up onto the curb and threw a scare into two small boys who were playing there.

Bukov had been watching for our arrival. He greeted us at the main entrance—introduced himself, shook hands and led us upstairs to his bed-sitting room. He looked about forty-five but he must have been at least fifty to have served in the army beginning in 1941, as he said he had. A spare man, ascetic features, short

139

grey hair shaped into a widow's peak. He wore a high-neck sweater and a pair of slacks that seemed much better tailored than most Russian clothes. He would not have been out of place in the same costume on the Riviera: he had the appearance of self-confidence and self-assuredness that you would expect of a tycoon or an aristocrat. My expectations began to drop the moment I set eyes on him. He looked the type who would stick to formal history and refuse to reveal any personal touches about the general whom he had served.

Bukov waved us to chairs. His room was archaically spacious, a Czarist anachronism of heavy carved moldings and a stone hearth on which a wood fire blazed. The furniture was old, steady, simple; with its row of windows and its high ceiling the room seemed under-furnished. He had no carpet and there was only one table which evidently he used for dining; it was near the back corner where there was a small stove and sink. An old desk with many scars squatted beside the corner window opposite. The panes allowed a good view of the rolling farm country that began immediately behind the boardinghouse.

The first hour was desultory; the conversation was the ordinary thing—he asked me about myself and my work, he gave a shorthand sort of self-summation (life-long bachelor, son of a tailor, not much of a reader but a great lover of music—he had a Gramophone and a surprising collection of recordings and his radio looked first-rate and expensive) and he asked me how I was enjoying my visit to the Crimea. The only remarkable thing I noticed was that he did not ask me very many questions about America.

I eased him toward the war and General Tyulenev and he followed my lead without resistance. Speaking slowly, selecting the dry phrases with care, he discussed the Caucasian, Ukrainian and Crimean campaigns from a semi-scholarly viewpoint more characteristic of a strategist than of an orderly. He spoke excellent Russian with a neutral Moscow accent; his vocabulary was formal. He said he came originally from Smolensk. I have said his reminiscences were on a grand strategic scale but they were enriched by many dramatic, if impersonal, details.

140

Thus, in the late summer of 1942 the Germans had been massed for an armored attack toward Grozny, and Tyulenev had learned through his intelligence branch that the German assault was to be determined and massive: the Wehrmacht had orders to break all the way through the Caucasus, on into the Middle East and on down all the way to Egypt to link up with Rommel. Tyulenev's job was to halt that blitz in its tracks, and to accomplish that purpose he mobilized nearly one hundred thousand civilians onto twenty-four-hour-a-day shifts to build antitank ditches and fortifications across the line of German advance ahead of Grozny.

Because he didn't use his own troops for these construction jobs, Tyulenev was able to muster a big enough fighting army to stop the Germans cold at their Mozdok bridgehead. They never went farther; winter came, and after that the Germans were on the defensive.

I had known all this before but Bukov gave me a number of details I hadn't seen. For instance the tank traps were devised by Tyulenev himself and were far more effective than the ones prescribed by regulations that dated back to the First War. They consisted of trenches dug across the roads and then covered with plywood or thin sheet metal and a thin layer of gravel. The bottoms of the trenches were mined. The Germans found it much harder to avoid a concealed trench than to maneuver through an ordinary field of pit-type tank traps; they lost hundreds of tanks in Tyulenev's mined trenches.

Bukov had quite a bit of that sort of thing. It was interesting but it didn't provide the personal glances I preferred. Nevertheless I did my best to pump him and we were still at it three hours after my arrival.

In the meantime Bukov had been a good host. He had been an officer's gentleman; he kept a neat home and served us little tea snacks cut into exact squares— bread and caviar and cheese—and he kept our glasses filled with beer. He kept the fire roaring and smoked a strong pipe of Russian tobacco; I thought it was the heat and smoke and the beer that put poor Timoshenko to sleep. He spent a while politely trying to smile and pay attention but he kept nodding and presently he dropped off, sliding to one side in his chair.

He hung there with his head lolling, supported on the arm of the chair, the fingertips of his right hand trailing the floor. Bukov smiled briefly in his direction and went right ahead with whatever he had been saying.

It had begun to drizzle in the middle of the afternoon but that didn't deter Bukov from rising to his feet and suggesting we go outside for a stroll and a breath of air. I needed a reprieve from the smoky stale heat of the room and I got up to go with him but I do recall making some remark about the rain; Bukov said it didn't matter. He had an umbrella and we walked through the town square under it, and along the pavement beside the railway track. Bukov kept talking steadily, a stream of wartime reminiscence; I stopped to make an occasional note and he waited patiently, his umbrella shielding my notebook from the rain.

Then we were past the edge of the village with the last house behind us and Bukov said abruptly, "Are you carrying a listening device?"

"No."

"Are you sure? Do you mind if we look?"

I stiffened but he waggled his free hand impatiently. "I have some things to say to you that shouldn't be overheard. Shall we make sure?"

"Do you mean to search me?"

His cool eyes appraised me. I wasn't afraid; it was more indignation.

Then he said, "Suppose I mention the name Nikki."

"How did you . . . ?"

"Let's be sure of our privacy first, shall we?" He nodded toward my clothing and now curiosity had replaced my indignation and I turned my pockets out for him. He didn't rifle anything, he just glanced at my possessions and then he moved up close to me and asked me to hold the umbrella while he had a look at the buttons on my various garments. "Sometimes they sew a button on your coat when you don't know about it."

"I doubt they'd bother in my case. I'm not a spy."

"They don't know that." He did a thorough job before he was satisfied. Then he indicated we should resume our stroll.

It occurred to me that Timoshenko's falling asleep had been very convenient to Bukov's purposes. I asked him if he had drugged Timoshenko and he admitted he had. "A sleeping powder in his beer. But he won't be aware of it. It will keep him out for a few hours. By the time he wakes up he'll find us just as we were when he dropped off." He tipped the umbrella back slightly to squint at the sky. "I apologize for this. But we needed to be out of earshot of whatever transmitters may be hidden on your friend."

"You mentioned a name just now."

"Nicole Eisen. Yes." He held up a hand to postpone my questions. "You had written her that you were coming here. She asked me to make contact with you."

"Why?"

"To introduce myself. It's possible you may have—let's call it inconvenience. With the authorities here."

"Why should I? Everything's gone quite smoothly. I've done nothing to annoy them."

"Sometimes it takes very little to annoy them," he said, very drily. "You know who I am and where you can find me. If you need my assistance at any time, I'm at your service."

"What sort of assistance?"

"Any kind. I hope the need won't come up. But if it does . . ."

"I think you've got something in mind. Something specific."

He said, "Naturally they're watching you very closely."

I knew that but I wasn't sure how much to trust him; it was even possible he was not at all what he pretended to be. I had written too many books about spies and double agents; for all I knew he was a Soviet agent putting on this little charade to find out if I had indulged in any clandestine activities which would cause me to be nervous enough to ask him for the assistance he so glibly offered. It could have been a trap; so I said nothing about having discovered for myself that I was under constant surveillance. I only said, "If they are they're wasting their time. I've got nothing to hide."

"This regime is infected by an epidemic of suspicion

143

and distrust. You're a very sensitive issue. There were people high-up who didn't want to give you your clearances to come here. They were overruled in the supreme councils but they're men who don't like to be overruled—they're watching you closely for a single misstep. That's all it will take."

"By 'they' I take it you mean the KGB?"*

"Yes. Specifically Andrei Bizenkev, the man who heads it now. He's an old-fashioned conservative Bolshevik. He wanted no part of this 'cultural exchange' you represent. He'd very much like to see you make a mistake. And it's possible if you don't do it for him he'll manufacture a mistake for you."

A frame-up. It sounded far-fetched to me. They hadn't harassed me at all up to now.

"I won't belabor it," Bukov went on. "Bear it in mind—act cautiously at all times and remember my offer of assistance if you require it. As I said, I hope you won't. My work has risks enough."

I assumed I knew the nature of his "work"; I further assumed he was fairly high in the fifth-column organization—partly because of his manner and partly because he could not otherwise be expected to know what the personal views and intentions of the chief of the KGB were.

I said, "Are you a Jew, Bukov?"

"No, I'm not."

"Then I'm not sure I understand your position."

"One does not need to be a Jew to be a man of conscience."

We went up the wooden steps onto the platform of the railway station; we had made a brief circuit along the road beyond town and had returned. The waiting room was empty—evidently no more trains were scheduled that day. Bukov collapsed his umbrella and we sat on a bench. The room was dim and unheated and we kept our coats on. He took out his pipe and tobacco

---

* The Soviet Committee for State Security (*Komitet Gosudarstvennoi Besopastnosti*)—the Russian Secret Police, the world's largest and most elaborate intelligence organization, founded and headed until 1953 by Lavrenti P. Beria, one of Stalin's closest and most vicious associates. It is a sort of cross between the CIA-FBI and the Gestapo.—Ed.

144

pouch. "We must return to the flat within an hour or so. Do you find it uncomfortable here?"

"No." It was a lie. I minded the chill; I was a soft American accustomed to central heating. But Bukov wanted to talk and I was curious to hear it; I was curious about him as well. "Conscience" was too broad and too vague a term to explain why a man of obvious ability and taste should take the deliberate and mortal risk of acting as a subversive agent in his own homeland. I'd seen the way he lived and he wasn't doing it for money (he had a legitimate office in the town, roughly equivalent to that of post-master, and the salary for that would be more than enough to pay for his rent and his phonograph records). Possibly he did it out of impulses toward idealism and adventure—but these again were emotional abstractions that explained very little.

Water dripped from his umbrella and made a little pool on the wooden floor. Bukov said, "Perhaps you're acquainted with the Universal Declaration of Human Rights of the United Nations."

It was more or less a question but he didn't wait for an answer. "Article Thirteen, Paragraph Two. 'Everyone has the right to leave any country, including his own, and to return to his country.' Do you know what it's like to be a Jew who wants to leave the Soviet Union, Mr. Bristow?"

"There's been a lot in our press. I have an idea, yes." I stirred; I was remembering what Evan MacIver had said.

Bukov went on. "Persecuting Jews is nothing new in the world. It's been going on in Russia for centuries. The pogrom massacres of eighteen eighty-one and the Civil War here, the purge of Jews in the nineteen thirties. In nineteen thirty-eight, after the pogroms, all the Jewish schools and institutions were closed in the Soviet Union. Not one has reopened. There are only some fifty synagogues left in the entire country—our Jewish population is around three million, you know—and I doubt there are ten ordained rabbis allowed to function in Russia today. Have you any idea what it must be like to be a Jew in this country, trying to accept the idea that your children will never read a Jewish book, see a

145

Jewish play, attend a Jewish school to learn Jewish history and speak his own tongue?"

His cadaverous cheeks were sucked in. He was watching me sternly. "Jews have always been treated as foreigners here. Worse than immigrants. On a Jew's identity card it says *Yevreika* and on his internal passport under 'nationality' it says *Ivrei*.* You meet people everywhere who voice their regret that Hitler did not finish off the *zhidi* and *Abrashki*.† Today all organized Jewish activity is considered Zionist plotting or anti-Soviet treason. If a Jew is too outspoken he is accused of deviationist crimes and he is shipped to Siberia for 're-education,' or he is forcibly confined in a mental hospital. Just last month in Sebastopol a young Jewish girl —I think she was nineteen—went on trial for sedition and anti-Soviet agitation. It was a summary half-day trial and they sentenced her to seven years in prison and five in exile. Now she was not particularly guilty of slandering the Soviet Union. She was guilty only of wanting to emigrate to Israel."

Bukov sat staring at a fixed point on the wall. His words were as formal as ever but passion had crept into his voice. "You know the name Maxim Tippelskirch, I think."

I stiffened. Haim's brother. I said, "He died in the war."

"Yes. One of his children survived. He was an infant. His name is Izrail."

"He's still alive?"

"I think so. He was taken into the home of a farmer who lived near the *shtetl* where Maxim Tippelskirch had his farm. This farmer was not a Jew. In point of fact he was an uncle of mine. Last year in the Ukraine they arrested Izrail Tippelskirch. He is twenty-one years old. They charged him under the Ukrainian Criminal Article One Eighty-seven with promulgating seditious slanders against the State. He was tried in Kiev on October the fifth."

Bukov stirred; he sat with his elbows on his knees, face hunching toward his hands; he began to rub his

---

* Respectively, "Hebrew" and "Jew."—Ed.
† Respectively, "yids" and "Abies."—Ed.

forehead fiercely as if to expunge the thought of the injustices he described.

"They sentenced him to twelve years in a forced labor camp."

I winced at his bitterness. He sat up then and reached for the handle of his umbrella; his hand grasped it as though it were a bludgeon. "Technically there is no single Soviet law which applies solely to Jews—anti-Semitism is more clever, more subtle than that in our People's Republics. But there's no end to their old tribal barbarities. The lip service changes but the hate is still there. People need to look for a hidden hand behind their own failures—and they always seem to find the Jews there. Thus, you know, the *Protocols.** And do not believe the *Protocols* are dead. If you read the official press you will see that the Zionist cartel is an imperialist tool—Zionism is the new Nazism, it is a Hitlerite global threat. They believe this. It is incredible but they believe this," he said at the weakening end of a breath.

Then he put away the umbrella and clasped his hands and said dispiritedly, "In your country I think you are getting tired of hearing about it. Perhaps you believe the propaganda that the Kremlin is so sensitive to your charges that Jews find it much easier to emigrate than they did before."

I said, "It's true, isn't it, that it's actually easier for a Jew to emigrate than for some of the other minorities —the Lithuanians, for example, or the Volga Germans?"

"These minorities aren't persecuted, are they?" he murmured dispiritedly. "I agree they should be allowed to go where they wish—everyone should. But the pro-

* *The Protocols of the Elders of Zion,* although it ramified from Berlin starting in 1919, was an invention of a Russian fanatic organization called the Black Hundred. The *Protocols* purported to be the minutes of several meetings of the heads of a worldwide, sinister Jewish conspiracy in which the Elders outlined their plans to overthrow all existing regimes and build a Jewish world empire. Obviously the *Protocols* were a forgery, and a crude one at that, but as ridiculous as they may have been, they were convincing to a great many people— including such Americans as Henry Ford and Father Coughlin. (*From Bristow's notes.*)

147

paganda is wrong. The truth is that the Kremlin has tightened its internal security, not loosened it. It has done this to offset the internal effects of its policy of relaxing tensions with the West. The KGB has been cracking down very hard on what it thinks are dissident groups—especially Jews. Let me tell you about a recent case. I'm very familiar with the details—I was involved in it."

I waited while he drew breath and composed his thoughts.

"The man's name is Levit. He's a chemist, not an important one. He was working in a plastics factory near the city here.* Now in order to leave Russia, a Jew must first have a relative abroad. You understand?"

"A vicious circle," I said.

"Exactly. So we have this function in our organization—we manufacture 'relatives' in Israel."

"I see."

"Levit was sent to me by someone who knows me. I took care of this for him. I told him what he had to do, I gave him a little pamphlet which outlines the steps you must take. He wrote a letter to Post Office Box Ninety-two in Jerusalem—the Jewish Agency—asking them to locate his 'relative'. in Israel, a first cousin whom we had manufactured for him. A real person, of course, but not actually related to Levit.

"Now in a few weeks Levit received a note from the Jewish Agency giving him the address of this cousin. Then Levit had to write to the cousin, asking him to send Levit a *vyzov*, which is an affidavit of the relationship, and an invitation to join him, and a promise to support him. This document has to be notarized, after which the Israeli cousin has to take it to the Finnish Embassy in Tel Aviv. The Finns handle these arrangements because of course the Soviet Union has no embassy in Israel.

"The *vyzov* has already been notarized but now it must be certified again at the Finnish Embassy, after which the cousin mails it to Levit. If Levit had been lucky he would have received it, but he did not, and we had to make the request again. In point of fact we

---

* Presumably Bukov was referring to Sebastopol.—Ed.

148

had to go through this four times, much to the inconvenience of the 'cousin' in Israel who did not live anywhere near Tel Aviv."

"You mean the Soviet censors were confiscating Levit's incoming mail?"

"Of course. It is standard, this sort of harassment. All right, finally Levit received his *vyzov*. That much had taken nearly three months' time.

"He took the document to the local OVIR and they gave him a form to fill out. For this form one must provide a stack of authenticating documents: a *karakterstika* from his place of employment, signed not only by his director but also by the Communist Party representative there and also by his trade union representative.

"No law forces these functionaries to sign such documents. They may call you a traitor, they may demote you, they may even dismiss you.

"In the meantime you are questioned by KGB agents. Your home is searched, your parents and relations and friends are interrogated. They are pressured by the KGB and if any of them weakens he will probably end up by testifying to your anti-Soviet activities so that the State can send you to prison on charges of treason or spreading Zionist racist propaganda or belonging to an imperialist Zionist ideological front."

He was speaking in a monotone now, repressing all emotion. "Levit was also required to get a paper from his landlord, and one from his children's teachers, and one from his wife's employer—she had to go through the same idiocy he went through.

"In the meantime we had sent our own people to talk with his friends and relations before the KGB could reach them, so that they'd know what to say when they were questioned. We had also exercised a little quiet pressure from various sources against both the Levits' factory supervisors. If we hadn't done so, the chances are the supervisors wouldn't have signed their *karakterstiki*. The supervisors weren't Jews, you see.

"All right, Levit got all these papers filled out and signed. I went over them with him to make sure there had been no mistakes in them. Then he took it all back

149

to OVIR in Sebastopol and paid a forty-ruble filing fee. After that he had to wait five months.

"At the end of the five months he was informed by OVIR that his job was sensitive and important. Therefore his exit passport and visa were being denied.

"I had expected as much, and warned him, but you can imagine the man's desperation. We convinced him to stick to it. He filed the necessary appeal. Three months later his appeal was denied. It was only then that I was allowed, by the regulations of our own organization, to act. Even so, in many of these cases we do nothing further. The applicant after another year's waiting is allowed to apply again."

"For an exit visa?"

"For a new *vyzov* from Israel," he said, utterly without inflection. "You must start at the beginning and go through the entire utter nonsense over again. I've known some patient Jews who were at it eight years before they got their visas."

"I gather it didn't take Levit eight years."

"The man hadn't the patience. He was beginning to drink a great deal, which was not like him—ordinarily drunkenness is a Slavic trait which the Jews despise. He and his wife were despondent. Their children were being subjected to cruel harassment in school. Both husband and wife had been dismissed from their jobs."

"If he'd been dismissed they couldn't deny him his visa again on the grounds of the sensitivity of his work."

Bukov nodded—that was true. "He might have been successful if he'd tried it again. But he'd have had to wait twelve months to start, and it would have been at least six months—more likely another year—before it ended. Two years, with no income. They were despondent enough to be talking about suicide. Both of them. They told me they had considered it. I was not prepared to take the risk they would do it."

"So you smuggled them out of the Soviet Union?"

"In some cases we merely arrange false papers—the *razrewenia* and the rest. In this case, for various reasons, that sort of forgery was impractical."

"What reasons?"

"Principally the psychological state of the Levits.

150

They were nervous wrecks, both of them. Very likely they'd have broken under the strain of interrogations and checkpoints, regardless of how serviceable their documents had been. If they'd exposed themselves they'd have exposed many of us too. We preferred to avoid that risk. So we smuggled them out, yes."

"How?"

"I'm not at liberty to explain the details. You understand."

"All right," I said. "Why have you told me all this?"

"To gain your sympathy. Do I have it?"

"Up to a point."

"Up to what point, Mr. Bristow? The point of willingness to help us?"

MacIver had been right. I felt as if Nikki had kicked me in the pit of the stomach.

I straightened up on the bench. "I don't think so. I'm sorry."

He didn't fight. "I understand. I had hoped . . ."

"Under other circumstances I might have." That was a shabby attempt and I regretted it the instant I had spoken. But I didn't retract it; it was too late for that.

I don't know if he understood what I meant. If Nikki hadn't chosen to take advantage of our relationship in such a way I might have been far more open to his suggestion. But I wasn't sure of that; I'm still not sure what I might have done under other circumstances. Anyone who is exposed to the product of the modern world's massive news-gathering machinery learns very quickly that he cannot possibly concern himself with even a small fraction of the injustice and misery that infects his planet. And since he cannot help *everyone* he soon becomes indifferent to *anyone*. I think this is really why witnesses to muggings watch but do nothing—it is why none of us wants to "get involved." We are assailed by too many appeals, all of them worthy; we are threatened by an avalanche of "problems" which cry out for "solutions"; finally in defense of our sanity we close our ears and isolate ourselves.

The moral rectitude of such a course is dubious but the pragmatic necessity is clear. In such a mood of defensive isolation I might well have reasoned that the Jews now had a strong and capable ally—the people and government of Israel—and that I, who was neither a smuggler nor a Jew, had no obligation to assist them. I might have; I might not. I can't say. The issue was clouded by Nikki's involvement in it; this was what I reacted to—it was my personal sense of betrayal that dictated my decision.

Bukov got to his feet, carrying the umbrella. "I apologize for taking so much of your time."

"It's quite all right."

"We'd better get back. Your friend will be waking up soon."

We walked through the dim empty station. As we passed through the door and he unfurled the umbrella he said, "Please remember my offer of assistance. If the need arises, I'm at your service."

"I shouldn't think you owe me anything."

"It wasn't intended as a bargaining point, Mr. Bristow. The two questions are separate. The one never depended on the other."

"Well since I'm not joining your fifth column I don't see how the need should arise."

"I hope it won't," he said with resonant sincerity, and we picked our way across the square, around the puddles.

11

THERE WERE QUESTIONS I should have asked Bukov but they didn't occur to me until we were driving back to Sebastopol that night with rain oiling across the windshield and Timoshenko hunching over the steering wheel, peering out, trying to keep the car on the road. I should have asked Bukov exactly what Nikki had told him about me—exactly what instructions she had given him, and what kind of help he wanted from me. Wasn't it possible that I was reading too much into it? Perhaps they only wanted inconsequential assistance from me—the sort of thing you would ask any friend who happened to be traveling in an area from which you required something.

I tried to believe that but it didn't work. Any trivial favor in the area could have been done by Bukov himself or members of his group. If they wanted my help it meant they wanted to use my mobility—the fact that I was soon leaving the Soviet Union. It could only mean smuggling, whether of documents or something else: information perhaps, the sort of thing you could carry in your head—verbal messages.

No, it wasn't that either. They already had lines of communication—otherwise how could Nikki have got the message about me to Bukov? It came back to espionage. The documents sewn between the layers of shoe soles; the microdot pasted onto your *carnet;* the spool of film imbedded in your bar of soap—all the tiresome rigamarole I had studied and written about.

I tried to find excuses but it was no good. She had tried to use me and it made me angry because it destroyed something precious.

Timoshenko was unaware that he'd been duped. He dropped me off at my hotel and from the shelter of the

153

portico I watched the car take off in splashing shards, sweeping through rainy puddles and flinging up arched sheets of water like a destroyer's wake.

On the opposite side of the street a dark car moved slowly, its tires hissing on the wet paving. It almost stopped opposite me. In the end it accelerated slowly and I watched it go out of sight. The rain made a black shine on the surface of the empty street and I felt anxiety: I realized it was probably the atmosphere but there had been something sinister about the slow passage of that second car and suddenly I was alarmed—wondering if it had been following us; if so, had Bukov and I been watched?

I retreated into the hotel. The woman at the desk nodded to me. I collected my key from her and went into the room. The chambermaid had turned down the bed and set the electric fire; it was warm and close and I was unpleasantly aware of the rank smell of my wet clothes. I opened the window a crack before I made ready to retire.

It had been a long and emotionally exhausting day but I was too keyed up to sleep. There was nothing to drink in the room. I lay staring at the darkness above me and listened to the rain trickle down the air shaft outside my window. There was fear in the room—I hadn't found it an oppressive room before but I did now. Fantasies ran away with me: what if the KGB had a make on Bukov and knew him to be subversive? What if I was now tied in to him by today's meeting? They would need no more evidence than that; I knew their methods. I wouldn't be the first American visitor they'd charged with improper activities. I recalled *One Day in the Life of Ivan Denisovich* and I pictured myself among Solzhenitsyn's starving convicts. . . .

I raged against Nikki. She had not only betrayed an intimacy; she had filled me with fear. It didn't matter that I had rejected Bukov's request; it mattered only that the request had been made at all. Cleverly Bukov had told me too much: by telling me these things in confidence he had made me part of his conspiracy whether I worked for him or not. I had an obligation to him now—an obligation to silence and secrecy—

which I shouldn't have had if he hadn't taken me into his confidence. Yet he'd told me nothing that could do important damage to his group. I knew the methods and the generic facts but not the details, not the names. He'd told me nothing the KGB didn't already know, except perhaps his own identity—if they didn't have him on file in the Arbat; and could I credit their total ignorance of his activities?

Bukov's revelations had served only one purpose: to bind me to him in secrecy. Because of Nikki he knew I would not voluntarily betray him; to betray him would be to betray Nikki. They had counted on that.

It was contemptible. They risked very little in asking me to risk everything; they were using a means—my relationship with Nikki—to further an end which they thought vital. It didn't matter whether they were correct about the morality and importance of the ends. It remained a cheap device and I was bitter. She had chosen this thoughtless way to bring us to a shabby ending. I felt hollow, emptied by a heartbreaking loss. There was no one, after all; in the dark room I heard the rain and my fear became terrifyingly lonely.

The work became a frenzy. It was all I had left. I sat hunched for uninterrupted hours at the long table in the archives with an endless rain beating at the high plateglass windows. My tired eyes raced across the pages and I clawed each paper aside to get at the next. My knuckles ached from jotting; my eyes burned, everything throbbed. I ignored the relays of watchers who kept surveillance from their shadowed corners and quietly sifted my leavings.

I had interviews in the city both Monday and Tuesday evenings. There were no further communications from veterans outside the metropolitan area of Sebastopol and virtually all the referral contacts from my interviewees were either close at hand or impossible distances away in other parts of the Soviet Union. As a result I decided to revise my schedule and spend at least one additional week in the archives while conducting as many interviews as I could on the weekends and during the evening hours when I was barred from the documents.

By that Wednesday I was too exhausted to keep my evening interview appointment; I canceled it and rolled into bed shortly after dinner but once again I couldn't fall asleep. Typewritten words—records, cipher decodes, dry matter-of-fact accounts of unspeakable atrocities—flashed against the insides of my eyelids like slides projected on a screen, painfully brilliant, confusingly rapid. I had worked myself very near a punch-drunk state of collapse. Reality had faded into vaguery and I had the strange sensation you sometimes have when you've gone too long without sleep or had a few drinks too many, that ordinary objects are just a bit too far away to be touched and that the voice which speaks to you from a nearby mouth is heard as if it issues from a distance away. When the chambermaid asked me a question I had to have her repeat it three times and still it came to me as if in a dream; finally I perceived she was asking if I would care for a flask of coffee and I nodded eagerly. But the coffee did not bring actuality any closer; it only kept me half awake during most of the night.

It may have been three o'clock in the morning or later; I was unconscious of time; images were still flashing in my mind. I was in that state in which associations flow most freely—half-waking, uninhibited, the brain able to make hitherto unrecognized connections between superficially unrelated things. And it came to me that in my scattered gatherings—a sentence here, a word there; clues and hints—I had accumulated enough information to solve the mystery of Kolchak's gold, if only I could fit the segments together into the proper pattern.

I dragged myself to the desk and switched on the dim little lamp and examined the notes from my pillow-case. I spread the fragments out on the desk and moved them around the way a street-corner charlatan moves the three walnut shells in the old con game.

I had far more than three notes. There were dozens. Somewhere there was a completion I hadn't seen—but whatever spark had shot into my mind in that half-dream had set fire to my awareness and I knew the pattern was there even though I hadn't yet recognized its shape.

I must have hung over those slips of paper like a raw-eyed vulture for hours, a claw occasionally darting out to shift one of them from here to there. The obvious cliché is the jigsaw puzzle but this wasn't that; it was more like a double acrostic in which a clue might not refer to the end reality; it might be merely a clue to another clue.

In the end I decided the best way to attack the problem was to do it right from the beginning by rewriting the entire thing. This would serve a dual purpose: it would force me to pay closer attention to every word and nuance, by copying all my scattered fragments into a continuum; and incidentally it would reduce my myriad scraps of notepaper to a workable one or two sheets, filled from margin to margin with tiny writing. Much easier to handle that way, and it gave me everything at a glance. I scribbled intensely and intently, fingers and head aching with splitting agonies; it took me back to college days—writing out the last notes for the finals. In the later stages I would have done this anyway; you try to get everything on a single sheet so that when you memorize it you do so visually: every item is remembered in its physical place on the page with relation to the other items so that you reinforce the process of memorization by a kind of visual cross-referencing. Soon I knew I would need to commit the entire thing to memory and destroy the documents before leaving the Soviet Union. By doing it now I would give myself more time to fix everything in memory.

I leaned on that reasoning because it meant that even if I came up empty-handed I wouldn't have been wasting this time and work. But not more than half an hour before Timoshenko was due to come and collect me for the day's servitude in the archives, I came up with hands filled: I found the elusive connection.

It didn't tell me where the gold was. But it told me where to find the single document that would pinpoint the gold's location. And I already knew that the document in question would be found in the archives: I had seen it listed in the card catalog at least a half-dozen times and I had passed over it blithely each time, never realizing its significance.

I bounced to my feet and strode back and forth in the little room, stopping to stretch; probably grinning like a fool. I throbbed with excitement. Five hundred tons of the Russian Czar's gold—and within hours I would know precisely where to put my finger on it.

What had been a distracting game was now a formidable reality. I knew the gold had been hidden again in 1944 and I had good reason to believe it had not been uncovered since then. Not even in a society as constricted as that of the USSR would it be possible for such a hoard of treasure to come to the surface without the world's knowledge. If the Soviets had found it and added it to their stockpile of gold, even without acknowledging the source, still the facts would have been reflected in their international trade dealings—and the word would have been spread by the world's gold-trading fraternity, a zealous body of men who miss nothing and who are keenly attuned to the slightest hints. And a sudden "find" of that many billions of rubles in gold would have been attributed to the Kolchak treasure regardless of what cover story the Russians might have attempted. No; the Kremlin had not been enriched by five hundred tons of gold at any time since 1943; no other country could have spirited it away without Russian knowledge; therefore the gold was still where it had been secreted thirty years ago.

And I *was* going to find it. Because, in some curious way, it was all I had left. I don't mean wealth; obviously I was not going to claim the treasure for myself. I was not thinking ahead far enough to worry about deciding what to do with, or about, the gold after I found it; it was enough to find it. Or so I thought. I must attribute my disregard of consequences to my confused mental state of that week—the reeling shock of Nikki's behavior, the dulled state of my reason, the overwhelming elation of this spectacular intuitive discovery. It was a period during which I'm sure any licensed psychiatrist would have found me certifiably, if temporarily, insane.

I remember the rain that morning. It seemed it would never end. It was after sunrise but the room drifted in a formless dimness around the puddle of yellow light cast by the lamp on the desk; the clouds must have been impenetrable because no daylight relieved the darkness of the shaft beyond my window when I lifted the blind to find out if my wristwatch was correct. It might have been midnight; I was ready to curse my watch as if it had joined the legion which seemed bent on betraying me; but then the old hall porter knocked —my customary wake-up call—and I went to the door in relief to unburden him of his tray with the *croissants* and the fresh hot coffee that this simple hostelry took to be a Continental breakfast.

I showered vigorously and changed into completely clean clothes—partly because like the successful marathon gambler I have always suffered under the illusion that neat cleanliness is an aid to keeping awake and alert under exhausting circumstances, and partly because today was to be a climactic, vividly-to-be-remembered day in my life and the occasion deserved the best I could give it. A starched shirt, an unwrinkled tie, my cashmere pullover and—despite the rain—my best Hong Kong suit. I buffed my shoes before slipping them into the rubber overshoes; I picked a bit of discoloring fluff from my hat and went out into the lobby to await Timoshenko's arrival in a euphoric condition of sartorial elegance. I even smiled at the forbidding woman at the desk.

Ordinarily Timoshenko's Volga would draw up at the curb outside the door and I would dive out to meet it before he could trouble himself to get out of the car. But this morning when a car slid into the space it was not Timoshenko's and I felt momentary irritation; it meant if I was to detect his approach I would have to wait outside in the rain and I was not prepared to ruin my clothing that way. No raincoat was proof against that downpour.

Then through the door's glass I saw two men get out of the car at the curb—it was a grey Wartburg—and to my surprise one of them was Timoshenko. The other, the driver, was a stranger to me.

Timoshenko looked uneasy. I pushed the door open and he grunted something to the driver behind him; then he said to me, "You must come with us to meet someone. I'm sorry, there'll be a delay getting to the museum today."

The driver's eyes pinned me back like a butterfly on a board. Timoshenko took my elbow and I slid into the rear seat of the car and stared at the noncommittal back of Timoshenko's head in silent terror.

12

THEY DROVE ME to a house on a height. In better weather it must have commanded a fine view of the city and the Black Sea beyond. It was one of those crenellated Byzantine houses, probably at one time the residence of Czarist aristocrats, somehow spared the destruction of the war.

Timoshenko's air was apologetic if not sheepish when we stopped and he quickly popped out to open my door. The driver came around and gave Timoshenko a suspicious sidelong glance before he gripped my arm.

The driver's arm pinched the nerve just above my elbow and I shook myself loose. Timoshenko cleared his throat pointedly and the driver didn't resume his grip on me; he only jerked his head toward the house and I stumbled through the rain with Timoshenko beside me, burly in his coat. The driver slid back into the Wartburg behind the wheel. I cannot remember what he looked like; only that he frightened me in spite (or perhaps because) of the fact that he hadn't said a word to me.

Timoshenko rang. After a brief wait a Judas hole at eye-level in the door opened, revealed a man's eye, and snapped shut; and the door opened.

The man was thickset and his flat face was expressionless; his eyes looked in two different directions at once. Timoshenko spoke my name and the man took our coats to a pole rack and then led us to a desk.

We were in a tall arched foyer. The closed shutters left it reduced to a greyish half-light. There was no furniture other than one hard wooden bench along the wall and the wall-eyed man's chair and desk placed across the center of the foyer. Bare, institutional, chilly.

The Russian pulled out his chair and settled behind the desk. "Papers."

His polite insolence was the sort displayed by a clerk in an exclusive shop. He only glanced at me twice—once when we first entered and now when he compared my face with the photograph on my passport. He went thoroughly through my papers, made an entry on a ledger by his elbow and handed my papers back to me. Finally he nodded to Timoshenko and indicated a high carved door behind him.

Someone opened the door from within and Timoshenko waved me inside; he did not come with me. I stepped in and the man at the door pushed it shut after me.

I remember being struck by the room itself before paying much attention to the two men it contained. It had an elegant spaciousness, the rich warmth of the style of a century ago; the ceiling was very high and the walls were hung, museum-like, with dim pictures darkened by age—portraits of Russian gentry, representational scenes of Sebastopol Harbor filled with sailing ships, hunting scenes. Heavy linen drapes of deep-hued velvet were looped back from the lofty windows and a fire blazed beneath the high carved mantel.

It was warm inside; the edges of the window panes were steamed over.

The man at my shoulder looked on with a poker stare; within a few minutes I realized he was mainly a bodyguard and of no significance—I don't recall his ever speaking.

Across the room a man sat behind a large table in a chair massively upholstered in luxurious dark red fabric and by his manner he was obviously the man I had been brought to see, or to be seen by.

His chair was arranged—probably deliberately—with its back to a window so that ordinarily it would have been hard to see his face against the light but in this weather the room's only real illumination came from its lamps and the fire on the hearth. He was writing—filling in a form of some kind. He glanced at me, beckoned me forward and lowered his head. Then he went on writing.

I crossed the room hesitantly, my shoes silent on the pile.

His rudeness gave me a chance to appraise him.

What little I gleaned from silent observation didn't reassure me. He looked about fifty, very thin but with wide Slavic cheekbones. He had a waxen face—rather pale. His clothes and hair and facial composure were carefully arranged. He wore a dark suit and a starched white collar with a square black bow tie; they made him look like a priest. Upon his lapel was displayed a discreet ribbon which represented some high Red honor.

He pushed the paper aside and looked up with startling abruptness as if to catch me off guard. "Mr. Bristow. Thank you for coming. It's necessary that I have a word with you. . . . My name is Zandor. Sergei Andreivitch Zandor."

He rose as far as the edge of the table permitted and extended his hand to me. We shook hands formally and he did not at first offer me a chair. His hovering smile masked an odd detachment—perhaps disdain. I detected in him immediately an essential coldness; and his voice and expression betrayed his homosexuality. I disliked him immediately and, surprisingly because he didn't look the type, Zandor was sensitive to the dislike.

I could see the quick cataloguing mind at work behind the scrutiny he gave me. A year from now Zandor would be able to testify to the color of my tie and the state of my shoe polish, and it was quite possible he would remember what was said between us in the exact words. He had greeted me in English; he was proud of his English, it was almost perfect.

"How does your work proceed, Mr. Bristow?"

"Quite well."

"Do you think you'll have time to finish within the limitations of your visa?"

In his circumspect manner Zandor somehow contrived to make the most innocuous remark sound like a threat. Uncertain of his objective, I said, "I think so. A bit more time wouldn't hurt."

"My ministry has asked whether there's anything you require that we haven't provided. Perhaps I can help arrange for an extension on your visa. What would you say? A fortnight? Three weeks?"

"That's very kind," I said. "Which ministry is that, Mr. Zandor?"

"Propaganda. The Ministry of Propaganda." I didn't believe a word of it.

He added, "That's a word which has unpleasant overtones in English, does it not? Here we consider it an honorable calling." There was a hint of asperity in his voice. His smooth smile tried to ingratiate but the eyes remained cold when they flicked casually across my face.

He waved me to a high-back wing chair near the corner of his table. While I was settling into it he said, "Would you care for coffee?"

"Thank you."

Zandor made a signal and the bodyguard turned to the door, his chin tucked in with disapproval; and went out. At the table Zandor had turned his attention momentarily to a stack of papers. He used his thumb to flip through them the way a bank teller would count money. His expression was one of acerbic boredom: superior, suggestive of *weltschmerz,* irritated at having to devote his important time to a case as trivial as mine. Beyond him through the high windows the sky was as grey as a sheet of metal. The rain seemed to be diminishing.

He put a finger on the stack of papers. "You have examined some very interesting documents, Mr. Bristow."

I froze up; I said, probably overcasually, "It's been a good opportunity—I'm very grateful to the Soviet government."

"You seem to have very wide interests, judging by the material you've asked to see."

A pulse thudded in my throat. I wondered if he noticed it. "Obsessive curiosity is the occupational malady of my profession."

"And so it should be, I'm sure."

He seemed given to the abrupt startling movement. He shoved his chair back, stood, went to the window and spoke with his back to me.

"Even today there are politicians in Bonn with a brown past, Mr. Bristow. The war is not a dead thing. Yet in Paris the young students ask, 'Hitler—*connais pas?*' To the young, words like Fascist and Hitler are mere figures of speech, to be applied indiscriminately

164

to anyone whose behavior displeases them. You know a year or two ago the British filmed a television program about Hitler in Berchtesgaden and Munich, and the actor who played the role was embraced by Germans in the streets. There were women who wept."

"I know there are still Nazi sympathizers."

"It could be stated rather more strongly than that, couldn't it? During the First War Germany was still a civilized nation. But no more. Not since Hitler. They stink of murder—they're a blight on our era."

The words were more forceful than the voice; Zandor spoke with a sort of sepulchral enthusiasm and it didn't ring true. He went on:

"It's too soon for the world to forget these things. Those who cherish fascism are still in positions to acquire power in the West, where their ambitions frequently coincide with those of the evil corruptions of capitalism. The Nazis must not be pushed away down the gratings of history. We all have an obligation to keep the lesson of the war vividly before the minds of new generations."

He turned to face me. My feeling was the one you get when you're sitting up late watching an old movie you've seen before. Not precisely *déjà vu;* more a sense that I had experienced this scene *too often* before—that the celluloid was brittle with age.

Zandor returned to his seat and stared—whimsically, I thought—at a point a yard above my head. "In the Soviet Union we were knocked to our knees by the Germans, Mr. Bristow. But we learned that an army could shoot very well from that position. Nevertheless it's an experience none of us ought to have to repeat. When the Germans took Russian prisoners they held them in concentration camps by the hundreds of thousands. The SS slaughtered thousands of Russians with machine guns. The Master Race hadn't the time to feed the rest of them so they starved them to death, about three million of them. The survivors turned to cannibalism and consumed the wasted corpses of their comrades. From Sebastopol alone, ten thousand Russian women were transported to the concentration camps in Germany. Most of them went up the chimney at Auschwitz. Not Jews. Russians."

It was tempting to riposte that conditions during the Stalinist pogroms and purges had been no different from what he was describing. But of course I didn't. He was watching me for a reaction—smiling slightly, but eyes at odds with his lips—and I only said, "I know these things, Mr. Zandor."

He picked up a pencil and held it upright, bouncing its point on the table. "We Russians are known for xenophobia. Granted. But I think when it comes to distrusting Germans you must concede we have a just point."

"All Germans?"

"Nearly all."

I said, "Even during the war there were Germans —high-ranking officers—who tried to do away with Hitler."

"Mr. Bristow, we're both aware that the plot to kill Hitler was carried out only after the plotters decided Germany was losing the war. The plot was hatched ten years too late, and it failed. It was hardly admirable. Since the war the Germans have done a remarkable job of convincing themselves that the treason of cowards cost Hitler the war—so that they have their excuse to exculpate the Nazis and restore Hitler's memory to untarnished greatness, which they have done."

"You're talking about a minority of Germans today."

Again the phlegmatic smile. "Perhaps. It's true that my aunt and two of my brothers were among those who did not return from Auschwitz." He spoke precisely, relishing the dry phrases. Yet it was complete sham: how cold he really was, how faithless—like a priest who only wore the collar because it gave him a sinecure—never any question of belief or real feeling. He was one of those clever ones whose existence is limned by the words with which they play—the ones who have not very much reality outside the words. His sophistication was amoral, the artifice of one who hadn't ever experienced a real emotion. He spoke of tragic atrocities—he spoke for the victims—yet looking at him, his eyes mirroring arrogant contempt, you could see he had never known anything of pity.

Zandor tucked his chin in toward his tie, probably displeased with my lack of zealous agreement but determined to carry on with his argument. If he was aware of my silent antipathy he gave no indication of it; but it may merely have been habitual remoteness.

He touched the pencil point to the stack of papers beside his blotter. "You've confined your investigations mainly to military operations with reference to the siege here?"

"That's right, yes." A sudden new line of questioning: and I was afraid again.

Zandor gave a gloomy sigh. "To be sure it's desirable that the heroism of Russian soldiers be emphasized in your book——"

"I fully intend to do that."

"——but isn't it equally important that you emphasize the crimes of the invaders? And don't you think——"

"I have no intention of whitewashing the Nazis."

"——don't you think history demands that you make clear the moral distinctions between German and Russian, if that is the correct——"

"Mr. Zandor," I said in an effort to be reasonable, "I think you're inferring too much from a glance at the kind of records I've asked to look at. The crimes of the Nazis have been documented ad nauseam and we have those facts available to us in the West, for the most part. What we don't have there is the details of the Soviet military campaigns which"——I added this as a palliative——"led to the great Red victory over the Third Reich. But you're mistaken if you've got the impression that I have any intention of ignoring the Nazi atrocities."

Zandor leaned forward, intending me to listen to him; clearly I had provoked him and he retaliated with schoolmasterish pique. "I've tried to complete my statement three times, but you keep interrupting. Now please let me finish."

I overturned a palm to indicate he had the floor. I caught a telltale twitch of his cheek muscle.

He said, "I have no doubt it's taken you many years' work to accrete your impression of the war here. If you hadn't been thoroughly grounded in your field, our leaders wouldn't have invited you to examine our archives. My government realizes you're a very serious student of history—that your views are of public importance in your own country and perhaps elsewhere in the world as well."

I was tempted to point out that he overestimated my importance. But I didn't wish to interrupt him again.

The bodyguard entered the room with a belated tray of coffee and placed it on the table by Zandor, retreating then to his former stance in the distance where he remained a silent surly presence, indifferent but not inconspicuous. Zandor lifted the pot and the coffee smoked as it poured from the spout. "Cream?"

"Just black."

"We've made unparalleled arrangements to give you access to an enormous volume of captured German records. Yet for the most part it appears you choose to ignore these. You've concentrated your efforts on patently insignificant Russian files—railway schedules, menus, interviews with veterans of the lowest rank. Now I'm aware of the phrase 'human interest' and its meaning, but if we have to conclude that you're merely researching the basis for a breezy popular magazine account of the war, let me caution you there may be—difficulties for you."

"The material you mentioned is a very small part of the whole. I'd think that was obvious."

"Let me give you an example, Mr. Bristow. We have on file a massive collection of Abwehr documents captured from the Germans in nineteen forty-four. Surely from the viewpoint of any serious historian—and particularly from the viewpoint of a historian whose work includes so many detailed books on military intelligence —these Abwehr documents ought to be a tremendous find. Yet you've spent less than two hours with those files."

"May I be allowed to explain that?"

"I wish you would."

"The Abwehr documents in your files are one end of a correspondence. You've got two kinds of documents in those files—the originals of messages received here, and the carbons of messages sent to Berlin. The fact that I spent two hours on those collections indicates my thoroughness, not my laxity. I've seen every one of those documents before. The carbons and originals of

168

the same messages were captured by the Americans in Germany in nineteen forty-five and we have them in Washington. Now in view of my limited time here, you have to agree I'd be wasting it if I devoted it to reviewing material I'd already seen."

The involuntary rictus of his smile betrayed him: he had known the answer before he'd posed the question. He'd only been watching to see how I would couch it. But knowing that only left me more baffled than before. What was he driving at?

He slid cup and saucer across the table and I had to get up to take it. The coffee was not very good.

He said, "I was trying to make the point that we've become quite concerned. I'd like your assurance that your account will be something more than mere journalism—something a good deal more substantial than the 'human interest' I mentioned."

"I'll be glad to give you those assurances. But I'm sure you know what sort of work I do. I'm sure that was clear before your government allowed me to come here."

Zandor stared at me for a dubious moment. Then he made a gesture—a movement of shoulders and facial muscles. It was as if to say, *Of course I know all this, but one has one's orders.* I still couldn't fathom his purpose.

I tried to drive the nail home. "I've gone to a great deal of trouble and expense to get clearances and come here to do this work. Is it logical that I'd go through all that for the sake of a superficial story?"

"Logic is a test of consistency, not truth. The publishers for whom you write are all subsidiaries of giant capitalist corporations. We're concerned about the risk of negative propaganda value in your work—perhaps not so much in what you wish to write, but in what your employers wish to publish. I'm sure you wouldn't willingly act as a lackey of corrupt imperialism, Mr. Bristow, but they've always had their ignorant tools, haven't they?"

"My publishers make no changes in my work without my permission."

"Yes. But American books are sold in West Germany, aren't they. The German translation rights can

169

be quite lucrative for English-language authors, I'm told. And I don't find it inconceivable that someone might suggest to you, merely in the interests of increasing the market for your book, that it would be politic perhaps to minimize the truths of Germany's crimes and to fill that space, instead, with charming trivial incidents out of the recollections of inconsequential foot soldiers and civilians. Isn't that possible, Mr. Bristow?"

I disliked him anyway; now I was annoyed and it made me reckless. "I didn't realize the common foot soldier was inconsequential in the proletarian state, Mr. Zandor."

He was taken aback. He had no sense of humor; he was stung by the rebuff. "I'm not a member of the Communist Party," I said. "I'm not even a fellow traveler. I intend to write as accurate and unbiased an account as I possibly can. Those are my assurances—they haven't changed since I came here. That's the most we would expect of any Soviet historian who came to the United States."

"You're suggesting——"

"I'm suggesting I came here under certain terms and conditions, and I've lived up to them. That's all."

Zandor picked up his coffee, sipped from it and peered at me over the rim of the cup. After he put it down in the saucer he spoke. "It's not for you to make terms, Mr. Bristow. It's for you to accept them." He spoke the sharp words as if they had been chipped out of hard steel.

"What terms am I to accept?"

"Perhaps I should remind you that Article Seventy of the Russian criminal code makes it a crime, punishable by seven years in prison, for any writer to disseminate slander concerning the Soviet Union—to disseminate it in the Soviet Union or abroad, it makes no difference."

I didn't reply to that; it would have been pointless. If the Soviet Union had expected me to slander them they wouldn't have let me into the country in the first place. Zandor was only throwing raw meat on the floor. And I was beginning to suspect his threats were empty; I wasn't sure of his position in the government but I doubted he carried the guns for it. It hadn't escaped my attention that there was every likelihood he had been

170

sent here by the KGB to intimidate me; Bukov had told me that Bizenkev had been against my visit from the first and this might be merely the KGB's way of keeping their oar in.

Zandor used the excuse of drinking his coffee to let the pause extend. Finally he put the cup down again, empty now, and put his cold eyes on me. "In the spirit of friendship I feel I must advise you that when the records of your researches are examined in Moscow— and that will take place before your departure from the Soviet Union—when the investigation is made, it will look much better for you if it is clear that the preponderance of your 'obsessive curiosity,' as you put it, has been devoted to matters of consequence. I would prefer not to have to add more long lists of menus and railway schedules to these summaries."

He tapped the stack of papers meaningfully and continued:

"By the same token you may decide to agree that it would be wise to continue your personal interviews with veterans who occupied more significant positions during the war than those you've seen fit to meet thus far. I'm sure men like the tank driver you interviewed, and the postal clerk Bukov, can contribute very little toward a real understanding of the German criminals and the genius of those Russian strategists who defeated the German war machine."

I might have pointed out Bukov's record as confidant of a key Russian general but I didn't; there was no point arguing with Zandor and furthermore I did not want to bring up Bukov's name. It was enough for Zandor to have mentioned it; it had struck a chill into me.

Zandor said, "I've taken the trouble of making a small list of names and addresses. These are all people of great distinction who have been asked to cooperate with you by granting interviews from their busy schedules. We've arranged tentative times and places for the meetings—you'll find it all here."

He produced a sheet of paper, neatly typed with names, places, dates and times; while I glanced at it I heard him say viscously, "I do hope you'll take advantage of this opportunity, Mr. Bristow."

There was the unspoken warning that if I didn't take advantage of it I was in great trouble.

I folded the list and slipped it into my pocket. "Thank you. I'll be happy to meet them."

There was a drawer on his side of the table. He pulled it open and swept the stack of reports into it, and snapped it shut. Then he stood up. "I wouldn't want to keep you any longer from your work, Mr. Bristow."

He walked me as far as the door. We shook hands and I went out into the foyer; Timoshenko broke out in a wide grin—as if he were relieved to see me again. I glanced back toward the door. The silent overpolite way Zandor closed it was an indication of his dislike.

"You had a good meeting, yes?" Timoshenko was eager.

"It was very good." I saw no reason to terrorize him. One of us was enough.

13

At some point along the drive back down from the heights to the city, I began to shake badly and I asked Timoshenko to stop the car. I felt faint and queasy; I stood by the side of the road getting a grip on myself. I'd faced up to Zandor with a cool aplomb that had taken me by surprise but now the reaction had set in and I was helpless to control it.

Timoshenko sat behind the wheel staring straight ahead. His knuckles were white on the wheel. If he looked at me it was only when my back was turned. I wondered how he sized it up.

Zandor was one of those men to whom deviousness is an entertainment. His threats had been obvious but he hadn't said anything explicit and that could be maddening, as he knew well. I was on probation without having been told the crime of which I was accused or suspected. Now I understood the emotions of Kafka's man on trial.

Were they onto my search for the gold? Or had they decided I was working with Bukov and his underground railway? Or did they suspect I was a CIA spy?

All my imagination needed was the knowledge that these wild things were at all possible. A year ago the Kremlin expelled a visiting American congressman* from the USSR after charging him, on the flimsiest suspicion, with spying for American secret police and planning to create subversion to incite Russians to betray their regime.

For all the talk of cultural exchange and dwindling barriers it's still a fact that the Soviet Union is ruled by a dictatorship. Like any other tyranny it suffers from

_____
* Rep. James Scheuer, Democrat of The Bronx, New York. —Ed.

the paranoia that results from the precariousness of its leaders' insecure positions. To maintain power they hand down arbitrary decisions from which their own citizens, let alone foreigners, have no appeal; and the mere suspicion of guilt is more than enough to lead to conviction and sentencing. Otherwise the dictators wouldn't survive in office.

So it didn't matter whether I'd done anything wrong; it mattered only whether I'd given them grounds for suspicion.

I didn't think I had. If I were under serious suspicion they'd have expelled me or arrested me; they wouldn't have turned me loose to go back to my work.

So they didn't have anything concrete. But it was always possible an attack was shaping up; since they weren't sure, they had to blanket all possibilities. So they warned me that I was under suspicion. It was a gesture; in specific terms meaningless. But I couldn't know positively that it was meaningless and therefore I would be off balance, perhaps frightened into abandoning my attack—if I'd had one in mind. Or conversely the warning might provoke me into an overt act that would give them a reason to arrest me.

It took time to reason this out but finally I was satisfied.

The cold sweat had dried on my face. I noticed for the first time that it wasn't raining. I had no idea how long it had been since the rain had stopped.

The church bells startled me, clanging from the city's crenellated onion domes. It was noon.

Half a precious day gone. But Zandor had offered to extend the visa. Because they didn't suspect me after all—or because they wanted to give me enough rope?

I had a misty *pointilliste* view from the edge of the hill road: the center of Sebastopol, the loop of the harbor. Here and there a surviving old building but most of them were square, modern, sterile: you didn't feel you were in old Russia. The city reminds one somewhat of San Diego with its tremendous naval base spreading out along the arm of the bay.

Sebastopol, my mother's birthplace. I had lived with its history for so long that it hardly seemed foreign to me. The bleak grey skies and the dark sea that lapped

174

against it, the stubborn stolid pedestrians, the sadness of its atmosphere. It was a city that had suffered; but it wasn't an ancient city. Grigori Potempkin created the port of Sebastopol in 1784 on orders from Catherine the Great.

The city was built to serve Russia's new Black Sea navy; Catherine had sent Potempkin, her lover, to build the port after Russia seized the Crimea from the Ottoman Turks. In 1787 the Turks counterattacked and the infant city withstood its first siege.

The Crimean War of 1854–1855—British and French fighting for the Turkish cause—put Sebastopol under cannon fire again and for eleven months the city heroically resisted. In 1914 the Turks attacked yet again, their navy shelling the city. After Kolchak's collapse in 1920 Sebastopol was Wrangel's headquarters and had to withstand the onslaught of Red armies while the White Russians made their last stand; and then came the Germans in 1941.

Such a city has a character and a spirit. I was trying to find these things. I knew the dry facts, the dates and the numbers and the details of record; I did not yet know the people. This was what Zandor pretended not to understand when he complained of the insignificance of the persons I chose to interview.

I went back to the car and asked Timoshenko to drive me to the archives.

Zandor had made an appointment for me that night with a retired navy commander who told me very little and conformed religiously to the party line. I left early and Timoshenko and I drove slowly through a swarm of sailors who were coming ashore from a ship that had just docked. We stopped at a nightclub where the music was loud and the crowd raucous; we drank for half an hour, Timoshenko in very good cheer. It was past ten when I returned to the hotel.

When I opened a drawer to get a clean folded shirt to lay out for the morning I discovered someone had searched the room. The things in the drawers had been crumpled by hands that had pawed quickly through. Someone had made a quick but thorough search. Oddly my notes themselves seemed to have been undisturbed.

Probably those who had been sent to search the place were not considered sufficiently literate in English to understand anything they might find in my writings. In fact it was probable that they hadn't really expected to find anything. I took it to be a message from Zandor —punctuation to his earlier warnings.

There was more, in the morning when I went outside to wait for Timoshenko. The man in the car could have been waiting to pick someone up and the man at the shop window could have been looking for a gift to buy his wife but I didn't think they were.

That day in the captured German files I found a document which confirmed everything I had assembled thus far about Kolchak's gold. I can recall it exactly; it is imprinted on my brain.

CERTIFIED TRUE COPY

Ministry of Transport & Communication
Railway Department—City of Chelyabinsk
12 April 1944
Certificate Number S.D.C. 4/1628

This clearance certifies that the goods wagons Numbers 1708, 1765, 1900, 2171, 2177, 2509, 2510, 2518, 2523, 2834 have been reserved by this Ministry for the transport of State Properties to Lugansk, and that by Authority of the Supreme Soviet these wagons must be cleared with utmost priority and dispatch at all points of transit.

—F. G. Grizodubov
Director, Railway Department   (stamp)

It was a forgery of course. But a good one. I saw no physical evidence to indicate it wasn't genuine; it was only the fact that it appeared in the German files rather than the Russian ones. It was a copy; the original had disappeared with the train. From its location in the files I knew something else as well: it was in one of the von Geyr folders dated November 1943 and it wasn't there by mistake; therefore the Germans had created the forgery well in advance of the need for it.

It was not the final clue I needed. But it was the last

link. It gave me the date and the route; I needed only one more fact.

Getting that fact was going to be harder than I had anticipated: Zandor had made it harder. The detail I needed was to be found in a large stack of documents which Zandor could only think trivial. Railway schedules to Zandor were on a par with café menus.

By now I had managed to reassure myself that the Zandor interview had had a silver lining: I convinced myself it demonstrated they didn't have any idea I was looking for the gold—that they didn't even know of the gold's existence, let alone my interest in it. I won't take the trouble to spell out the chain of reasoning by which I came to that conclusion; at best it was rationalization. In any case I allowed myself to see no reason to abandon my pursuit of the treasure. The only problem was to misdirect Zandor's attention.

There was no way to get the answer without looking at that stack of railway schedules. I couldn't hide the fact that I was looking at them. The best I could do was sandwich the file number into the middle of a list of varied requests for all kinds of transport and supply records, so as to suggest I was analyzing the enormous job the Russians had done to supply their armies in the south (while Hitler let his troops starve to death). I even made awed remarks—along those exact lines—to the woman at the desk. I hoped my friend at the corner table overheard me.

I left the archives that day in a disoriented daze—half euphoric and half terrified. I had done something for which—by Soviet standards—I could be shot.

Timoshenko was sensitive to the vibrations. "You have found what you were looking for, yes?"

"I guess I did," I confessed; and he beamed and insisted we have a drink to celebrate.

The drink became several drinks and we were both in high cheer that evening. But the hangover set in at about the time I returned to the hotel. I began to tremble when I pulled the three tightly rolled documents out of the sleeve of my jacket. They weren't notes of mine. They were original documents and I had stolen them from the archives, rolling them like straws and sliding them up my sleeve like a cheap gambler hiding aces.

Unless they had seen me purloin the three papers—and they hadn't or they'd have arrested me on the spot—they weren't likely ever to discover that they were missing. Railway schedules are not numbered individually. The same file number appears stamped at the top of every paper in the folder. With anything as commonplace as marshaling records they'd have had no reason to make a specific note of each sheet of paper. It was possible they had a notation of the total number of papers in the file but I doubted anyone would bother counting them—there had been at least five hundred in that file—and even if they did make a count they'd have no way of proving I was responsible for the discrepancy. Not if they didn't find the documents on me.

I unfolded a map and studied it, and studied the papers I'd stolen; and then I destroyed the three documents by flushing them down the toilet in tiny pieces.

With them went the last written record of the final hiding place of Kolchak's gold.

THE NAZI SCHEME*

1.
BETWEEN THE WARS

[From 1920 until 1944 the gold of the Czars rested undisturbed in its hiding place in the Siberian mountains. Speculations and conflicting reports to the contrary, it did not fall into the hands of partisans, Atamans, Reds, Whites, or the remnants of the Czech Legion. Buried under the rubble of its caved-in hiding place, it remained undiscovered and untouched while the world changed.]

* Both the title and the organization of this section are the editors'.

In Bristow's manuscript, the foregoing pages contain numerous oblique references to World War II. These would make little sense to any reader who was not acquainted with the history of the war in the USSR. Therefore the editors have deleted nearly all such references from the narrative; we have combined them, together with other material, in a separate section here, in order to put everything before the reader with the minimum confusion and obscurity.

This section, therefore, is compiled mainly from Harris Bristow's working notes; from passages deleted from the foregoing manuscript pages; from the transcribed interviews with Haim Tippelskirch; and from a summary outline which Bristow prepared in 1971 as a basic framework for his Sebastopol project.

For certain events we have no other guide than the cryptic references in Bristow's Vienna manuscript, since his Russian notes have been lost. Therefore, in a few cases, we have been forced to draw inferences. They are so labeled.

As in the Kolchak segment, material supplied by the editors appears in brackets, while the Tippelskirch statements appear set off in quotation marks. But it must be understood that this section is a re-creation of Bristow's notes rather than an

In the decade that followed the Russian Civil War the Soviet state did not, as Marx would have had it, "wither away." Instead it became ever more totalitarian after the ouster of Trotsky and the death of Lenin made room for the imposition of the absolute dictatorship of Josef Stalin.

The Communist state was threatened by "capitalist encirclement" and Stalin used that rationalization to justify the intimidation of the populace, the imposition of extreme propaganda measures and the infliction of the great purges which disposed of all suspected opposition to his despotic regime.

Vast numbers of the original Bolsheviks were forced to fabricate "confessions," were tried publicly (but hardly fairly) and were brutally executed. Ten million persons were sent to the forced labor camps of the NKVD. The purges eliminated the entire Lenin Politburo, the entire old Bolshevik movement, and the entire leadership of the army, the state police, the trade unions and the Communist Central Committee. All of them were replaced with men whose sole qualification for office was their loyalty to the *vozhd* (roughly, the führer), Josef Stalin.

Because Stalin's purges weakened the Red Army and the nation disastrously by massacring most of their leadership, Stalin was not nearly ready for war when Munich came about.

But neither was Hitler. The Nazis wanted a guarantee of Soviet neutrality (in the event of a "dispute" between Germany and Poland) just as badly as Stalin wanted time to mobilize. As a result, on August 23, 1939, the Molotov-Ribbentrop pact was signed to guarantee mutual nonaggression and divide eastern Europe into "spheres of influence" which placed Finland and the small Baltic states under Russian "protection."

---

edited version of an existing manuscript. The words are mainly Bristow's but the connectives are the editors'. To mark all of them would be to create pages so cluttered with ellipses and brackets that they would be unreadable. In all cases, any fact or event which is not from Bristow's material is clearly marked as such, by appearing in brackets or in a footnote. But we repeat that Bristow did not actually "write" this section as it now appears.—Ed.

[In the meantime] the center of the universe was still Berlin. Foreign correspondents drank their days away at the Adlon Bar and occasionally went up along the Wilhelmstrasse to watch Hitler on the balcony review the troop lorries that rolled past. The dictator with his Chaplin mustache watched his thousands of mesmerized youths shout their *"Sieg Heils"* and spoke to them in his guttural hypnotic rant, rousing their apocalyptic fervor to a frenzy, preparing them in the moral twilight of the Third Reich for *Mitteleuropa's Götterdämmerung.* The accumulated sadistic malice of human history, which was to find expression in such souvenirs as the human-skin lampshades of Ilse Koch, made the world a clinic for the grotesque evil of the Nazi experiments in racial purification and mass death; and found its voice in the cloying martial sentimentality of the Horst Wessel Song.*

Adolf Hitler's compelling voice inspired his brown-clothed followers to offer their lives in the service of the immortalizing nobility of Destiny. Hitler convinced Germany (as he had convinced himself) that he was of divine origin—that Providence rendered his pronouncements Infallible; that German honor and German glory demanded the Aryan world conquest; that the Fatherland's insidious enemies—the Communists, the Jews, those who had heaped upon Germany the ignominious betrayal of Versailles—must be crushed.

Of course the German mind was diseased. Of course the Nazi upheaval was an aberration—mankind throwing a tantrum. Of course Hitler was mad: a man whose most intense gratification derived from the ultimate act of obeisance—kneeling before a woman so that she could defecate and urinate upon him. Of course the deranged sycophantic parasites who surrounded Hitler fed on his weaknesses and influenced his bestialities. Of course the circumstances and conditions were "unique." Yet: of the two nations, Russia and Germany, it was not Germany in which a small minority imposed its will on an unwilling population; it was not Germany in which, by apathy or outright partisan revolt, enormous

* Evidently this carefully typed paragraph was to have been the opening passage of Bristow's history.—Ed.

segments of the population resisted the despotism of the regime; and it was Germany—not Russia—in which the committed successful revolution arose among the workers and trade unionists. The Nazis were the revolutionaries of the 1920s and their movement was fundamentally proletarian: a blind, nonintellectual will for change. Their revolution drove to the right, not the left —a fact overlooked by those who insist that revolution is always a function of the left—but nevertheless it was a populist movement and there was never any coherent resistance movement during Hitler's lifetime in power. Thus while Russia merely tolerated evil, Germany gave it active and undivided support—and one may argue that in the end there wasn't a penny's worth of difference: mere tolerance of evil is an evil in itself.*

One week after the Molotov-Ribbentrop pact was signed, German Stukas and Panzers overran Poland.

In the Katyn forest near Smolensk some five thousand ranking officers of the Polish army were slaughtered by execution squads. The Germans were blamed for this, the first mass atrocity of the war. In fact it was the Red Army which massacred the Poles at Katyn— to eliminate any possibility of a Polish military reformation around their cadre of leading officers.†

At the end of November 1939 the Soviet Union invaded Finland, committing one million troops in thirty combat divisions against the Finns' nine divisions (two

* This paragraph was written longhand on a sheet of Army & Navy Club (Washington, D.C.) stationery; the evidence suggests it was written by Bristow in 1972 during the period which he characterizes as "argumentative" and "opinionated" —the summer when he became briefly notorious after his appearances on television interviews. Probably he would have toned down, or eliminated, this passage in his full draft of the work. But it serves here to emphasize his state of mind at the time; that is why we have elected to include it.—Ed.

† This information comes from notes Bristow made in London in 1972. The British Official Secrets Act specifies that official records may be made public after thirty years. Bristow was among the first historians to have access to these reports from the British ambassador to Poland, confirming the role of Russian executioners in the Katyn massacre.—Ed.

hundred thousand men). To Stalin's chagrin the Finns chopped the Red Army to ribbons. A peace was signed in March 1940 by which Finland ceded about 12 percent of her territory to Russia; but Stalin gave up his plans to occupy the country. He had lost two hundred thousand lives—nine times the number of Finnish casualties.

The Russo-Finnish War was militarily and politically indecisive. The Finns gave ground but did not give up; the Russians gained little of value. Perhaps the most significant result of that otherwise inconclusive campaign was its effect on Hitler's appraisal of Soviet fighting strength and ability. A relative handful of plucky Finns, neither mechanized nor particularly well armed, had made mincemeat of one million crack Red Army troops.

It suggested that Moscow was highly vulnerable.

2.
OPERATION BARBAROSSA

[Preparations for the German invasion of the Soviet Union were made under the code name *Plan Barbarossa*. The plan had two objectives: first, to attack by surprise and destroy the Russian army at the border, so that the Russians could not retreat into the vast interior of the country to regroup; second, to drive at high speed into the populated industrial heart of European Russia and seize the major cities.

[The invasion was launched from Poland, spearheaded across north-central Russia in the direction of Moscow, then dispersed in fast-moving armies to the north (Leningrad), the center (Moscow) and the south (Stalingrad, the Ukraine, the Crimea, the Caucasus).]

Communists and Jews were two groups which rapidly merged into one in Nazi rhetoric. Bolshevism became a Jewish conspiracy (as it had been earlier to the White Russians); the Soviet government was Jewish and its leaders were Jews—Stalin, Beria, all of them.

A Jewish government obviously did not represent the Aryan people of Russia; or even the Slavs (although to the Nazi ideologists a Slav wasn't much better than a Jew). The Jew was subhuman: he was not a human being, he was vermin—a symptom of degrading putrefaction. This pitiless racial mysticism of the Nordic Germans led at first to national policy—the clan oaths, the marriage permits, the exhaustive racial "hygiene" investigations—and then quickly to foreign policy, where it became a reconfirmation of the abiding German distrust of Russian communism.

Germans understood—and quietly approved—Hitler's strategem of neutralizing the Reds (the real enemy) with the nonaggression pact while crushing the rest of Western Europe in 1940, to prevent a stab in the back from that direction when Germany went to war against the Soviet Union. The pact had been a mutual convenience and everyone recognized that—the Russians as well as the Germans. As a result, by the early summer of 1941 both sides were preparing for the inevitable conflict, and the German attack did not surprise anyone in the Kremlin; only its timing did.

The Luftwaffe and Hitler's two hundred divisions attacked without warning just after midnight in the dark morning hours of June 22, 1941—a Sunday.

Within a week the Panzers had utterly destroyed fourteen entire Red divisions. German planes went over with a great abdominal rumble, dropping sticks of bombs and vomiting parachutes. The guns—both sides still used horse-drawn artillery—produced brutal casualties because neither side was entrenched. It was a war of movement with no time for fortification; where the invader met the resistance of bunkers and defensive lines of earthworks, he bypassed them and left them isolated for the second and third waves to mop up.

The Germans took the Ukraine at a rate of eleven miles a day despite fierce resistance. The retreating Russians left scorched earth.

The initial victories were easy. Hitler's contempt for the Red Army seemed justified. The Russians were throwing Cossack cavalry divisions at him—horse against the might of German armor!

184

Stalin's reaction to disaster was very nearly the same as the reaction Hitler would later display when the tables were turned. Stalin's orders forbade retreat or withdrawal *under any circumstances:* retreat was treason and traitors would be shot. The result was that entire divisions stood their hopeless ground and were slaughtered or gathered into the vast bag of prisoners taken by the Germans.

[By September the Germans had taken nearly a million Russian soldiers.]

Operation Barbarossa was on schedule. But then Hitler made the crucial error.

The German generals intended to meet the Red Army at Moscow. The battle would be decisive. Everything was committed to it—until Hitler decided it was necessary to take Leningrad, the industries of the Donets, and the Crimea. To accomplish these dubious purposes he diverted hundreds of thousands of men from the center prong and sent them south.

[The diversion not only cost the Wehrmacht in vital strength; it also cost time, for reorganization and resupply.] When Hitler ordered the resumption of the concentrated attack on Moscow it was nearly mid-September, and it was too late. Napoleon had reached Moscow on September 14 but the Russian winter had defeated him; Hitler had not learned from history.

There had not yet been a single successful Russian counter-offensive. In late September Kiev and Vyazma fell to the Germans; von Rundestedt and von Bock took 1,200,000 prisoners. North of them, Army Group Center pressed toward Moscow in October and captured another 600,000 men. At this point in history *the majority of Russia's soldiers had been taken prisoner by the Germans.**

Red reinforcements moved in from the Far East but not nearly fast enough to keep up with the attrition. By November Moscow was under fire, Leningrad under siege, and the entire Ukraine was in German hands.

On November 10, 1941, in his underground command bunker at the Kremlin, Stalin held a conference

* The clause is underlined in Bristow's notes.—Ed.

to analyze the state of the war. It was bleak. The Germans were within twenty-five miles of the Kremlin and a German tank unit had penetrated the outskirts of the city itself on the north; only one railway—to the east—was left uncut.

The war looked just about lost, on all fronts.

The reasons for the staggering German victories of 1941 were varied and numerous but one significant factor was the Russian unwillingness to fight.

Stalin's terrors had created in the population an unparalleled hatred and fear toward the regime. The collectivization of agriculture under the forced programs of commissars and soviets had cost the lives of millions of farmers and had "relocated" forty million others to Siberian *kolkhozi* and forced labor camps. The purges by the GPU and Beria's secret police had created still more fear and fury.

By October even Stalin had to acknowledge for the record that many Russians at the front were throwing down their arms and welcoming the Germans. So unreliable did Stalin deem his own population that he pleaded with Roosevelt and Churchill to send their troops to fight on Russian soil.*

"Treason? † Perhaps it was. You recall Talleyrand's definition—treason is a question of dates. A charge leveled by winners against losers. I think to the Russian people it was not a question of treason but of patriotism. The strength of a nation in the long run is no greater than the people's measure of themselves, and the Russian people were ashamed, you know. Ashamed they had let Stalin do these things to them. At least that is my estimation, but remember, it comes from a Jew; it is biased.

"I was not in Russia at this time; I was there later of course, more than once. What I tell you about these times is what I have learned from many people.

"In my brother's village no one had been informed of

---

* In October 1941, for example, Stalin cabled Churchill an urgent request for thirty divisions of combat troops. (*From Bristow's notes.*)

† Transcribed from the Haim Tippelskirch tapes.—Ed.

the Final Solution at that time. In fact the German frontline soldiers had not been informed of it. To the Russians of nineteen-forty and forty-one the Germans were a trustworthy people—reliable and civilized. It had always been so, had it not? German civilization was the model upon which the Czars had based Russian society.

"One Ukrainian told me that when the Germans arrived in his district they were courteous—almost gallant —and some of the villagers came out with flowers to meet them, and the Germans cursed the inefficient Russians for not having built railroads and roads enough to support the *blitzkrieg*'s supply lines, but they were laughing while they cursed.

"At first the rumors of mass brutality were met with disbelief. No one thinks himself a poor judge of human nature, and the first Germans into Russia were simple soldiers for the most part—not SS, not Gestapo. That all came later.

"My brother lived in a village east of Kotelnikovsky. Not the Ukraine, really—southern Russia, near the Caucasus. The Germans didn't get that far at first. Not for nearly a year, in fact. But in the meantime the refugees who managed to flee without being caught by the Germans brought the news with them."

[The news was of incredible bestialities.]

3.
SEBASTOPOL* AND THE LARGER WAR

In October 1941 the Germans overran the whole of the Crimean peninsula, isolating Sebastopol against the sea.

---

* The great bulk of Bristow's material is devoted to Sebastopol, but much of it has no bearing on the central thrust of this book. The extremely brief summary here is sufficient to lay the groundwork for the narrative which follows, concerning the German attempt to bring the Czarist bullion out through the Crimea in 1944. In the meantime we shall have to hope that someday Harris Bristow is able to complete his definitive work on the siege of Sebastopol.—Ed.

The Wehrmacht (the Eleventh Army under von Manstein) made repeated efforts right up to year and to broach the city's defenses and succeeded in pushing the defense lines closer to the populated center but each German assault broke against the fervor of Russian resistance and when the winter rains stalled further German attempts the city was still holding out.

For months the suburbs burned. The pungent stench was nauseating—a clinging acridity of burning wood and flesh—but a good part of the time it was driven back across the German lines by prevailing winds.

Then, in May 1942, the Russian counteroffensive at Kerch collapsed and the German forces there were freed to wheel toward Sebastopol. The population moved into caves and bunkers; the ordeal of German shelling became uninterrupted. Early in June the Luftwaffe assembled a force of several hundred bombers and the Wehrmacht brought up a mammoth railroad gun, the siege cannon "Dora," designed to smash the Maginot Line. The German 105s, the German bombs, the German siege-gun shells destroyed Sebastopol's airfields and cut off the sea-lanes of supply. The rest was obvious.

[The Germans took ninety thousand prisoners and called it a great victory; but Stalin was not dissatisfied since the siege had tied down von Manstein's three hundred thousand men for two hundred and fifty days during which they might have made a decisive difference on the center fronts.]

[Perhaps the turning point had come as early as December 4, 1941, when Zhukov and Vlasov at Moscow blunted the German drive. Vlasov's daring counterattack broke through the German lines and halted the advance; then it snowed; Stalin's fresh Siberian units had time to reach the front and the Germans fell back from Moscow's suburbs under their attack.

[For the most part the war was stalled in its tracks by the severity of that winter. Casualties were high, the fighting savage, but the Germans were no longer in motion; Stalin had time to build new armies and train them and—with the aid of lend-lease—equip them.]

Neverthless after the spring thaw the relentless Teutonic march resumed. Russian resistance was heavier, better organized, and the news of SS atrocities had firmed up Russia's will to fight; but German air and armor kept the invasion alive and in the summer of 1942 the German hordes smashed through to Stalingrad.

Krupp shells destroyed the city but not its inhabitants; the defenders held. And in November 1942 the Red Army counterattacked: surrounded the Germans and obliterated half a million of Hitler's soldiers at Stalingrad.

It was on November 19, 1942 that the German advance became a retreat. From that date on, there was no further possibility of a Nazi conquest. By 1945 the Reds would push the Wehrmacht all the way back to Berlin.

4.
KRAUSSER AND VON GEYR:
THE HUNT FOR TREASURE

Gruppenführer Otto von Geyr arrived at Tempelhof on November 8, 1942, and was collected by a command car which took him silently through the blacked-out streets to the Chancellery where he met for nearly an hour with Hitler's deputy, Martin Bormann, in a conference that also included SS *Reichsführer* Heinrich Himmler. No minutes of this meeting were kept. But later that night, von Geyr and Himmler went together to Himmler's office in Prinz Albrecht Strasse and Himmler's staff notes, dated November 9, indicate that the subject of discussion was *Standartenführer* Heinz Krausser's dispatch of September 13 concerning the possible whereabouts of the five-hundred-ton Czarist gold bullion treasury. The phrase "Siberian iron-mine shaft" appears in the staff notes.

[Perhaps it can be assumed that the conference at the Chancellery had to do with the Reich's need for hard currency and the plausibility of the Krausser report with reference to that need. Subsequent events suggest that Bormann ordered von Geyr to proceed to organize a search for the reputed gold treasure.]

The key figure in the investigation was Krausser, who as head of *Einsatzgruppe* "E" had unearthed the first references to the Kolchak cache. Heinz Krausser was thirty-nine, a veteran of the First World War on the Western Front; in 1920 he had joined an anti-Semitic organization sponsored in part by exiled Russian monarchists, and in 1927 he enrolled in the Nazi Party, when he was a foot patrolman on the Munich police force. Several years later, when the SS was organized under Himmler, he was absorbed into it as a drill instructor with the rank of captain.

Krausser's zealous anti-Semitism, his combat background, his youth, and his cynical if not fatalistic sense of *Realpolitik* made him stand out even among his SS comrades. It was not surprising that Krausser was selected to lead one of the new *Einsatzgruppen* murder battalions in the Russian campaign of 1941.

The official photographs show a thin man of moderate height with a prominent triangular nose, eyes hidden under bony brows, a surprisingly full sensuous mouth and a veined bald skull. (Evidently he had begun to lose his hair in his early twenties and had elected to shave his skull thereafter.) His black-collared tunic conceals the double-lightning SS tattoo on his forearm but one can be sure it was there. He wore the long black cavalry boots of an officer and the Death's Head insignia on his high-crowned, black-billed garrison cap, which in the photographs is invariably clenched at his side by the pressure of his elbow. His letters from the Eastern Front—to von Geyr and to his sister (he had no wife)—indicate that he was a highly demonstrative man dominated by crude passions.

He was filled with vitriol toward "the Jewish vermin" and "these Russian swine" but at the same time he was very sentimental about Christmas and wrote long maudlin passages—how he missed the candle-lit windows, the decorated trees, the laughing children. In 1942 he was nearly forty years old but his letters home are the letters of youth: callow, unsophisticated, cynical but with a fatalism that left no room for compassion, even toward himself.

Demonstrably a sadist, he doubtless looked forward keenly to his own violent destruction at the hands of infuriated would-be victims. Twice in his letters to von Geyr* he expresses surprise that the sheeplike prisoners do not at least make an effort to overwhelm their German murderers-to-be, whom they outnumber by factors of hundreds to one.

Despite his masochism and fatalism he was ambitiously an opportunist. He declared it was one of his keenest hopes to make Battalion "E" the most "successful" of all the *Einsatzgruppen* (that is to say, to murder more Jews than any other Group murdered) in order to bring himself to the Führer's grateful attention. Evidently Nirvana to Krausser was to stand at attention while the Führer in person pinned a medal on his tunic.†

"I never met this Krausser but I knew his kind. I knew these instruments of Germany's glorious historical mission to cleanse the world of Jews. They were mediocre men you know, not great fire-breathing villains twisting the ends of their mustaches. They were utterly ordinary. In all of them you saw a great self-pity—they wanted someone to sympathize with the distasteful job they had to do. Once I overheard two SS *Leutnants* talking, complaining, and then a *Stürmbannführer,* a major, came into the place. He had heard some of what they were saying.

"He said to the two subalterns, 'You don't like your

* By apparently meaningless coincidence, according to Bristow's notes, von Geyr had married a woman who in turn was related vaguely to Krausser (Frau von Geyr being the aunt of the husband of Krausser's older sister). "The correspondence" (between Krausser and von Geyr), Bristow observes on a note card, "shows no visible affection between the two men." Apparently Krausser's insensate brutality dismayed von Geyr, while Krausser in turn thought of the elder officer as an old-fashioned militarist with outmoded notions of morality and lack of proper devotion to the Führer. It appears both men were correct in their appraisals.—Ed.

† Krausser never realized this ambition, although in 1944 his name was among those singled out by Hitler for posthumous recognition: into the file stamped "Deceased" was inserted a commendation by the Führer and a citation for the Iron Cross. (*From Bristow's notes.*)

orders, do you?' And then there was a pause, nobody said anything, and afterward the *Stürmbannführer* continued, 'You don't like your orders, but you will obey them. If you were Russian soldiers you probably wouldn't. Which is why we are winning and they are losing.'

"They were always pouring sentimental tears for their own exile—from their wives and children at home, from German food and German this and that. Always they sought excuses—those pious patriotic euphemisms they used in order to convince themselves that mass murder was not a crime.

"At this time there were a number of national units that helped the SS assassinate Jews. These were guard units mainly. The Slovak Hlinka Guards, the Croat Ustasa, the Ukrainians and the Rumanian and Bulgarian *Fascisti*. Now I went from Palestine into Europe by way of Italy in the end of nineteen forty-two. I was sent from Palestine, I was in the Mossad then. I had been provided with papers and uniforms which identified me as a Gestapo *Ortsgruppenleitung* with the military rank of *Hauptmann*. You know it isn't true that the Gestapo wore those civilian overcoats and trilby hats with the brims turned down. In military areas the Gestapo wore uniforms just like all the other Germans. It was the grey Wehrmacht uniform. The boots and headgear were black like the SS, including the scuttle helmet, but the long leather coat was brown.

"My papers had been prepared by the Mossad. We had discussed my identity at great length.

"It was decided I should appear as a Nazi bureaucrat, inspecting the Eastern Front with orders to report on the efficiency of the *Totenkopfverbanden*. Those were the sentry units which guarded prisoners and disposed of the mass dead and that sort of thing. Essentially they did the work that was too menial for the heroes of the *Einsatzgruppen*. You see in this way I was protected from too close contact with the SS officers who commanded the *Einsatzgruppen*. Those people—like this Krausser—were naturally very suspicious, and if they thought I had been sent to spy on them, I'm sure some of them would have sent angry inquiries to Berlin, demanding to know what this meddlesome Gestapo

Hauptmann was doing interfering with them. Obviously I couldn't afford that sort of inquiries. So I was sent to examine the efficiency of these subordinate groups—the Croats and Slovaks and Bulgarians and so forth. That was my cover.

"Of course there was no Israel then. We had no official standing in the world. As you know, Roosevelt and the others found the Zionist cause suspect and contemptible. But our people were being slaughtered. The world knew this, but chose to ignore it—to pretend it wasn't happening. You would read in the American press about the heroic resistance of the brave Russian people but you didn't read much about the Jews dying by the tens of thousands.

"In Palestine we also knew it was happening. But like everyone else we had only hearsay evidence. The purpose of my trips into the Soviet Union during the war was to bring out real evidence.

"It was not feasible for us to infiltrate the camps in Germany itself. The security in those camps was very tight. It is quite true—although one is tempted not to acknowledge this—that many Germans who lived quite near the extermination camps actually had no inkling of what went on inside.

"At the time of my first journey they had not yet devised the death chambers, the Zyklon poison gas. The only gassing was done with gasoline exhausts in mobile vans. There were a few such vans in Russia but most of them were in Poland. In Russia the murders were done in the open, mainly by gunfire or flamethrower. There was no great amount of security to circumvent. For the most part, the *Einsatzgruppen* didn't mind having spectators around. It gave them an opportunity to share their shame.

"I cannot use words to describe myself at that time —my state of feeling. It would be useless. To speak of these things at all, one must be utterly factual, utterly emotionless. It was not the first time I had betrayed my people—I had turned my back on them in the war twenty-five years earlier, I had denied I was a Jew. Now I went into Hitler's world in the guise of Gestapo.

"I was, of course, not the only agent sent in. I believe I was the only one to survive the war.

"I know of one who broke. He had to witness the extermination of a hundred Jews in a village in the Ukraine, and he seized one of the Spandaus and turned it against the other machine-gunners and the officers. They say he killed more than a dozen SS before they shot him down. Perhaps he was an idiot, perhaps a hero; in any case it is impossible not to understand what forced him to do this. At the time I thought him a fool. I felt sorry for him—his lack of strength. Since the war I have realized how wrong I was to feel that way. But you must see how, at that time, it was necessary for me to feel that way. It was the only way I could do what I'd been assigned to do.*

"I had a miniature camera. The assignment was to secure photographic and documentary proof of the Nazi atrocities. This then could be released to the world. In our naïveté we believed that the world could not continue to ignore the facts once we had presented such irrefutable evidence."†

"I arrived in Poltava in December of nineteen forty-two. The area was the headquarters of *Standartenführer*

* Elsewhere in the interviews Haim Tippelskirch makes it fairly clear that he volunteered for the assignment, but only because he felt that his background made him a good choice for it. Tippelskirch here does not take credit for the initiative, but apparently the idea to attempt these evidence-gathering missions was largely his own.—Ed.

† Tippelskirch and his fellow agents brought stolen documents and photographs out of the Soviet Union on at least five occasions during the war. These were copied *en masse* and distributed to government officials and organs of the press in many nations, including the important neutrals; the Zionists also tried to persuade the British and Americans to drop leaflets over Germany in order to reveal to the German people the monstrous proportions of the Nazi atrocities. But almost all the governments and newspapers who were approached by the Zionists with these materials paid little heed to it. They "considered the source"; they were not altogether convinced that the photos were not fakes, the documents forgeries. Indeed, the press generally refrained from printing the photos not only because their origin was suspect but also because they were "too gruesome." This evidence was only exposed to full public view after 1945, during the war-crimes trials.—Ed.

Krausser's *Einsatzgruppe,* but as I have said I never encountered Krausser face-to-face. I did meet two or three *Scharführeren* and a completely insane *Haputscharführer* [respectively, SS sergeants and a master-sergeant] who were under Krausser's command. Later, sometime in nineteen forty-three, I was to meet a man from my brother's village whom I took into my confidence. In the end I assisted him to escape from the Germans and the Russians and brought him back to Palestine with me. His name was Lev Zalmanson, if it matters. He was a man of volatile emotions and extremely quick intelligence. I felt he would be a valuable addition to our small force. In Palestine over a space of some weeks I had an opportunity to learn from him almost all the details of the story I'm about to tell you. Unhappily he began to brood on the events, he became terribly depressed—pathologically so—and then he suddenly turned violent and had to be confined in an institution. Not long after that, he committed suicide.

"Now I shall tell you about my brother and Heinz Krausser. You will understand that my information comes from Lev Zalmanson, and from things told to me by the three SS sergeants I have mentioned."

"My brother had become very religious. Have I told you that? After he returned from Siberia. He worked for some years as clerk to an apothecary in a *shtetl* near Poltava, and then around nineteen thirty he moved to a poultry farm outside the village. He had married —I never met his wife—and there were three children. He took a job as director of the workers on this farm; I believe I've mentioned Maxim's extraordinary leadership qualities.

"He was still a young man but the community regarded him almost as an elder, because of his wisdom and leadership. He wrote me that he would like to have taken up formal rabbinical studies. But this was not allowed under the Soviet regime. Still, one could almost say that my brother became a rabbi, although an unordained one.

"The Soviets had boarded up the synagogue and there was no rabbi nearer than forty or fifty kilometers away. As a result, the poultry farm became a sort of informal community center. When the Red Army began to fall back through the village and it was obvious that the Germans would be upon them at any moment —this was in August or the beginning of September, in nineteen forty-two—the people gathered at the poultry farm.

"The people knew the Germans would be upon them in a matter of days—possibly hours. They didn't know what they should do. They had heard of the atrocities of course; the village harbored a number of refugee survivors of the Nazi murders to the west.

"There were partisan bands in the hills. Fighting both the Germans and the Reds. It was suggested the people desert the village and join the partisans.

"Many people rejected this idea because their wives and children and the old people couldn't possibly survive winter encampment in the open with the partisans. Besides, the partisans were not Jews and would not welcome them except perhaps at gunpoint.

"Some others suggested they form their own partisan band—not to fight but to stay out of the hands of the Germans. It was then suggested that perhaps the village should retreat eastward, *en masse*—into those areas which were far beyond the German advance.

"Zalmanson told me this idea [that the entire village retreat toward the Caucasus] was the most popular one until one of the Ukrainian refugees pointed out that no one had the necessary internal passports, and that in the Ukraine he'd known of a case where a *shtetl* tried to flee *en masse* and had been machine-gunned off the road by a retreating Red Army battalion, because they were in the way.

"And then as always there was the question whether the children and the old people could survive such a march.

"The people prevailed upon Maxim for his opinion. Maxim had witnessed the winter retreat across Siberia with Kolchak and he knew too well what flight would mean to these people. None of them was equipped for survival under such circumstances. These were not soldiers, not nomads, not outdoor people in any way. They were villagers and a few farmers.

196

"He told them they must stay. Stay here and pray that the Nazis did not come to the village.

"If you have seen the German army move at night you do not forget it. The heavy measured tramp of their boots, growing louder. The soldiers' faces blackened with burnt cork, the ribbons of light stabbing through the slits of the blackout headlights on the vehicles. The silhouette of an officer up in the turret of the thirty-seven-millimeter gun of a *Panzerwagen,* talking into a radio, calling down artillery on some suspected shadow ahead—first the rushing approach of an HE shell, then the ground shuddering.

"At my brother's village the infantry stopped just short of the town. A scout company went among the houses to make sure it was secure, but the main body encamped outside the *shtetl.* The soldiers unfolded their shelter-halves and dug holes while the villagers watched. Whenever a German patrol came close, the villagers would put their hands in the air to indicate their non-combatant status. Many of them went around with white handkerchiefs displayed at all times.

"These Germans did not arrest them. They hardly paid attention to them at all. Civilians were of no interest to the Wehrmacht as long as they stayed out of the way. The soldiers were too tired for sadistic sport.

"Zalmanson said they all trembled in terror that whole night, but there were no incidents and the next day the Germans folded up their shelter-halves and moved on past the village, leaving only a small squad to secure it.

"The sound of the guns dissolved to the southeast. The German squad kept to themselves, having commandeered a farmhouse on a small height overlooking the village.

"The lines of battle had veered away to the south, and there were no heavy movements of Germans through the area; the rear echelons and reinforcements had gone past to the south, on their road eastward to the fighting. For a few days it appeared there was room for hope that the Germans had forgotten their existence in the little valley.

"Finally, of course, some sort of minor official of the

German Occupation arrived in the village in the sidecar of a motorcycle, and that was that."

"It was in September that this Heinz Krausser came on the scene. The *shtetl* was only one of several on his list.

"He arrived in one of those open armored cars and he was carrying a Schmeisser machine pistol in one hand. His headquarters platoon was with him—fifty or sixty men. They went through the village tacking up posters on the walls, ordering all Jews to present themselves at eight o'clock the next morning in a field at the edge of town, for what was called "registration and resettlement." At the bottom in very large letters it said *'Bei Fluchtversuch Wird Geschossen'*—anyone who tries to escape will be shot. I have seen these posters in other villages.

"The SS went through people's houses, looting them. They did everything except rape. They didn't wish to be contaminated by contact with Jewish women. Zalmanson told me there were no rapes reported in the *shtetl*. These SS were often expert rapists. Many of them were only sixteen years old.

"Krausser was a different sort, much older than his troops. At his home in Bavaria, I was told by one of the sergeants, Krausser kept a Rumanian slave in the kitchen and a young Jew was chained outside the house like a watchdog.

"Zalmanson described him to me—he had a shaven head and one of those inhumanly monotonous German voices. He would walk strutting around the village square, slapping the Schmeisser into his open palm. He had a crude sort of humor—very cynical, a sort of dull sarcasm. The sergeant told me one of Krausser's favorite remarks—'Our little war is going better. Much better than next year.' He was referring to the fact that there wouldn't be so many Jews to kill next year. Otherwise the story would not ring true. I think he was a fatalist, but not a defeatist, and anyway at this time it still looked as if the Nazis were winning the war, didn't it?

"The village was not fooled by the resettlement announcement. Too many refugees had told them what happened to villages where the Jews lined up for 'registration.' In the afternoon there was a meeting out at the poultry farm—the Nazi SS had not come that far yet. Zalmanson was there, and my brother.

"It was too late to flee, yet there was no other choice. They did not know what to do. The SS were already setting up Spandaus on tripods along the edge of the field where the people were ordered to assemble in the morning. A truckload of shovels had arrived.

"They must have been chilled by the hopelessness. You know the kind of paralyzing fear which prevents flight?

"Zalmanson said my brother withdrew to meditate privately. When Zalmanson came upon him, Maxim was retching into his handkerchief.

"Dear God we can never forgive them! Never in a thousand years!

"Zalmanson told me he saw Maxim's face drawn with pain. But Zalmanson had no way of understanding the dilemma my brother faced. The community was scheduled for annihilation—this is what Zalmanson knew, and he attributed Maxim's agony solely to this. I never told Zalmanson the truth, but the events themselves can only be explained by the assumptions I must make."

"Maxim had a giant's gentleness. He had made himself over into a man of faith, a man of peace. Through that blind indifference of fate he found himself, as I did, a forgotten survivor of that terrible Civil War in Siberia.

"Whatever material loyalty he owned, he felt he owed to the Jewish people of his homeland—those whom we had betrayed by denying them. Obviously he was no more a Communist than I am, even though he had elected—almost as a sort of penance—to remain in Russia. He had no allegiance to the Moscow regime.

"We carried in our heads the secret of that heavy royal treasure, buried in the Sayan heights. Neither of us had ever revealed the secret.

"Why? Well that is easiest to explain by asking another question: to whom could we have revealed it? The Red government? Hardly. Some other government? What for?

"I had thought of discussing it with my fellow Mossad people but it seemed pointless. Granted we needed money, we were chronically without it in Palestine. But you cannot simply go into Siberia and remove five hundred tons of deep-buried gold. Or so I assumed. And also of course we had no way to know whether the gold had already been removed from its hiding place. In fact I rather took it for granted that it had. I assumed the Bolsheviks had got it, in the end. Evidently Maxim did not make the same assumption; at least he acted as if he had not.

"So we kept the secret because there was no one to whom we could usefully reveal it.

"But then Krausser came to the *shtetl*."

"I have pieced these things together. Many of them are guesses but I shall relate them as if I know them to be fact; the outcome we know.

"At first Krausser refused to listen to my brother's pleas for a hearing. He had heard Jewish pleading before, he was not interested. But Maxim did get the ear of an amused junior officer, a Waffen SS *Hauptmann*.

"Maxim implored this *Hauptmann* to persuade Krausser to spare the village. In return for the lives of the Jews, my brother offered to tell the Nazis where to find the gold we had buried for the Admiral.

"I have said my brother acted as if he assumed the gold was still where we had hidden it. Perhaps he did not believe that any more than I did; perhaps he only wanted to make the Germans believe it.

"Now I am on uncertain ground. I cannot describe the sequence of events, only the possibilities.

"It is likely, to me, that this *Hauptmann* was unimpressed by my brother's wild story. But perhaps he repeated it at the evening mess, and perhaps his fellow young Hitlerites agreed that there was probably nothing to it—a desperate lie by a cowardly Jew trying to save his skin—but *if* there were any truth at all in Maxim's story, it was possible they would find themselves in serious trouble for failure to report it.

"A hypothesis. A report goes to the *Oberst*—Krausser. Krausser feels there is probably nothing to it, but it cannot hurt to listen to the Jew—the story sounds entertaining.

"I know from Zalmanson that my brother was granted an audience with Krausser that night. I do not know what was said; one can guess.

"My brother is earnest, compelling. Perhaps he begins by demanding the lives of all surviving Russian Jews in return for leading the Germans to the gold. Krausser replies caustically that even if this fantasy has truth in it, the gold is hidden a thousand miles beyond German lines in the deep heart of the Soviet Union. What good is this to the Third Reich?

"But Maxim is adamant—persuasive. Krausser hears him out. Finally Krausser probes: an offer. If what Maxim says proves to be true, the villagers will indeed be spared. His promise, on his word as a German officer.

"Not the villagers, Maxim insists. Consider the value of this hoard. Billions of Reichsmarks. Billions. All the Jews who are still alive must be spared.

"The village, Krausser says. Only the village. Gold is not that important. Important but not that important.

"Now Maxim sees that there is no hope of gaining a wider reprieve. The *shtetl,* only the *shtetl.* Yet Maxim knows about German honor. He insists that he be given a guarantee of safety for the villagers from a higher, more responsible official than Krausser. He picks a name out of the air, a name he has heard—General von Bock's name because von Bock is known, even to his enemies, to be an honorable old-fashioned soldier.

"A guarantee in writing, personally signed by von Bock. Only then will he reveal the location of the gold.

"Now it goes through Krausser's mind that he could torture this Jew and make him talk. But he is impressed by Maxim. Maxim is a very big man, powerful. His eyes are calm and level. He has lived with torture half his life—the torture from within. He will not break easily. It would take a long time and the results are never guaranteed: men under torture have willed themselves to die. In any case it would take time and these SS do not have a great deal of time. The Nazis are always in a hurry. There are other villages: Jews to kill.

"My brother gains a temporary reprieve. In the morning the villagers queue up for registration. The twelve hundred and seven men, women and children are

201

stripped of their valuables and ordered to wear Star of David armbands at all times—and then they are released to go home.

"Krausser allows an appropriate interval to pass and then in due course a written guarantee over General von Bock's signature is presented to my brother by Herr Krausser. Two or three army command orders, bearing von Bock's signature, are shown to my brother so that he may be sure the signature is genuine.

"Krausser speaks with feigned anger, talking very fast, insisting that my brother realize that the reprieve remains only temporary until it is ascertained whether his story is true. Until that time the *shtetl* remains in jeopardy, and only if the gold is found will the Jews be spared. In the meantime the village must consider itself Nazi martial law.
collectively under arrest and subject to the strictures of

"Actually what has transpired in the interval, one must assume, is a series of communications between Krausser and General von Geyr, between Krausser and other officers, and between Krausser's superiors and Berlin.* Krausser was not an educated man—I doubt he had any Russian history, I doubt he knew whether there ever had been a Czarist treasury, let alone what happened to it. Confirming those details of Maxim's account which *could* be proved must have taken some part of this time.

"Now everything the Germans learn tends to support the authenticity of Maxim's story. In time, as we know, an expedition was sent to look for the gold. But in the meantime. . . .

* Haim Tippelskirch's estimate of probabilities was remarkably accurate. Bristow's files show that this correspondence began with Krausser's dispatch to von Geyr, 12 Sept. 42, and that it followed very much the pattern suggested above. According to passages we have deleted from the foregoing portion of Bristow's manuscript, Bristow found several documents in the USSR which added details—nothing extraordinary—to the manner in which the German High Command slowly became convinced of the possibility that Kolchak's gold was still buried in the Sayan Mountains and that Krausser's reports were more valid than had first been assumed. Krausser was commended for his initiative in the Maxim Tippelskirch case.—Ed.

"The village had been spared, it appeared. The Spandaus had been dismounted from their tripods. The main body of Krausser's force had moved on to some other slaughtering ground. According to Zalmanson, a platoon of Waffen SS under the combined command of an SS *Leutnant* and some sort of Gestapo official was left to maintain German order in the *shtetl*.

"Krausser himself would reappear from time to time —at intervals of four or five days—to meet with his *Leutnant* and, two or three times, in private with Maxim. Maxim never told anyone what was said in these conferences. The villagers knew he had saved them somehow, but no one was able to persuade him to explain it—not even Zalmanson.

"Rather than indicating relief and triumph, my brother became morose and despondent and would not speak to anyone except in grunts. He withdrew completely into himself.

"Late in September the fall rains came, and then an early winter."

"I never saw this von Bock document. Zalmanson did not see it either. Certain things he said were what led me to believe it must have been produced by Krausser. Besides, I knew my brother's thinking—his way of thinking. I'm sure there must have been such a written guarantee. Zalmanson said that my brother had intimated that von Bock had personally decided to spare the *shtetl*. Maxim wouldn't have made that up.*

"I have good reason to suspect, however, that to whatever extent this letter existed, it must have been a forgery.

"On October fourth, late in the day, Krausser's battalion returned to the *shtetl*. They came in motorized sleds, the big ones that carried thirty men each. I can remember the grating roar of those machines crossing the valleys of the Ukraine a year later.

"Krausser did not arrive with the force. The SS men posted themselves in the town and said nothing—not a

* Nowhere in Bristow's manuscript or materials does such a letter appear, but apparently Bristow was willing to believe Haim Tippelskirch's hypothesis. It does fit the facts, whether or not it is accurate in every detail.—Ed.

single word—to the inhabitants. No questions were answered. There were several incidents, Jews being knocked down in the snow and trampled, that sort of thing. After dark the Germans became steadily more belligerent, although they still did not speak to the people except to bark obscenities or arrogant orders at them.

"You must recall the mentalities of these necrophiles. This village had been denied them for weeks—they singled it out for special hatred. During the night several Jews were murdered by the SS swine. The corpses were left in the streets, mutilated horribly. Zalmanson told me of the naked severed arms of a small boy lying shriveled in the slush, and an old man's head impaled on a staff before the old synagogue.

"Zalmanson knew what these things portended; he went around to the poultry farm and tried to persuade my brother to join him and many others in attempting to escape in the night.

"My brother refused to go.

"One can spend hours speculating on his reasons, and many more hours recounting the details of the flight which Zalmanson described to me, but there's no point in it. My brother stayed, he wouldn't budge. Zalmanson and perhaps eighty others crept away in the night. He himself was with a party of eight, of whom he was the only survivor in the end—the seven others were killed by the winter, or the Germans, or the Cossacks. . . .

"I have no further firsthand reports of what happened in the *shtetl*. I do not know whether Krausser arrived and took charge of the slaughter personally; I suspect he must have, he wouldn't have missed that. Undoubtedly they followed the usual pattern.

"My brother undoubtedly protested. Equally undoubtedly, once he saw the hopelessness of it, he did not resist. In a way I'm sure he welcomed his death."

German documents indicate that *Standartenführer* Heinz Krausser was relieved of his command of *Einsatzgruppe* "E" temporarily, on October 7, 1942, and given a special assignment.

A set of RSHA travel orders from Himmler's office in Prinz Albrecht Strass sent Krausser to Kiev, apparently for a meeting with *Gruppenführer* Otto von Geyr and others.

A new unit was established on paper with the designation *Jagdsonderkommando Ein,* reflecting the crude sense of humor of—probably—Himmler; *Jagd* means "hunt" but *Goldjagd* means "gold rush"; an SS *Sonderkommando* was defined as a probe unit assigned to special duties. Krausser, with no promotion in rank, was placed in command of *Jagdsonderkommando Ein.*

At this point Reinhard Gehlen's branch of the Abwehr—the German secret intelligence network—was incorporated into the operation, along with the captured ordnance section of Field Marshal von Paulus' headquarters battalion. The purpose of the former was to provide intelligence, false documentation and training for the members of *Jagdsonderkommando Ein;* the purpose of the latter was to provide uniforms and equipment from captured Russian sources.

It is mentioned in Krausser's dossiers that he spoke Russian, although there is no indication of the degree of his proficiency. All the others who were assigned to his *Jagdsonderkommando* were Russian-speaking Germans.

The actual operating force numbered three officers, nine noncommissioned officers and seventeen enlisted men.

These personnel were drawn from SD, *Ordnungspolizei, Sicherheitspolizei* and line-Wehrmacht units; they were specialists in varied fields, the one common denominator being their knowledge of the Russian languages. Among the members of *Jagdsonderkommando Ein* was a disproportionate number of automatic weapons experts, railroad men and commando-demolitions specialists.

One of Krausser's two lieutenants was a former civil engineer with a background in earth-moving operations. The other had been recruited from his post as deputy commander of the railroad marshaling yards at Dresden; in civilian pre-war life he had been a locomotive driver and had spent four months working on the Trans-Siberian Railway during the period of nonaggression-pact *detente.*

The recruiting and training seems to have taken a

surprisingly long time—months, stretching nearly into a year. One might suspect unusual inefficiency among these Germans; however, a closer examination of the documentary record implies several contributing factors.

Like most military intelligence operations, the Abwehr was a far poorer performer than its propaganda would have us believe. Its reports from Siberia, as relayed to von Geyr and Krausser, were woefully skeletal; evidently its personnel in Siberia was almost nil. Krausser kept demanding more details about railroads and defenses in the Sayan district and along the route from there to the Crimea; he kept getting long-winded gobbledygook which boiled down to, "We don't know, we're guessing."

Furthermore, a minor smallpox epidemic in Rostov —where the unit was in training—killed off three members of the *Jagdsonderkommando* and evidently these men's specialties had been vital to the plan, so that everything had to stop and mark time while three replacements were found and trained.

After that, Hermann Goering had to be brought into the plan at top level in order to justify Himmler's request for long-range air penetration of Siberia into the Baikal border area, and evidently Goering thought the whole plan idiotic and it took time for Bormann and Himmler to change his mind.

Of the various delaying factors, however, none was so important as the crucial lack of intelligence provided by the Abwehr. Krausser insisted, in a series of dispatches that range in date from March to October 1943, that there was no possibility of success if the operation had to be undertaken blind. He insisted on specific intelligence of the defense and transport in the area: particularly, he needed to know the exact details of operating schedules along the Trans-Siberian, and the exact disposition of repair and marshaling yards in the vicinity. The need for this information becomes more obvious the more one understands the nature of the *Goldjagd* plan. (That was its code name, inevitably.)

From the outset it is clear that von Geyr, more than any of the others, fully comprehended the magnitude of the logistical problems. The gold might or might not be where the Jew had said it was; but there was a good chance—every piece of intelligence suggested the Jew's story was true. Himmler probably reasoned that even if it proved false, the most he could lose would be twenty-nine men; in terms of odds, the potential reward was well worth the cost and risk.

But von Geyr's reports and dispatches indicate that he was the first to grasp the obvious logistical difficulties. Gold is unlike paper money, diamonds, and other valuables; it is incredibly heavy. The fact that the Czarist treasury weighed in the neighborhood of five hundred tons was deceptive, because it was a highly concentrated tonnage in terms of size-*vs*.-mass. You could not begin to fill a five-ton lorry with gold. If you did, its axles would collapse instantly. Five tons of gold takes up the space occupied by less than half a ton of crushed rock.

The original Heydrich-Krausser plan evidently was based on the assumption that the entire bullion hoard would fit inside the fuselages of twelve or fifteen four-engine airplanes. In terms of size and space this was true; in terms of weight it was absurd. Such a load would instantly crush the floor out of any airplane, even if such an airplane were capable of lifting that much weight. And the load capacity of even the greatest four-engine bomber or transport was more like ten tons than five hundred; a capacity which had to be reduced still further by the need for extra-range fuel tanks.

Apparently, however, it remained to Hermann Goering to shoot down permanently the idea of flying the gold out of Siberia. He only needed to point out the consequences if even one of the airplanes were to be shot down over Russian territory with its load of bullion.

Other proposals were then advanced, and one by one destroyed by careful reasoning; in the end it was von Geyr whose idea provided the solution. The only reasonable means of getting the gold out of Siberia was to employ the same method of transport that had been used to take it to Siberia in the first place: the railway.

The track of the Siberian railway from the Sayan

district made a relatively straight line west as far as Kuybyshev, whence a variety of switchings from track-line to track-line would bring the train southwest toward the Ukraine. Once in German-occupied territory, it could be driven straight to the Polish border and its contents then transferred to a Western train on the European track-gauge; or—and this was far less desirable on account of the risks—the train could turn south out of the Ukraine, cross the Crimea and deliver its cargo to Sebastopol, thence to be shipped by sea through the Dardanelles. (In 1942, while the Germans still held the Mediterranean, this was a viable possibility; by the time the mission was actually undertaken, it was not.)

In March 1943 the von Geyr plan was settled on. The delay had already amounted to nearly five months. Because the von Geyr plan was clandestine in nature, the training of Krausser's force had to be rigorous and painstaking: every man in the force had to be able to pass as a Russian.

Documenting, equipping and costuming them took more time; not only did they have to look like Russians and talk like Russians, they also had to know enough about their own manufactured backgrounds to satisfy the suspicious, and they had to know enough contemporary Russian cultural history to sound authentic.

Under the coaching of Abwehr agents and various Russian prisoners-of-war, they made steady—but not exceptionally fast—progress in their effort to become Russians, and between the strenuous care of their training and the slow excavation of intelligence of Siberia from the Abwehr's espionage field agents, it was the autumn of 1943 before von Geyr felt confident enough to report to Berlin that Krausser's team was ready for action.

It had been decided that the *Jagdsonderkommando* would travel as a special unit of Soviet Transportation Corpsmen, led by a first lieutenant (the *Leutnant* who had been a locomotive driver) and chaperoned by a Communist Party commissar—a role played by Krausser himself, in the familiar grey choke-collared uniform

208

of the Red Army, with the insignia of a commissar in place of officer's epaulets.

The other lieutenant (the one who had been a civil engineer) played the part of a Russian army engineer officer, also a first lieutenant: again, a role close to his actual status.

The cover-story postulated that Moscow wanted a military survey of the iron mines to determine whether it was feasible to reopen them for wartime production. The expedition would have an air of authenticity to it, and even though everyone in the Sayan knew that the mines were empty of iron, no one would be likely to question the Kremlin's bureaucratic decision to have them reinspected at such a time as this.

Along with the cover story went various sets of forged orders by which the bearers were authorized by the Kremlin to commandeer such rail transport and dispatching priorities as might be needed to transport ore samples out of the district. The signatures on Krausser's phony orders were those of the highest—and thus least-to-be-questioned—authorities: Malenkov and Marshal Zhukov.

Krausser's detachment carried reams of documents designed to meet almost any foreseeable contingency. The files of Abwehr, Wehrmacht and RSHA records include copystats of billeting requisitions, orders allowing Krausser to commandeer provisions and tools and equipment, personnel orders (with the names left blank) authorizing the detachment to impress civilian workers into labor companies if it became necessary to repair the tracks and roadbeds of abandoned mining railways, and disciplinary authorizations by which Krausser—as People's Commissar—was empowered to arrest, sentence and even execute officials who refused to cooperate. The latter were designed mainly with railway dispatching controllers in mind; once the train was loaded the Germans wanted to get it across the Soviet Union as quickly as possible.

On November 23, 1943, the bogus Russians were flown to a Luftwaffe military airfield near Donetsk, where they were fed lavishly and spent the night in Luftwaffe officers' barracks.

The mission was scheduled to take off at 0430 hours

the morning of November 24. The transport was a captured four-engine American long-range bomber, a B-24 Liberator, painted over with Russian markings to resemble the lend-lease aircraft with which the United States had been supplying Russia since 1942. The Liberator model had been selected for several reasons: its range (about 2,400 miles); its ability to fly at altitudes above most antiaircraft capacities; and the fact that many of the American-built planes had been delivered to the Soviet Union over the Alaska-to-Vladivostok Lend-Lease route, so that Siberian soldiers were accustomed to seeing the twin-tailed four-engine bombers overhead.

German antiaircraft batteries in the Donetsk region had been advised not to fire upon a single Liberator with Russian markings during the morning of the twenty-fourth. By the time the plane crossed the front lines into Russian-held territory it would be too high to be hit by antiaircraft bursts fired by either side; portable oxygen equipment had been provided for the twenty-two additional passengers, since the plane had been designed to accommodate a crew of seven.

The plane had extra fuel tanks on board but these would not be sufficient to make a round-trip flight. The pilot and his three-man flight crew had orders to drop Krausser's group by parachute, then turn southeast and attempt to reach the Japanese-held airfield at Huhehot in northern China. If the fuel didn't last, the crew was to bail out and make its way on foot to the nearest Japanese base.

At cruising speed the flight from Donetsk to the Sayan district would take some sixteen hours; the take-off had been planned with a night parachute-drop in mind. The deep Siberian snow was expected to make for soft landings for the parachutists. They would be dropped from an altimeter height of eighteen hundred meters, which meant their drop to the high ground would measure some two hundred meters or less; a short drop which guaranteed no one would be frost-bitten by the frigid air in the drop zone.

The weather went bad, unexpectedly, and takeoff had to be postponed twenty-four hours. A snowstorm then set in which lasted nearly two days, and meteorological estimates of the weather in the Sayan district were disappointing. Krausser had to drop into the right area or risk being isolated in freezing mountain fastnesses; furthermore, the jumpers had to be able to see their drop zone or they risked death in a blind jump. For those reasons the weather in the drop zone was more critical than the weather at the takeoff point, and in the end the Germans had to wait ten days before a favorable forecast allowed von Geyr to give them the go-ahead.

On the morning of December 3, 1943, the *Jagdsonderkommando* took off.

The absence of records to the contrary suggests that the drop was made as planned.*

Met records show it was a typical Siberian winter: a great deal of snow lie, temperatures subfreezing but not severely so, as they were farther north in the tundra, storms frequent—one or two a week—and high winds the rule.

Krausser's *nom de guerre* was Ivan Samsonov; his railroad lieutenant went under the name Yevgeni Razin. The Red Army mess hall at Tulun issued twenty-eight meal tickets to First Lieutenant Yevgeni Razin on December 8; this may indicate that Krausser ("Commissar Samsonov") found billeting and meals elsewhere, since he was not an army officer.

The next trace of the *Jagdsonderkommando* does not appear until December 24, when a conscript labor battalion (60 percent men, 40 percent women) was assigned to Lieutenant Razin on temporary assignment. Provisions and camping equipment sufficient for four weeks' work were issued to the labor battalion at Cheremkhovo. The next day, December 25, Razin signed—with an endorsement by Commissar Samsonov

---

* Bristow made a note to inquire of the Japan Defense Agency whether they had any record of the landing of the bomber in China on December 3 or 4, but he hadn't done so before his trip to Russia. The spoor left by Krausser's commando in German and Russian records was cryptic at best. This portion of the narrative is mainly an editorial extension of Bristow's notes and the conclusions he reports having drawn from his study of Russian documents in Moscow, Kiev, and Sebastopol.—Ed.

—an official requisition by which he commandeered the use of two steam locomotives, seventeen goods wagons† and one passenger car. This train was assembled in the yards at Zima, the nearest marshaling area to the Sayan.

The request for a labor battalion indicates that by that date—December 24—the Germans had located the right mine. Now they were ready to have the roadbed and track repaired so that they could move their train close to the mine in order to load it. But Krausser's requisition of heavy lorries and a caterpillar-tread front-loader was not made until January 5, 1944—an indication that the repair of the railway took nearly two weeks.

On January 8 the construction equipment—the lorries and bulldozer—were winched onto flatbed cars coupled to Krausser's train; that same day, the labor battalion was released to return to its former duties. Indications are that the Germans transported the members of the labor battalion back to Zima aboard the train, dropped them off, loaded the digging machinery onto the train, and left Zima for the return trip to the Sayan mining district—all on the same day, January 8.

On January 15, 1944, Krausser's train was cleared through Krasnoyarsk (the principal marshaling yard of the Yenisey-Sayan district); it was now on its way out of the area, en route to Omsk and the Ural Mountains. Checked off against the train were bills of lading alluding to ore samples, construction materials and six goods-wagonloads of "leaden ingots" billed for delivery to an ammunition factory near Stalingrad. One assumes the Germans had simply painted the gold bullion with grey metallic paint, disguising it as lead—a rather bemusing trick of alchemy.

The train drove westward at a steady rate of 250 to 300 miles a day, receiving priority routing through the crowded switching yards and depots of Anzhero-Sudz-

† Kolchak's train had numbered twenty-eight goods wagons, but those had been armored. The newer Russian rolling stock was more capacious and sturdy than that of Kolchak's time. German engineers had made a careful study and come up with the figure of seventeen wagons. It may be worth mentioning that the Russian railway system had a much wider gauge than the railroads of Western Europe.—Ed.

hensk (January 17), Novosibirsk (January 18), Barabinsk (January 19), Omsk (January 21), Petropavlovsk (January 22) and Chelyabinsk (January 25).

It is at Chelyabinsk that the main lines divide and scatter. Krausser's train moved west into the Kuibyshev along the Moscow line as far as the junction near Ufa, then branched south to the city of Kuibyshev and then southwest on a dogleg to Orenburg and Uralsk in the Kazakhian People's Republic. The line goes west from Uralsk and crosses the Volga at Saratov. [The distance to Saratov along this indirect route was more than 1,100 miles from Chelyabinsk but] the *Jagdsonderkommando* train covered it in a little less than three days —an indication of the urgency the Germans must have felt by then. Villagers along the right-of-way must have been awed by the sight of such a train highballing westward, powered by one huge steam locomotive at the front and another at the rear. Undoubtedly this haste must have drawn attention the Germans would prefer to have avoided, but by this time Krausser must have learned about the alarming conditions at the front; hence the train's acceleration. The *Jagdsonderkommando* and its booty were suddenly caught up in a desperate race against time. . . .

5.
WAR'S END

In 1942 Zhukov stopped the German *blitzkrieg* on the doorstep of Moscow and destroyed the myth of German invincibility.

On war maps the battle lines moved relentlessly westward. For 1944 Hitler committed two hundred combat divisions to the Russian Front but it was pointless.

By the beginning of 1944 the Germans were being driven rapidly out of the Crimea and the southern Ukraine. Marshal Vatutin had pushed the Germans west out of Kiev in 1943 and by January the Germans were in full retreat toward the Polish and Rumanian borders; the German lines fell back almost a steady two miles a day during the first four months of 1944, at first wheeling back on a hinge at Odessa but then pulling back almost in parallel unison after Odessa fell to the Reds.

The collapse of Odessa left the Germans with only one Black Sea harbor to sustain her naval force—open at all costs. In the meantime, Heinz Krausser's Sebastopol—and Hitler ordered that Sebastopol be kept planned primary route—into Kiev—had been stoppered by the Russian advance: the Red Army stood astride the railway and there was no way to get a train across the front lines, as there might have been if the city were still contested.

It left only the Crimean alternative; and the Red Army had already regained a foothold on the peninsula.

Krausser's train, at the end of January 1944, was in a race with the Red Army to reach Sebastopol. The route von Geyr and Krausser had worked out is probably the route Krausser intended to follow: cross the Dnieper at Alexandrovsk; down through Melitopol, then across the steppes to Taganach; then over the railroad bridge onto the Crimean isthmus, and thence across Crimea into Sebastopol.

What happened to the Germans at Sebastopol is a matter of record; what happened to Krausser, his train and his *Jagdsonderkommando* is not.

Sebastopol was the Nazis' Dunkirk. The city had been leveled in the early months of the war; but the harbor was intact and the German Black Sea navy used the port as its principal base, mainly for the purpose of intimidating the vacillating Turks and supporting the German war effort in Greece.

After the fall of the southern Ukraine, the Crimean peninsula was cut off from overland communication with Germany and the use of the German Black Sea navy as a support unit in Greece became impossible because the navy had no access to supplies from Germany. Nevertheless Hitler seemed more preoccupied about the possibility that the Turks might enter the war against him than he was about the fact that the Russians were already destroying his armies. At least that is the commonly accepted historical explanation for his maniacal—and evidently pointless—defense of Sebastopol. It is possible [although there is no proof yet] that one reason the Führer needed to keep the port open was his expectation that *Jagdsonderkommando Ein* would still manage to break through the Russian encirclement somehow and deliver into German hands the billions of Reichsmarks' worth of gold which by now must have assumed the proportions of a magic talisman in Hitler's deranged thoughts. (Clearly it was far too late to *buy* a victory.)

The German *Festung Sewastopol* did not manage to match the Russian record for withstanding a siege.

The Russians took Sebastopol in four days. Total German losses were in excess of one hundred thousand.

When the city fell on May 8, 1944, there was no sign of Heinz Krausser, his *Jagdsonderkommando,* his train, or Kolchak's gold.

The clues are cryptic.

[Every time a train stops to take on water or fuel, or switch engines, or be shunted onto a siding to await the converse passage of another train, some yard bureaucrat must make a twitch in his logbook. Railroads everywhere are like that: records are kept of the location of every engine and every railway car at all times because it is the only way for the system to keep tabs on its rolling stock. In wartime some of these regulations were disregarded, and even when they were obeyed the records did not always survive. But each train is assigned a dispatching number which it retains as long as it retains its entity as a *train:* that is, from the time it is assembled until the time it is dispersed and its pieces of rolling stock are used to combine in other trains.]

. . . .*Train #S-1428-CB, 3000 kilos coal. . . . T #S-1428-CB, north switch 1100 hrs 28 Jan 44. . . . S-1428-CB held 2325-0118 hhs for priority routing Troop Train V-8339-CJ. . . .*

The spoor of Krausser's train could be traced from its starting point in Siberia to the marshaling yards of Saratov, at the northerly edge of the Volgograd Reservoir. From that point to the Crimea, however, is a distance of more than one thousand kilometers by rail,

215

and there are several alternate route approaches. The wake of Krausser's train, beginning in February 1944, becomes progressively harder to find.

[This much is revealed by the surviving records:] On February 3 the train passed through the rail junction at Balashov, taking the westerly branch; on February 9 it appeared in the vicinity of Kharkov, heading for Poltava; on February 12 it reappeared at Kharkov, apparently having turned back after Krausser had found out the state of the war front ahead of him. The German lines were now well to the west of Kiev, or some six hundred kilometers west of Kharkov.

The train wasted at least another week in false starts in a westerly direction before Krausser apparently decided he had to give up that attempt and strike out along the alternate route instead—toward the Crimea.

An adamant official in the switching yards at Gorlovka held the train up for two and a half days on account of priority munitions movements; that this took place is not surprising—Krausser had had amazingly good luck up till then in keeping his train moving—but there is the curious fact that this delay took place on February 28 through March 2, 1944; the train had taken more than two weeks to traverse the three hundred kilometers between those two points. No dispatching records from intermediate stations have turned up in Russian archives. Apparently Krausser had been held up—once or several times—en route to Gorlovka.

One pictures the frenzied desperation with which *Jagdsonderkommando Ein* now faced the passage of every day, every hour. And now, on March 2, the dispatcher at Gorlovka only allowed the train to leave in one direction—eastward. Documents show that "Lieutenant Razin" was ordered to get his train out of the way because of urgent priority trains which were continuously arriving from the north. The train left on the evening of the second, going in the direction of Lugansk, where duly it arrived on March 4—nearly a hundred kilometers farther from the German lines than it had been two days earlier.

No further specific records have turned up. The train disappears at Lugansk, still some six hundred kilometers from the Crimea.

The records of a Red Army Graves Registration team for April 13, 1944, show that eighteen Russian soldiers were buried the preceding day on the outskirts of a deserted Jewish *shtetl* about fifteen kilometers northeast of Rostov, near the Don. Listed among the dead are First Lieutenant Yevgeni Razin and People's Commissar Ivan Samsonov. The names of the sixteen remaining dead are the same, with certain variations in spelling, as the Russian cover-names of sixteen enlisted and noncommissioned members of *Jagdsonderkommando Ein*. Cause of death in the GR team's report is listed as "combat casualties the result of warfare, probably against counterrevolutionary bandits"—a customary euphemism for partisans. [The anti-Communist Ukrainian army was fiercely active in that area during that period.]

The GR report leaves eleven commando members unaccounted for until one examines the attached lists of personal effects found on the bodies. On the body of "Commissar Samsonov" were found the metal Russian identity tags and papers of the eleven remaining team members. [One must conclude they had died in earlier engagements and been buried by the survivors.]

As a result it is clear that the twenty-nine men of *Jagdsonderkommando Ein* were wiped out without exception. [However it is also evident that the bodies were found many miles from the nearest railway track; that it is not possible for twenty-nine men to carry any significant portion of five hundred tons of gold on their persons; and that in any case no gold was reported to have been found on or near the bodies. Furthermore there is no record of the reappearance of the Krausser train *as a train:* that is, as an assembled entity. There are, however, ample records to prove the reappearance of several goods wagons and both locomotives which had been assigned to the train.] Both locomotives appear in an April 17 report from the marshaling yard at Donetsk, where they were used in assembling a munitions train which was dispatched to the front at Korosten. Of the numbered goods wagons, three appeared in April at Makeyevka and two others were incorporated into a heavy-weapons train being assembled at Gorlovka on May 3.

[The conclusion to be drawn from this seems inescapable: Krausser must have removed the gold from the train, hidden the gold, moved the empty train to one of the busy switching yards in South Russia, and abandoned it there, after which he must have concluded that the only recourse left open was to make his way back to Germany and report on his mission, in hopes von Geyr or someone else in higher authority would be able to come up with a new plan for extracting the treasure from Soviet territory.

[The original plan had been to smuggle the train through battle lines by taking advantage of the tactical confusion that had existed in late 1943 in several cities in the Ukraine and South Russia, where portions of the cities—Kiev for example—were in the hands of both armies. Under such circumstances it would have been possible for a train to cross from the Russian-held sector into the German, probably without being fired on. But by February 1944 there were no cities still in German hands except Sebastopol (which was inaccessible to Krausser) and those cities to which rail tracks had been destroyed by bombardment—a fact Krausser must have learned in his several unsuccessful forays west into the Ukraine in January and early February.

[Thus for the second time in twenty-five years the gold of the Czars was removed from a train and hidden. No subsequent Soviet records even so much as hint that there has ever been a suspicion in that country that the treasure may be buried near the banks of the Don in South Russia. The annihilation of *Jagdsonderkommando Ein* guaranteed that no one in Germany could make even a wild stab at the eventual disposition of the gold—not even those like von Geyr who were intimate with the plan to extricate the treasure.]

Erysichthon offended Ceres; in response, Ceres punished him with an insatiable appetite. Finally he ate himself.*

---

* This notation, on a 4 X 6 file card in Bristow's files, seems a fitting conclusion to his account of the war.—Ed.

THE VIENNA MANUSCRIPT

III

---

* The narrative resumes where it was interrupted. Perhaps it should be repeated that the section and chapter divisions herein are the editors'.

Within the next few pages the manuscript becomes a sort of montage of brief chapters held together with paper clips and written on papers of different kinds. The section which follows this one, for example, is written in pencil on stationery of the Hotel Schloss Hohensalzburg, a small hotel near the Makartplatz in Salzburg, Austria. Evidently the present section was written at the beginning of May 1973, but there are indications that Bristow did not write this final part of his manuscript in the order in which he later assembled it (by numbering the pages). He added some interior sections after writing some of the final ones. This accounts for the fragmentation of certain passages.—Ed.

14

I COULD HARDLY go out into the mountains, dig around and find out if the gold was hidden where I thought it was.

And if I had done so, and found it—what could I have done about it?

The three yard-records which I destroyed were evidence that Train #S-1428-CB was en route from point X to point Y to point Z. It left X and arrived at Y; it left Y but never showed up at Z. There was no rail junction between the two points; the train could only proceed to Z, or reverse and return to Y. It did neither. Therefore the train must have been unloaded at some point between Y and Z, and the train then broken into two trains (it had two locomotives, one at either end); the two half-trains then went in opposite directions, each bearing a new designation number—forgeries provided by Berlin, again. These two empty trains were dispersed from points Y and Z, their rolling stock used in the assembly of new trains.*

By destroying the documents I made it impossible for anyone else to discover where the gold train had been unloaded.

* Elsewhere, in a section deleted earlier by the editors, Bristow speculated on how the gold might have been hidden: "Several possible methods. (A) Much industry had been moved to Siberia. Spur rail lines remained, now unused. Some went through tunnels. Unload gold inside tunnel, then demolish both openings at ends of tunnel as if air-raid bomb damage. (B) Old smelters—numerous in South Russia. Slag piles—enormous. Pile up gold in area of slag heaps, cover it with layer of slag. (C) Several lakes and reservoirs adjacent to spur RR lines. Sink gold in one of them. It won't corrode. (D) Several new highways then being laid & paved for military transport. Lay gold in road-fill, then pave over it. (E) The traditional way: dig a hole and bury it."—Ed.

It was a hazardous act; I knew that. It was also crucial; I only inferred that.

Self-evident: I destroyed the evidence to guarantee the secret would remain my own. Why? Perhaps sheer egoism, megalomania. I can't account for all my motives, particularly in my recent actions; I've been too pummeled to retain much insight.

The act was an impulse. A Freudian would insist I had prepared for it by doing a great deal of unconscious reasoning. After all I had expected to find the gold, or at least hoped to; the solution was a sort of emotional triumph but not altogether a surprise. Destroying the evidence did surprise me in a way; I hadn't premeditated it. But when I actually found those documents I knew I couldn't leave them there. Couldn't let anyone else find them. I had followed a chain of reasoning; anyone else could follow it too.

I gave myself several reasons to justify the act. I remember most of them. They were voiced in the encounters that took place during the next weeks; there's no point in spelling them out twice. Basically my reasoning wasn't all that different from the reason why Haim or his brother hadn't ever revealed the location of the Sayan cache. What decided me was the same question that had decided the Tippelskirch brothers: to whom could I reveal what I knew? And why should I, and what purpose would it serve, and whom would it benefit; and so on.

The day after I destroyed the stolen documents I returned to the archives as usual and went to work. To do otherwise might have raised suspicion; I didn't want to attract attention to the files I had requisitioned yesterday.

I told myself I'd solved the mystery of Kolchak's gold; I told myself it freed me to focus on what was still the real job—reconstructing the story of Sebastopol.

But it wasn't possible to keep from thinking about it. Working out schemes. Fantasies about going in search of the gold with a spade, a pick, hiking boots and a knapsack. I excused them by thinking of them as exercises.

I tried to throw myself into the work with renewed concentration. I divided the next several days between industrious file-riffling in the museum's reading room and conversations with Zandor's hand-picked interviewees. Three of them gave me surprisingly useful information. Timoshenko chaperoned me to the meetings with his customary good cheer, and continued my informal introduction to the city's night life, such as it was.

Then a Thursday,* a day that remains as clear in my mind as the day of a marriage or birth or death.

I left the museum at noon to walk off tension and look for a tavern for a midday drink. It was a balmy day. The street was busy with lunch-hour pedestrians. They walk stolidly because they have to, they're not strolling for exercise. There is never a great deal of motor traffic in Russian cities but the street was noisy with trucks and coaches and the poorly muffled growlings of Russian-built cars.

A man stood on the opposite sidewalk and his eyes flicked across me. Anywhere else I'd have thought nothing of it—a meaningless glance in a street. But it alarmed me. I sensed his eyes on my back when I turned to go down the street.

A block distant I looked back; he was no longer at his post.

I went fretfully on. I knew the neighborhood now; I carried my lunch into a small tavern on a side street and ordered the local wine. People milled in and out; I recognized none of them.

I examined my observational abilities: I set myself the task of reconstructing his appearance.

Unextraordinary. A large man but not huge. No hat, no topcoat. A blue suit cut to reduce a paunch. A somewhat rubbery face, dark hair combed straight back without a part. Round features. Nothing about his eyes; I hadn't been close enough; I had the impression however that he had hairy hands. Not a Slavic appearance; neither square nor swarthy. Western European, then—or more likely a Russian from the White country to the northwest. But I came back to the suit: not Moscow serge. A little baggy but that was from lack of pressing; it had been a well-cut suit, probably a

* Probably March 22, 1973.—Ed.

223

fairly decent fabric. Something German about it; something distinctly un-Russian.

Or was it one of Zandor's people? I remembered his fastidious dress.

Then I remembered Vassily Bukov: the indulgently tailored slacks.

I finished the carafe of wine and left the place. The traffic was noisy. I didn't hear his approach and I was startled when he spoke.

"Please don't look at me, Bristow. Study that radio in the window."

I saw his reflection ripple across the shop window as he moved past my shoulder and bent to try his key in the door lock of a parked Moskvitch. He seemed to have trouble getting the key in. He had too much of a belly on him to be able to bend down comfortably.

In the racket I could barely hear him. "I'm an American. You're in trouble, Bristow. We've got to meet tonight. Half-past six, leave your hotel and turn right—north. Keep walking up the street until we pick you up. If you're being followed we'll spot it and you won't be contacted. In that case stop and wait by the phone kiosk at the corner by the postal exchange—we'll call you there with further instructions. Got it?"

"Yes. But what danger——"

"Shut up. Beat it."

He got the door open and slid into the car. It pulled out into the traffic and I took my eyes off the display of radios and cheap clocks in the shop window.

Central Intelligence Agency, obviously. Their penchant for trench-coated melodrama is infamous.

But he'd scared me. I kept my fears buttoned down tight because if I let my imagination go I knew I could go to pieces.

The breeze blew the smell of diesel exhaust across my face. A block distant, smoke spurted from the tailpipe of the blue-suited man's ramshackle Russian car. I remembered him stooping there, fiddling with the key and very carefully not looking in my direction; probably talking out of the side of his mouth like a ventriloquist. Something comical about it: the television absurdity of it.

I went back to the museum but my nerves were in a bad state.

The street meeting he'd proposed was one of the standard ploys to reveal shadows and make safe contact. Abwehr and MI-6 agents had used it in Madrid and Lisbon and Istanbul. It didn't prove my blue-suited man had any imagination; it only proved he'd read the book. Mine or his agency's manual.

I dismissed Timoshenko for the evening and at half-past six I left the hotel and went up the street as instructed. The postal exchange was nine blocks distant. The sky was heavy with clouds; it was cool and a bit steamy. Caution had led me to carry the most important of my notes in the pockets of my suit; they made bulges here and there but my coat concealed them.

A woman like a bosomy Druid waited patiently by a cable pole for her dachshund to finish. I went past her trying to gauge the light automobile traffic in the street beside me. I did not detect any sound or reflection of a car moving along behind me at walking pace, but then they wouldn't have handled it that way. They'd be hanging back a few blocks watching me—watching what happened behind me.

I made no effort to disclose a tail. It was up to my contact to discover him. Those are the rules of that game.

I did not know what to expect. There were too many possibilities; guessing was pointless. Danger, he'd said. . . .

I reached the postal exchange without contact.

Suddenly I realized what a poor scheme it was. *They disclose a tail on me.* So I'm under surveillance. Now I'm supposed to answer that telephone? They're idiots. The minute it rings and I answer it, whoever watching me knows I'm making a contact.*

* Italics supplied by the editors. Written in growing haste, some of these passages are characterized by muddled verb tenses and uncertain syntax. As much as possible, we have left the wording alone, feeling that the best editing is the least editing.—Ed.

If my erstwhile friends were watching me from a car —he had implied they were—it would take them a bit of time to get to a telephone. I turned abruptly and walked back the way I had come; I wanted to be away from that kiosk before the telephone in it began to ring.

Half a block ahead of me a man turned into the entrance of a building. When I passed it he was not there; he'd gone inside. He'd been vaguely familiar; I'd seen him before—possibly at the museum. One of Zandor's? My backtracking had caught him off guard; I wasn't supposed to have seen him.

A block farther I made a right turn and strolled down a side street. I didn't check to see whether Zandor's man was behind me; there was little doubt of it. I didn't want to return directly to the hotel because he would have been puzzled by my direct hike to and from the corner where the postal exchange stood. This way I might still persuade him I was simply out walking, limbering up the joints, with no particular destination in mind. I took a circuitous and unhurried route back to the hotel.

I insert these details because it illustrates Ritter's* clumsiness and helps to show why I later resisted his approaches. "Intelligence" is a poor word for the operations of most espionage and counterespionage organizations. An unpleasant number of their actions tend to serve as self-fulfillment of gloomy prophecy. On the way back to my hotel I had ample time to reflect angrily that even if I had not been in "danger" before, Ritter's stupid plan would have guaranteed it in the end, if I'd obeyed his instructions.

By nature the operation of intelligence activities is supposed to be passive. All too often it fails in that objective because in the course of gathering intelligence

* Ritter, of course, is the name of the man in the blue suit. Below, Bristow gives him more of a formal introduction. As mentioned earlier in the notes, these passages were added as insertions in the manuscript after Bristow had completed the basic structure; they are written on odd scraps of paper with such indices as "page 382-A, -B," and so on, to indicate where Bristow wanted them to appear.—Ed.

the operative brings attention upon himself and his illegal behavior. This in turn creates exactly the kind of international "incident" which Intelligence, ideally, is supposed to prevent. If I had more time and felt more level-headed I could turn all this into an amusingly comic sequence; essentially that's what it is, once you remove to a certain objective distance. But I was not, and am not, in that luxurious condition. I was afraid.

I was on my way out of the hotel to wait for Timoshenko's arrival.* A familiar man was coming up the sidewalk toward me. I almost suffered cardiac arrest when he reached inside the lapel of his coat but what he produced was an envelope; he approached with the envelope extended toward me.

He identified himself stiffly as Yakov Sanarski and waited for me to open the envelope; I found that it contained a new, revised visa. It extended my permit by five weeks.

He asked if this was satisfactory and I tried to look pleased. "Tell Comrade Zandor I'm very grateful to the government."

Sanarski bowed with a formal little twitch of a smile and walked away, back the way he had come, to a waiting car he had parked awkwardly at the very corner of the block, sticking out into the intersection. He drove away and I stuffed the new visa into my already overcrowded pocket.

Sanarski was the man who had been following me the previous afternoon, to the postal exchange and back. This morning connected him beyond question with Zandor; so at least I had confirmation—I knew who had me under surveillance. This relieved me somewhat. It makes things a bit easier when you know who your antagonist is.

Trepidation thundered through my blood through the whole morning. I couldn't suppress the American agent from the center of my thinking, but there wasn't a thing I could do that would alleviate the tension; the next move was his to make.

* This is the next morning—probably Friday, March 23. —Ed.

He made it at the same hour as yesterday. I went out during the lunch hour for that purpose—in case he was waiting for me as he had done before. I walked slowly along the exact route I'd followed yesterday. There was no sign of him. I reached the tavern and went in.

The place was not terribly crowded; about half its chairs were occupied. One of them was occupied by the American agent. He didn't look at me.

I couldn't very well sit with him; in any case I didn't want to. By destroying state documents I had already committed a grave offense but there was a good chance it wouldn't be discovered—ever. Unless that was what the agent had been referring to yesterday when he'd warned me of danger. But I'd just about convinced myself that couldn't be it. If they knew about the theft of the documents they'd have arrested me, not given me an extended visa. I hadn't done anything else to put me in trouble and I didn't intend to, certainly not by making open contact with the American.

I took one glass of wine at the bar, intending to leave immediately.

From a corner of my vision I saw him get up to leave. He counted coins gravely in his palm and pressed them down onto the table singly, pocketing what was left; he still had his hand in his pocket when he came forward toward the door. His route took him immediately behind me. He jostled me. When I looked around I heard him mutter "Sorry" in Russian—not very good Russian, a terrible accent. He went on outside. His hand was no longer in his pocket.

I finished the wine, giving it a good five or six minutes. Then I went back to the men's room. I was alone in it; I reached into the outside pockets of my coat and found the note, crumpled into a tight ball like something a schoolboy would put in a slingshot. I smoothed it out, read it, tore it up and flushed it away.

It told me to leave the museum at two o'clock and stroll down to the Square of Fallen Warriors, then take the tram up Nevsky Boulevard. There were detailed instructions, what to do step by step. The last sentence was, "Be careful—they are onto you." It was signed *K. Ritter.*

I could only obey it or ignore it. The vague silly warning had its intended effect; I obeyed it, half in fear and half in anger because there was no need for such cryptic melodrama.

Procedures for disclosing and shaking a tail are numerous and they differ according to the purpose of the procedure. It is relatively easy to "ditch" clandestine pursuit if you don't mind his knowing he's being shaken. It is considerably harder to make the ditch look like an accident: that is, to put him off the scent and make him think it's his own fault. He must not know that he has been spotted; he must not know that you have shaken him off deliberately. Yet all the same you must lose him. It isn't easy but classic patterns have been laid down; fundamentally the choice of method must be determined by the number of shadowers who are in play.

I knew the textbook methods and Ritter's was one of them. The instructions in his note had professional weaknesses and that was one reason for my anger. Had I obeyed his specifications methodically I wouldn't have lost the tail. He hadn't taken into account the possibility there would be more than two of them.

I threaded the bleak massive monuments of the Square of Fallen Warriors along a random choice of footpaths. A pale sun filtered weakly through the haze but it was not a cold afternoon; there were overcoated figures on the park benches. I kept an eye out for an approaching tram and when one came in sight I timed my stroll to meet it when it stopped at the corner of the square; I swung up onto the steps and eeled inside without looking over my shoulder but the reflection in the opposite window gave me a glimpse of two long-coated men jogging toward us from the footpaths of the square. Neither of them reached the tram; we were in motion before they reached the curb.

From my seat I saw a four-door Volga squirt across the boulevard; the two men climbed into it and it followed us.

My instructions were to leave the tram at its second stop, four blocks from the square; this would have been sufficient to lose a pursuer on foot but Ritter hadn't counted on their having a car. They could keep up regardless of how far I chose to ride.

Better to risk missing the meeting than to let them see I was trying to lose them. Therefore I had to make it look as if I had a legitimate destination in mind; you can't just ride a tram four blocks and then get off in the middle of nowhere.

As you follow Nevsky Boulevard across the horse-shoe-shaped hillside that contains the city and harbor of Sebastopol, you enter the city's commercial district. Here are the monolithic state-industries stores, the consumer-goods sales and services, the maritime offices and executive buildings from which the activities of the port are directed.

All right, I was on a buying expedition; what did I need that was important enough to take me away from the archives in the middle of the afternoon? I finally decided on a hat, since I wasn't wearing one; I had one in the hotel room but I could get rid of it later and pretend I had lost it. The forecast called for snow and windy cold days ahead; obviously I needed a hat.

It was flimsy but it would have to do; in any case with luck I wouldn't be asked.

In heavy *centre ville* traffic I dismounted from the tram and made my way into the crowded GUM emporium, threaded the throng, picked out a dark Russian hat with earflaps and a lining that was probably rabbit, and stood in the queue that you can't avoid whenever you shop for anything in the USSR. With an expression contrived to combine impatience with boredom I let my glance flick from display to display and from face to face, turning on my heels with irritable restlessness; and spotted my two pursuers busily inspecting a table of yard goods where they looked as out of place as two bulls in a hen yard.

When my turn came I paid for the hat and walked through the store without hurry, ambling past counters of clothing and hardware, stopping now and then to examine something of passing interest. A pulse was battering in my throat but it was not so much fear as the excitement of challenge: the kind of thrill a small boy feels when he tries to get away with something against the rules. I was, I must confess, having fun.

It was fun only so long as I managed to disregard Ritter's warning of danger. At the moment I was in no real and immediate danger because everything I did could be construed to have innocent plausibility; I was the only one who knew an adventure was taking place.

I had roved deep into the half-acre store and there were at least four street exits available, one on each side of the building. I knew there were two of them and a third man outside in a car, probably waiting at the curb by the door through which we had entered. The two on foot had to follow me because there were too many exits; otherwise they'd have posted themselves by the exits and simply waited for me to leave.

My purpose at this point was to get rid of that car. I did it by wandering out of the store through the back door. A stout woman was entering as I left; I held the door open for her and used that movement as my excuse to turn. Smiling in response to her "Thank you" I was able to pick up a glimpse of my two stolid watchers: one was coming idly toward me and the other was striding away purposefully toward the far end of the building, where obviously he would get in the car and come around the block.

Carrying the new hat in my hand I went up the sidewalk to the nearest corner and turned right. This put me out of their sight and I knew where all of them were: one man following me down the sidewalk, one getting into the car, one behind the wheel. I turned into the side entrance of the store and reentered it quickly, before the man on foot behind me had time to reach the corner and see me go inside.

For the first few paces I hurried; I went off at an angle from the side entrance into a crowded area of small refrigerators and television sets where citizens stood gaping at these marvels of consumer technology. As I entered the group I fitted the new hat onto my head and turned up the collar of my coat. The man following me was looking for a hatless man with his coat collar lying flat.

I pushed through the knot of gawkers and made my way through fifty yards of men's clothing, neither idling

231

nor hurrying; I went out the front door—the door through which I had originally entered the store—and of course by now the four-door Volga was no longer there, having gone around the block in search of me. I crossed the thoroughfare quickly and boarded the south-bound tram which took me back along Nevsky Boulevard the way I'd come.

We made about two blocks and through the rear of the tram I saw the man who'd followed me afoot come out of the GUM and stand on the curb looking baffled. The car emerged from the side street and drew up before him. It was facing away from me. The second man climbed out of the car and the two of them stood there talking and gesturing disgustedly, and then we made the bend up the hill and they were out of sight.

At the next corner I left the tram and walked spirit-edly uphill along a side street of cheap concrete apart-ment blocks; I crossed one intersection and paused to catch my breath from the climb. No car was turning into the street below me, nor was any pedestrian in sight. I went up another hundred yards to the next main boulevard which ran along parallel to Nevsky, and waited for the tram with my back to the corner of a building so that if they drove by along Nevsky and looked up along the side streets they wouldn't see me.

The tram seemed forever coming. But my shadowers did not appear and finally I rode back toward the Square of Fallen Warriors, left the tram four blocks short of the Square and walked uphill along a silent street of two- and four-family houses with the Mediter-ranean roofs the Sebastopolites affect. I was now back on the route Ritter had specified in his letter of in-structions; I was about a half hour late.

It was quite possible he wouldn't wait for me but I didn't hurry. Nothing attracts attention so quickly as the sight of a running man.

At the top of the hill I surveyed my backtrail and saw nothing alarming. A woman pushed a baby car-riage along one sidewalk and three people were stand-ing on a porch talking; a delivery van moved across my line of sight a block or two below; I saw no Volga sedan, no men in long coats. I turned into the People's

Park for Culture and Learning, followed the pathway around the perimeter of the auditorium and left the park at its upper end, following my assigned route. I was quite certain no one was following me now; I'd stopped twice in the park to scan the paths and although I was not alone in the park there was no one moving in my direction.

Two blocks along Maxim Gorky, then turn right and walk one block along Arbat, turn left. The car was there—the same little Moskvitch he'd had trouble unlocking yesterday.

"I'd about given up on you."

"There were three of them and a car. I had to lose them first."

"Then they're serious about you. You can see for yourself you're in trouble, Harry."

He had an accent that wasn't quite American and I gave him a close look as I pulled the passenger door shut. He stirred the shift lever and we moved away from the curb.

"I'm Karl Ritter. Born in Germany, if you were wondering—they tell me I still have a bit of an accent."

"You've managed to half scare the pants off me. I'd like to know why."

"Let's go where we can talk. I can't drive and talk at the same time. I'm one of those people who have to do one thing at a time."

We went over the ridge toward the suburbs. The sky was becoming more heavily grey. Ritter looked over-crowded in the driver's seat, his belly almost pressing the lower rim of the steering wheel. He kept banging his left knee on the column when he clutched to shift.

I said, "You almost railroaded me into trouble twice. I'd like an explanation."

"You'll get one, Harry."

He got to first names too quickly; it was another thing I didn't like him for. And the accent made me think of Henry Kissinger.

He drove the car with earnest aggressiveness but not well. He kept both hands rigidly on the wheel and tended to overcorrect; it wouldn't have been a relaxing ride under any circumstances.

"Here we are."

It was a featureless two-story block of flats, probably not more than ten years old but crumbly around the edges as if the building had been poured in one continuous dump of concrete and it hadn't set properly. Ritter jammed the Moskvitch into a space at the curb and grunted getting out of the car. He walked me to the door and turned to survey the street before he came inside. He pointed to the stairs and we went up and along a narrow corridor with a bare concrete floor. It was reminiscent of American federally financed housing for the poor. Square, functional, bleak; there was no décor.

Ritter opened a door with a key and we went into an apartment furnished with a nondescript potpourri of battered chairs and tables; it looked like a careless bachelor's residence and there was an unmade daybed, Scandinavian style—a platform with a thin mattress on it, the sheets and coverlet thrown back and rumpled. Two interior doors gave onto a tiny bathroom and a separate kitchen that was large enough to contain a small table and two chairs. Ritter went directly into the kitchen and beckoned me to follow; when I entered the small room he closed the door behind me and said, "Have a seat."

I concluded he had chosen the kitchen because it had no windows. It was not a comforting conclusion.

Ritter said, "I swept it this morning. There are no bugs. I'm sorry if the precautions seem excessive, but nothing can be assumed to be private over here."

He was one of those people who get too close: his nose was inches from mine and I could smell the tobacco on his breath. I sat down at the table to put breathing distance between us.

Ritter fixed me with baggy eyes. They were pale blue, rather watery. He turned to a cupboard and found a bottle of vodka inside. "Drink?" He seemed to feel a compulsion to act the host.

"Is this your apartment?"

"No."

He seemed to be looking for drinking glasses; he

234

wore a preoccupied look as if he couldn't remember whether he had packed his underwear.

I said, "All right, damn it. Who the hell are you?"

"Me? I'm just a civil servant with a slight sinus condition." The flash of a grin across his swollen face. He found tumblers and put them on the little table; sat down, took out a cigarette and flicked it against the back of his hand. Then he hung it in his mouth unlit and reached for the bottle to pour.

Finally he spoke. "It's kind of a low-budget safe house. We borrow the place when we need it. The owner works days. He's one of our people, works for my firm."

"What firm would that be?"

He waved the cigarette. "Hell, you know." Lit it with a wooden match and waved his hand to extinguish the match. "Just looking out for the interests of our citizens abroad."

I was rigid with suppressed feelings. "I'm waiting."

"Harry, you're in trouble two ways. You know what they are."

"Do I?"

"One, the Jews. The KGB already suspects you on that one. Two, the gold. They haven't tumbled to that yet."

I don't know how well I concealed my consternation. He had chucked a hell of a big rock into the pond. I had to make an instant decision: how to reply, how much to give in.

His elbow was on the table and instead of lifting the cigarette he ducked his head to reach the cigarette with his mouth. His eyes were puckered by suspicion.

In the end I chose not to say anything.

He waited awhile; then he said, "Come on, Harry. You're trying to hunt lion with a peashooter. You're unimportant, you know that—you're not hurting the Reds and you're not hurting us. You're just hurting yourself. A little while and Moscow's going to have all the evidence they need to slap you in prison on some vague grounds and say it's necessary in the interests of national security. You'd have a hell of a time proving it was a frame from inside a Siberian work camp.

You'd just be an entry in a file someplace. And then they go to work on you with all those Manchurian Candidate techniques and whatever else they're using to take the place of the rubber hose. When they start that you might as well give them everything you know because they're going to get it out of you anyway. And then afterward they're finished with you. You freeze to death or you have a fatal fall in the shower bath or you're charged with assaulting a prison guard and attempting to escape, and they execute you. I could give you a list six pages long. Is that how you want it to end up? Don't you see that you can't . . ."

He blustered on until he heard himself; then he stopped, embarrassed because I hadn't given him any visible reaction; I'd just waited him out.

Ritter dribbled ash on his coat; he brushed it off and sat back and crossed one fat leg above the other. It hitched up his trouser cuff: his sock had fallen down and the calf of his leg was pale and slightly hairy. "No comment? I'll say this for you—you've got the balls of a brass gorilla."

"Ritter, you're certifiable, do you know that? I simply don't know what you're talking about."

"A word of advice, Harry—the innocent act is contraindicated. It's too late to do anything about the Mossad group, you've already been linked to them. Getting out of that mess would be like trying to get your virginity back. But the gold, that's something else."

"What gold?"

He shook his head in exasperation. "Look, as soon as you calm down and quit lying to me we'll have a conversation."

I said, "I find you amusing up to a point, Ritter, but you've passed it. I still don't know what you're talking about and I can only conclude that you've been making assumptions based on assumptions and you've reached some wild answers."

But it wasn't getting me anywhere and I saw I was going to have to put it so bluntly that he could not go on evading it without exposing the truth. I said: "You don't seem to get this yet. I have no way of knowing who or what you are."

236

"I told you. Just a civil servant trying to earn my gold watch."

"All right, but *whose* civil servant?"

Suddenly he got it. Recognition was mirrored transparently in his eyes and his face dropped a foot. "Oh, for Christ's sake."

"I've got to see some credentials."

"I haven't got any. I couldn't very well, could I?"

"Then we're at an impasse, aren't we?"

I had only his word for it that he represented American interests. He could have been one of Zandor's people trying to trip me up—testing me. Nothing he had said or done precluded that possibility. It would serve the interests of Zandor and his superior, Bizenkev in Moscow (who had opposed my visit from the beginning), to toll me into a trap by encouraging me to confess my anti-Soviet sins to a Soviet agent in the guise of an American.

He pushed his chair back against the little piece of wall beside the door; he sat with one knee bent, foot against the table, the other foot on the floor and his head resting back against the wall. He took a drink and then spoke in a voice made breathless by the vodka:

"What would it take to convince you?"

"I don't know. That's up to you."

"The business about the Romanov gold reserves. I got that from Evan MacIver. The Russians don't know about it yet."

"Assuming we both know what you're talking about, how would I have any way of being sure the Russians didn't know about it?"

"If they did you'd be sweating out a torture cell right now."

"And what *am* I doing right now?"

He smiled. "Your daddy must have been a lawyer."

"What are you really doing here?"

"MacIver told me to bail you out."

"What's your title?"

"I'm a programming officer."

"In the field?"

"Sometimes we work in the field."

"What's MacIver's title?"

"Assistant Deputy Director of Programming." He hacked out a dry smoker's cough. MacIver was a heavy smoker too. "None of that proves anything, does it. I could have got all that from one of your books. Or if I was a KGB agent I'd know it. Look, I'd better spell it out for you."

It was about bloody time.

Ritter was forty-nine years old. His parents had emigrated from Germany in 1937 when he was thirteen; they had settled in Boston and joined the German-American Bund, which he thought ridiculous. He broke openly with his parents at the beginning of 1942 when he was eighteen; he had not yet received his draft notice but he volunteered and was taken into the army.

According to what he told me, he was approached by OSS recruiters in 1943 but was turned down after an FBI security check revealed his parents' affiliations. Ritter went into army intelligence instead and spent two years in Italy, France and Germany, mainly spying out soldiers who profiteered on the black market.

When the Central Intelligence Agency was formed in 1947 out of ragtag remnants of OSS, MI and other security groups he went in as a legman and was used extensively thereafter in foreign postings because with his German appearance and accent he was not likely to be taken for an American agent. But the fact that he was not a native American militated against his being promoted to any office of administrative importance within the excessively chauvinist agency.

In the sixties he got another black mark against him because he was one of Cord Meyer's people engaged in recruiting for the CIA on U.S. campuses and when these activities were made public the pressure from the liberal wing had truncated several promising careers, Ritter's among them. He had found himself doing tours of duty in Iceland, Chile and Thailand.

Then in late 1971 he had been recalled to Washington by Evan MacIver, whose protégé Ritter had become, when MacIver was promoted to the post of Assistant Deputy Director of Programming.

In the Washington area one out of nine federal employees works for the Central Intelligence Agency. It is funded by vouchered but confidential Class "A" funds audited only within the Agency itself; the budget is hidden within various federal programs including the Defense Department, the National Aeronautics and Space Administration and various executive departments. Called the Agency by outsiders and The Firm by insiders, CIA has its headquarters in the midst of four hundred acres of trees near the Memorial Parkway inside the belt Interstate Highway 495 near Langley, Virginia; the building is modern, imposing, suitably enormous (it rivals the Pentagon in size) and shaped rather like a gigantic Louis XVI palace with two vast courtyards and endless interior corridors. A significant part of its square footage is below ground level. It is an enormous satrapy under the director who controls the operations of some two hundred thousand employees who are engaged in espionage, deception, insurgency, dissemination of propaganda, analysis of intelligence, counterintelligence, "black propaganda" (the publication of forged documents to embarrass the enemy), "black documentation" (the preparation of false facts to be fed to enemy agents), and "political action"— the euphemistic term for disintegrating or overthrowing a nation's government while leaving the appearance that the government collapsed from natural causes. The Programming Division is known informally as the department of dirty tricks and it receives the largest share of CIA's budget and personnel.

The operations of such an organization are complex because it is not enough merely to attain an objective; in order to succeed, the Agency must also conceal the fact that the objective has been attained. Ideally the Agency should be able to conceal the fact that it has even tried to attain the objective.

Unfortunately these ideals are rarely met in practice.*

Ritter's explanation—his "spelling it out"—was rambling and anecdotal. In substance what he said was that

* It is probably clear from the context that Bristow added this passage and inserted it here. Henceforth such insertions will not be pointed out unless it seems important to do so.—Ed.

Evan MacIver had become concerned about me after my affair with a known Mossad agent ripened; that the Mossad connection began to worry the Agency when it became clear I was going to Russia; and that because of these things and the gold, the Agency took a bet on me—so they "ran" me in a sense, with MacIver serving as a sort of Control. (I recalled that lunch in Washington when MacIver had said, "I think you get your nocturnal emissions from dreaming you'll find that gold of Admiral Kolchak's.") Ritter revealed that in November 1972 the Agency had assigned "a warm body, full time" to retrace my steps through the files of the National Archives, to find out what I'd found.

"Also," Ritter said, "you were pretty specific about what you'd found, in your letters to Mrs. Eisen."

I stared at him.

He said, "We didn't get it from her."

"Then you opened my mail."

"Inside this room I'll admit that. Outside I'd have to deny it."

"How?"

"A man on your house in Lambertville. Raided your mailbox every morning. Look, we had to."

My house in Lambertville is on a dirt road that serves half a dozen farms. It was my habit to go to the post office only to buy stamps; I mailed everything from my own mailbox, where the rural-route carrier picked it up.

I'd written about some of my discoveries to other friends as well, and to my agent and editor; I presume MacIver's "warm bodies" prowled those as well.

I said, "Then you took this gold thing seriously."

"Five hundred tons of raw bullion. How many dollars on the open market? Five billion? Maybe it sounds far-fetched to you, Harry, but we couldn't afford not to take it seriously. Especially with you bedding down with an Israeli agent."

I felt a hot suffusion of angry blood in my face and I was tempted to tip the table right over against his ballooning belly.

He must have begun to see cracks in my composure long before that but he hadn't let on; now he said, keeping most of the sarcasm out of his voice, "You begin to get the picture. We can keep tabs on you. We can read everything you read in the free-world collections. We can even follow you right into the Sebastopol archives. But we can't see the same stuff they're letting you see. There's just no way for us to get to that stuff, not with anybody who'd know what to look for."

He stabbed a long cigarette at me as though it were a pistol. "But you know what to look for, Harry."

I didn't tell him I had destroyed the documents which could put "Paid" to the whole thing; I didn't tell him much of anything. He was doing the talking. I was too stunned to do much more than absorb his revelations.

He said, "That's about the size of it. You believe I'm who I say I am?"

"I do now."

"Then why don't you work for us?"

"I'm not that hungry."

"I find that hard to believe, Harry. We know your financial picture. You had to stretch things to come over here at all. You're going to have to sweat like a coolie when you get home, just to pay your back bills. Now, you can't touch that treasure and you know it. What are you going to do, carry five hundred tons of gold bricks in a false compartment in the bottom of your suitcase?"

"You don't really think I came over here to steal five hundred tons of gold?"

"No. But I think you came over here to find it. Now about working for us—there'd be a fat finder's fee. A real fat one," he said obliviously. "We'll get you a Panama bankbook—Panama banks ask even fewer questions than Swiss ones."

"You'd be buying a pig in a poke. I haven't got any gold."

"You can't afford to stick to that line, Harry. It's inoperative. The Organs* knows you talked to Bukov.

* "The Organs" is professional argot for the Soviet KGB. —Ed.

They're just biding their time, waiting until they get you pinned like a butterfly on a board where you can't even keep flapping your wings. They mean to cancel your ticket, Harry, and here you're trying to climb a greasy pole all by yourself. You're just hastening toward doom, you know, and I can assure you you'll catch something you weren't chasing."

"You mix a mean metaphor."

"Sooner or later you'll tell me where it is."

"Sooner or later you'll tell me why I should know where it is."

"Because if you hadn't found it," he purred, "you wouldn't deny you were looking for it." And he beamed at me in triumph.

I am not expert at thinking on my feet. I do my best work at a typewriter when there's time to reflect and to compose and to polish. This is one reason why I never would have made the grade as one of Fitzpatrick's favored round-table wits.

What I said, with literal truth, was, "I haven't found an ounce of gold, let alone five hundred tons of it. But let's assume I did find it. What then?"

"Then you tell us where it is and you're off the hook."

"What do you mean off the hook?"

"Harry, at this moment in time you're the only human being alive who's had access to the records on both sides of the Iron Curtain."

"So?"

"You're the only human being alive who's in a position to find that gold."

"Suppose I couldn't find any records over here to support my investigation."

"You'd have said so a long time ago."

"What do you think I've been trying to tell you all afternoon?"

"It's a little late to ask me to believe it now," he said, "but let's get back to the original question—what happens now. . . ."

He was right. If I'd opened the conversation by admitting I'd been looking for the gold, but adding that I

242

hadn't been able to find it, he might have believed me. As it was I'd put my foot in it with too many palpably false denials.

"We're onto you," he went on, "and I rely on your own knowledge of the intelligence apparatus to tell you what happens next—or if not next, at least soon. How long does a secret stay secret, Harry?"

"Don't play cat and mouse. I'm tired of it."

"We have people in The Organs. Not higher-ups, but people. Double agents. That goes without saying, right?"

"Go on."

"From extrinsic evidence"—he pronounced the phrase with a precise Germanic inflection that made it sinister—"we can assume they have people on our side. Once in a while, you know—a piece of fact gets into their hands that they couldn't have obtained if they didn't have double agents in our gang. I mean, a couple of hundred thousand employees, Harry, I don't care what kind of security clearance you run, you're bound to turn up a few rotten apples, aren't you?"

"In other words if the CIA thinks I've found five hundred tons of gold, then it won't be long before the KGB will think it too."

"That's the size of it."

"You're saying if I don't play ball with you, you'll turn it over to the KGB."

"That's unfair."

"The hell it is. If the gold exists at all it's in Russia. There's no way for you to touch it anyway. If you knew where it was, you could only use that knowledge as a bargaining point. Trade it to the Russians for whatever you happen to need from them this month. So that's the threat, isn't it?—either I find the gold for you or you trade *me* to the KGB and let them get it out of me. That way your hands stay clean."

He brooded at me; I said, "It doesn't matter to you. You'll trade them the gold or Harris Bristow, whichever's easier. That's what we're really talking about, isn't it?"

"You've got a low opinion of your country."

"The CIA isn't my country."

"Is Nicole Eisen your country, then?"

243

"If I had that information do you really think I'd give it to the Israelis?"

"It wouldn't be the first time a citizen betrayed his country for the love of a woman."

"It's not America's gold," I said. "Whose country would I be betraying?"

He was shaking his head in feigned exasperation. "You've got a hole in your argument. What makes you think the only thing we could do with that gold would be to turn it over to the Russians?"

"I suppose you'd just send in a fleet of trucks under the cultural exchange program and cart it off to Washington?"

Ritter said, "Well there might be ways. Didn't the Germans almost succeed? If you forge proper-looking papers you can get away with all sorts of things. If we did it right and did it fast enough they wouldn't even get curious until it was gone. Then all they'd find out is they should have got curious a lot earlier."

"Is that what MacIver thinks? You people are incredible."

"Just tell us where to look, Harry."

"Even if I knew, why should I tell you?"

An insidious assumption hid behind Ritter's coaxing. It was the same flummery used by the witch-hunters who insist that if you don't cooperate with the House Un-American Activities Committee, you are perforce a traitor. Such illogical reasoning ridicules the democratic concepts of liberty: it denies any right to privacy—the essential freedom without which there are no others.

I was no longer prepared to accept my-country-right-or-wrong simplifications. To study and write the history of CIA blunders and atrocities is to put an end to innocence. . . .

In January 1942, a month after Pearl Harbor, the American freighter *Absaroka* was torpedoed just outside the harbor of Los Angeles. A month later a submarine shelled an oil refinery near Santa Barbara. In one of my books* I reported that the two attacks, as

_____

* The reference is to Harris Bristow's *The War in the Aleutians* (New York, 1969). Clearly Bristow felt compelled to

well as several other incidents along the West Coast of the United States and Alaska, were perpetrated by Japanese I-class submarines. As a result of these shellings the California Hearst press began a banner campaign against the "yellow peril" on our beaches and not only was the reality of war brought home to American soil, but thousands of Japanese-born American citizens were rounded up and herded into concentration camps in the Southwestern desert for the duration of the war. Subsequently I learned that the Japanese navy had no fleet submarines in American waters at that time; and recently declassified Pentagon files prove that the attacks on the West Coast were ordered by Washington and that the high-explosive shells were fired by American ships. At the time, Harold Ickes privately justified these cynical acts as being necessary to morale. (They have a Watergate ring to them: there is nothing new under the sun.)

Then of course there was the incident of the American shipload of mustard gas which blew up in an Italian harbor and killed a thousand people. And the OSS-Mafia alliance in Sicily. And then the overthrow of the Guatemalan regime by the CIA in behalf of an American corporation. And the Bay of Pigs, the Powers U-2 fiasco, the Dominican Republic, the abortive CIA attempts to bomb Duvalier's palace in Port-au-Prince, the Agency's overthrow of Prince Sihanouk in Cambodia, the Air America bomb-runs over four nations in Indochina, the CIA-IT&T attempt to overthrow the elected government of Chile, all the chilling secret maneuvers designed to make Latin America safe for the United Fruit Company, the Bolivian and Venezuelan fiefdoms of American oil companies, the massive CIA support of feudal despots in Arab oil basins while the right hand of the Administration gave lip service and jet planes to Israel. . . .

I knew that Haim had been right after all. In South Russia squatted a motionless pile of metal which in its way could be as destructive as fissionable uranium: on

explain why he refused to cooperate with the CIA's Karl Ritter; therefore he added this passage to the manuscript. It appears to be one of the last segments he wrote.—Ed.

the open market, several billions' worth of gold bullion —enough to topple governments, enough to decide wars.

In November 1968 the Western monetary system depended for survival on the strength of the West German Deutschmark which was backed by a gold treasury no greater than Kolchak's.

Put it in CIA hands and who could be sure what use it might be put to? Or allow the CIA to put it in Soviet hands: same question. Or perhaps more so: Russia has always been, and still is, a nation in which all policy is controlled by a small band of totalitarian leaders who are restrained by no law, answerable to no one, and educated abysmally in the realities of the outside world.

My question put Ritter at a loss: evidently it hadn't occurred to him that I wouldn't recognize my obligation to prove my patriotism by handing over the gold to the CIA. He tried to conceal his indignant outrage; he tried to act contemptuous: "I'm empowered to offer you a sizable finder's fee."

He said it too loudly.

I must have been in a state of emotional idiocy—an aberration from which I would soon recover in terror —but just then I was acting far more professional than he was and that was another thing he couldn't take. He'd been prepared to deal with a garden-variety scholar and we both knew what that was: probably gutless and naïve, certainly eager to bow before the whim of Authority. He found himself dealing with a self-assured lunatic who wouldn't knuckle under. It had to be disconcerting; had I been in his position I'd have burst a blood vessel.

"Listen to me, Harry. I'm making you a hell of an offer. Millions. If you turn it down there's nothing I can do for you. You understand what I'm saying?"

"I understand threats. You're very handy with the rack and thumbscrew, aren't you? You use bribes and blackmail and threats, and then you tell me I ought to do it because it's the right thing to do. Good God, Ritter, you can't preach patriotism and morality at gunpoint."

He became very sibilant and German again. "I would

246

suggest you consider the fact that you are in no position to dictate to me concerning such things as morality and patriotism." I waited for him to call me *Herr Bristow* but of course he didn't, that was only the black comedy inside me.

"I don't know where your gold is. You may believe that or not—I don't much care. But you can't trade me to the Russians if I haven't got anything they could use. You can't turn me over to them if I'm worthless—all that would do is destroy your credibility with them."

Of course I was bluffing but he couldn't know that.

I stood up. "They're going to wonder where I've been. It's almost five."

"You went for a walk to soak up the atmosphere of the city. After all you're writing a book about it. It isn't your fault they lost sight of you."

He hadn't risen from his chair; the back of it was against part of the door and he had my way blocked. I said, "If the way you handled my getaway this afternoon is an example, you'd never get near that gold—even if I found it for you."

"It must have been the first day they used the car and the third man on you. I've had them under the eye for forty-eight hours. The plan would have worked perfectly well if they'd followed yesterday's pattern."

That began to bring me back to earth. I put both palms flat on the table and leaned toward him. "Ritter, what made them change the operation *today?*"

"You must have done something to alert them."

"I did nothing. It had to be you. They spotted you, you clumsy bastard."

"Don't be an idiot. I've been in this game long enough to know when I've been blown."

"Sure you have."

"You're rattled after all." He was pleased. "It wasn't me, you know. Probably they observed your little ballet of indecision around the telephone kiosk last night. That might have been enough to make them increase their suspicions."

"And just who set up that charade?"

"I did. I was mistaken. I'm to blame, I accept the responsibility, and I apologize."

247

"I don't want your apology," I said. "I want your absence."

"I'm afraid that wouldn't conform with my orders."

"And you're a good German, aren't you."

He tried to ignore that. He said, "You opened a door a moment ago. You said, 'Even if I found the gold for you.'"

"Figure of speech. An army of searchers might find it, if they had twenty years to search for it."

He levered himself to his feet, grunting, one hand against the table for support. "I don't believe you."

"Ritter, I'm not responsible for your speculations."

"Think about this, Harry. In their country the incumbents get to count the votes. In their country ten million of you may get purged out of existence any minute, at the whim of some fool with red stars on his epaulets. You can't publish what you want to. You can't even think if your thoughts don't conform to the party line. You can't go where you want to go, you can't even have a conversation without worrying about whether somebody's going to inform on you. You can't agitate for reform, you can't defend yourself against phony charges. The freedoms you take for granted——"

It was all true and I was tired of it because it was beside the point. I cut him off: "The freedoms which you're asking me to give up so that I can safeguard my freedom. Aren't you bombing the hamlet in order to save it?"

"Nuts. I'm asking you for only one thing—a piece of information which isn't rightfully yours anyway."

"What makes it rightfully *yours?*"

"We're both Americans."

I laughed in his face.

He said patiently, "Harry, it does make a difference. I won't torture you or throw you in prison. I draw the line at that."

"There are heroin pushers who draw the line at rape. I'm not impressed by people who draw lines."

"You ought to be. If you were having this conversation with Zandor there'd be blood coming out from under your fingernails."

He led the way out of the dreary apartment and we went down the stairs. I said, "And now?"

248

"Now I take you back to your neighborhood and you walk back to your hotel."

"Just like that?"

"What did you expect me to do? Hold you prisoner until you capitulated?"

The temperature had dropped sharply under a pewter sky. We crowded ourselves into the little car and he got the engine going and waited for it to warm up. Our breath fogged the windshield. Ritter said, "Do you mind if I make a suggestion? It's for your own good. I think you ought to inform Comrade Zandor of the location of the treasure before you leave the Soviet Union. If the information was already out of your hands, your government wouldn't have reason to harass you."

I said, "What have you got to gain by advising me to spill everything to Zandor?"

"Just cutting my losses, Harry."

"No." I reasoned it out. "You'd have to inform Zandor in advance that I was going to volunteer the gold to the Soviets—as a favor to you. That way you'd get the credit, you'd still get reciprocity from Moscow. One good turn."

"The KGB might get that impression," he murmured. He switched on the defroster fan but it didn't work very well. "Actually the way you'd better do it is write the information in a letter and mail it just before you fly out of the country. That way you'd avoid the tedium of questioning. No point taking unnecessary risks, is there."

"I wonder how many people you've blackmailed into doing the right thing."

"Then you'll do it?"

"I told you before. I have no idea where the gold is. The whole thing's a fantasy. Yours and MacIver's."

He put the Moskvitch in gear.

15

He reached across my lap to unlatch the door.

I walked back to the hotel and fifty people seemed to spring out of the cement. None of them accosted me but I felt eyes on me.

In the lobby I found Yakov Sanarski and Timoshenko playing chess.

Sanarski greeted me without smiling and I explained my disappearance when he requested the explanation. I was not sure if he believed my story but he didn't challenge it. He would report to Zandor and it would be up to Zandor to decide.

I did not want to be alone in my room. I pulled out a chair and watched the chess match. Timoshenko was an aggressive but careless player and Sanarski mated him easily. Then the KGB man went off, to a phone or a car, and Timoshenko asked what might be my pleasure for the evening; we had no interviews scheduled for the day. I was in a stage of delayed shock, the tremor starting in; I left the decision to him and resorted to my room to clean up and change. I remembered to put the old hat in one of my coat pockets and when we got to the restaurant I managed to leave it on the hat rack there.

I kept up with Timoshenko drink for drink until it occurred to me that if I had ever needed a clear head in my life it was now. The music was frenetic and earsplitting in the place and Timoshenko was enjoying it hugely, stamping both feet to keep time. There was no need to make conversation with him. The vodka in my blood made it easier to shut out the frenzy of the place; it helped to clear the nervous fears from my head and allow me to concentrate.

In the beginning the gold had been an orphan abandoned on my doorstep and I'd had the freedom to accept or ignore the responsibility of it. But I hadn't covered my tracks well enough and the CIA was onto it, and Ritter was right—it wouldn't be very long before Moscow got onto it too.

It meant I was under pressure of time. How long did I have? I didn't know. I might have a month; I might not have forty-eight hours. The KGB was behind Mac-Iver and Ritter, but how far behind?

At intervals I was disgusted by my own smug and pious moralizing. The rest of the time I thought myself a man of principle. But the road to hell. . . . I had to consider the temptations of chucking it in. I could still turn back; I still had options. I could give it to Ritter or give it to Zandor and I would be off the hook.

But it was too late for that because I'd taken the baby in off the doorstep and now it was my child.

I did not sleep. The rest of my life hung on the decisions of that night: I vacillated but I couldn't procrastinate because soon they would take the decision out of my hands. I had to decide *now*.

But there were so many sides to it and I was cursed with vision that was too clear. I began to see myself contemptuously as a fool who insisted on equivocating about the state of the exact temperature while the building was burning down over my head. I entertained so many *but-on-the-other-hands* that by the dark small for the sake of having it done with: remember the hours I was ready to take any decision at all merely Kurosawa scene where the Samurai warrior reaches a crossroads, tosses his staff spinning in the air and walks off in the direction indicated by the fall of the staff? The toss of a coin had distinct appeal.

In the end I had to capitulate. As long as two conditions were met I could evade the final decision until I'd had time to study it. The two conditions: I had to keep the secret and I had to keep my freedom.

The one depended on the other, so that I really had to meet only one condition: I had to remain free. Free of coercion, free to move about, free to think, and free to put into execution whatever decision I arrived at concerning the gold.

Reduced to that simplicity, my course of action became clear. I had to get out of the Soviet Union.

The afternoon with Ritter was a Friday and I had the weekend ahead. There were three Saturday interviews on the schedule: a morning interview in the city and two meetings later in the day in Crimean towns.

The plan I worked out was simple enough to work. I got somehow through the morning interview with Timoshenko sitting bored off to one side; when we left the retired navy commander's house I suggested lunch and it was no great challenge to make sure Timoshenko consumed several beers before we left.

It was a bitter cold day but the snowfall which had been forecast was holding off. We drove past the suburban rubble which hadn't yet been rebuilt; we went north and occasionally from the hilltops the sea would come in view, overhung by heavy clouds.

According to plan Timoshenko pulled over to the side of the empty road and got out of the car to relieve himself. There were farm fields on either side of the narrow strip of road. When Timoshenko turned his back to the car to unbutton his fly I climbed across into the driver's seat and drove away, leaving him staring at me in the rearview mirror with confounded amazement, shouting and waving.

It was a rotten trick to have played on him but I hadn't been able to work out a better plan.

I used the Intourist map to guide myself in a wide semicircle to the east and south around Sebastopol. It took me nearly three hours to reach the village of Bykovskiy; I kept to the back roads, most of them unpaved. Several times my passage drew the stares of farm people who rarely saw automobiles.

I entered Bykovskiy along a side street and parked the car in a quiet corner that wasn't visible from the square, the station or the main road. When I got out of the car I felt bulky; my pockets were crowded with everything I dared take with me. The main bulk of the notes was in the briefcase in my right hand but I hadn't trusted the gold notes off my person in weeks and these were in my pockets.

I had the new hat pulled down over my head, the coat collar turned up; I put the car keys in my pocket —I might need it again—and went along behind the row of buildings that fronted on the village square.

I had to show myself on the square briefly but no one seemed to take an interest in me; it was cold and those who were abroad were intent on their own business. I entered the building and went directly up the stairs, turned along to the door and knocked.

There was no reply. I tried the knob; it was not locked; I let myself into Bukov's patrician quarters.

He wasn't home. I laid my coat across my briefcase and sat down to wait for him.

Twice I heard trains come to the depot, stand hissing awhile and proceed. It grew dark; I didn't dare light a lamp. After a while I found myself standing beside the front windows watching the occasional vehicles that moved in and out of the square. Timoshenko would have thumbed a ride by now and Zandor would know I had broken my tether; the search would be on, and they'd think of this place soon. If Bukov was away for the night I couldn't wait him out but if I left this place there was no other place to go. . . .

I kept vigil, watching for Bukov, watching for anything that looked like an official car.

In the beginning the plan had seemed simple and foolproof but now I saw all the things that could go wrong with it. In the cold room sweat stood out on my face. Now and then something snapped in the dark and I had to take a very careful grip on myself and not relax it for an instant: if I fell apart it would be all the way. A tic set in at the corner of my mouth, my sphincter contracted, I had to keep wiping my palms dry against my hip pockets; and time seemed to distort itself in an Einsteinian way, terror affecting the speed of time in an inverse geometric ratio. It became a kind of marijuana atavism: all the senses drawn to their taut limits, a fine alertness to every subliminal sound and movement—and the conviction that I could parse each passing second.

As a trick of preserving sanity I kept reassuring myself it was the right gamble, the best odds: I kept telling myself I hadn't made a mistake by not simply applying for an early exit visa and a new Aeroflot ticket.

I reviewed the reason a dozen times. The answer did not always come up the same. The trouble was I had to deal with probabilities rather than facts. Logic is no better than its premises and mine were uncertain. I'd had to make assumptions and act as if they were facts; but suppose they weren't true?

I'd accused Karl Ritter of basing assumptions on assumptions; now I was doing that. They went like this:

Assumption: Ritter was not lying when he said the KGB suspected I was involved with the illegal Jewish emigration underground. There were too many ways he could have been right. First there was the fact that Andrei Bizenkev* had opposed my visit from the beginning; naturally Bizenkev would have ordered a full-scale investigation of my background and affiliations and therefore the KGB could have been aware of my close association with Nikki, my extended sojourn in Israel and possibly my connection with Haim Tippelskirch, a known spy. Second there was my prior visit to Bukov. Putting that together with my known contacts with Israeli agents, the KGB had to be "onto me" even if it was for thoroughly erroneous reasons.

Assumption: Zandor had put a third man and a car on me immediately after he'd extended my visa. That had the earmarks of giving a man enough rope to strangle himself: they'd given me a longer tether but they'd strengthened it.

Assumption: When I had dropped out of sight for nearly four hours yesterday Zandor would not accept it as an innocent lapse. He might assume I had slipped my leash in order to make contact with Zionist agents. Whatever he took it to mean, it could only increase his suspicions.

Up to that point I was on firm ground. Those assumptions were sensible and conformed with the facts. The next assumptions were far more shaky since they were based on nothing more substantial than guesswork, in-

---

* Director of the KGB in Moscow. These paragraphs (beginning with "I'd accused Karl Ritter . . .") again are Bristow's inserts, afterthoughts to explain his actions.—Ed.

254

tuition, knowledge of espionage history and practice, and odds. All these assumptions could be challenged easily; but standing together they made an imposing whole.

Assumption: Zandor knew who Karl Ritter was.

I had no idea what cover Ritter was using; he hadn't told me. From his look and his background I thought possibly he was in the Crimea in the guise of an East German minor official. From what Ritter himself had told me I knew he hadn't operated behind the Iron Curtain very often, and not at all in the past six or seven years; nevertheless he was a ranking CIA agent and I could not safely take it for granted that he was unknown to the KGB. Obviously he thought his cover was secure or he wouldn't have been in Sebastopol, but I didn't put much faith in Ritter's feelings; he had illustrated his ineptitude more than once in his clumsy attempts to make contact with me—and if an amateur like me could see the weaknesses in his game-plan then it was a fairly good bet the professionals of the KGB had tumbled to him by now, or would do so in short order. That being the case I couldn't count on the fact that the KGB wouldn't trace Ritter back to that safehouse apartment in the suburbs, and find witnesses who'd seen us enter or leave the place together, or who'd seen me in Ritter's car. There had been people who'd seen us in the tavern near the archives, and Zandor's own agents had seen Ritter trying to fit his key into the door lock of the Moskvitch beside me; perhaps up to now those agents didn't realize what they had seen but if Zandor showed them a photograph of Ritter and asked them if they had seen this man with me, they'd remember it: they were trained to.

It was a shaky assumption—that Ritter's cover was blown—and there was a good chance I was wrong. But Ritter was a fool and I couldn't count on his competence. If I acted on the assumption that he had *not* been blown, and it then turned out I was wrong. . . . It was safer to assume the worst.

Assumption: Ritter was right when he said the KGB would soon discover my interest in Kolchak's gold. It is not true that the CIA and the KGB are riddled with each other's agents but it is true that there are leaks, which each organization makes constant attempts to caulk, never with complete success. In my opinion there are advantages to these rifts in secrecy because they provide safety valves and often they prevent either side from springing unpleasant surprises on the other. But they also lead to a situation in which wherever Mary goes, her Lamb cannot be far behind her. The speed with which Zandor got word of my search for the gold would depend largely on how much importance the CIA attached to it; the fact that MacIver—a functionary of high rank—had been assigned to the case made it clear enough that The Firm took my search seriously indeed. (Evidently they had been taking it more seriously than I had, at first.)

I therefore had to accept the probability that the KGB would learn of my interest in the treasure. The moment that happened, I was locked in; there was no chance they would let me out of the country before they squeezed me like a lemon. And the operative factor here was my total inability to put a time limit on it. If I could be sure it would be two weeks before the KGB caught up with this business then I still might be safe in applying for an early exit. But I couldn't be sure of anything of the kind. For all I knew the word was already on the wire from Moscow to Zandor. There simply was no way to guess; and therefore I had to assume the worst and act accordingly.

Finally, although this was perhaps of lesser importance, there was the fact that I couldn't go to Zandor with a request for early exit without further arousing his suspicions. Two days after my visa is extended? He wouldn't buy it unless I had an ironclad reason, and there was no excuse I could think of that would convince him. At the very least, such a request from me would only persuade Zandor to redouble his efforts to find out what chicanery I'd been up to. If he did that he might find the real answer—and once again the result would be my incarceration and interrogation.

I went endlessly up one side and down the other and the answer usually came out the same. There were too many ways for them to nail me, too many risks in staying put and waiting for the bureaucratic machinery to convey me legally out of the country. If nothing else, I wasn't sure I could stand the constant terror of never knowing when they would reach out for me.

The alternative was to escape illegally—a breakout —and while the risks here were as great as the other, at least I had the spiritual advantage of having made the decision myself, having taken the initiative and having been able to weigh known risks.

Also there was a bleak satisfaction in using Nikki's organization to get me out of this mess: in some emotional way which I deliberately avoided analyzing, I blamed Nikki for having got me into this.

There was snow. I moved back and forth like a caged animal taking exercise—aimlessly, looking at my watch, waiting; I drank a beer from Bukov's cupboard, moved an ashtray on the desk, stood at the window growing sick with tenseness.

Then I saw him coming across the square in the snowfall and I tensed like a runner in the starting chocks because he wasn't alone.

An older man walked with him, in step; they were deep in conversation. An argument, from the gestures. A local friend—or one of Zandor's people? It was a feeling like ice across the back of my neck.

I watched them come toward the downstairs door to the building; suddenly I broke out of my paralysis. I couldn't take the chance. I backed away from the window, picked up my things and strode across the room: in the darkness I barked a shin on something—made a small racket and whispered sibilant invective through my teeth, and wheeled out into the corridor. I pulled the door silently shut and crept quickly to the ascending stairs and went up to the next landing, the top floor. I heard the main door open, heard their voices and shrank back against the wall opposite the balustrade. They wouldn't see me unless they came partway up the top flight of stairs and if they did that I had no escape anyway unless I chose to burst into someone's flat.

They came up the stairs two flights below and I tried to listen to their conversation—to identify the man with Bukov—but I only understood about one word in five because they were speaking in a Crimean Tatar dialect but then I heard Bukov pronounce my name. I couldn't

257

make out the context and in my present condition I was not prepared to make fine distinctions among tones of voice. I froze; I felt a insistent hammering behind my eyes.

I heard Bukov open the door to the flat and they went inside. I did not hear the door close; I stayed where I was with the pulse shaking me like a pneumatic drill. And then I heard Bukov, very distinct, in Russian: "He has been here."

There followed the other man's short grunt and then footsteps into the hall.

Bukov said, "Harry?"

I didn't stir.

He started up the stairs.

I turned, ready to break into the nearest door but his voice arrested me:

"He's a friend, Harry. It's all right."

Only half trusting him I went down slowly and he retreated to the landing to wait for me; he was talking to the other man who was inside the flat: "Draw the drapes before you switch on the light." Then turning to me: "Where did you leave the car?"

I had to swallow and clear my throat. "Behind that row of shops." I pointed through the wall to my right.

I heard drape cords slide; a light came on, splashing a yellow fan along the floor through the open door. Then Bukov's companion appeared there, blocking the light. He was a big greying old man who had been red-haired; he had coarse features, there was a heavy roll to his lips. Bukov was arctic and aloof. "You'd better give the keys to Pudovkin."

Without objection I produced them and handed them to the old man. They disappeared into his fist; Bukov ushered me toward the door and Pudovkin went down the stairs quickly, still in his overcoat.

Bukov shut the door behind us. "Pudovkin spent ten years of his life hunting down Germans in Johannesburg and Buenos Aires. He's one of the best we've got."

"You expected to find me here."

"Don't be so awed. Your escape stirred things up. The first thing they did was alert all border stations, and I have people at several of those. I've had the word for several hours."

"They moved fast. I left my driver in the middle of a dirt track in the wheat farms. I didn't see any telephone lines."

"He picked up a ride with a lorry. It only took him twenty minutes to reach a telephone. Was it that same fellow who came here with you?"

"Yes. Timoshenko."

"Pity. He's an inoffensive sort. They'll have his hide for this."

"It wasn't his fault. They ought to see that."

"I'm sure they will—but they've got to have someone to vent their rage at. Would you like another glass of beer?" He asked it drily; he'd picked up the glass I'd left near the window.

"You offered me your help," I said. "That's why I came."

"I hope you've got a first-class reason. You're putting us all in jeopardy."

"I had very little choice. I'm sorry."

"I'm sure you've considered what you're doing—the consequences. You'll be an outsider forever, you know. You're consigning yourself to exile—a blind wandering to an unknown destination. You're not the type, Harry."

It took me a moment to catch up with him: then my head rocked back. "How do you know that, Bukov?"

"You found the gold, didn't you."

It was Karl Ritter all over again. I sank into a chair, raging in hopelessness.

"You'll be an outsider everywhere until you share the secret with someone."

Someone entered the building and Bukov listened to the climbing footsteps because he knew the tread of each of his neighbors and acquaintances. He relaxed before I did. The steps went on up the second flight. Bukov said, "Comrade Litvinov," in a tone Napoleon might have used in pronouncing Wellington's name.

I said, "I didn't find anything. But they think I did. I won't be tortured for something I haven't got." It was the story I'd decided on—to use in case I had to. It had become necessary far earlier than I'd anticipated.

Bukov was remarkably uninterested. "In any case it's still my job to assist you. I gather you wish to get out to the West."

"It's a terrible imposition."

"Don't apologize. I offered our help. We've rather expected you to accept the offer."

I didn't want to think about that at the moment; it had too many implications I wasn't prepared to face.

Pudovkin came up the stairs and Bukov, recognizing his step, met him at the door. "Where did you put it?"

"The railway motor-pool garage. I smeared the number plates. It's just another official car—they'll be a while noticing it." Pudovkin shrugged out of his coat. "There's a man standing by the station trying not to look like an agent. I think I know his face—I've seen him in Yalta."

"Naturally. They know their man might come here for help."

I half rose from my seat; Bukov waved me back. "It's taken into account. But we'd better not stay here any longer—he may take it into his head to come up and inspect the premises. Come along—bring your things."

Thinking he had a rear exit in mind I began to put on my coat but he said, "You won't need to wear it." I gathered up the hat and my case, hung the coat over my arm and followed them out of the flat.

We went up the stairs, Bukov several steps ahead of me; he reached the landing and surveyed the hall before he motioned us to follow.

A key from his pocket: he unlocked a door and let us into a dark room, stuffy with disuse. Pudovkin silently closed the door and Bukov hit a light switch—a ceiling fixture flickered and brightened.

The room was windowless and not more than twelve feet square. It contained an old desk, four straight wooden chairs and a row of shelves on which stood dusty bound volumes of postal and railway regulations. "My office," Bukov explained. "I rarely use it. I'm afraid you'll have to sleep on the floor. There's no heat but we're in the center of the building, it won't freeze here. You'll have to rough it."

"For how long?"

"Until we can make the arrangements."

"I feel like such a bloody fool," I whispered.

"No need to keep your voice down. Litvinov is stone deaf and there's no one else on this floor. The railway department uses most of it for storage of records. But one word of caution—don't let Litvinov see you, he's the sort of old woman who loves to inform."

"Is it risky living in the same building with someone like that?"

"Quite the contrary. He's a good cover."

There was a door in the wall behind the desk. He went to it and opened it. There was a cupboard the size of an ordinary clothes closet with shelves across it at two-foot intervals. The upper shelves held rows of green metal file-card boxes; the lower two shelves were empty. Bukov knelt and pulled the lowest shelf out. It slid away easily in his hand. He pointed at the back of the cupboard.

"If you hear someone approaching, slide through. The rear wall is a door on spring hinges. You'll find yourself under the eaves. It will be very cold but they won't find it if you remember to slip the shelf back into place behind you."

I nodded. It wasn't the first time he'd used this room as an underground railway station. He'd designed the cupboard for that purpose.

Pudovkin had a heavy voice like lumps of coal rumbling down a metal chute. "You'd better keep your things in that cupboard while you're here—in case you have to hide them quickly."

I put the briefcase, hat and coat on the floor of the cupboard and Bukov closed the door on them. "You'll have to wait until morning to use the lavatory. Can you hold out?"

I said I thought I could. "After Litvinov goes to work you'll be free to move around during the day."

"Tomorrow's Sunday. Will he go to work?"

"Yes."

Pudovkin said something in dialect; Bukov gave it a

moment's thought. "It might be wise." He turned to me: "How committed are you?"

"To what?"

"This nineteenth-century romantic gesture of yours. How great is your rage to survive? Greater than your rage to escape?"

"I don't follow."

"If they cornered you—would you prefer death or capture?"

I said, "What are you offering me? A cyanide capsule?"

"A pistol. Do you want one?"

"I'm not much good with them."

"It doesn't take much marksmanship to put the muzzle in your mouth and pull the trigger."

I pictured myself sitting in this room for an indeterminate time, counting the walls; I foresaw the increasing waves of depression and anxiety; finally I said, "I think I'd rather take my chances without it."

"Very well. I'll bring food and drink." Momentarily his austere features softened. "Don't break yourself on the wheel of fear. There are places where the borders are quite porous—with any luck we'll get you out. We've done it with hundreds, we know the drill. Does it matter to you where you break through?"

"I'd assumed you had a limited number of routes— I thought I'd better leave it to you."

"All right." He glanced briefly around the room. "I'm sorry you'll have to be incarcerated here. I know you'd rather be a moving target. It can't be helped, for the moment. Arrangements must be made—it takes time. Now. What about your linguistic aptitudes?"

I gave him a list of the languages I spoke; he needed that because it limited the identities he could manufacture for me.

I brought out my wallet. "I'm not offering a bribe. But I've got some money, in dollars. Can you change them into rubles without too much trouble?"

"Of course—and for a good deal more than you could." He counted the bills. "Would you like some sort of receipt?"

"Don't be ridiculous. I meant the money for your use. There'll be expenses getting me out."

262

He divided the bills into two stacks and proffered one of them. "You'll want money after you're out. You'd better keep this."

I took it back without arguing. His eyes went beyond me to Pudovkin but it was to me that he was speaking: "When you go, Pudovkin will accompany you partway. You'll want to get to know each other a bit."

Instead of leaving the room then, Bukov settled into one of the chairs and crossed his thin silk ankles. Specks of dust twirled in the light. "Please try not to concern yourself with too many details. Under great stress you will naturally find yourself worrying about trivialities but I must ask that you leave everything to us. Our organization has several people in it who know where many bodies are buried—we'll be able to obtain *bumagi* for you but you must leave the choice of identity to us. If you balk at anything at the wrong moment it could set us all right back to the wrong side of square one—you understand?"

"I put myself in your hands," I answered. "I'm very grateful."

Pudovkin jerked his head up as if he had just had an inspiration. He spoke a name.

Bukov shook his head. "No, I won't use him. He has a fourteen-year-old daughter, he's vulnerable. All they need to do is hint that she can't be protected every minute—she could be raped by bandits. To prevent that, all he'd have to do is expose us. I won't use him for anything more than innocuous errands."

"Then who?"

"Don't worry. You won't have to carry it all the way."

"I wasn't thinking of myself, Vassily."

"I know you weren't." Bukov smiled a bit. "One of these days you may begin to agree that my sense of security is as thorough as your own. I'm not a brash youth any longer, Mikhail."

I was left out of this; watching the two of them I saw they were very old friends, it was more than a political alliance. Neither of them seemed the sort of man who communicated emotion easily but there was a bond of great warmth between them. Possibly Bukov had begun as the older man's protégé.

Bukov got up to leave us then. On his way to the door he paused. "Perhaps I should mention this—not to terrify you but to make you see things realistically. You can be sure that more than normal pressures have been applied against Sergei Zandor. To lose you would be to risk his position in the KGB chain of command. He has orders to bring you in alive of course —but he may be tempted to exceed those orders. You've given him a very bad time. You understand?"

"Yes." The warning was: do exactly as you're told and don't mess things up for us because we could all get killed as a result.

Bukov nodded. Then the two of them left me.

In a little while he returned with a tray of borscht and Beluga caviar—an absurd combination but nourishing enough. He made a list of my clothing sizes.

On his way out he said, "Try to sleep."

"Yes."

"I rather approve of you."

"Do you?"

"How did Nietzsche put it? 'Audacity is essential to greatness.' You have the essence of greatness, Harry."

He went. I prowled the chamber for a while; pulled down a dry tome and read half a page and put it back; finally I rolled my shoes into my jacket to improvise a pillow, switched off the overhead light and lay trembling in the dark with my overcoat for a blanket.

16

ON TUESDAY* Pudovkin brought a parcel into my cell and unwrapped it with a certain *voila* flair—it contained the clothes I was to wear.

"We've laid on the truck for tonight," he told me. "See if everything fits."

"We're going out tonight?"

"We're starting tonight." He had a dry deflating manner sometimes. I had learned that Pudovkin's character was summed up largely in his Scandinavian thoroughness and impartiality: a cautious man with the patience for details. It had probably kept him alive. He seemed stolid but he had a good quick imagination; you needed that too if you were to anticipate the opposition's movements. Pudovkin's other *persona*—the visible portion of his iceberg existence—was that of a retired foundry official. Because he was retired from daily employment he enjoyed a certain freedom of time and movement which made him invaluable to Bukov; I gathered Pudovkin rarely had time to relax but that was the way he wanted it. He reminded me of the retired police lieutenant who can't stand being out of harness and sets up his own security-detective agency—"just to keep a hand in," but ends up working twice as hard as ever before.

For Pudovkin there was the added spice of illegality and the added strength of having a cause. Like Bukov he was not himself a Jew but to Pudovkin that was beside the point.

He had brought food also and I cut into the fresh loaf; the rich heavy smell invaded my nostrils and I ate while I unfolded the garments.

* March 27, 1973. Bristow had arrived at Bukov's on the night of Saturday, March 24.—Ed.

Several plans had been studied and rejected. At first there was the idea of smuggling me down to the Black Sea resort of Sochi and shipping me out as a deckhand on a tramp, but I had no nautical experience and we had to scotch that one. In any case there were too many checkpoints and bottlenecks; and the constant reinforcement of the Mediterranean Red fleet through the Dardanelles meant the waters would be alive with navy vessels practicing their boarding techniques on every passing freighter.

Our scheme was limited by the variety of OVIR blanks and forged passports available in the Bukov cell's collections. It was also limited by my physical and linguistic markings: for instance I could not pass as a Cuban or Chilean, nor as a Russian for that matter—not only because of my height and coloring but also because the Soviets are far more meticulous in examining their own citizens who try to leave the country than they are about foreigners.

Bukov was adamant about one thing. I was not to cross through any international checkpoints in the Crimea. In the first place the Crimea was where they were looking for me; in the second place if I were caught too close to home it could bring down Bukov and his entire cell and he was quite right in refusing to take that risk. But it made our planning far more difficult because it meant I had to get to the mainland across the narrow isthmus at Armyansk, or cross Karkinitskiy Bay by small boat, or ride the train across the causeway from Dzhankoy to Genichesk—or, and this was what we settled on, due east across the length of the Crimean peninsula to the Kerch Straits and across to Taman by small boat. Once in the Georgian heights of the Caucasus it would be possible to motor southeast along the mountain roads above the Black Sea to the rugged Turkish border country; slip across into Turkey and escape through Asia Minor.

It meant a journey of nearly two hundred miles across the Crimea by road, followed by a ten-mile boat crossing and then the run down through the Caucasus which would be about five hundred miles of mountain roads to the Turkish border. There were OVIR barriers at several points to check travelers' internal passports; we would be able to avoid some but not all of them and I had to have papers. Therefore I became Georges Lapautre, a Communist labor-union functionary from the St. Chamond small-arms factory near Lyon. I was visiting the Soviet Union to learn about the fine points of worker organization in small-arms plants, of which there are a great many in the southern part of the USSR.

The suit was a cheap ready-to-wear one of Marseille manufacture; the hat was marked *Italie*—indicating it had been imported into France—and I asked Pudovkin where the devil they had found it but he only shrugged it off as if the wardrobe department had ten warehouses of clothes for every specification. That was not the case and I knew it and after a while it occurred to me that perhaps they had chosen the French identity because that was the one they had clothes for.

The shirt and underwear were French products but the shoes were Russian. "I'm afraid your feet were the wrong size," Pudovkin said. "If you are asked, you mistakenly stepped in fresh tar and it ruined your old shoes, and you bought these here. You won't be asked."

I had a look at the French passport—the photo was mine, Bukov had taken it. The rest looked completely authentic except for a few details. According to the passport Georges Lapautre was forty-two, where I was thirty-four; Lapautre was some two inches shorter than I, but weighed nearly the same; Lapautre had blond hair.

I considered the evidence before me. Finally I said to Pudovkin, "Georges Lapautre is real, isn't he."

"Why?"

"The only false thing about this passport is my photograph in it. And the suit is a little too big in the waist and a little too short in the trousers. And it's an ensemble—he bought the tan shirt and the brown tie to go with the brown suit. He's dead, isn't he?"

Pudovkin smiled. "You don't think we would murder a man merely to provide you with a suit of clothes and a French passport?"

"I'm not too happy about wearing a dead man's clothes."

"They're not contaminated. He wasn't diseased. Anyhow we've cleaned them."

"How did he die?"

"He fancied himself a swimmer. He died in the Black Sea last summer—of drowning. It happens every few weeks in the resorts. I'm afraid we make it our business to make off with the property of such people. It's a bit ghoulish—but no one's harmed."

"Don't the Soviet authorities know he's dead? Hasn't this passport been canceled or revoked or something?"

"This one died in Sochi," Pudovkin said. "The commissar of the police in Sochi is one of us. The deceased was buried under some other name. Of course his OVIR visa expired months ago, and his travel permits from point to point. Yours are forgeries."

"Where are they?"

"We'll have them ready by the time we leave tonight."

"I'll be passing right through Sochi. What if I meet someone who knew him?"

"He only went there for a week's holiday at one of the *pensions*. I believe he died his third day there. Not many people would have known him—or are likely to remember."

An hour later Pudovkin returned to collect my own clothes.

"What do you want with them?"

"One of our people will leave them in the lavatory of the railway station in Sebastopol."

I felt I was in competent hands.

The hair bleach was crude stuff but it made me blond enough. I had been using it since the day before Bukov had taken my picture for the Lapautre passport. "You'll have to shave as often as you can. The darker stubble would give you away."

"I'll remember," I said. He'd packed a razor in my kit. I was to wear heavy-rimmed glasses at all times: they contained plain glass lenses. Pudovkin instructed me to slouch my shoulders and walk with short strides; it would make me appear shorter. And to let my mouth hang open all the time. "It gives you a vacant expression of innocence—and it changes the shape of your face."

He wrapped the razor and my notes in brown paper and tied it with string. "You'll have to leave the briefcase. Do you have everything?"

I had transferred things out of my old pockets. I said, "Everything I need, yes."

"We might have made it a suitcase but a man with a package draws less attention."

"You've thought of everything."

"Let's hope we have."

Pudovkin wore black stovepipe boots up to his knees. Cord trousers and a heavy short coat and a soft motoring cap. He looked like a truck driver; he was supposed to. "Let's go down," he said, and we left the chamber. I found I was moving with a prowler's predatory silence, my heart pounding, watching the deaf informer's door; we slipped past it and went down the stairs into Bukov's flat.

The lights were out and it was dim, the windows defined by dreary winter twilight. Pudovkin shut the door and produced an automatic pistol—one of those flat dull nine-millimeter guns stamped out in a Czech works. He popped the clip into his hand and worked the action with the air of a man who knew his weapons. When he put it away again I saw that he carried it in his belt, without a holster. That was according to the rules: it's not impossible to ditch a gun but you can't hide a holster when it's attached to your belt.

Bukov was an amorphous shape in the poor light. "It's time."

I said, "I don't know how to——"

"Never mind that. You'd better come over here."

He led us to the front window and pointed across the way. I had not been out of the cell in three full days and the heavy lie of snow on the square took me by surprise. It was not snowing at the moment. The shadow was where he had to be, on the right-hand side of the square just inside the window of a café, at a table near the door with money by his wine so he could leave instantly without arousing the waiter's ire.

Bukov said, "He wouldn't recognize you as you are now, but he knows everyone who's entered this building. He didn't see you enter it. He can't see you leave it."

"Is there a back door?"

"No. There are windows."

"All right," I said.

"Pudovkin will have to leave alone by the front door —the man saw him come in. You understand?"

I turned to Pudovkin. "Where do I meet you then?"

"Remember where you parked Timoshenko's car?"

"Of course."

"That street. Fifty meters farther along it. You'll find an old grey lorry standing there. Get in behind the wheel and wait for me."

Bukov said, "If you're challenged you're just waiting to pick up a friend. The cargo is wool coats, the destination is Kerch. If anyone wants to see the shipping documents they're in the glove box with the keys to the truck."

"That gun you offered me when I first came. Maybe I'll take it now."

"No," Bukov said. "We can't have shooting here."

The three of us went down to the ground floor. I shifted my grip on the paper-wrapped parcel; my palms were slick. Pudovkin stopped at the foot of the stairs and watched Bukov guide me to the rear of the corridor; the sill was low but the building was constructed on a slope so that it was a good ten-foot drop to the bank of snow beneath.

Bukov frowned. "Wait here a moment." Then he left me; I saw him circle past Pudovkin and then his heavy shoes thudded the stairs going up. I bit my lip; what if someone should enter just now, or pop out of a doorway along the hall?

Bukov came trotting down with a high pair of rubber overshoes. "You don't want to ruin your shoes, do you."

"Are these your own?"

"I'll get another pair. Put them on."

"Thank you."

I balanced myself against the window jamb and tugged them on over my shoes. Bukov slid the window open. "All right?"

"I've been privileged to know you," I told him. "Isn't there anything I can——"

"Just don't lead them back to me if you can help it. They know what I am but they think if they leave me free to operate I'll lead them to others. I won't, but they don't know that."

"They won't leave you alone forever."

"I know that. But in the meantime we're getting a great many people out. I'll have no regrets when they come—I just don't want to hurry them."

"I understand."

I thought he smiled; in the dimness it was hard to be sure. He offered his hand. His grip was firm and quick. "Give Nikki my love."

"I——"

But he urged me out the window. I hung by my fingers and let myself drop. The snow cushioned the fall but I lost my balance nonetheless and had to brush myself off; when I looked up the window was sliding shut.

The truck swayed when Pudovkin put his weight on the running board and swung himself into the cab. The door chunked shut and he reached across my knee into the glove box for the keys. "I'm sorry it took so long. I had to throw him off the scent, that fellow in the café."

"Did he try to follow you?"

"No, but he knows who I am. I couldn't let him see me come this way. I had to come the long way round."

The dusk had turned to night. He ground the starter and the engine caught; I heard the ratchet of the hand-brake.

The truck had been driven to pieces. We rattled around the village and went bucking and pitching down the country lanes, snarling through the gears. He said, "We're a little heavy. It really is a cargo of coats. I'm afraid it won't be a fast journey—we'll be lucky to make the coast by dawn. I've got to stay on the back roads."

"Then we'll be crossing the straits by daylight."

"No, it's better to lay over and cross by night. There's a house we'll use."

It began to snow again. Through the batting windshield wipers I saw the forests slide past. We snored and growled up the low hills, the truck shuddering with the strain. There are thick woods inland on the peninsula; at the crests the wind has made the trees hunchbacked. The wind of our approach stirred the trees and pillows of snow fell with plopping crunches, now and then on our hood; several times we had to stop and get out to clean it off. Pudovkin said, "I have tire chains but I hope we won't need them." His voice was thin against the racket.

There was nothing for me to do. He had to concentrate on his driving; the roads were narrow and steeply treacherous. I tried to doze. Into my inert grey weariness fell the occasional pebble of apprehension and retrospection: I was a fool, there was no way out of this, I'd been unforgivably callous in involving Bukov and his people in this because it meant I was no longer risking merely my own life but theirs as well.

We ran on into the snowy night along the narrow hill tracks. We crossed above a lake, faintly shining in the night—the ice on it gleamed where the wind had cleared the snow from it. The truck was not insulated and had a poor heater and its window seals were all gone; the wind bit my ears.

During the past three and a half days I had numbed myself with introspective rationalizing and fantasizing. At times I'd had to fight an overwhelming yearning for Nikki, whom I had tried to put out of my thoughts until then; I could see her clearly, her movements and poses and faces—I remembered the way her hair had looked against the pillow; I could hear the cadences of her voice. She was personal and specific in my vision. The nerve ends of my hands and lips remembered with exquisite agony the sweet warm textures of her body. Now Bukov's parting comment brought it all back again and I drowsed fitfully in the lurching truck with Nikki on my mind, wanting her and blaming her, loving and hating, and now wondering: would I seek her out, once I was out of the Soviets' reach? Would we meet—and how would it go? Did I have anything to say to her beyond accusations?

My anguish was the torture of questions without answers. The faces moved across the screen of my eyelids: MacIver. Haim Tippelskirch. Zandor. Timoshenko.

272

Karl Ritter. Vassily Bukov. And Nikki. The faces I had never seen—Kolchak, Maxim Tippelskirch, Heinz Krausser—and the dream of gold.

The snow stopped falling before dawn but it had dropped heavily on the hills and we had to use the chains; it took a long time to wrestle them onto the tires and we were still west of our destination when the light came.

The dawn sky had a bruised coloration and it promised to be another oppressive grey day; the trees were limp and heavy, the crumpled folds of the hills were blue with dull shadows. The truck's window crank, designed by some sinister idiot, hammered the side bone of my knee.

A small stone farmhouse on the left: Pudovkin swung the wheel and we angled across into its yard. I stiffened.

"We'll lay over here."

He drove it right into the barn and a man came down from the house, a big man with his face glowing in the chill wind. We dismounted from the truck and Pudovkin smiled but the farmer did not. Pudovkin had begun to utter a greeting but now suddenly his voice stopped, as if someone had shot it.

I said, "What is it?"

The farmer only shook his head and closed the barn behind us and took us to the house. He was reaching for a wide rake when I went inside with Pudovkin.

The woman was stout and I heard the cry of an infant somewhere in the house. Pudovkin and I stood in the kitchen stamping and blowing through our cheeks. Pudovkin pulled off his gloves and blew on his hands. "Hello, Raiza."

"You're still too thin," she said.

"Boris has a long face."

"He heard something. I don't know."

Through a steamy window I saw the farmer raking the yard, obliterating the tracks our truck had made.

Pudovkin said, "We haven't eaten all night." He took me through the house and showed me the bathroom. I heard his footsteps recede; the farmer banged into the house and they talked in the kitchen. I could hear the voices, not the words.

I let the water run until the rust cleared out of it. The trickle spiraled down an icicle that hung from the spout. When I turned it off the waterpipes banged. I found a towel and scrubbed my face warm.

I found Pudovkin at the kitchen table, his jaws ruminating bread. "We've had a little trouble. The man I was to turn you over to—he was to take you across to the mainland and drive you down the Caucasus. He's been arrested."

I sat down very slowly as if the chair might break under me. "Then they know."

"No. The man's a Jew, they arrest them for sport. It doesn't mean this has anything to do with you."

The farmer stood at the stove, brooding, his nose tucked inside the upturned collar of his coat. "Perhaps you'd better change your plans, Mikhail."

Pudovkin said, "The car is ready on the other side?"

"Yes."

"Then we'll have to go as planned. Our papers go with that car, not with any other."

"Suppose Leonid gives them the plate number?"

"Will he?"

The farmer turned. "He won't volunteer it. But if they put pressure on him. . . . You can't hold that against a man. Anyone would break."

Pudovkin said. "But they'd have to know what to ask him."

"They may know that he arranged for a boat. I don't altogether trust the man he got the boat from. The man's a gentile."

"So am I," Pudovkin said.

"I trust you, Mikhail, I do not trust this man who has the boats."

"Then why use him?"

"In the winter our usual man takes his fishing boats to the yards at Yalta for refinish."

They excluded me. I was apart but not aloof. I couldn't interfere; in any case the only thing I could do to change things would be to walk out. I considered it: at least it would take the burden off these people. It was none of their blame.

Pudovkin said, "Suppose we tried to get a different boat tonight. From someone else."

274

"We might try. I doubt it would throw them off."

"It might keep us out of a trap. If the man's informed they'll be watching to see who comes to use his boat."

The farmer left the house almost immediately and without any further talk; it was settled.

Pudovkin took me into a bedroom. "You'd better try to sleep. We'll be leaving at night fall. I'm afraid you'll be burdened with my company for another few days. I'll have to take Leonid's place with you. It will be all right."

I said, "You were planning to turn back here—do it. Just tell me where to find the car on the other side. I can drive myself."

"You wouldn't get fifty kilometers. Put it out of your mind. And don't be gallant—don't run away to save the rest of us. If you're caught we're all caught. You need my help and I need yours. You see?"

He was right; I had to give that one up.

I slept through a snowfall and at dusk we had to shovel the barn doors clear before we could bring out the truck. A surly wintry evening; we ate quickly and washed down the food with strong local wine. I shook hands gravely with the farmer's wife and then the three of us set off in the truck. I rode in the middle and tried to keep my knees out of the way of the shift lever. Boris, the farmer, was driving: he would drop us and take the truck back to his farm to await Pudovkin's return.

I said, "What about the load of coats?"

"I delivered them this afternoon," Pudovkin said.

"You've had no sleep at all then."

"There's plenty of time to rest when we're dead." He seemed pleased with himself.

We reached the coast several miles south of the city of Kerch. A man stood on the stony beach holding the bow rope of a dinghy. The farmer introduced him and Pudovkin shook his hand; I saw money change hands and then Boris was bear-hugging all around and walking back up to the road. I felt lucky to be still wearing Vassily Bukov's knee-high rubbers; we shoved the dinghy into the surf and clambered into it and the boatman picked up the oars. Above us the truck began to move up the road and the weather swallowed its lights quickly. We pitched out through a crashing froth that soaked us with freezing spray but the boatman was superb with his oars—we never shipped a wave.

The fishing boat lay at anchor without lights; we climbed over the low transom and the boatman fixed the dinghy to its davits and went forward to start his engine. Pudovkin and I went below. The crew cabin was tiny; there were four hammocks and it stank of fish. The engine came alive with a guttural growl and we heard the anchor cable scrape; a few moments later the cabin floor tipped underfoot as the stern went down with the screw's bite.

"It's twenty-four kilometers by the route we'll take," Pudovkin said. "We'll be about four hours."

"You'd better sleep, then."

"I intend to."

I left him cocooned in a hammock; I went up to the wheelhouse. I've never been a good sailor and I knew I couldn't take the confinement of that stinking closed crew cabin; on deck in the air I might make it without losing my stomach.

We ran without lights and the boatman kept her throttle at something like half speed because he didn't want excessive noise and he didn't want to throw too much of a visible wake. We were quartering across the current that flowed through the strait from the Sea of Azov into the Black Sea; it was a rough ride and I clung to handholds.

For two hours we rode the bucking deck together and never learned each other's names; I think we both felt it was better not to know. We exchanged meaningless small talk, neither of us giving anything away. He told me a little about fishing and a little about the waters hereabouts.

In mid-channel we hit a crosschop of conflicting currents that was too much for me and I had to hang over the stern rail at one side of the dinghy and cat up my dinner. The rest of the ride was agony.

Once he throttled down and I looked up in alarm; after a while I caught sight of lights moving past our port side in the distance. The boatman identified it as the night ferry to Kerch. We pitched derelict in the sea's short chop until distance absorbed the ferry.

After midnight we went ashore in the dinghy and Pudovkin paid the boatman the second half of his money. Again the handshake—in contrast to the ritual bearhug of friends—and then Pudovkin and I climbed the steep rocks in a frigid wind. I could hear the chatter of my own teeth.

"I'm afraid we have a walk ahead of us. I didn't trust him enough to have him put us down too close to the car. Are you up to it?"

"Is there a choice?"

He laughed and went striding toward the coast road, setting an example I'd have been embarrassed not to follow since I was half his age. On the boat I'd been convinced I could survive anything so long as it was on dry land but now I found the bite of that arctic wind and the lash of driven snowflakes to be equally painful. I've never thought myself a hypochondriac but that night I had visions of trenchfoot and frostbite and pneumonia.

I don't know how long we walked. I had passed the point of exhaustion and had made a fine discovery: there was no such thing as second wind. But it was still dark when Pudovkin led us down a snow-covered side road that appeared to be nothing more than dirt-track ruts with tufts of weed sprouting from the center hump. We had a limited amount of light, reflecting down from the underbellies of the clouds; it had stopped snowing at some indeterminate time in the night and Pudovkin said the lights were those of a town beyond the ridge inland of us. Whenever the wind let up we could hear the crash of surf below to our left. There was a gothic wildness to the night: snow-mists swirled around us and the wind had a dismal voice.

I bumped into Pudovkin's shoulder before I realized he had stopped; belatedly I saw that the snow-covered mount in front of us was a car—a Volkswagen by its shape. We batted the two-inch white cake off the windshield and rear window and then Pudovkin opened the door to release the catch of the front hood.

He stood looking into the orifice. "You'd think there'd be a shovel. Well we'll have to make do." He handed me the jack handle and went at it with his gloved hands. It was impossible not to admire his self-control. We shoveled snow clear of the exhaust pipe and scraped purchase-tracks for the wheels and then we let the wind blow us back to the car. At least there were chains on the rear tires.

Pudovkin found the key under the seat and we had some trouble before the car would start. From the diminutive size of its oval rear window I assumed it was very old—early nineteen-fifties at best—but after a great deal of weak grinding it caught and Pudovkin revved it mightily. He made sure it was warmed enough not to stall before he tried putting it in gear.

The night's coat of granulated-sugar snow treacherously concealed an underlayer of glazed ice; we skidded loosely all the way out to the main road but the chains kept us moving. When we reached the road I said, "Shouldn't we sweep over our tracks?"

"The wind will do it for us."

We jingled slowly south and in a little while daylight began to flood across the ridges, scattering the shadows.

I tried to navigate but the map of Georgia and the Caucasus was not of the finest scale and did not show all the back roads; often we reached intersections not indicated by the map and had to guess. We were trying to avoid the seaside resorts but at the same time we could not afford to take the main inland routes because they were summer roads high up in the Caucasus and if you got stuck in snowdrifts up there they would be carrying your body out in the spring. The late snowfall had been a bad break all around; it restricted our choices of routes, it slowed our travel and it left tracks.

On the stretches between resort towns we tried to get down onto the main roads because they were plowed clear; along here we removed the chains and Pudovkin drove too fast for the roads, the tires leaving black smears on the oil-smudged curves, the beetle running along with a complaining rubbery whine.

On the northern approaches to Tuapse we stopped at a government pump to fill the tank and put oil in the crankcase and Pudovkin asked the attendant about the weather to the south. There had been less snow down there, the man said; he heard Sochi was completely snow-free.

We had come only a bit better than a hundred miles since dawn and it was already afternoon. We'd last eaten at midnight—food we'd carried ashore from the boat—and we were famished; we bought bread and tinned herring and beer and I purchased a cheap composition suitcase because my paper-wrapped bundle had been ruined by last night's weather. When we returned to the car Pudovkin said, "If we run straight through we'll reach the border by tomorrow night. What do you say?"

"I'll take another turn at the wheel, then."

He'd been reluctant to let me drive before; he was still reluctant—he loved to drive, particularly on bad roads. "I should have been a taxi driver or a racer," he said. "Isn't it childish?"

We ate on the move and then he spread the map across his knees and directed me to the left up a steep pitted asphalt street; we had to get around Tuapse because at this time of year the police would notice any strange car in the deserted streets.

The detour took us well back into the hills before we could turn south again and the snow was deep along the shoulders; we had to put the chains on again.

Darkness fell and there was no moon—the clouds were still with us. We crawled because it was hard to see: the line of definition was poor between what was road and what was not road. The country there is jagged and humpy and the hills are studded with low scattered trees. Down below along the coast it is semi-tropical with palmlike vegetation and white-roofed seaside houses but these hills, footing against the mysterious Caucasian Mountains, are as primitive as something in Nepal. It is twenty miles between habitations and there are no towns; the roads at best are farm-truck tracks and our game antique beetle had as much trouble as it could handle.

Go a little higher in the mountains to the left and you would find yourself in valleys inhabited by tribes of prehistoric persuasion among whom the people grow to fantastic ages and technology is unknown. The hold of

Soviet civilization is precarious on these fringes and nonexistent in the interior: like the role of colonial forts on an African frontier in the eighteen fifties. Bukov had elected this route for that very reason but it didn't make the journey any less alarming: only the fragile heartbeat of our antique Volkswagen kept us alive. Chilled beyond the poor heater's capacity we labored through the hills and I think privately both of us prayed, each in his own way, although I doubt Pudovkin was any more religious than I.

In predawn murk we reached a signpost and found we were several miles southeast of where we thought we were. We had to backtrack to an intersection and turn west toward the coast to avoid being forced up into impassable mountains.

We were beyond Sochi now, somewhere above Sukhumi, and there was no alternative but to drop straight along to the main coast highway and follow it south.

"There is a checkpoint below Sukhumi. Too many arms smugglers trying to sell in Turkey. They have deliberately made this bottleneck—everyone who goes south must go through there. The alternate back roads have been closed off by explosives."

"Then we'll just have to find out if our papers are good enough."

"I'm not concerned about the papers. But we've left possible leaks behind. Leonid, the one the police arrested. The man who has boats—the one Boris doesn't trust. Or that one who took us across the straits. The checkpoint may have been warned."

"Why don't you turn back, then. I'll go on through alone. If they take me at least you'll have time to get out of the country yourself."

He said, "I don't wish to leave. It's my home."

Ten minutes later he broke the silence again. "I had better tell you the plan in any case. You will have to do the last of it yourself since I am not going to cross the border with you."

"I thought I was just going to walk across through the fence."

"That used to be possible. But on account of the arms smuggling they have mined the border."

I took my eyes off the road to glance at him. Bukov hadn't said anything about mines. I suppose he'd seen no point in alarming me more.

"Batumi is the Soviet border city. A village, really. Just before you reach it there is a fork, and we will take the Armenian route to the left, toward Leninakan. At one point about five kilometers south of Batumi the road skirts very close to the fence. There are guard towers—machine guns and searchlights. About one kilometer past that point, I will let you out of the car and you will be on your own. You will be about five hundred meters from the fence. There are a good many trees but not close together enough to be a forest. There is a metal culvert in the road which marks our spot. If you walk toward the fence from that culvert you will find a narrow foot track marked by four trees which grow along an exactly straight line. You have to be looking at them from the culvert to see the line because from any other angle they are just four trees among many. If you walk that straight line, keeping just to the left of the trees—within arm's length—you will not step on a mine. It is a route we have used several times. We had to dig up two mines and de-activate them, and replace them.

"Now the time to cross is at dusk, because the searchlights are least effective and daylight is poor. If you move slowly and watch the lights you'll get through. The nearest searchlight tower is about two hundred meters from the point where you will cross. The fence itself is nothing, a few strands of barbed wire like a cattle fence, but the top strand is electrified with a very high charge. You must go through between the bottom strand and the middle one. Then you are in Turk territory but you must cross about twenty meters of open ground into the trees beyond. You are safe once inside those trees. You understand all this? I'll give it to you again before we get there, but I want you to be making yourself ready in your mind. The trick of survival is to move slowly. Slowly. Every muscle screams to run but you must remember to be slow. All right?"

"Yes. I'll remember." My pulse thudded just thinking about it.

"There is a goat track up the river valley on the Turk side. Follow that path to the left about three kilometers and you will come to a road. A dirt road, but it has a fair amount of traffic from the coast. From there you should be able to get a lift into the town of Trabzon, only be sure it is not a Turk army vehicle you try to flag down. You have the Turkish visa among your new papers?"

"Yes."

"Then you should have no trouble, but avoid the army while you are close to the border. Sometimes they tend to throw refugees back across to ingratiate themselves with the Soviets."

"I understand."

"In Trabzon there is a *taverna* run by a man called Pinar. Remember the name."

"Pinar," I said, and repeated it.

"He has worked with us for many years. He will see to your needs and provide transport for you at least as far as Ankara or Istanbul. After that you must make your own decisions."

At half-past ten that morning, freshly shaved, we approached the checkpoint and were halted in the stalled queue of traffic awaiting clearance. There were half a dozen lorries and two or three cars ahead of us.

Pudovkin was rehearsing what he would say. He wasn't speaking aloud but I could hear the tongue drumming against his palate.

He had the wheel now; he thought it would look better. He had an Intourist identification card and was going to try to pass as my guide and overseer.

It was raining now, the downpour slanting into the glossy pavement and melting what snow was left; the Soviet guards stood at the zebra-checked crossbar steaming in their heavy wool uniforms. I was rigid with fear: what if they didn't like the look of the contents of my suitcase? The water-soaked note cards, the admixture of Russian and English script. . . .

We had scraped off our stubble in melted snow with hand soap for lather and my cheeks stung with shaving rash; my feet were frozen even though I had dried them repeatedly; we had eaten the last of the bread and herring and my stomach growled incessantly; I knew they would take one look at the pair of us and yank us out of the car. . . .

From the side of his mouth Pudovkin said, "Mainly they will look for weapons. The south of Russia has many arms factories—as you are supposed to know, Monsieur Lapautre—and this means that guns are easier to obtain here than in any other part of the Soviet Union. Workers try to sell them on the black market in Turkey."

"What about that pistol of yours?"

"I left it where we shaved," he said.

It only chilled me more: now we were weaponless. Then I realized how foolish the thought was. There were six guards at the checkpoint and each was armed with an automatic rifle slung across his back. One light pistol wouldn't have made a tinker's difference if it had come to shooting.

Then it was our turn. In their grey uniforms buttoned to the choke collars they leaned down at either door and asked us to step out of the car. The guard on my side was young, red-faced; I noticed the frayed cuffs of his uniform.

"*Bumagi*," he said—papers.

Several of them were glancing at us. I tried to keep my hand steady when I reached for my—Lapautre's passport and documents. I heard Pudovkin saying we had nothing to declare, we were on our way to the small-arms assembly plant at Tblisi. I tried to find belief or disbelief in the soldiers' faces but they only looked professionally stern. Beside me a lorry driver climbed into the back of the truck; evidently the driver was a frequent passerby and the sentry nodded and smiled in response to something he said, but then that sentry's eyes came around toward me and his face turned cold. I endeavored to look impatiently bored with the bureaucratic idiocy of it but I was convinced the contrivance was transparent. . . .

The youth didn't give the passport back to me. He held it in his hand and walked around to the front of the Volkswagen. I thought he was staring suspiciously at the front number plate and my throat turned hollow but then his partner reached in past Pudovkin to pull the release and the youth opened the trunk.

He removed my suitcase and set it down on the wet pavement and pried up corners of the trunk lining. He took out the spare tire and shook it, weighed it in his hands and put it back. Then he opened my suitcase. I tried not to stare. He pawed through the single shirt and pair of wet socks I had replaced last night; he riffled two stacks of notes and then put one finger on the floor of the suitcase while he reached around under it with his other palm—testing the thickness for a false bottom. Finally he closed the suitcase and politely laid it back in the trunk. I breathed.

His partner was down on one knee on the far side of the car looking at the understructure, his rump showing past the front-sloping fender.

Pudovkin, yawning, patted his lips and turned to glance at the clock mounted on the side of the checkpoint shack. The truck beside me growled through, the gate came down again and another truck pulled in.

They gave us back our papers. Pudovkin had to sign something and then we got back in the car and drove through the raised gate. Sixty yards beyond it was a café-bar and Pudovkin pulled in there. "Hungry?"

"My God, I never want to go through that again."

He grinned at me. "You get used to it."

"I'd rather not have to."

The place was obviously a popular pit-stop for those who had had to wait on the queue at the checkpoint; we had to wait again but finally we bought wine and cheese and bread and went outside to get in the car.

A sentry at the checkpoint shack was talking into a telephone, looking up and down the road. I began to freeze up. Pudovkin went around the front of the car to the driver's door. I saw the sentry's arm come up, pointing our way; he took the phone away from his ear and shouted something.

Pudovkin said under his breath, "You didn't hear him. Get in—quickly."

I jackknifed into the car and Pudovkin had it rolling before I had the door shut. We swung out into the road

284

and his foot was on the floor. We were nearly through the bend before the first bullet starred the glass of the rear window.

We had a jump on them because they had to get to a car to chase us but the road ahead ran right into the town of Poti; they would telephone ahead to put us in a vise. We had to get off the coast highway and I unfolded the map with badly shaking fingers while Pudovkin wheeled recklessly past slow lorries on blind bends.

"Not the first left," I said. "It loops back. Take the second turning."

He pulled out to overtake a bus and there was a van coming toward us but Pudovkin kept the throttle down and the van nosed down under pressure of panic brakes; we squeezed through ahead of the bus and when I threw a wide-eyed glance at him Pudovkin's lips were peeled back in a fierce glowing rictus. I clung to the strap with one hand and tried to keep the map in focus with the other. "It ought to be soon."

The old car had a top of not more than a hundred kph—about sixty miles per hour—and Pudovkin was getting every ounce of that out of it. Once we hit the hills we wouldn't be able to make even that much speed.

I kept glancing to the rear but the starred window made it hard to see. Pudovkin had an outside mirror on the door and he was using that. He said, "No sign yet. Those trucks are holding them on the bends back there."

We had a straightaway now and at the end of it was the fork; I pointed wildly and he said, "I see it," but he hadn't even lifted his foot off the gas. He wanted every inch of space he could get between us. At the last instant he jabbed the brake and we swung up the hill violently, weaving on the springs, the tires wailing.

On the map there were choices and I said, "We could take the first right—it runs parallel to the highway. But they might look for us there."

"What else is there?"

"If we stay on this road it bends south. There's a turning about—" I measured the map's scale indicator with my eye and transferred it to the road's black line—"about fifteen kilometers. It goes back in the mountains but the map shows a river there—it may be a valley. It cuts back across toward Batumi beyond that."

"Batumi's what we want."

"Have we got any chance at all in this thing?"

"We have with me driving." He grinned like a lunatic.

The tires snickered on the curves and Pudovkin drove at breakneck pace, using his horn on the blind turnings. We were climbing steadily into the foothills of the Caucasus range above the widening coastal plain of Poti and looking off to the right I could see the patchwork of farms on the flatlands—and a spume of spray on a wet road arrowing up toward a bisecting point somewhere ahead of us. It was quite distant; I looked away and looked again and it was still there, the wake of a fast-moving car. I pointed and shouted. Pudovkin nodded.

It couldn't be accident. That one was coming up to block our route; he'd been signaled from the checkpoint. They'd have other cars on the other roads by now as well.

Pudovkin said, "We'll just have to beat him to the crossing."

The transmission was whining in third. Pudovkin cut across the insides of all the bends without taking his foot off and we were on two wheels more than once. The rain had quit but the surfaces were still wet and there were patches of mist; we burst through them like a projectile.

At intervals the road lipped out and we had glimpses of the flood plain from ever higher points. The car was out of sight in the lower hills somewhere. I tried to judge his course by the map but there were too many roads out of Poti. Most of them crossed the one we were on.

I saw the first intersection coming at us and I jammed feet and hands forward to brace but Pudovkin roared straight through it and the lorry to our left hit his brakes with an indignant yelp of horn. We rammed through a stand of timber and crossed a ridge and I saw the pursuit off to our right angling toward us from below. It was a big Skoda, black with four doors, a heavy Czech saloon climbing the steep rises with the arrogant power of its two-and-a-half liter engine.

The roads met at the head of an open meadow and we were watching each other as we squealed toward it. I saw one of the windows roll down and a weapon appear—something squat and ugly, a submachine gun.

We were into the crossing ahead of them and then the road made a painful turn: Pudovkin down-shifted for it and we almost rolled over but the wheels came down on the high crown and he accelerated us out of it.

We had a third of a kilometer's straight run and Pudovkin disengaged his seat adjustment lever and pushed the seat all the way back; slid down until he was sitting on the back of his neck, eyes just high enough to see over the wipers through the crescent of the steering wheel. "You'd better get down."

I followed his example and my knuckles went white gripping the hand strap. He had his driving: I had nothing but hopeless panic.

The big saloon closed rapidly on the straightaways but we had quicker brakes and better turning balance and Pudovkin regained the lead every time we hit bends. He had the engine full-out and I was waiting for a piston to burst through the engine block. In the end it wasn't the Volkswagen which kept us out of their range —it was Pudovkin's skill. A better driver at the wheel of the Skoda would have made better miles out of the big car's horsepower. As it was, we'd hit the intersection nearly a quarter of a kilometer ahead of them and they'd lost a little ground making the turn but since then we'd lost a little bit of our lead with every hill.

It was their climbing power that made the difference and Pudovkin saw that. He spun the wheel at the first right-hand intersection and that put us into a down-slope of ruptured third-class mountain road. Rocks and stunted trees whipped by my door handle at shoulder height and one uncertainty would smash us on the narrow bends but here the horsepower was equalized and we had gravity on our side.

But instinct made me grope for the map and when I

had it before me I yelled at him desperately: it was a dead-end road.

"How far?"

I had squirmed around to peer out the back; through the splintered glass I had glimpses of the black snout of the Skoda. Not far back—not far at all: on a straight run they'd have been shooting, at this range. I could almost read the number plate.

"How far?"

"Not more than five kilometers."

Now we ran out onto a shelf, close under the windward side of the mountains with a sheer cliff dropping away on the open side to our left; the tires chattered and whimpered on the bends and I saw the Skoda sway out onto the cliff-cut road behind us. And suddenly I realized we were losing speed and I stared at Pudovkin in horror. "What's the matter?"

He didn't answer but I saw his foot was off the gas. He had his right hand wrapped around the handle of the handbrake between the seats but he hadn't lifted it yet. Ahead of us the road swept out of sight to the right around what appeared to be a very sharp bend —hairpin on a pivot of rock, and no guard rail at the outside. I spun my head to search for the Skoda but it took no finding: on the straight run it was barreling down on us like a black locomotive.

"Now hold tight." Pudovkin was pulling the handbrake and I knew instinctively why: for some reason he wanted to slow us down without flashing the red brake-warning lights on the back of the car. At the same time we were swinging out into the left-hand lane of the road—the outside lane above the drop—and at first I thought he was giving himself the widest possible angle from which to hit the right-hand hairpin bend ahead. But it gave the Skoda its chance and I saw dust squirt from beneath its rear tires as the driver gave it full speed and I shouted at Pudovkin because I was sure he hadn't seen the Skoda's move:

"They're going to overtake on the inside."

"I know. Hold tight."

A runoff ditch skewered the road and we crashed through it with a jar that made the beetle jump and scrabble but Pudovkin kept it away from the lip of the cliff. He was still far over to the left and the Skoda was within a hundred feet, roaring down the inside lane; the snout of the submachine gun appeared at the rear left-hand window and I shrank down in the seat.

The bend was coming at us and Pudovkin had the brake up several notches in his fist; we were slowing disastrously and the Skoda pulled almost even with us and I knew they were going to push us over the edge. I heard the submachine gun and then I felt the terrifying first touch of the Skoda's bumper nudging our rear fender and I knew we would go over.

But then Pudovkin yanked the handback all the way up and because the emergencies were rear-wheel brakes we didn't lose traction: we were stopping precipitously and I saw the Skoda shoot past and suddenly its driver must have seen the trap because I heard the wicked grab of his tires on the gravel when he jabbed his foot-brake. The submachine gun roared virtually point-blank in my ears and I hunched my head down into the corner between the seat and the door; I did not see the rest but I heard the sickening shriek of burning rubber and the long jangling crunch when the Skoda went over the hairpin edge ahead of us—the bouncing impacts as it went down the mountain, the brittle shattering of glass and the long echo of crumpling steel as she hit bottom. Then I could hear the insistent steady cry of the jammed horn and I knew it had to be final.

Only then did I realize that we were not moving: the ratcheted handbrake had pulled us to a halt within six feet of the lip.

My skin crawled when my emotions realized how close it had been. I turned to Pudovkin.

He was dead. The submachine gun.

17

THE BULLETS had taken him straight through the temple and the neck. I had never seen a man shot dead but there was no question he might still be alive; nevertheless I tried to find a pulse and of course there was none.

Breathing deeply and regularly in a feeble attempt to calm myself, I left the car and staggered to the crumpled edge of the road where the Skoda had gone over. I doubted any of them in that car could be alive; something else concerned me and I needed to check it because I didn't trust my memory—all I'd really had were frightened glimpses of the car.

The wreckage was crumpled and distorted. It had come to rest on one side wedged into the boulders more than a hundred feet below me. It was too steep a pitch to climb down without wasting a great deal of time. Nothing but boulders and loose sliding shale chips of rock, slightly reddish in the grey daylight. At the bottom a sinuous stream glittered and on the opposite slope a high tower of raw stone loomed like a gallows.

What I was looking for on the Skoda was a whip aerial; I didn't recall seeing one but I needed to know. If it had an antenna then it had a two-way radio.

There was none in sight but then I realized it would have been the first thing to break away.

The Skoda had been crushed flat; its entire front axle had come away with one wheel and tire attached —it lay in the stream below—and the squashed condition of the roof left no likelihood anyone had been left alive. The doors had sprung open but from this angle I couldn't see inside the wreckage: the rear deck-lid had come awry and lay across the upper side of the car.

On rubber knees I climbed back to the Volkswagen. We had left great ruts in the soft road. They veered close to the edge at several points. I remembered in a jumbled way that the gun had been firing before we stopped and I realized that Pudovkin had died while we were still moving: only the ratchet on the handbrake had kept us from going over after his lifeless thumb had gone slack on the button.

The bullets had shattered both windows, his and mine; the interior of the car was jagged with splintered glass and I had no recollection of that happening. When I touched my cheek my fingers came away sticky with blood that was already beginning to congeal in scabs: I had a number of small cuts and hadn't even noticed.

Of course the engine had stalled out—the car was still in third gear—and I didn't know if it would run again. I saw no bullet holes in the rear engine area. Both sides of the car were riddled and when I began to pull Pudovkin out of the car I saw that the expanding bullets had exploded away fist-sized chunks of the driver's door. He had great wounds in his upper chest and shoulders that I hadn't seen earlier. The gun had been firing down and I had been slumped below the sill of my window; the bullets had angled above me and down.

I handled the old man with gentle care—it's odd how gently we treat the dead—and now my mind was working with a curiously cool detachment: my reasoning was ruthless and clear. I couldn't take the time to bury him, I thought, but then I knew I couldn't leave him in the road for the birds to pick at. I carried him to a trough in the shale above the road and piled some rocks on him and then went up above him and kicked at the shale until a little slide started. It covered most of him and I did the rest with slabs of loose rock.

The car started and I jockeyed back and forth to get it turned around. I had a last look at his grave and dragged a hand down my face and then I began to go to pieces: the shakes hit me.

I had to sit there with my fists locked on the wheel and ride it out. The car stalled but I didn't try to re-start it. I went a little mad. Flashing visions like DTs veered kaleidoscopically across my eyes. I was like something at sea in a hurricane. The only thing to do was hold on tight.

The bottle of wine we'd put in the car a moment before they'd identified us from the checkpoint was still intact on the floor of the back seat. I drank a good part of it and gulped air in long drowning spasms. My face was stinging with thick fever-sweat that ran into my eyes and dripped off my nose.

I scrubbed my face with a cloth and it came away dark with half-scabbed patches of blood. I threw it down amid the broken glass where I had been sitting before; I cranked the starter and after a long time the engine caught, and I drove shakily up the way we'd come.

The car had no fuel gauge but I was sure there was at least a half tank. By the map it wasn't much more than a hundred kilometers to Batumi on the border. The tank hadn't been punctured and the engine was running as well as it had before—roughly, but turning. The car would do it if I could. But all South Russia was looking for me—looking for this car—and I was overcome by the futile certainty of failure while at the same time I knew there was nothing else but to keep going, pushing whatever luck I had left. Bukov had said, *I know you'd rather be a moving target.* Moving or dead; had that Skoda had a radio?

With shattering violence freshly implanted in my mind I drove the hill roads like an old woman, stopping at frequent intervals to question the map. The country became steadily more barren, vegetated by what in the States I would have taken for clumps of piñon and scrub oak and juniper. I was in the lower mountains with the Black Sea's floodplain down to my right, occasionally visible through notches in the hills; the roads were narrow dirt tracks, still muddy in low spots. If it hadn't been a Volkswagen it might not have got through some of them; I had to rock it out of the mud twice.

This was the border country between Georgia and Armenia and it was so sparsely inhabited that the map showed every farm cluster and hamlet as a town. It was possible to avoid them all by judiciously selecting secondary roads which crossed at junctions between settlements; but this took time and added miles. I passed only four or five moving vehicles in the course of the entire afternoon: they all gave me terror but they were local people, farmers and deliverers, and none challenged me. It is a country filled with fear of strangers and although they must have been curious about the battle-torn condition of my car they'd been conditioned by a brutal life to mind their own business.

It was not going to be possible to reach the border in time to go through the wire at twilight as Pudovkin had counseled. The next best time would be dawn, so I had the hours of the night to use; this being the case I knew it would be wisest to abandon the car somewhere on this side of Batumi. The car was more easily iden-tifiable than I was. They were looking for two men in an old black Volkswagen; alone and on foot I'd have a better chance in the populated area. I'd have all night to walk it.

. . . . I found a rutted driveway that seemed long disused; I left the car there, far enough into the scrub to be invisible from the road. I took the suitcase and the map and walked, eating cheese, finishing the wine, clinging to the hem of hope.

Batumi has the weary look of dusty jaundice peculiar to arid bordertowns everywhere. The buildings are shabby stucco in faded pastel colors—tile roofs and splintered grey doors, filthy windowpanes and rammed-earth streets. Grimy people sit on the porches in the last of the day's warmth, drinking beer or smoking opium. Red slogans are daubed everywhere. The only vehicles I saw were the occasional small decrepit bus and now and then a military sort of police vehicle sliding among the town's lights.

It is a river-delta town and there are clumps of mossy trees. I stayed close to these, in deep shadow under the valedictory light of dusk. I judged it the best time to move through the town: people were still abroad. The suitcase was in my hand, tacky with sweat; every hundred feet or so I changed it to the other hand. My groin itched with fear but I kept moving.

Ahead of me a bus stopped and picked up two people who'd been sitting on a bench. It pulled away and I sat down on the bench to rest my legs. After a time

I saw a fat woman approaching the bench; I got up and moved on.

It was quite warm at sea level. I walked with my open coat swaying behind me; I must have been an odd sight, a tall man in a flowing greatcoat with a suitcase, striding through this town of dark swarthy people.

Then I saw the border crossing—the barred gates and machine-gun towers, the road narrowing to a single lane between sentry windows. Even at this hour there was a little queue of trucks on either side of it. I turned sharply left and walked south through narrow streets with the lights fading behind me until I came to a crossroad that took me along to the dusty Leninakan highway. I was unused to hiking and my ankles were beginning to flop loosely; I had the rest of the night to make a few miles and so I took it unhurriedly.

Now and then the lights of a moving vehicle would warn me of its approach and I would step off the road until it had passed. Once it was a truckload of soldiers singing gustily in the night; the call of their voices rang long after they'd passed.

The river was somewhere just beyond the fence and the growth of trees was heavy except along the cuts that had been made for the road and the border. When the road went close under the guard towers I forked away from it to the left and stayed inside the trees, groping parallel to it until I was past. Searchlights on the towers made steady crisscrossing patterns like inverted air-raid lights, throwing tactile yellow beams through the warm river mists.

I made that entire journey in a state of mind that can best be described as invulnerable euphoria. I was in a kind of shock and not fully aware of the dangers. It was almost as if I were an explorer on an expedition through uncharted country: I was curious, I behaved rationally in avoiding unnecessary exposure, I moved along steadily to conserve my strength—but I had blocked from consciousness all true realization of the odds against me, the absurdity of my solitary pilgrimage, the fact that I was undoubtedly the target of one of the larger manhunts ever to have taken place in that forgotten corner of the world. Possibly it was this obli-

viousness which had saved me up till then: I had not
roused suspicion by skulking stealthily through Batumi.
I had walked through it like an interested tourist. Had
I not been in shock I'd most likely have done something furtive enough to give myself away. It is one thing
to know the spy's dictum—*Act naturally and everyone
will assume you belong there*—and another thing entirely to do it without being paralyzed or galvanized by
fear.

In the car with Pudovkin it had been different. Even
in full chase we'd had each other's courage. There is a
certain exhilaration in sharing risks; perhaps it is only
childish *macho* but it not only had bound us together,
it had prevented either of us from becoming fearful
enough to think of surrender. Alone it is something
else. You can be tempted to give yourself up merely for
the sake of having the company of your captors. Solitary flight is the most harrowing of all because a social
animal has few defenses against it. This sense of awful
aloneness nibbled at the back of my mind but my
strange oblivious catatonia defended me, prevented it
from crowding everything else out of my spirit. I'm
sure that was the only thing that kept me going.

Now, finding the culvert and knowing it was Pudovkin's because I could sight straight along the row of
four trees, I saw freedom just beyond the barbed wire
and felt certain I would make it. There was no alarm.
The searchlights fanned across the fence in swift arcs,
throwing surreal patterns that etched the thicket of
branches in strange movement. Wind soughed in the
trees and the thud of a diesel generator was a faint
distant mutter in the night.

I moved forward along the line of four to within a
hundred feet of the fence. Then I laid my coat and suitcase on the ground and sat down on the coat with my
back to the bole of a swamp-maple sort of tree.

The searchlight was a good distance away—at least
a couple of hundred yards to the right. It touched this
point of fence and moved on a few more yards, inter-
secting the beam of the next light, then sweeping back
across its arc. The light it threw was somewhat dis-
sipated and considerably weaker than at points nearer
the tower.

The towers stood above the treetops on wooden lattice structures; there were platforms halfway up and I'd seen similar towers in Germany. There would be a shoulder-wide hole in the platform and a rope ladder fixed to it. When the guard went up he drew the ladder up after him. It prevented insurgents from storming the platforms and taking over the machine guns. The tower would be manned by two sentries: one on the light and one on the gun. The range to this point in the fence was approximately two hundred yards from the tower to my right and nearly two hundred and fifty from the tower to my left. A machine gun is not precise at that range but of course if you throw enough bullets you have a good chance that one of them will hit whatever you're aiming at. These were probably Kalkashnikov guns with a high rate of fire.

The open cut between Russian trees and Turkish ones had been timbered off and bulldozed to weeds. It was about fifty yards wide, a swath with the fence running down its center. Pudovkin had suggested the main line of defense was the mine field; the fence was secondary but I had to remember that electrified top strand. The three-strand fence stood about a yard high or a little better on wooden posts set eight or ten feet apart. You had to run twenty or thirty yards, get through the lower gap in the fence, and cross another twenty-yard flat into the farther trees.

I timed the searchlight sweeps. They didn't work in unison; they didn't always cross each other because sometimes they were both moving in the same direction. It made the intervals impossible to time precisely.

Generally it seemed about thirty seconds from the time one light hit the end of its arc and the time it made a complete circuit to that point again. Since the light crossed this point in the fence twice at this end of its arc it meant there was about a twenty-five second dark interval—provided the second light was moving in a pattern directly opposite to that of the first. That coincidence seemed to take place every ten or twelve minutes.

I had several hours to make these calculations and

I made them with cool aplomb. The insensate stupidity had not worn off.

It was a warm night but I shivered through it.

I made my plan on the basis of a shallow depression in the earth about eight feet this side of the fence. When the lights crossed the little hollow they left it in shadow. It was a few feet to one side of the straight line of the four trees and that meant it might contain a land mine and so I spent at least two hours working on alternative ideas but none of them worked; it kept coming back to that hollow because I wasn't going to have time to make the whole run in one go, not when I had to stop and get through the fence midway. The strands were less than a foot apart and you couldn't simply dive through them. I was going to have to make it in two runs and the only place I could stop was in that hollow. If there was a mine in it I wouldn't have to concern myself about getting through the fence.

At an ordinary walking pace you cover about five feet a second. Sprinting over short distances you can multiply that by four. If I ran full tilt I could reach the fence in four seconds to sprint to the far trees without being picked up by the light. But Pudovkin had pointed out the fallacy in that. The first thing they'd see—light or no light—would be a running figure. You had to move slowly.

Walking slowly it would take me at least fifteen seconds to reach the fence. That was why I had to use the depression.

Behind me the sky pinked up with heavy clouds: dusk, then dawn. Fear began to pump the sweat out of me now.

I had to wait for that moment when the searchlights were almost equaled by the growing daylight: when everything merged into a common murk.

The trees made a mosaic against the clouds. I left my coat on the ground; it would only impede me on the barbed wire. I picked up the suitcase.

Sky merged with earth along the uncertain eastern horizon. I turned away from it and faced the fence. The beams were no longer visible but you could still see the yellow disc of light sliding along the ground, growing parabolically longer as it approached the end of its swing. It was no longer distinct at the verges and I knew it was time to go; never mind the synchronization of the farther light.

Up on one knee. I'd studied the line all night; I'd memorized it. The only place I might hit a mine was the hollow. Reckless: the hell with it, *go*.

The light swept past the hollow, faded, came back faintly. When it crossed the hollow again on its return sweep I walked out of the trees.

I moved low to the ground and slowly, very slowly, bent double with my breathing tight and shallow, my sphincter contracted, my palms damp, sweat running in my eyes. I kept looking both ways at the towers because if a light or a gun muzzle began to swing too fast my way I was going to run for it.

The cliché is that time slows to a crawl in such circumstances: that one's feet seem to drag leadenly, every lurching step is an agony of needle-pierced nerves, all the muscles are drawn so tight they twang with vibration and the impulse to break and run wildly is almost overpowering. The cliché is true. There is no way to remember it all clearly but it lasted subjective *hours*. I had the suitcase clutched to my chest as if it would shield me against bullets; I moved like a man about to retch—and I was ready to. Somewhere in my head a clock was at work and at hourly intervals I knew another second had passed—yet at the same time the instants raced by in such a blur that I knew I wouldn't nearly have time to reach the hollow before the lights came swinging back and the guns opened up. . . .

When the pale searchlight pinned me I was lying bolt still in the hollow because they would spot movement before anything else. I didn't stir—and the light moved on. There was no land mine, but I didn't even think of that until after I was belly-flat in the depression.

I felt it return across my back: felt it because I'm sure I didn't see it. The daylight seemed to be strengthening with incredible haste. They would spot me now without the lights. . . .

Wait now until they've begun to turn and look another way—wait for the light to circle away. Now. Up. Three strides to the fence. I went against it prone—laid my knee across the bottom strand to bend it down; lifted the upper strand.

The sudden noise of a man's shout tore a gash through the fabric of the dawn. I could not look up: I *could not*. It was like burying my face in the pillow, that inability to look—as if by not looking I would prevent them from shooting. . . . I rolled through the narrow gap in the wire. My suitcase caught and jerked me around and I knew there was no way to free it and I left it there and ran—*ran*, diving and zigzagging with my soles slipping on the damp weeds, legs pumping, arms driving, my eyes only on the Turkish wood that meant life.

The stutter of the machine gun was curiously far off but then above the roar of my ears I heard the bullets whack past me and I learned that all the writings are wrong: bullets don't whiz or whistle or fan the air, they *crack* like explosives when they go by—a sonic boom. I listened with compulsive curiosity to this phenomenon and then I was tumbling, sliding in among the trees and the guns were chipping bark and twigs above my head: I scrambled and pawed into the wood and at some indeterminate moment the guns stopped and I was alive.

I crawled deep into the forest. A crescendo of pounding blood pulsed in my head. I stood up and kicked out, flexing legs and arms recklessly to find out if I'd been hit. Then I stood with the sweat drying on me and pressure drained out of my head and I had to sit down quickly and tense the muscles of my stomach to keep from passing out.

I fought it desperately. After a very long time I was able to get up. With a deep drained ache in all my fibers I began to limp toward the river.

❦ 18 ❦

TRABZON. I caught a raw whiff of the sea. A bright light at the far side of the bay stroked the water with a pale rippling stripe. I was riding on the half-exposed springs of the seat of a ruined Dodge pickup truck beside a Kurdish woodman. The pickup bed was piled so high with cordwood that logs rolled off now and then and lay obstructions in the road behind. I was not trained to divide his language into words, nor he mine; we shared the word "Trabzon" and occasional sidewise smiles that strangers use to indicate to each other that they are not threatening.

A waterfront town: whitewashed stucco, bleached sidewalks constructed of cement and seashell. At the single loading dock a freighter stood with its hull broken amidships into a hinged loading ramp. Wiry workmen in greasy fezzes and white peon clothes made ant streams in and out of the hold, unloading her into a corrugated metal warehouse under high incandescent lights.

The woodman let me off in the center of town. Veiled moslem women peered from shuttered windows. A boy pedaled by on a bike. The cars parked at the curbs were mostly American-made and always very old: 1953 Plymouths, 1957 Chevrolets. One of them was pale green with TAXI painted freehand in yellow on the door. I approached the man who leaned against its fender. *"Traverna?* Pinar?"

He smiled at me as if I were a buffoon; shook his head and said something very rapid. But he was pointing at a doorway less than half a block distant. I nodded and smiled and said thank-you and went there. It all reminded me of Mexico—some fishing town on the Gulf of California coast. All except the profusion of straw-laden donkeys and the occasional camel. But the architecture and the smells were the same. Children plucked at my clothes.

And the smell in the taverna. Alcohol and tobacco: the spilled-beer aura of a bar anywhere. The room was crowded with dirty little checkerboard tables; it was near eight o'clock and midweek, the place wasn't teeming, but it was the kind of low-roofed room that felt crowded even with half a dozen people in it: the air was thick with heavy body heat.

There was a bar, topped with linoleum and bordered by dull chrome. The lights were weak. A full-bosomed woman came to wait on me. She had long wiry hairs on her legs. I said, "Is Pinar here?" and when she looked puzzled I tried it in German and in French. In any case she understood "Pinar" when it appeared in each language and finally she tapped my arm —*Wait here*—and went away through a rear door.

A tired gnome served me food and beer at one of the tables. Globules of fat swam in the soup but I ate ravenously. I wished I had my pipe to smoke afterward. I sat back to wait for the woman, for Pinar. I was fighting to keep awake: I was wound up too tightly, to the point where I was convinced everyone who spoke within earshot was shouting—at me. I'd gone too long without sleep and I felt drunk, in that stake of inebriation where nothing I saw quite made sense anymore: perspectives were off, shapes were out of kilter, lights were blurred and too bright.

I knew I had to keep a deliberate grip on sanity because I was close to losing it.

The wind kept a branch scratching on the side of the *taverna*: I was irritably aware of it until someone switched on a scratchy little radio and turned it up too loud—the heavy twanging racket that passes for rock-and-roll east of Brindisi: one of the many things like ouzo and kebab and olive oil which the Greeks and Turks deny they have in common.

A pulse drummed blood-red behind my closed eyelids. All my muscles were inflamed; my face was sore and scabbed from the glass cuts; my hands were skinned raw. I must have looked monstrous in my torn clothing. The beard stubble had grown perceptibly to

301

the touch and my Russian shoes were scarred beyond repair.

Someone shook me gently by the shoulders and I almost bolted out of the chair. It was the buxom woman: she had a dark crickety little man with her. "Pinar," she said proudly, and went away.

One eyebrow went up disdainfully as he looked at me. "Yes, luv?"

"You're Pinar?"

"Yes, luv. I have rooms, if that's what you've come to find. Can you pay?"

"I've got money." It penetrated that he'd taken one look at me, *dishabille* and all, and instantly spoken English. "I've just come through the border. Pudovkin told me to come to you."

Pinar sat daintily down on the edge of the chair beside me. He perched on it nervously. His hands fluttered when he spoke. "Pudovkin, luv? What did he say about me, then?"

"Only that you could help me."

"Help you do what?"

It stopped me cold, that question. I'd sustained myself with a goal: the goal was this place, this man; it had been a long time since I'd thought farther ahead than Turkey, which meant freedom, and Pinar, who meant help.

Finally I said, "I've got a Turkish visa. I suppose I'll be all right here?"

"Of course, luv." He touched a tear in the sleeve of my jacket. "What a frightful mess you are. We'll have to get you cleaned up. Do you have a name, luv?"

"Bristow, Harry Bristow."

His face changed.

Pinar had half a dozen boardinghouse rooms on the floor above the *taverna*. By the time I had bathed and attempted to shave around the wounds, the dark woman had brought clean clothes for me from somewhere and a pair of Arab sandals. The clothes were a poor fit but I managed; anything would have done.

I stretched out fully clothed on the bed and was unconscious before I thought to turn off the light.

Two days in that place and I slept almost all of it away. Once—the second afternoon—I walked through the inferior regions of the town and bought a pipe and a pair of oxfords for my feet. I sorted the handful of note cards I'd had in my pockets—I'd lost a good many with my coat, unthinkingly leaving them in the pockets when I'd abandoned the coat. Most of the rest had gone with the suitcase on the barbed wire. The ones I'd kept in my pockets were those tracing my search for Kolchak's gold and I no longer needed most of them because the most likely hiding place was burned into my memory cells too brightly ever to be extinguished. Late that afternoon I took the cards downstairs and threw them into the black wood stove and watched them turn to ash.

Pinar caught me at it but concealed his curiosity. "Feel ready to talk, luv?"

"I think so."

"Shall we have a drink then?" We had the place to ourselves. We took glasses of wine to a table and Pinar raised his drink in toast: "To your adventure."

"I could do without any more of it."

"Well, what now? Most of them I send straight on to Tel Aviv by way of Piraeus. I suppose I could arrange passage for you to the States, but you might find that more easily done at your own consulate in Ankara."

"I'd rather not advertise my whereabouts to the consulate."

"I see. Like that, is it, luv?" He had an insidious smile—as if we shared some clandestine purpose. Like an elbow nudge in the ribs. And always the single lifted eyebrow, the supercilious curl of lip. He reminded me a bit of Zandor, the aura of homosexuality; but Zandor was a mover. Pinar was only a connection: a man whose existence was like that of a crossroads, defined only in terms of those who touched his life briefly on their way to some other place.

He contrived to be dainty and motherly; he succeeded only in being somewhat sleazy and conspiratorial. "Well then. A ticket to the States, will that do it? Can you pay?"

I'd counted my remaining travelers checks; I could

303

make it if I wanted to. For forty-eight hours I'd been asking myself about the next step. I hadn't answered yet. "Let me stay a few more days and get it sorted out."

"No rush, luv. My house is your house."

On the following morning after a predawn rain I went down to the rocky shore and watched the gulls. Trying to decide. If I went home would MacIver leave it alone? Not bloody likely. They would put on all the pressures—everything from the revoked driver's license and the IRS audits to the pressures on my publishers.

But if not home—where? Tel Aviv? Nikki?

I was a little old to run to a woman's arms for succor; and Nikki was no longer mine. Or at least I was no longer hers. Indirectly it was Nikki who'd got me out of Russia alive but I still felt that annoying suspicion, that accusatory anger. When I began to analyze it I saw how flimsy it had become but still I couldn't shake it off. I could go to her but would I ever trust her again?

What else was there? Bukov had said it: *Exile—a blind wandering to an unknown destination.*

I had to think about the rest of my life. Planning like a college boy trying to decide on a profession the night before commencement. How real was Ritter's threat? Was I finished as a writer?

What if I flew to Washington and walked into MacIver's office and told him where to find the gold?

It would get them off my back. I was sure of it.

But if I did that it would negate everything I'd done. Pudovkin would have died meaninglessly.

I recoiled at that reasoning: it was the justification all the fools had used for keeping the Indochina war going long after it had been patently lost. *Don't let the soldiers die in vain.* It's specious reasoning—contemptible.

And it had nothing to do with the issues. The facts hadn't changed in a week: the reasons for my keeping the secret were the same now as they had been in Sebastopol. There was enough gold in the cache to inflate currencies to starvation levels or to slaughter thousands of people and I had refused from the outset to be the instrument of any such catastrophe and that fact was

304

still the same. I'd believed it and I'd been willing to sacrifice Pudovkin's life for that belief—and Bukov's and several others' along the way—if it had come to that—because at the time I'd been willing to sacrifice my own as well. This was what would have been in vain if I changed my mind now. And it was a guilt I couldn't face.

Nor was I ready yet to face the only real alternative. I returned to the *taverna* still having made no decision for myself and feeling like some dreary imitation of Hamlet.

Coming along the street I looked more closely at the front of the *taverna* than I'd done before and saw that it had been covered with a new façade. Somehow that made it look worse than the old building around it: renovation hadn't disguised its age, only shown someone wanted to disguise it.

It took a moment for my eyes to accommodate to the dimness inside. I was still by the door when Pinar greeted me there and led me through the room with the clandestine indifference of an arch headwaiter leading the way to an undesirable table. "I've got someone you'll want to meet." We went through the back door and past the foot of the stairs and he twisted the knob of a door which I had assumed led into some kind of office. I hadn't been inside it before.

Pinar's hand fluttered at me. His cowardly half smile warned me. When the door swung out of the way I saw a bookcase, two empty chairs, a scrofulous little desk and a man sitting behind it with a rowdy grin on his face.

Evan MacIver.

19

"WHAT ARE YOU doing here?"

"You may as well shut the door and give us a little privacy." He gave Pinar a look of ill-concealed revulsion and Pinar bowed his way into the corridor.

I kicked it shut with my heel. The little room was filled with the stink of Pinar's cloying after-shave. Mac-Iver was puffing smoke into it.

"Well, Harry." He almost managed to make his voice sound cordial. His face didn't match it. The wide grin had been triumphant, not friendly. He looked a little bloated and pasty as if he'd spent the past twenty-four hours sleepless on airplanes.

"How did you find me here?"

"We have ears everywhere," he muttered. "You made a hell of a run. I never thought you had the guts for that kind of thing. How'd you manage it?"

"One day I'll put it all down in a book and send you a copy."

"Send me the very first copy, Harry. And put in it where you found the gold."

"I didn't have it in mind to write fiction."

He made a tent of his fingers and peered through it slyly. "I had a long talk with Karl Ritter. He half believes you. But then he doesn't know you the way I do. I remember a term paper you did on whether or not Hemingway stole his story 'The Killers' from some yarn by Stephen Crane."

" 'The Blue Hotel.' "

"Yeah. You asked for an extension so you could do more work on it. The professor thought it was the usual undergraduate stall. It wasn't, remember? You just couldn't let go of it until you had the answer. You're a reporter is what you are. Snout like a hound. No—you lied to Ritter. If you hadn't already found it

306

you'd still be up there looking for it. So let's not play pretend, shall we?"

"I'd still be there looking for it now if I had a choice. I had to run—I'd be on a prison hospital table now with scopolamine needles in me if I'd stayed." I sank miserably into a wooden armchair: putting on an act for him. "Evan, I didn't want to be tortured for something I don't have. Of course I looked for anything that might tell me what happened to the gold. I found out a great deal. The Germans sent a commando team into Siberia to find it in forty-four. The commando team never came back. I can give you all the details you want, but that's what happened. It won't help us find gold. Dear God, all I want to be is left alone."

MacIver pasted a cigarette to his lip and gave me a bloodshot look before he lit it. "You went into Russia what, seven weeks ago? Sometime early February, right? So you haven't been up on the news, I gather."

If he meant the sudden new tack to unbalance me then he succeeded. "What news?"

"There's been another monetary crisis. Raids on the dollar. We had to devaluate twice. The Bonn government had to buy up a hell of a lot of dollars. And we've had to agree to support the dollar *with gold*. To save us from financial humiliation. Us, Harry—the United States of America. Sticks in your craw a little, doesn't it."

"Not particularly. If the States can't compete with the rest of the world, we deserve devaluation."

"A six-billion-dollar trade deficit, currently," he murmured, not with great conviction. "You know why? Because we've still got to pay for renewing our own outmoded factories. While Japan and Germany are outbidding us on everything because we rebuilt both countries from scratch after the war with brand-new modern industries. *We* did that, Harry. General George C. Marshall and the United States of America."

"Don't wave flags at me."

"Do you know what the U.S. gold reserves at Fort Knox amount to?"

"No."

"Some of the bullion's earmarked for foreign credits.

307

Know how much we're left with that we can call our own? About twelve billion dollars' worth. Twelve billion. If we had that Russian gold it would increase our reserves by more than fifty percent. Does that mean anything to you?"

"Not a thing. Don't feed me well-marinated platitudes, Evan. The dollar isn't tied to gold anymore. Nobody cares if Fort Knox is empty."

"Wrong. Gold is power."

"That's the disease, isn't it. The overwhelming need for power."

"Would you rather see it pissed away to support the dollar so the Reds can take over everything?"

"Frankly, Scarlett. . . ." I was in one of those reckless flip moods again.

His congested face was becoming orange with fury: he wasn't reaching me at all and he couldn't stand that, he couldn't get a grip and couldn't find the right place to stand and he must have hated me then. I saw it wasn't getting us anywhere and I began to get up to leave but he barked at me, "Keep your seat, Harry, I'm not finished with you," and his voice pushed me back down into the chair.

He was playing with an unlit cigarette as obstinately as a bored child, squinting through the smoke of the one that hung from his mouth. He peeled it off his lip and lit the new one from the stub of the old; stubbed the butt out and only then lifted his head. His glance came around toward me like the slowly swinging gun turrets of a battle cruiser. "It's time for you to bite the bullet, Harry. You may think you've had a rough time up to now but you just haven't got the slightest idea. You've subjected yourself to an incredible self-inflicted hatchet job out of some weird sense of principle, and I guess you've suffered a little, but if you don't quit this game right now, there won't be enough left of you to make a barbecue sandwich."

"Go to hell, Evan."

"I guess I'm on my way. For what I'm going to have to do to you."

"I suppose you'll start by holding my hands out on the floor and stepping on my fingers."

He didn't reply. He swiveled his chair until his back

was to me. Smoke drifted around his head. He tipped back, the red neck creasing white. "It's a dicey business, Harry. Individuals don't matter at this level."

"I know. I'm expendable."

"So am I. If I don't get what they want from you, my ass is grass."

"I'm sorry."

"The hell you are." He still had his back to me. "But I am. The damnable thing is, to an outsider like you I look like a pretty big guy. I mean I've got a big job. They pay me a lot of money and I've got a rank that's just about equivalent to lieutenant general. I whistle and twenty thousand people jump through hoops. People hold doors for me."

Now he swiveled to face me. He laid both arms out along the desk top. "But there are people in Washington—I'm not even big enough to see over their desks. You understand who I'm talking about?"

"Yes."

"They know about you, Harry. They know about your train of gold. And they also know that you and I are friends."

"Used to be friends."

"Yeah." He dragged his hands back off the desk and unscrewed the cigarette from his mouth. "They expected I might go soft on you. Because we used to be friends. So they didn't have any choice. We're gladiators, you and me. They threw me into the arena with you and they locked the gate behind me. I've got no exits, Harry. The only way I can go back is with your scalp. Otherwise I might just as well join the Watergate crowd or bury myself right here in that faggot's backyard."

"I'm sorry. I can't help you."

"Bastard." Then he reached inside his coat and withdrew a revolver. Its orifice swung toward me. "You still think I'm kidding, or bluffing."

"I know you are. That's a stupid mistake. Don't point that thing at me when you're not ready to kill me with it. Kill me and you'd never have a chance of finding what you're looking for."

Now he grinned. "Actually I wasn't thinking of using it on *you*."

"What do you want me to do? Talk you out of suicide?"

"Why don't you try. Start by telling me where the gold is. Just think, Harry, you've got a chance to save an old friend's life."

"Actually I'd rather you shot *me* with it."

"Shoot you? As you pointed out, Harry, who would that profit?"

"Everyone but you," I said. "Now who's playing games? You thought the gun might scare me. It didn't. Why don't you put the damn thing away before it goes off."

He slid it back under his coat. Not sheepish: brash. He said, "Up till now I never realized what a tough hundred-proof son of a bitch you really are. You'd make one hell of an agent. Brains and guts. What'll you take, Harry—Ritter's job? My job? I'm due for the chop anyway."

"Do you mind if I go?"

"In a minute. We're waiting for someone."

"Is that all we've been doing? Stalling for time?"

"It's a way to pass the time. But don't think I wasn't telling the truth. They've got my ass in a crack, old buddy. You're the only one who can get it out. You're forcing me to make it hard, but hard or easy I'm going to make you do it."

"Who are we waiting for, Evan?"

It was as if he hadn't heard the question. He went on:

"You could still do it easy. Think about whether you'd rather have it in the Kremlin or the White House. Think about democracy—corny as that may sound. The innate good judgment of the American man in the street."

"That good trustworthy American Christianity. It wasn't the man in the street who ordered the bombing of Nagasaki."

"You really don't believe in it, do you?"

"The apple pie way of life? Sure I do."

"Democracy."

"I don't believe power can be trusted. I don't trust Brezhnev and I don't trust Mao and I don't trust Nixon."

"Right now this minute, Harry, you've got more power than most people in this world."

"No. You only think I have. I've got no gold mine in the sky. I'm sorry you convinced them I did. It's back-fired on you, but there isn't a thing I can do about that."

"You make me sick. Aren't you tired of this yet?"

"Tired to death of it."

"Then quit it, Harry. Tell me when the auction was supposed to start."

Of course that was it. They had sat around a great long table at the CIA Director's conference one morning and they had come up with the auction because it smelled right: it fitted their conspiratorial way of thinking, it was exactly what each one of them would like to do if he had the chance. They were people so corrupted by their own cynicism they couldn't credit anyone else with a morality any higher than their own. Somebody had said, *Sure, that's exactly the way Bristow will do it,* and they'd all nodded in agreement because it was just plausible enough and it sounded dirty enough to appeal to them.

It was a mark of my own naïveté that I hadn't thought of it myself. I wouldn't have done it—I wasn't gaited that way, wealth wasn't my goad—but if my mind had been working more clearly I'd have known that was how they were thinking and I'd have known why all of them were taking me so seriously: they didn't want me to get loose where I could force an auction. I hadn't anticipated it at all, so I was just as shortsighted as they were.

I said, "No. No auction, Evan. Think about it and you'll see why it couldn't be done."

MacIver cleared his throat. He sat there with his hands intertwined across his incipient paunch. "God damn it."

"You're all clowns," I said. "You've done it again, Evan. The CIA working in mysterious ways its blunders to perform. You see how funny it is?"

"Do I look amused?"

"I wish you had the grace to. You used to have a pretty good sense of humor."

"I never laugh when there's a gun jammed up my ass."

"You put it there yourself."

"Please don't tell me it's poetic justice, Harry." He spat something out; I saw that he had bitten his cigarette cleanly in two.

He said, "You win that round on points, Harry, but I still have to win the fight. Now either you throw the fight or I knock you out. Your choice. And I still don't think you want——"

An obsequious knock at the door cut him off. Pinar opened the door.

"Here?" MacIver asked.

Pinar nodded. "Upstairs, as you wished."

MacIver noded. "About time. Harry, go up to your room. I'll see you again later. But one thing first. This building is surrounded by our people. If you try to leave and they haven't had a signal from me, they'll turn you back. As painfully as you make necessary."

"That could be a bluff."

"Try it and see. You're welcome to."

"You've laid on an expensive production here."

"It'll be cheap at the price," he drawled. "Go on upstairs like a good boy."

He'd regained his self-confidence. It was more than I could say for myself. I went along the hall with Pinar; he left me at the foot of the stairs.

When I put my foot on the step a new realization grenaded into my mind: I knew what I would find in my room. It had to be; it was the only way MacIver could have known I was in this town. I went upstairs with slow uncertainty and hesitated outside my door with my hand on the knob.

I opened it and stepped inside and suddenly I was face to face with Nikki.

"Hello, Harry."

SHE WAS SITTING on my bed with her knees drawn up against her breasts and her head tipped to one side on her folded arms, watching me. She'd been sitting that way for quite a few minutes, I thought, burying her face in her arms.

I pushed the door shut behind me—slowly, almost reproachfully. "Then it's true what they say. It really is the crossroads of the word. Wait long enough in Pinar's *taverna* in Trabzon and sooner or later everybody you know will come by. *Mazel tov,* Nikki."

"Please don't make jokes."

She wasn't wearing her glasses. The nearsighted agate eyes squinted at me, pressing at me curiously like diamonds etching against glass. She looked very slender and very tense, hungry for something: information? Forgiveness?

Her soft and always slightly breathless voice: "Harry. Please let me talk to you."

Now she uncoiled. She stood up hesitantly, her fingers at her throat. Her dark hair was plaited at the side of her head. I hadn't really remembered how gamine and lovely she was: I thought I had, but I hadn't. Even now—bedraggled and dispirited, rumpled and untidy and too tired to care—she was so very lovely.

"Somebody had to tell MacIver where to find me," I said. "I didn't think it was Vassily Bukov. And it couldn't have been Pudovkin, he's dead."

Her head jerked back as if I'd slapped her; she swung away from me and swung back again, her face crumpling.

"He was driving. They machine-gunned him. I was lucky, they missed me."

313

I watched her face adjust to it. I said cruelly, "You and MacIver."

She pinched her lower lip with her teeth. I said, "I liked Pudovkin. He was a gentle old man. How well did you know him?"

"Well enough to like him. I'm sorry, Harry, I didn't know."

"You knew the risks. You set the whole damned thing up. Didn't you."

Taut anger ground itself into the lines around her lips. "I'm responsible for it, yes. For his death. Yes."

"Don't get maudlin. It's a privilege I'd just as soon not see you luxuriate in. How long have you been in this with MacIver? From the very beginning?"

"Yes."

"From the night we first met?"

"Yes."

"MacIver set it up for us to meet there as if it were an accident. Is that the way it worked?"

She nodded her head.

"And Haim Tippelskirch. It must have been his idea at the beginning. He was the one who'd been obsessed by the gold for fifty years."

"Harry, you don't understand. Please——"

"I will not be your wailing wall, Nikki. You hung me on puppet strings and made me dance across an emotional minefield. I owe you nothing." I stood there with my fists clenched at my sides. "Nothing."

She lifted her chin. Very soft: "Are you the only one with principles? Are you the only one with a private line to God? How are things on Mount Olympus, Harry? Will you let me talk to you? Will you listen to what I came here to say to you?"

"When you've said it, you'll go," I said. "And you'll take MacIver and his wolf pack with him."

"I'll go, yes. I can't answer for him."

"You sicced him onto me. You can get him off me."

"It's not like that. We had the plan but it was Mac-Iver who provided you. That wasn't my idea. I'd never heard of you."

"Sure. I was a total stranger. That made it a whole lot easier to play your badger game—you didn't have to worry about feelings. All you had to do was act like a hooker, the hundred-dollar kind who says I-love-you between humps."

She squeezed her eyes shut. "Please. That's not true. Dear God it wasn't like that, Harry. Falling in love was the worst thing that could have happened, but it did happen and I wasn't acting. It wasn't supposed to happen. All I was supposed to do was to get you to Israel so that——"

"So that Haim could work on me. He wasn't really retired from the Mossad at all, was he. He was right up in the top echelons—right up to the day of his death."

"Yes. That's true."

"Fifty years he schemed to get at that gold."

"No. It wasn't until the nineteen fifties. After there was an Israel."

"It had to be someone above suspicion. Someone acceptable to both the Americans and the Soviets. Certainly not a Jew. Someone who could get access to the records in both countries—and someone who had an interest in the gold so that he'd know what to look for, and look for it. *Was* it MacIver who picked me? Or was it Haim? He knew my books."

"I don't know, Harry. I can't answer that. I wasn't there when they had their first meetings. It was several years ago, I'm sure. I only came into it a little while before you met me."

"Well you sure as hell made up for lost time, didn't you?" I swung away heavily; I couldn't bear to go on looking at her.

"Wait...."

"I won't leave," I said. "Not until I've heard the whole story. You've got the floor."

Her words came in a headlong rush as if she were talking compulsively to hold herself together.

It must have seemed an even more fantastic scheme at the outset than it had proved to be in actuality. The fountainhead was Haim Tippelskirch.

"Haim said there must never be forgetfulness or forgiveness of evil," she said. "He said it was a debt we owed the dead and the living equally. The Russians must not have that gold. Nor the Germans. Too many

Jews died for it. I remember one of those foolish old men saying something about God's will. Haim reminded them of their Torah—God does not intervene to redeem man's duties to his fellow men."

The gold belonged to Israel by moral right. That was Haim's idealism. His realism was that it would be a cold day in hell before the Soviets would let a Jewish researcher into their archives. An innocent dupe had to be found. Nikki did not use the word dupe but it was what she meant.

It was all such a long chance. Haim was the only one with faith in it because he was something of an amateur historian himself: a student of military history, a student of Germans and Russians. He knew the German penchant for record-keeping and he knew if they'd moved the gold they'd have left paper tracks. He also knew one other thing he'd never told me:

"Our people went into Siberia in nineteen sixty-two to look for that old iron mine. It was empty. That was how we knew the gold had been moved."

Another thing they hadn't told me: Haim himself had sought access to the American files, on the pretense of writing an article for some European quarterly on the subject of World War II in Russia. They hadn't let him in because as soon as the security check began they discovered he was an agent of the Mossad and that was what put MacIver on him.

MacIver wanted to know what interest the Mossad had in those records and Haim told him the truth because he knew it was never going to work without outside help; and the United States was the firmest ally Israel had, despite suspicions and reservations on both sides. Clearly the dupe had to be an American historian and sooner or later the American authorities would have to be brought into it because too many of the documents were classified.

It was no wonder I'd got access to so much material that had never been exposed before: The CIA had been opening all the doors ahead of me, unseen by me.

It was CIA agents in Moscow who confirmed that the Soviets were ignorant of the gold—its original hiding place as well as the fact that it had been moved some-

316

time between 1920 and 1962. Since the Soviets didn't have it and no other country or individual had produced it, it could only have been rehidden, and probably still inside Russia. All this merely confirmed what Haim had already intuited.

I had to be kept ignorant of the scheme because there was always the chance the Soviets would tumble to what I was doing; that they would either shut down the archives to me or interrogate me. In either case the gold would be lost again but if the Soviets interrogated me and found out that the CIA and the Mossad had put me up to it there would have been hell to pay. At least if I didn't know who was calling the shots I couldn't tell the Russians.

The best my puppeteers could do for me was put me under the protective wing of Vassily Bukov because he had a far more viable organization in the Crimea than the CIA had. Unfortunately this had backfired because my visit with Bukov had inflamed the Soviets' suspicions.

In the end I was to have been persuaded by the CIA to turn over to them whatever I discovered about the gold. Originally this debriefing was not to take place until I was safely out of the Soviet Union after having completed my research there. But Bukov had reported that Zandor was breathing down my neck too closely; that the Russians might lock me up at any time; and therefore Ritter had gone in, ahead of schedule, to find out as much as he could.

"What if I'd told him I knew where the gold was? What if I'd specified a location?"

"What do you mean?"

"He'd have killed me, wouldn't he? To keep the Russians from squeezing me."

"No," she said vehemently. "He had orders to get in contact with Vassily. Together they were to smuggle you out safely."

Something had convinced Ritter that I'd found it. Probably the poor way I handled the meeting with him. I'd given it away, or Ritter thought I had—it amounted to the same thing. The screw was cranked a few turns tighter and I did what I had to do: I broke and ran, and was delivered onto MacIver's doorstep, or Nikki's, on schedule.

"All right," I said. "What's supposed to happen now?"

"To you? You were supposed to tell us where the gold is."

"I didn't find it, Nikki."

She had nothing to say to that.

I said, "Suppose I'd found it. Suppose I told you, or MacIver, where to find it. What would have happened then?"

"They expect to make a trade with the KGB. It's a lot of gold, Harry."

"Yeah. I know it's a lot of gold. One million pounds of it. Troy. What was the trade for?"

"Gold."

"Trading gold for gold?"

"Have you ever heard of washing money?"

"Like gangsters?"

"Yes. That was the plan."

Organized crime takes in enormous sums of money but it can't be spent overtly because that would bring the Internal Revenue people down on the spenders. It has to be "washed" first—funneled through a Mafia-owned legitimate enterprise, such as a gambling casino, where it can show up as acknowledged gross receipts, then be balanced off against operating losses so that the income tax is minimized.

Nikki said, "The Russians have five hundred tons of Spanish gold in the Ural vaults."

"Five hundred and ten."

"All right. There are two plans, really. One is to persuade the Russians to give that gold back to Spain. The United States and Israel will get a substantial portion of it from Spain in what will be written up as repayment of foreign-aid loans."

"I didn't know Israel had lent money to Spain."

"It would funnel through Washington."

"What was the second plan?"

"Repayment for World War Two lend-lease. Direct payment, in gold, from the Kremlin to Washington. To equal exactly half the value of the gold we led them to."

"And you think the Russians will go for either one of those?"

"Either they will, or they don't get the gold. Half of it is still a lot of gold for them to keep. More than two billion dollars' worth."

I said, "And Tel Aviv ends up splitting fifty with Washington, whatever the Russians pay?"

"Yes. We're a silent partner. The Russians might not go for it if they knew we were involved. We're not exactly political bedfellows."

"An unwise turn of phrase, Nikki."

She flushed to her hairline. "Harry——"

"Let me tell you something. I didn't find the gold. That leaves all of you looking pretty foolish, doesn't it? Maybe it makes it a little easier to see things clearly —what you've really done."

"To you?"

"To both of us. All of us."

"It was worth the cost. It had to be."

"The Nazis and the Communists have a phrase for it. To use a knotty overworked saying, the ends justify the means. Any means."

"Don't try to put words in my mouth, Harry. You act as if you're the only one who's got a right to principles. I've got principles too—things that come higher than my feelings about you or anyone else."

"It ain't the principle, it's the money."

"I hate you when you make cheap jokes, Harry. It's beneath you."

"So is theft."

But I remembered the documents I'd stolen and destroyed.

"Theft from whom?" she said. "Whose gold is it? The Czar's?" She stood up. Her shoulders went up and her face lifted. "Let's talk about another principle. We made it possible for you to do your research, Harry. Without us you wouldn't have found a thing. You probably wouldn't even have got clearance into the Soviet Union at all. It was a sort of bargain, even though you were forced to sign the contract without reading it. That's regrettable, but we kept our part of the bargain. You got everything you wanted. You've got your book to write. You've got the fantastic story of the gold to tell the world. Nobody will stop you from doing that—as long as it's not published before we complete our arrangements with the Russians and the gold changes hands. You're alive, you've had an adventure——"

"And Pudovkin is dead, and my notes are hanging on a barbed wire fence in Russia."

"We'll get them back for you. We'll make it part of the deal with Moscow."

I thundered at her. "What deal with Moscow? Don't you understand? Don't you listen? I found no gold. *No gold.*"

"You're lying, Harry," she said. She turned her bitter face toward the window. "And how about that for principles."

"You all keep telling me I'm lying. As if by saying it you can make it so."

"Don't you think I know you well enough to know when you're keeping things back, Harry? You were never a good liar."

"I thought I knew you pretty well too, Nikki. We do make mistakes about people, don't we?"

"You found the gold, Harry. If you hadn't you wouldn't have stolen those papers from the archives."

"It was one of Vassily's men. He was in the wagon watching you. He saw you roll them up and slip them into your sleeve. Now you didn't steal them for the information they contained—you could have taken notes. You stole them to keep anyone else from finding what you'd found. It had to be the gold, Harry. Nothing else would have made you do that."

I had sagged into the chair; she came to me and the touch of her fingers on my shoulders was electric. She murmured, "Harry, you're destroying yourself. You take it all upon yourself and it's not even your responsibility to bear. Would the world fall down if you kept your part of the bargain? Harry, what have you got to gain from sticking this out? What will it accomplish?"

"Sometimes you can't go by that. Maybe it's just the rationale of a lost cause." I was whispering, I think. "Something stupid. But you go along all your life thinking you're honorable and principled, and then just once you're up against it. You can't turn away. You can't even pretend it didn't happen. You just have to go ahead. Stubborn. Just because it's a matter of principle. Even if it doesn't accomplish a damned thing except your own destruction."

I looked up at her and she was leaning toward me, an eager posture. I said, "Does that make any sense to you, Nikki? Any sense at all?"

She walked away from me. Around to the far side of the bed. She sat down on it—sat there not moving for the longest time. Her face was tipped down, huddling; her hair fell around her ear and bared her white nape.

When she began to shake I went to her. She must have been weeping for quite a while—great racking silent sobs. "For myself," she said. "For what I've let myself become, Harry. It's a vile business." Her hands wrenched at each other. "It contaminates everyone who comes in touch with it."

"I have to know something, Nikki. Coming here—was it your idea or MacIver's?"

"He told me you were here. He make it clear he wanted me to come. But I wanted to come."

"All right. But to talk me into giving you the gold—was that your idea or his?"

"You're asking me whether they forced me to do it, aren't you?" She was still looking at her hands. Her cheeks were wet.

"Yes."

For a little while she didn't speak. I had no patience then; I said, "I've been wondering what sort of pressure they might use. Michele?" Michele was her little girl, in Switzerland.

Finally she said, "It's kind of you to try to find excuses for me, Harry."

"Probably being kind to myself. I didn't think I was that good at misjudging people. Particularly people I had reason to believe loved me."

"Maybe we've both always been too selfish to give up anything for each other. That's what you used to say in your letters."

"I said that because I hoped you'd try to talk me out of it."

321

She wiped her face with a corner of the coarse sheet. "You just don't understand about us."

" 'Us'?"

"Israelis."

"That's true. I've always hated fanaticism. It gets in the way of everything real," I said.

"Real—like love?"

"Yes."

"In a utopian world there'd be no conflict between those things. But we don't live in——"

"Stop it, Nikki. You're only repeating all that about ends justifying means."

"I know." I could barely hear her. "A few days ago —you probably haven't heard—there was a Libyan airliner. A civilian plane, forty or fifty passengers. It strayed off course over Israel. We'd had threats from Al Fatah—that they were going to fill an airplane with high explosives and crash it in Tel Aviv. So our air force shot the plane down. There weren't any high explosives. Just passengers."

I sat by her and felt her spine beneath my fingers. Her voice went a little sour then. "You and I—it's a desperate thing with us, isn't it? It's fatal but it's serious. I think I'm not enough of a professional, Harry—I'm too much in love with you."

"Would you want to be professional? These agents I've seen—MacIver, Ritter, Zandor, all of them—they may be enemies but they're co-professionals and there's something sick about that. They've got the kind of mutual respect you'd have thought died with the aviators, the ones in silk scarves in the First World War. Their talents mean more than their allegiances. You don't belong in that company. MacIver's got the character of a billy goat. He's spiritually color-blind. He doesn't know loyalty when he sees it. He doesn't know truth when he sees it. The highest accolade any of them can pay another is to say he's 'a real professional'— even if he's an enemy. All right, on a certain level that's understandable, maybe there's even a way to admire it romantically. But it's got to put you in mind of the German rocket scientists who're working for Moscow and Washington now—or the professional mercenaries who don't care which side hires them."

At least she was listening to me. I said, "You're not one of them."

After a time she whispered, "I should have been. Then I'd have been able to live with it."

Her arms were folded. She leaned against me, moved her face, kissed me without stirring her arms. I put my hands softly on her cheeks, holding her without pressure. It was a kiss only of the lips, and gentle: yet it rocked me down to my feet.

She was still breathing warmly in my arms when I awakened at sunset. She wasn't asleep.

I said, "Think of it this way. If you leave gold alone long enough it'll sink right into the earth, grain by grain. Specific gravity."

She tried to smile. "There's that strange streak of old-fashioned gallantry in you. It's always confounded me." She had undone her hair before; now it flew and swayed when she sat up and shook her head in negation. "I suppose happiness exists only in the imagination."

"You're burnt-out and hungry and in desperate need of a drink, I think. It's still better than dead. Why don't we go down and eat?"

"MacIver is waiting down there."

"All right." I felt drained. "We may as well go down."

"No. Harry—he doesn't know about the documents you stole."

"He doesn't know," she insisted. "He's only guessing. Hoping. I'm the only one who knows. Bukov and I."

I said, "So you didn't really trust him after all."

"No. . . ."

"Is that the only reason you kept it to yourself?"

She began to dress—the same travel-rumpled clothes. She was a long time answering; finally she looked at me. "That's right, isn't it?"

"What is?"

"I kept your secret."

"It won't be our secret very long, Nikki. You can't be Bukov's only contact in Tel Aviv."

"No, I'm not."

"Then sooner or later they'll query him and he'll re-

323

port to someone else next time. It may have happened already."

"No—MacIver would be hammering at the door."

"All right," I said. "But that's not the point. Look at it, Nikki, face up to it. You could have burned your bridges by telling MacIver about those documents. But you didn't. You kept my secret."

We went down into the smoky crowd and the woman with hairy legs—Pinar's sister—brought us wine and soup and a small local fish, the *rouget*. I did not see MacIver. Pinar pirouetted in and out of the room. We didn't speak of much of anything until after the meal. Then I said, "MacIver wanted you to seduce me into spilling it."

"I suppose he did. He didn't put it like that."

"He thought it."

"To hell with what he thought," she said.

She was very quiet that night in the room. I kept trying to talk to her but she would shut me off.

In the morning with early sun streaming through the cracks between the curtains she said, "I'll have to go down and talk to him."

"Go ahead."

"You're trusting me again, Harry. Bad habit."

"I seem to have become accustomed to risk-taking."

"I won't tell him. Not until you give me permission to."

"Do you think I will?"

"You'll get tired of having the world against you. I'm sorry but that's the way it will be. It won't be MacIver, Harry, it'll be you. You'll grind yourself down and finally you'll give in."

"I don't think so. Eventually, to you, I might. Not to him. Not to any of them. But I'd be an old man. Like Haim was."

"Or like Haim's brother. What if they took me for a hostage?"

"I can't answer that. Are you planning to suggest it to him?"

"No." She was hurt, badly hurt.

"I didn't mean to be harsh. It's another one of those things that's become a habit."

"I've earned it," she said. "It's too bad we don't live in the same world, you and I." She went downstairs to talk to MacIver.

I went out onto the sidewalk and watched the camels parade by. It was going to be a genuinely hot day—the first I could remember in more months than I wanted to recall.

When she met me there the liveliness was coming back into her; she was in a higher mood than before; the sun lit the blue of her eyes as she turned, and her smile was as good as a kiss.

"I've got a car," she said. "He trusts me to watch you. Anyway you wouldn't survive in this country on foot. I'm not to take the main highway. Maybe we'll drive down to the shore."

She hurried ahead, hips animated, fine legs scissoring; I caught up and took her arm.

The car was a Mercedes Benz coupe, the little one with a great deal of glass. She got behind the wheel and there was a satisfying rumble from the hood.

She drove three blocks to a filling station and had the tank topped up although it had been nearly three-quarters full and that was when I realized. . . .

Ten miles west of the town she stopped on the highway shoulder. I let her get out of the car. I didn't open the door for her.

She wasn't looking at me, her face was averted. We didn't speak.

She slammed the door and I slid over into the bucket seat behind the wheel. I knew she would wait at least until sunset before walking back to town and telling them I'd overpowered her and taken the car.

In the mirror as I pulled away I saw her give a careless salute and walk away toward the sea, kicking stones with long languid thrusts of her feet.

EDITORS' EPILOGUE

There is a postscript to Harry Bristow's story.

The Central Intelligence Agency has refused to comment on the Bristow manuscript, only offering to read and criticize it before publication—an offer the editors declined. The CIA will not acknowledge that there is any Evan MacIver on their roster; it would be against Agency policy to do so.

Inquiries have been made of American consular officials in the Soviet Union and it would appear there is no such person as Vassily Bukov anywhere near Sebastopol. Quite possibly Bristow changed that name, and several others, for obvious reasons.

There is, however, a real Nicole Eisen. On June 14, 1973, Mrs. Eisen sold her co-op apartment in Tel Aviv, taking a loss because of the speed of the sale. On June 23 she left Tel Aviv at the beginning of a paid three-week vacation from the Israeli tourist office, which employed her on the record. She boarded an El Al flight with connections to Rio de Janeiro, traveling alone and with only hand luggage. On June 24 she left her hotel in Rio de Janeiro and has not been seen since, apparently. Official Israeli sources have refused to comment on her disappearance.

Since we received Bristow's manuscript and letter from his agent we have had no communication from him.